Family
Passions

By Betsy Aswad

Winds of the Old Days
Family Passions

Family Passions

A NOVEL
Betsy Aswad

The Dial Press
DOUBLEDAY & COMPANY, INC.
GARDEN CITY, NEW YORK   1985

Published by The Dial Press
Copyright © 1985 by Betsy Aswad
Manufactured in the United States of America
First printing

Library of Congress Cataloging in Publication Data

Aswad, Betsy.
  Family passions.

  I. Title.
PS3551.S9F3   1985   813'.54   84-25989
ISBN 0-385-19346-7

FOR BOB HAMMER, ". . . poet . . . pilgrim . . . preacher
. . . walkin' contradiction;
Partly truth and partly fiction"

and

IN MEMORY OF THE JAMES BROTHERS—
Henry and William—who lived long and never closed their minds

ACKNOWLEDGMENTS

Carole Paul and Suzanne Locklair, who unwittingly "composed" Tradd Baynard with all her Southern belle ways;

Don Barr, who told me about ligands and spectrometers, and his wife, Edythe, who delivered him up to me;

Patty Wilson, who gently demanded each new chapter;

Jem Aswad, my son and toughest critic, who ungently demanded each new chapter;

Molly Friedrich, my agent, who defined the book, and Mindy Werner and Allen Peacock, the editors who refined it;

My mother, Jane Becker, who is a whiz at galleys;

The Tioga Point Museum at Athens, Pennsylvania, who let me copy, not by machine but *by hand,* material on Queen Esther, material with which I took egregious (but not outrageous) fictional liberties;

John Murray Cuddihy in whose book *The Ordeal of Civility* (Basic Books, 1974) I stumbled on Freud's letter to Karl Abraham that Chloe Otway in turn stumbles on in Seven; and Larry Murray, whose song, "The Lights of Magdala" (Prodigal Son Music, 1974), flickers through Jason Baynard's sermon in Five; and

Dick, Jem, and Kris Aswad, who endured the awful presence of a writer in the family.

The motive for metaphor, shrinking from
The weight of primary noon,
The ABC of being,

The ruddy temper, the hammer
Of red and blue, the hard sound—
Steel against intimation—the sharp flash,
The vital, arrogant, fatal, dominant X.

Wallace Stevens,
"The Motive for Metaphor"

ONE
". . . One Big Blooming Buzzing Confusion"
Tuesday, June 18

That Confusion is the baby's universe; and the universe of all of us is still to a great extent such a confusion. . . .

William James, *Psychology*

Jason Beauregard Baynard III swung one army-surplus duffle bag over a shoulder and kicked the other before him through the door of his bedroom onto the coco matting of the upper piazza. Oleander, pale yellow and ubiquitous, clambered over the railing from fat clay pots at the edge. From the fluted pillars that supported the overhang, wisteria and trumpet creeper fought for control of the old palmetto taller than the house that charted two lifetimes between the upper and lower piazza. Jason looked up at the palmetto's fan of leaves, its ephemeral wisps and tufts of Spanish moss motionless as mist in the moist heat of the early morning air. Jason leaned on his elbows over the railing and let his eyes slide gradually down the trunk of the palmetto. Oleander fell and bruised on the neat bricks of the garden walk below. On the back of his neck, the sun poured slow, thick as honey, hot, sweet; and the stultifying fragrance of the air quivered his nostrils. He sneezed. Civilized! The most civilized town in the world. Civilization. The very word was like a sneeze.

Jason sneezed again. No breeze from the harbor, hot, thick air, oh, God, the cloying scents of Old Charleston, a walled and concentrated garden club for ladies in fussy pastels and hats and gloves. I'm allergic to Old Charleston! Jason sneezed once more, with great satisfaction. He gathered his duffles in his arms, a fat lumpy heap, and dropped them over the rail. He looked down. Crushing oleander, the duffles crumpled together on the garden walk like a body with all the bones broken.

Jason turned to contemplate the palmetto again. It had grown. When he and his sister, Tradd, were children, the palm fronds had still encroached the upper piazza and you had to duck under jagged petioles to reach the trunk. He saw Tradd's disheveled raven-colored hair, her skirts hitched up, her tender knees twined around the trunk, as once, on his dare, she'd humped down the tree, monkey-style. The bark had scraped the skin from the insides of her legs; she'd literally dripped blood. Their housekeeper, Jessamine, had wrapped Tradd in her dark chocolate arms: "Hush, baby, let us not alarm your mama. We'll do for you, and then we'll get *you* some ice cream while I pound your brother's smart ass." Jessamine raised a clenched fist toward Jason, transfixed on the upper piazza.

Years later, also on his dare, a spirited and lovely girl had climbed the palmetto to spend a wild, mad night with him; ah, she knew how to dare. Smiling a little, Jason looked down again, his eyes settling on a stylized octagon of hybrid yellow roses. Her name ended in something like "-anna." Susanna? Joanna? No, no, they followed Jesus in Luke 8. Ladies who also knew how to dare, however.

Whatever-her-name-was lived in Ansonborough, a few blocks the wrong way from St. Philip's, and Jason's mother had actually and seriously dubbed her "the upstart." Why did he remember that instead of her name? She was working at Cypress Gardens that summer to earn tuition for sophomore year; she wore demure hoop skirts and pantalets all the month of June (Jason had disrobed her once, thus attired: "Don't pull, Jason honey. Locate the drawstring, and carefully untie it, like a birthday present. I reckon gentlemen were more patient then") and water-skied for show through haunted cypress trees in July. Her arms and legs were strong locked around him, but she'd prudently used a hammer and pitons to climb the palmetto to his bedroom. He'd gotten laughing when she left at dawn, removing the pitons on her way down; he'd gotten laughing and couldn't stop. She shook her hammer at him: "You hush, Jason. You're not scared of your mama, but I am. Hush laughing!" With alarm their gardener Robert had examined the symmetrical etches in the palmetto trunk and conjectured the interloper must have been a small, reckless, tusked animal. Three years later, the girl had married someone in Congress, and Tradd had sent Jason the clipping with her own scrawled caption in red ink: "The upstart starts up, brother mine. Where're *you?*"

Jason felt a little irrepressible smile at the corner of his mouth as his senses remembered the taste of the girl who'd climbed up, the gold-dust breathiness of her laughter, the texture inside her like wet velvet clinging. She came with a guttural deep in her throat, and if you were kissing her her breath rasped like fine sandpaper in your mouth: irresistible. Her back arched— Jason took a deep breath and willed his body's inevitable response away. Upstart.

Deliberately he eyed the trunk of the palmetto again. Stripped of petioles, it appeared smooth as a weathered column. With both hands he grasped the trunk—about twenty-two inches in circumference, he reckoned, the size of a slim girl's waist. It wasn't as smooth as it looked. He sat on the railing and, feeling very tentative, raised his knees to grip the trunk. He tested the surface of the bark with his sneakers. Tradd had tried to do it all with her legs and feet. Jason let go, let his arms lurch him down, hand under hand, bizarre jerky motions, down the tree. Civilized! Apelike, the thrusting staccato rhythms of sex, arms taking the weight, the body driven, detached and animal and absurd.

His feet hit the garden walk. He stood up, light-headed, his biceps and thigh muscles shaking a little. He wiped his hands on the backs of his shorts. Noted his knees and calves were skinned on the insides. Felt the pain with pleasure and with pleasure looked up the palmetto trunk. Met the disapproving eyes of his mother.

"Oh, *Jason,*" she said.

To avoid her eyes (with her favorite "boys will be boys" expression therein, though the boy be twenty-four), Jason swooped low in a parody of a bow. "Morning, ma'am," he called mockingly up.

"You've decided to stay for breakfast," she said. Neither interrogative nor declarative: clearly an imperative.

He sighed. Not another good-bye! He'd told her last night at Perdita's, expansive over she-crab soup and champagne, "This is a glorious send-off, Mother. Don't wake up tomorrow. The prodigal son's just here overnight. Keep it light, Mother."

Jason collected his duffles, one over either shoulder. He went along the garden path to the wrought-iron gate that opened on Meeting Street. To capture the prevailing breezes, most of the piazzas of Old Charleston faced side gardens, southwest toward the Ashley River. Only one narrow and deceptive end of the Baynard house faced the street, that end secret with solid shutters on the windows. The closed town-house facade masked a pillared Georgian mansion with an English garden flaunted on the side, the inhabitants living life, as it were, sideways. Jason closed the gate behind him and latched it in the intricate Baynard way. There were already tourists on Meeting

Street, peering through the grillwork and the oleander into the garden.

"Good morning." Jason smiled at them with just the practiced proper balance of welcome and reticence he had been taught as a boy. "You are privileged to live in a beautiful and an historic area, Jason. Your behavior must be exemplary of courteous and cordial Charleston; you are a living survivor of the Old South. But you must always, always, do you hear? remember to lock the gate."

Jason stashed the duffle bags in the boot of his old Triumph parked at the curb. He found his battleship-gray sports car a satisfactory statement against the floral splendor of the artfully weathered brick street. The car denied the rampant gardens; it denied color that had no function; it was, indeed and in fact, a Triumph. So was he. He wore faded khaki shorts and an old white shirt. His hair was too long, unkempt and curly, its tawny gold already mottled with silver at twenty-four. He liked the silver. It helped him jump borders of age. He smiled at the tourists again as they pretended not to be peering at his garden. There were two ladies, one in lilac, the other in lapis lazuli linen, escorted by a gentleman in a gaudy Hawaiian shirt. Jason smiled terminally; he entered the lower piazza at the big black door to the right of the garden gate. Behind him, over his shoulder, he could feel the tourists gape for a glimpse of the interior. He left the door wide open.

"Close the door, Jason!" His mother's scandalized voice.

He felt the door whoosh shut behind him. His mother put her hand through his elbow and led him along the gallery to the morning room, chattering lightly, spattering a delicate, inconsequential, relentless fountain of words. She smelled of lemon verbena. "I've sent Robert down to the harbor for shrimps; no, don't you stiffen up, Jason, the shrimps won't take but a minute, and so fresh, just out of the harbor, and then you can be off, on your journey northwards"—a light, bitter laugh—"to bring your peculiar salvation, your, ah, gifts— isn't that what you call them?—yes, your *gifts* to the benighted and the barbaric, but here you can sit with me now, just a moment, in my morning room." The Elfe breakfast table was set, exquisitely, for two: a yellow rose next to each place setting, goblets of grapefruit juice in silver bowls with cracked ice, a plate of benniseed wafers, the tiny Elfe chairs invitingly, charmingly askew.

"Hellfire," Jason breathed.

His mother seated herself and arranged her skirts. She fixed her eyes on her plate, then looked up at him from under her lashes. ("Equivocate a trifle, *just* a trifle," he heard her voice counsel Tradd years, oh, years ago, "before you encounter a gentleman's eyes directly. Then use your eyelashes.") "Hardly appropriate language, I must say, Jason, coming from you," her voice said now with mild reproach. "Nice talk!" She began to pour coffee from the silver urn. She tinkled a little silver bell. Jason sat down carefully on the little chair opposite her. He had to clamp his knees together to get them between the table legs. Ironically he and Tradd hadn't been allowed in here as children, when they would've fit. "Arvella! Where is that girl?" His mother turned her head and delicately screeched, "Arvella!" The new girl appeared in the doorway, flustered. Her feet tangled over themselves. She wore tennis shoes. Her hair was in corn rows. Jason couldn't believe his eyes. His mother would eat this girl for breakfast.

"Robert jes got here with the shrimps," Arvella said. Jason's mother made an exaggerated gesture of dismissal.

"You really don't mean to forgive Jessamine?" asked Jason. "You've actually hired this girl?" What can I do? his mother's eyebrows eloquently inquired. He'd gleaned last night they'd had one of their Byzantine squabbles, she and Jessamine.

"Jessamine," said his mother, shaking her head sadly, "is *emancipated*. Jessamine has taken to selling flowers up near the corner of Meeting and Broad." She gestured vaguely northward. "I swear, Jason, she has stationed herself at that corner so as to serve as my nemesis."

Jason sputtered on his coffee, laughing. She'd surprised him. "Probably," he said.

"When your sister was here last month—quite alone and without her husband, Jason! And refusing to wear anything but blue jeans, no matter where we went—she spent three hours up at that corner talking to Jessamine right on the street. Then afterwards the house was full of the most peculiar 'flowers,' because, you see, Tradd took it upon herself to purchase *all* of Jessamine's flowers. I've brought you a present, Mother, she said when she came in, her arms full of flowers, some of them nothing but *weeds*, but I said most cordially, Thank you, honey, it is so seldom she makes even a token display of filial affection for me, and then I had to find out later from Robert that Tradd was up there all the afternoon at the corner of Meeting and Broad, visible from Chalmers, sitting on the pavement just like trash amid the daisies and the violets and the bignonias. Jessamine wears a *turban*," she moaned softly.

"All the flower venders do," countered Jason. "It comes, more or less, with the territory." He held a pack of cigarettes in his hand, as if to palm it, hoping she'd notice and he wouldn't have to ask, May I smoke?

"They do *not*. I've noticed lately that a considerable number of them have taken to wearing hats. Gaudy, vulgar hats, but hats, Jason. You may smoke."

"Thank you."

"You and Tradd," she ran on, "inevitably the first question that issues forth from your lips is Jessamine, Jessamine, how is Jessamine? where is Jessamine? never how am *I* doing or feeling or coping, not a word about me. I'm thinking the mammy system is insidious, separating mothers and children, and Jessamine was all your father's fault, she was!" *I have got to go*, Jason thought loudly into the reproachful pause. His mother altered her pitch two decibels, her tone to lugubrious. "Speaking of whom, Jason, I would like you just once before you embark on this feckless journey northwards to look with me quietly at the books, the volumes, in your dear father's library. They are untouched—but for dusting—since his death, as you well know, Jason, untouched and waiting on you, Jason, and it isn't too late even now to abandon your humanitarian foolishness and take up where your poor, poor daddy left off."

In his mind, Jason saw the lawbooks of Jason Beauregard Baynard II (and of Jason Beauregard Baynard I, some of them, for that matter) ranged behind glass in the library: Blackstone, Coke, *Corpus Juris*. On the desk (not an Elfe, a veritable giant of a desk), the cut-glass decanter was kept, as if in memorium, half full of the bourbon that had carried his father off rather young, when Jason was eight and Tradd was six. Your traditional Southern tragedy after all, Jason wryly thought, the principal cause of early demise among your intellectual Southern gentry: Jack Daniels.

"I always did think your innate and inbred propriety would triumph," his mother mused on, "if only you would not be so proud and stubborn and stiff-necked, Jason—"

Arvella entered with the shrimp. The aroma of bacon drippings and onion, green pepper and Worcestershire Sauce swirled around the morning room. It cut through the floral scents deliciously; it eclipsed them, as with a wink. All conversation ceased as Arvella fluttered and cringed to serve the Charleston breakfast shrimp and the grits.

"Thank you, Arvella," sighed both Jason and his mother in unison. Jason abandoned his cigarette to a silver ashtray. Arvella stumbled out, dangling her tray from a limp wrist.

Jason allowed himself one heavenly bite, a tooth exquisitely pierced a shrimp fresh from the harbor, and then he could not refrain from picking up his mother's refrain.

"You know," he said reasonably, "some mothers might consider it the height of 'propriety,' to have a son who next year will be"—he timed it carefully, as for a hypothetical audience—"ordained a Presbyterian minister."

"Elements. A careful and decorous combination thereof." Chloe Otway was devouring a grapefruit more or less whole. She stripped the peel but ate the large segments whole, seeds and rind. Deliberately she stuck an index finger in her mouth to clear it of seeds; then she dipped the same index finger into the sugar bowl in front of her and licked the finger. All around her the blue-and-white-checkered tablecloth was littered with peel and seeds (she had not wanted to dirty a dish). A bowl heaped high with grapefruit centered the table. About to leave on summer vacation, Chloe and her husband were attempting to clear the larder.

Across the table from Chloe, her husband, Tony (almost twenty years an expatriate Englishman, still somewhat to the manner born), ate his grapefruit in neat halves, sugar sprinkled thereon, with a sharp-pointed spoon of old coin silver. But, Chloe pointed out, neatness aside, he was dirtying a dish. And a spoon. He was a chemist; she was a biologist; and while they both veered rather often into biochemistry (Tony was working at the moment on polydentate ligands), their attachments to their respective disciplines remained staunch. In fact, for some time now, they had been debating with great (if illogical) glee how said respective disciplines motivated their approaches to grapefruit consumption. Tony's lab, Chloe argued disparagingly, was always fussily immaculate, you could eat off the tables, drink out of the beakers; but, sputtering, Tony protested, the lab had to be neat, the methodology painstaking—how else to procure accurate data? Chemistry was denied the looseness, the sloppy dissections biologists so loved, plunging their eager little hands into the blood and the mire—

"But a chemist," Chloe said as she licked sugar from her finger, sucking it, "even if he risked an explosion, might discover something radically new if he tried for random combination. Instinctive science. I think we should get back to instinctive science."

"But your hypothetical—and quite mad—chemist wouldn't know what he had found. Nor could he ever find it again," Tony objected.

"It's your basic East versus West argument," Chloe asserted. (No holds barred, she was switching the grounds of the discussion to the philosophical.) "You know—'Flower in the crannied wall, I pluck you out roots and all.' Like an Oriental, a Buddhist, I am appreciating the whole of the grapefruit. Whereas you"—she waved an airy, derogatory, sticky hand—"are dissecting it."

"I just leaped to the opposite conclusion." Tony leaned forward and smiled at her over the table. "*You* are plucking, roots and all. Your whole approach is violent, much more Western, if you will. Swilling all that acetic acid." He frowned. "You did drink your pint of milk this morning, didn't you?"

Chloe made a face. Her voice went flat. "Yes. God, Tony, I hate milk; it makes me feel like a child. I'd almost rather aggravate the damned ulcer. Fight fire with fire. Du-o-de-nal," she enunciated ironically, curling her upper lip.

"Chloe."

"Oh, I won't. I'll try. I promised to try."

"I ought to warn you, I took your microscope out of the car. And your books. You'll have to be more clever than that to hide Gray's *Anatomy* in a Volkswagen."

"Oh, damn!" Chloe's eyes went hot with rising, angry tears.

"Love, you know what the doctor said—"

"Per-fo-rate," she said, teeth clenched.

"Lots of milk, no work, no worry this summer. Vacation. Idle and cavort. Read murder mysteries. Gain some weight. I say, love!" Tony got quickly up; he went behind Chloe and put his beautiful, limber hands on her hunched shoulders. She was snorting and snuffling, trying not to cry. He kneaded the tight muscles of her shoulders; she rolled her neck and breathed deeply. "I say, let's abandon the rest of this acid," Tony said. "Five grapefruit. Poison! Let's get moving. Let's get on the road."

"I suppose Krishna won't spurn the grapefruit."

"And Krishna will water the plants."

"Is the car all packed?"

"Yes, love, and Sir Isaac is waiting with admirable patience in the back. I couldn't budge him. He's afraid we'll leave him behind."

Chloe laughed. "With Krishna. Sir Isaac hates Krishna."

"Chloe, dig up Sam's letter, will you? For the directions." He smiled at her. "And, of course, for the style. I'll clear up here."

Chloe got up from the table. Like her husband, she wore white jeans and a faded-blue oxford-cloth shirt. Both in their early forties— she forty-two, he forty-four—they looked (and sounded) much younger. Both lean and lithe with dark silky hair (Chloe had started to let hers grow, she wasn't sure why), they looked alike from the back: vaguely androgynous, long-legged, high-flanked, with slouched, vulnerable shoulders. From the front, however, there was an agreeable polarity of coloration. Tony's eyes were as blue and straightforward as clean-split aquamarine, and his fair English skin flushed pink at the cheekbones. Chloe's skin tones were gold; her eyes, which slanted rather wickedly, were a lucent khaki-green, eyes that perceived acutely and with wonder; she took great joy in the visual. Her eyes also affected people, dazzled them a little, drew and flustered them; this was fun, of course, but a power she tried not to abuse, for she had a husband so easy for living with, talking with, even for casual walking with, it would be sheer folly to be wanton with her eyes.

Eyes, she always tried to tell herself firmly, were for seeing, not for showing. As legs were for walking. Dreamily Chloe watched Tony's legs walk around the table and began to imagine walking around the yet unseen (but surely emerald-green) Lake Lenni Lenape with him. Whenever they walked together, it was like dancing; their strides paralleled naturally, such incredible luck, and it always delighted her, this physical congruence, this kinship of the body. Chloe moved fast to nudge Tony's hip with her hip; he smiled at her, nudged back. "Get moving, woman."

It was unfortunate, Chloe reflected as she indeed got moving, that she and Tony were nothing alike inside where, ultimately, it counted. Their temperamental disparity was beginning to show. Easy Tony was blessed with easy, efficient internal organs. Her own volatile sensibility was making marks: the duodenal ulcer, the dicey thyroid, the blood pressure, the hyperventilation. Which came first? she wondered, as she wandered from kitchen to living room, checking for forgotten items: Did my biochemical construction make my temperament or vice versa? Does one become angry because adrenaline is released, or does one's anger activate the adrenaline? Either way, she decided with puritanical asperity, one is to blame, one is responsible. I deserve my ulcer.

Her lovely living room diverted her, its creamy high-ceilinged walls with the frieze of absurd little cherubs holding hands. Or were they seraphs? Some of them had four wings, some six. She and Tony were not quite sure what sort of winged creatures populated their frieze. Mostly the fat little faces simpered benignly, but, upon occasion, in the right light, the right mood (making love on the floor, for example), the plaster expressions went erotic, they positively leered down at one. Chloe smiled at the red wool couch, the Wassily chairs. On the coffee table, her nasturtiums were still blooming from last summer, a horticultural phenomenon. She touched a leaf of her *Ficus benjamina* in the corner. Agile as a dancer (externally her body was youthful, perfect), she squatted down to make sure her note was still taped to the huge clay pot: "Krishna, a whole wine bottle full daily." Something wrong with that. What was wrong? Krishna's English, while flamboyant, was not much on idiom. He had trouble following her conversation, although he covered his bafflement with silly, effusive smiles. Chloe read the note again. Dear God, Krishna would give the tree *wine*. She snatched the note off the pot.

"Tony, how am I going to word this?"

Tony shifted the grapefruit peels to one hand, read the note, and laughed. "Maybe wine'll make it grow figs," he said.

"D'you think 'one wine bottle of water'? With water underlined?"

"That's ambiguous. How about 'one bottle of water'? Leave the wine out of it."

"How'll he know what bottle? I always use a wine bottle."

They stood, two scientists, pondering this. They were both full professors; their publications numbered in the hundreds. Chloe was head of her university's biology department; Tony had once been considered (with a group of others) for a Nobel Prize. Over the note, they inclined their heads at an identical angle; she bit her lower lip; he pulled at his earlobe. The air swirled with their thinking, buzzed over the problem of how properly to instruct their summer housesitter, an Indian physics student, in the watering of their *Ficus benjamina*.

"Krishna's a Hindu, I don't think they drink wine," tried Chloe.

"I don't think any religion forbids giving wine to plants."

"I guess not. I mean, who'd think of it? What religion would bother? Krishna would probably think wine was some brutal Western custom."

"I have it!"

"What? What?"

Tony brandished the hand holding the grapefruit peels. "We place a wine bottle next to the tree. We append the note to the bottle. The note will be revised to read 'Krishna, give one bottle of water daily.' "

"Perfect!" Chloe kissed her husband's cheek in an effusion of admiration. "Brilliant!"

Tony basked. Then he said, *sotto voce*, "One more thing, love. Krishna, with great delicacy and tact, has confided to me—"

"What?" Chloe leaned towards his whisper with some alarm.

"He can't read your handwriting."

"Oh, you."

"I'll write the note. Move your arse, woman. Sam's letter."

From the top shelf of the bedroom closet, Chloe extracted a shoe box full of letters from Samuel Coleridge Barnes, professor of English, last of the great letter writers, dear Sam, her one link with her rapidly dwindling family; she often felt herself the breathless survivor of a shipwreck or fire, for they were all gone: parents, brother, sisters. Childless, she and Tony clung together, adrift. Even Sam wasn't a blood relation, what was he? he was her nephew-in-law, Chloe computed, but kin for all that, metaphoric kin, blood brother, incidentally married to her niece, Abbie, the daughter of her eldest sister. Abbie was, in point of fact, her closest living blood relative. Chloe, the youngest child of her parents, was an anomaly and an accident, closer in age to Sam's and Abbie's generation than her own. She was a year older to the day (Valentine's Day, of all days) than Sam; and their disciplines clashed, their sensibilities grated, his prose style drove her up the wall; yet in the ten years since she and Tony had been in Cambridge, Chloe and Sam Barnes had sustained a loquacious, vibrant correspondence that somehow kept the kinship system open, the epistolary glee alive. "A letter from Sam!" Chloe still exulted to Tony, whenever she found one, riffling through the mail in the hall downstairs. Tony pretended to be jealous.

Replacing the shoe box, Chloe opened the last letter, and walking

backward, she sat carefully down on the bed's patchwork counter-
pane, not to muss it—Krishna was so particular, a regular princess
and the pea he was, so much for the Hindu bed of nails!—and started
to skim Sam's letter for the relevant directions. But it was no use
skimming, she was immediately hooked; she pulled up her feet American Indian-fashion and read the letter through:

> Lenni Lenape (an
> intentionally cryptic
> location, to be illuminated
> later when your curiosity is
> at fever pitch)
> Memorial Day

Dear Chloe,

My right thigh is bloated to an alarming degree; I caught just a
glimpse of the scurrying creature who bit me, and it was an arachnid.
I remain firmly convinced it was a Black Widow, but Abbie says I
would be already dead if it were. While I attempt to divert myself
from the neurotoxic symptoms that multiply about me here in my
idyllic boathouse study (aren't you curious?), I'll use the time, the
brief precious time before paralysis and death, to gasp out a letter to
you, my faithful pen pal.

So you have an ulcer, old girl? Congratulations. In this academic rat
race, an ulcer, especially of the exotic duodenum, constitutes a badge
of honor. All I've been able to manage thus far is a spider bite (and
quite hideous it is), but give me time.

Many thanks for the kind words on *Thorns of Life*. I could tell you
had actually read it, was mightily pleased. I am presently puffed up
(this spider bite is rendering my diction positively biblical!) with a
kind of ingenuous, awed pride, for my royalty checks indicate *Thorns*
is being ordered as a standard text for fall in many Romantic poetry
courses throughout the country—even at Princeton! Not bad for
one's first book, though one be older than Byron when he died (not to
mention Keats and, excuse the expression, Shelley); but who thought
that I would ever write a *book?* However, pride goeth before falls, and
in an aberrant moment I consented to write, *before fall*, a monograph
for a series entitled, with spare elegance, *Poets*. The monograph I
agreed to write is on Blake. Don't ask me why Blake. I am sick to

death of Blake. I am longing to talk to Tony about Blake—despite his long sojourn in America, Tony must hide vestiges of English sensibility somewhere about his person. I am rather desperate. Anglophile that I have always been, I am shocked that the English would actually take to their collective bosom such a madman as Blake and rank him with Donne and Browning. I mean, really!

> And did those feet in ancient times
> Walk upon England's mountains green?
> And was the holy Lamb of God
> On England's pleasant pastures seen?

Anyone but Blake I'd say was speaking metaphorically (irritating as even that would be), but, damn it, I'm beginning to think the man *means* it: Jesus was once tripping through English meadows. It is downright *Mormon.*

Speaking of which and to get out of that boring shoptalk paragraph somehow, my life has lately been a positive burden from Mormons. Last month, two young men in black suits came to the house in town, Mormons on their missionary year, and Liz and I were friendly (Liz said later one of them was "cute") and hospitable and plied them with refreshments they could not imbibe. (My daughter, who is addicted to Pepsi-Cola, now drinks "that carbonated stimulant" with an evil glint in her eye.) Offered cocoa, the two Mormons treated us to a stern diatribe against chocolate; apparently there is internecine strife in the Mormon Church about chocolate, and both of our visitors wanted to go on record as staunchly anti. Finally and reluctantly, after some debate, they accepted (honest to God) *Popsicles,* which they licked while I sipped whiskey in a properly hangdog and defiant manner, Liz having skulked off, presumably for a bit of the bubbly.

The two Mormons and I discussed their religion. Politely I objected to their treatment of blacks (besides polygamy, that was offhand all I could summon to mind about Mormonism), and they became very excited and allowed that, yes, they did, despite official statements to the contrary, still mistreat blacks, but had "very liberal views on women." Turned out this did not mean a return to polygamy as I initially hoped, but that they "even let our women preach."

To get rid of them, I accepted a *Book of Mormon.* To what has become my enduring regret, I read it. You know I will read anything.

(Yes, I do read your articles, and Tony's too, although his chemical formulas—especially those fancy spiderweb [!] constructions—stymie me somewhat. I try to view them as esoteric works of art, illustrating matters beyond my comprehension. I enjoyed you particularly, by the way, on "The Genetic Inferiority of the Y Chromosome"—what an underhanded feminist trick! You should be a Mormon; they'd even let you preach.) At any rate, I read the *Book of Mormon* with mild interest (it's not a bad yarn for a seventeen-year-old with a wild imagination), and when the two young men returned, I casually referred to my reading. They nearly embraced me. I was all alone. I was damned frightened. They were ecstatic. I got the idea that even their prophet Moroni was ecstatic somewhere, and I expect them here daily, even in the wilderness of Lake Lenni Lenape, probably with Moroni in tow. As a matter of grim fact, Jos. Smith, Jr. hung out around here, circa 1825, seducing farmers' daughters, I believe. So my Mormons will doubtless make a pilgrimage here, and when they do you will be able to meet them.

For (at last to the point of this interminable letter!) *you* are to make a pilgrimage here, you and Tony. Abbie, Liz, and I are adamant. Where we are is at a lake (pronounced Len-ni Len-a-pee) in a handsome cottage that proves to be, along with innumerable car dealerships and a whole block of buildings, a part of Abbie's inheritance. The cottage is vast, delightful, and needs filling with family. I seem suddenly to have been seized by the urge to be the father of a large brood, and to the end of painlessly humoring this urge, we have managed to acquire, when school lets out, a Wilson nephew and niece, Abbie's brother's children. (Your great-nephew and niece, it occurs to me, old girl. I've instructed Liz to start calling you Great-aunt Chloe.) Betsy, you'll recall, is fourteen, just Liz's age. Bill is nineteen and is on a football scholarship at Syracuse. He is burly, but no dolt, being a quarterback. He will live here but work during the day on construction, earning more money than you or I. Their mother is seizing the cash from her own belated legacy to go to Columbia for a crash MBA. Thus, Abbie and I, Liz, Betsy, and Bill will be ensconced by the fire but rattling around this big cottage. We absolutely require you and Tony. Abbie and I long for a resident bridge table. The place is a charming anachronism. There is no television. Our telephone rings two longs and a short. Or is it two shorts and a long? No matter. We will amuse ourselves with parlor games, charades and twenty questions, as they did in Jane Austen's time. I will (dreary thought) chip away at Blake daily in the boathouse.

Which I'd relish sharing with Tony. He can set up test tubes; he can blow the place up for all I care. The editors of *Poets* will surely understand why the Blake volume perished. You, I gather from the exasperated tone of your last letter, are under orders to rest and drink milk. The milkman cometh daily for the ulcerated. Abbie has planted a vegetable garden. The place reeks of health and morality.

Should you be loath to leave the cosmopolitan environs of Cambridge (note how cleverly and exhaustively I counter any possible argument), I can even offer you selected ethnicity here: for example, a Jewish contingent on the northeast corner of the lake, cut off by the inlet and a stand of trees. Just ten years ago, local legend has it, "they" managed to grab a toehold, although the antiquated Charter of the Lake remains opposed—the most shocking document imaginable (yes, I do read anything). It doggedly forbids "those of semitic or negroid persuasion"—I ask you, *persuasion?*—to swim in its waters. If you have any venturesome black friends, I urge you to bring them; Matt Bernstein (a charming man, editor of the local *Bugle)* and his family have already swum from my dock, and I'd like to agitate (muddy?) the waters even more.

The General Store, called "Esther's," is owned and run by a woman who claims to be a descendant of Esther Montour, an Indian queen of notably bloody inclinations (single-handed, she tomahawked and scalped fourteen hapless settlers at the Wyoming Massacre to avenge a son), but the present Esther is redheaded, freckled, and dumpy (although sharp-tongued, now that I think of it. "If anyone knows where the Heineken is, Sam Barnes, *you* do," she once said to me).

Directly in back of us, just across our little bridge and the road, there's a tiny old German fellow named Otto Dolch who plays every Sunday morning on his loudspeaker, very loudly, scratched records of German marches. I awake groaning, fantasying I am in Berlin about to hear the Führer speak. Why on Sundays? it occurs to me. Why German *marches?* But Otto has a volleyball court and tennis courts, a basketball court and a baseball diamond. A sign at the entrance to his property says, "FOR THE KINDER OF LENNI LENAPE." His lawns are terraced and decorated with odd seating affairs: covered

wagons, oriental chaises, Victorian love seats, perfect places for neck-
ing on chilly nights. (Do you still neck?)

And should you fancy Elizabethan culture, due south of Otto's
playground, the head of my department has a cottage, an incredible
bore named Harold Fanshawe, a Shakespeare specialist. We cordially
loathe each other. He seethes with rage (I can feel it, across the road)
that my cottage fronts the lake while his does not. He has two teen-
aged daughters, homely girls named (honest to God) Olivia and Viola,
from *Twelfth Night*. Harold covets my beautiful daughter; he probably
loosed the Black Widow who bit me; enough of Harold.

What more? Abbie, Liz, and I burn to have you here. There is a
roadhouse cum bar and country-western band called the Lake Lenni
Lenape Inn; there is weekly garbage collection; there is a Presbyterian church dated 1846 which Esther (the redhaired Indian) tells me
will be manned for the summer by a seminarian from Vanderbilt.

Oh, I saved the best for last. We have bountiful and sublimely witty
bathroom accommodations. In the kitchen, stark and unenclosed,
there is a toilet just sitting there, between sink and stove. Upstairs,
there is a mundane, ordinary bathroom and also a monumental one,
with two toilets side by side, one white, the other magenta. Each has a
matching washbowl. The bathrooms alone are worth the trip.

Always,
Sam

Chloe laughed, a rich, throaty laugh. She inspected the meticulous
map under the scrawled signature, a map drawn, she surmised, by
Abbie, Sam's wife, who also appended the laconic note: "Chloe,
there's no washer and dryer. Bring warm clothes, insect repellent,
blankets, and *pillows.*" I wonder how Sam and Abbie are doing, Chloe
mused briefly; I never thought they would last this long. Sixteen
years. Whee. Then she heard the honk of the Volkswagen; she got up,
smoothed the bed, and, briskly, with her long-legged boyish stride,
left her apartment without looking back. When she emerged from the
front door, their Old English sheep dog, Sir Isaac Newton, poked his
shaggy head through the sunroof of the Volkswagen; she laughed into
his wild and woolly face.

"The Massachusetts Pike to Albany," she said to Tony, getting in
beside him, "then Eighty-eight to Eighty-one to the Pennsylvania

border where we follow the Susquehanna and it starts getting compli-
cated." Tony started the car. They turned at the corner, and Chloe
said, "Do you realize, Tony, I am the only one left of my generation?
I'm a God damned *matriarch.*" He patted her knee. He started singing,
"It's a long way to Tipperary," and she chimed in. They drove by
Harvard Yard. "Good-bye to Piccadilly. Farewell, Harvard Yard!"
They hit the Longfellow Bridge singing at the tops of their voices,
and Sir Isaac barked percussion through the sunroof.

3 CHARLESTON, S.C.

Next to his Triumph, Jason stood at the curb on Meeting Street and tried to read his battered road map. It was tearing on the creases. Too much road, he thought, feeling dizzy, tasting shrimp in the back of his throat, fumbling the Eastern states from the south to the north section. The driver's seat of the Triumph did not look inviting. On Saturday morning, he'd been still in Nashville at Vanderbilt, taking notes on Luke-Acts in his carrel in Divinity Library. By Sunday morning, he'd been up in the Great Smokies just over the Carolina border at a place called Pisgah, named after the biblical mountain at the end of the Dead Sea. The Dead Sea Scrolls were probably in better shape than this road map, thought Jason.

Sunday morning in a black church on Pisgah with his roommate Calvin, also black, a middle-class, but street-smart refugee from the Upper West Side of New York City, romantically seeking out his Southern "roots" at Vanderbilt. "Africa's just too far back, man. And Mississippi, where my great-grandparents came from, is too scary." Calvin was serving his summer internship as pastoral assistant to a Baptist preacher in a mountain parish. Calvin's church had been . . . fun; Jason brought it back through his ears, the music and the joy, the feet stamping, the rollicking, wholehearted hymns. "Now you have to come to *my* church," Jason called to Calvin, waving out of the Triumph, just yesterday morning.

His own church. Nobody's assistant, he. He would be *the* pastor: Pastor of the Lake Lenni Lenape Presbyterian Church, somewhere (although not, apparently, on his road map), somewhere on *faith*, in Pennsylvania. Pisgah and Lenni Lenape, bizarre fields for education. What did Lenni Lenape mean? Something to do with Indians, Jason reckoned. He'd look it up. The boot of the Triumph was crammed with books: his Depression-vintage Britannica picked up at a sidewalk sale, a stack of hasty summer loans from Divinity Library; New

Testament stuff mostly, for the Luke-Acts paper, but also an intriguing batch of books on American church history. His grim Hebrew
books, his Greek New Testament, and the gleaming, newly purchased Aramaic text for fall: at last, the language of Jesus. The department held out Aramaic as the plum, the carrot beyond the barbed
goad of two years of biblical Hebrew and Koine Greek. At long last,
one became eligible to study the homely dialect Jesus had spoken
every day.

The morning sun was merciless. Jason felt melded to the pavement
of Meeting Street. He winced sideways toward the piazza gate to
where his mother, oh for God's sake, had collected not only Robert
but also that idiotic Arvella to bid him Godspeed. Young massa off to
the wars. Jason crumpled up the map and threw it on the seat: 26 to
95 to Baltimore, 83 to Harrisburg, follow 11/15 and the Susquehanna,
then it got complicated. He shoved back the top of the Triumph,
folding it down, fastening it on sprockets, feeling relief his hands still
functioned. What kind of madman shinnies down palmettos before
breakfast? He rubbed his hands together and went to the piazza gate.
He shook hands with Robert. Robert was crying—he always cried at
departures. When Tradd left on her honeymoon on Valentine's Day,
Robert had howled. (Of course Tradd had been crying her eyes out
too. She'd wept out loud coming back up the aisle, while Whit, the
bridegroom, looked at her in alarm.) "Buck up, Robert," Jason said
now, gripping the old man's frail shoulder. " 'Bye, Arvella." He
smiled at her. Arvella giggled. Jason kissed his mother. Some tourists
stopped across Meeting Street to watch.

"Do write, Jason." His mother flaunted what he and Tradd called
her "smilin' through face" bravely.

"I'll write." Waving, Jason got into the Triumph, settled his body
gingerly into the sticky, familiar leather seat, waved wearily again
after he'd started up the motor, setting up a roar through Old
Charleston. His mother and Robert and Arvella stood at the gate like
a triptych of the Old South, and when he turned the corner at South
Battery, Jason glanced back and could see them still waving.

4 LONDON, ENGLAND

"Daddy, I really mean it; do I have to say it again? I will not go on another honeymoon." Elise Barnes clenched her fists in the pockets of her navy-blue school blazer and rocked back and forth. She was freezing. It was winter still in her father's London flat; probably nobody'd been in it since winter; there was a horrid, musty smell of cold mildew. Elise wrinkled her nose. She'd noticed out of the corner of her eye, as for a ransom note, that they'd come by the Piccadilly Eros and Leicester Square to get to this grubby bachelor *pied-à-terre*, her dad's borrowed "digs"; but for all the sense of place she had, she could be floating somewhere over London in one of his private planes, never quite landing.

Jack Barnes ("John Keats Barnes" on his birth certificate and "Mad Jack" to his friends) sat at the scarred kitchen table, drinking a pint of ale. Ale was all there was in the fridge; Elise had looked. Her father had grown a beard since she'd seen him last at Christmas, a pirate's beard, curling and wild, streaked gray, blond, black. It was funny that the beard made him easier for her to buck, to stand up to—he didn't look altogether real, Elise decided. He looked like he was in costume for something.

"Elise, baby," he said now in the soothing tone of sweet masculine reason dealing with feminine hysterics, "you've never objected to the honeymoons before."

"I was too young to know what was going on," she retorted.

"Ah—" Watching him swallow as if to digest that, Elise tried an airy, sophisticated toss of her head to underline in pantomime, so there, now she did know what went on on honeymoons, no thanks to him, no thanks at all, nor thanks to any of his wives. She'd known, of course, from other sources about sex in the abstract, but she had not known about the explicitly sexual connotation of honeymoons; and now she felt (not without some justice) that this connotation had been intentionally kept from her; she became, in retrospect, a dupe, a buffoon. "Oh, Elise always comes on my honeymoons," she heard Jack's stale joke vibrate through layers of time and restructure her past.

What there was of it. Elise was just sixteen, the sheltered product of her father's restless, peripatetic life, a daughter picked up and dropped in private planes and Maseratis by this man, her father, a roving journalist and a much married man. She'd been at school in Grenoble, in Seattle, in Berlin, in Geneva, was now on her summer holiday from an Anglican girls' school in East Sussex. Jack Barnes was appraising her, frowning up and down her body, a bit taken aback by her sixteen-year-old presence—at least she hoped he was taken aback she'd grown up. She felt herself blush, deplored her school blazer and the long auburn plait down her back; she knew she didn't look sixteen at this particular moment, although with her hair loose, flowing down past her waist, she could look—she had it from her friends—absolutely smashing.

Of middle height, Elise appeared almost achingly small-boned, light of body, narrow. Wiry and strong, a splendid scrapper on the hockey field, she still looked as if she'd break; she was accustomed to being treated as fragile. She hated it, the kid-glove treatment. Her face was narrow at the temples, wide at the cheekbones, pointed at the chin; her cheeks looked as if she were sucking them in. Her eyes, deep-set under her forehead, were dark amber flecked with gold, eyes the color of her hair. "Red hair and red eyes," her friend Daphne described her with a droll little moan, "and yet you're beautiful, Elise. It isn't fair." "Why, she's all eyes and hair!" Jack's bride-to-be (Elise characterized Pamela thus, ironically, in her mind) had cried on Christmas holiday, meeting her. "Mad Jack, she is exquisite. Just look! those sooty eyelashes."

As if she were a doll and not a person, Elise reflected now grimly. "Daddy," she argued, "Pamela won't want me on the honeymoon. It isn't fair to Pamela. The wives must have hated my being on the honeymoons."

"Elise, you got on with the wives a damned sight better than I ever did. Now spare us these schoolgirl dramatics." She scowled at him. He grinned wickedly at her, switching to another tack before she was ready. "Examine your logic, baby doll. You were willing, even eager, to travel with Pamela and me in sin, yes, in sin, baby; didn't you learn about that too, in the loo, at St. Catherine's? Now you balk at travels with a respectable married couple. I thought you'd be pleased. You like Pamela, don't you? Pamela is crazy about *you*— "

"Bloody hell!" Elise exploded. She crashed her fists on the table, taking pleasure in the pain. She stood, breathing hard, staring him down. Jack Barnes stared back a minute, then began to laugh. He covered his mouth with his hand, resting his elbow on the table. His shoulders shook with laughing.

"You look like—do you know what you look like, Elise?" Elise felt her jaw tighten. The roving journalist was about to deliver one of his Pulitzer Prize-winning metaphors. Jack Barnes uncovered his mouth. "You look like an angel who just said bullshit." He laughed again, his soundless, uncontrollable laugh. He raised his hands, thumbs touching on the horizontal, in half a square to frame her face. "You look like Juliet suddenly telling old Capulet to fuck off."

Elise gulped. She felt an unwilling giggle in her throat. She sat down at the table. Her father smiled at her. "Well, baby doll," he said, "what're we going to do with you?"

Elise felt her eyes open wide. She squared her shoulders, so as not to look like a waif. ("An exquisite waif," had been how Pamela summed her up.) She'd not really expected to win this contest with her father, had merely wanted to go on record as rebel. What would become of her? Mentally she located her school friends. "Perhaps," she improvised, "I could join Daphne and Jane in Scotland . . ." She had no idea where in Scotland they'd be by now, Jack had fetched her so late. Inverness? "Rebels," her mind parroted Sister Maria, the history mistress, "should always have an alternative in mind, in case they win. Otherwise," Sister Maria said, nodding solemnly, "they're no better than anarchists."

Jack Barnes shook his head. "I want you in the States," he said. "Pamela and I are going to settle down in the States where there's still someplace to rattle around in. We're going to buy a house in the country."

"Where?" Elise raised one skeptical eyebrow, defying Carol, Jack's fourth wife (the wife before), who'd once gasped, scaring the wits out of Elise, "Don't raise that eyebrow! You'll make a wrinkle!" "Where are you going to settle?" Elise repeated.

"Someplace we like on the honeymoon. Maybe in the West," he said breezily.

"I'll believe it when I see it," said Elise.

"You wait." He raised a finger, wagging it. "You'll see. It's time I wrote my long-threatened memoirs." He winked. She laughed. "Volume One," he proclaimed. "Mad Jack Barnes's Early Years." He cocked his head, listening to the rhythm in the air. "Or maybe The Early Years of Mad Jack Barnes. Which d'you think?"

"I don't care what you call them," Elise said, "but I'd certainly like to read them. I don't know anything about your early years."

Jack quaffed ale and sat silent for a moment. He wiped foam from his beard. "Sam," he said. He slapped the table. "That's it. Sam."

"Sam who?"

"Sam, my brother," said Jack reproachfully. "Oh, come on, Elise, don't play dumb. You know Sam. You met him several times." She stared. "Well, several times as a baby," he amended. Then he smiled a faraway smile into space. "He and your mother got on—oh, hell." His eyes misted.

Elise waited. He couldn't bear to think of her mother. He still couldn't, although it had been thirteen years since Leslie Barnes had . . . well, sky-dived to her death. Through years of being asked how her mother died, Elise had not been able to come up with a more solemn and respectable description, although sometimes she lied and said, "in a plane crash," an answer that tended to elicit a more unequivocal sympathy than "skydiving." In Elise's imagination, the legendary scene unfolded as a montage in slow motion, almost a cartoon with bright primary colors: a red plane, blue jump suits, yellow parachute; Jack and Leslie in the air, the one chute opening, the other not, Jack's mad, desperate hands grabbing air, as Leslie went down, down. How could her father still fly? Elise wondered now, watching him almost critically, for he flew with wild glee whenever he got the chance, kept a plane in London, another in New York. Why did he remind himself? she mused, pondering this weeping man's stubborn defiance of fate and of gravity.

Jack pounded the table and snuffled his nose in a brisk way. "Every time I hear from Sam, he asks us to visit. I got a book from him in the post the other day, and he'd written on the flyleaf, 'How about sending Elise for the summer?' " Elise felt her mouth fall open. "A book he wrote," Jack went on. "Some thorny English lit nonsense. Sam's got a daughter too. I met *her*, as a little kid."

"You mean I had a real invitation?" A dart of anger, sharp and pure, directed her words. "You never told me I had any real place to visit." Jack looked away, down at the table. "You always make me feel you're the only family I've got." Elise took a deep breath. "It's no wonder I look like a waif. I *am* a waif."

"Baby doll." Jack reached across the table and trapped her hand. "Don't look like that. Honey, you're all I've got. I didn't want to lose you." His eyelids sagged; his voice lost its buoyancy, went hoarse and heavy in the air. "Don't think I haven't suffered over Sam's invitations. I've felt guilty about them for years." *How many invitations?* Elise wondered; then Jack gave her hand a slack, exhausted squeeze that stayed a weight and pinned her hand to the table. "Oh, hell, can't you see it? At a certain age, there's nothing in creation so God damned seductive as a settled family. Say you were ten or eleven. You'd have visited, and, God almighty, they'd all have loved you"—he smiled at her, a moony, downsloping smile—"because who could help it? Then Sam and Abbie'd start feeling sorry for you, and they'd say, 'Elise, stay on, go to school with Liz, you'd see your father just as much as you do now, go on his honeymoons with him.' By now, honeybunch, you'd be *theirs*. Would you like that?"

Elise looked at his large, lugubrious self so pathetically slumped in his chair; and she pushed the warm family portrait he'd painted out of her mind, let the names fade away, insubstantial: Sam, Abbie, Liz. "Oh," she said, pulling her hand away from under his, flexing the pins and needles away, "I'm happy, Daddy. I like being"—she parodied what he called himself—"a wild expatriate fly-by-night's daughter."

He didn't laugh. He cast a shrewd eye on her. He sat up straight now, alert and powerful and sly. "Do you think," he asked her speculatively, "you're old enough now to risk a summer with your Uncle Sam?" He pointed a finger at her. "You'll come back to me?"

"Of course I'll come back to you," said Elise.

"Well, then it's settled," he said. Wait a minute, she thought with alarm, what have I agreed to?

"Well," said Jack heartily, putting a hand on either corner of his end of the table, "Uncle Sam it is." He levered himself up as if doing a push-up, muscles straining the armholes of his ancient herringbone tweed jacket. "Uncle Sam. How's that to cushion your reentry into the States? Uncle Sam." Settled, is it? Elise was thinking, as she grimaced automatically at his bad joke. She had again the fantasy she was in a plane over London, a plane Jack was taking through all his favorite flips and plummeting, mad dives. A mere passenger along for the ride, she fixed her eyes on him, steadying herself. "Pretty bad, I agree," Jack said. "We'd better call Sam. Get this show on the road." He fumbled in his jacket pocket and pulled out his tiny address book. He was a broad-shouldered man who blundered through rooms, yet his handwriting was as fine and as delicate as his daughter. Elise focused her attention on the address book where his unruly, sprawling acquaintanceship was recorded in a script that emulated a medieval manuscript. She watched his big hands turn the little pages.

"Steady Sam," said Jack. "One address for sixteen years. One English department for sixteen years." He shook his head. "One *wife*, for Christ's sake." He looked at his watch. "What time is it in the States? Five hours. Two o'clock here. Fourteen minus five. Nine o'clock in the morning. A good, respectable time to call."

Jack came around the table and put an awkward hand on Elise's shoulder. She felt her whole body flow toward the hand's warmth. "Will it be okay, baby doll?"

"I expect I can always join you on the honeymoon"—she tipped her head to look backward up at him—"if it doesn't work out."

"Honeybunch, I'll be joining *you* if the honeymoon doesn't work out." He laughed loudly, a fake, hearty laugh. Elise smiled, but her eyes ached a little, as at an ending she wasn't sure was happy.

5 CHARLESTON, S.C.

Jason turning north on East Bay gunned the Triumph, inhaled salt
sea air off the Battery, sped as if from the hounds of hell. He wanted
to whoop and holler. He felt a wildness in his chest. From inside his
shirt he freed the two medals around his neck (hidden from his
mother, who'd have been horrified, as horrified as if he'd gotten himself tattooed): the cross Calvin had hammered out of a tin can while
Jason watched, amazed, and the coupled Alpha and Omega in old
gold, given him by that dark-haired girl he'd spurned in the spring.
Looking down, Jason approved the wry antinomy of tin and gold, the
two chains tangled across the worn oxford cloth of his shirt.

His lips played with the word "spurn." He'd been spurning girls
for two years now, not exactly as a vow of celibacy (although it might
come to that), more as a recognition that the wild oats hitherto sown
had been enough, would serve. His senses were sharper thus, spurning. His senses hummed. Some of the girls had been hurt, two had
gotten angry, but the dark-haired girl in the spring had been, well,
what else to call it? impressed. She'd hung an old gold medal around
his neck, appointed herself Mary Magdalene to his Jesus, followed
him (at a discreet distance) through the streets of Nashville.

"Oh, whee!" Calvin had laughed under the willows in Centennial
Park. "Mary's sandals are too much!"

Magdala on Galilee, Charleston on the harbor. St. Michael's bells
clanged, jangled nine o'clock. Into Jason's ear, with the bells, a stern
edict came: "Remember the rector." Jason braked, turned abruptly
into narrow, brick-walled Longitude Lane, racketing the Triumph
along the skewed bricks of the alley. He turned (illegally) up Church
Street and headed for St. Philip's. As the car bumped across the
quaint cobblestones of Chalmers Street, "Don't look left," something
warned. Good advice, he answered back, allowing into his mind, reluctantly, the word "schizoid." The left and right lobes of his brain

were more aware of each other than most people's, he knew. He could feel the clicks back and forth between logic and imagination. He also knew a psychiatrist would say his resident voice (if such soundless words could be called "voice") replaced a father who had died too soon. Jason could imagine the casual psychiatric shrug: "It's a conscience, that's all. Don't, for God's sake, get that mixed up with *God.*" Jason laughed. He kept his eyes straight ahead, teased though they were leftward down Chalmers to Meeting where Jessamine beturbaned might be hawking flowers at the corner. A turquoise-blue turban, he imagined. Imagined himself caught like his sister Tradd in Jessamine's magic, prattling free as a child to Jessamine all the day long.

Jessamine would know about Tradd. All about Tradd. Hellfire, he hadn't the *time.* Jason drove up the rise to St. Philip's and parked his car (illegally) in front of the portico. He stopped in the portico, his favorite place in all of Old Charleston, favorite because it looked out of Old Charleston. Ah, the kingdoms of the world. Behold the kingdoms of the world.

On the other side of the rise an ordinary business district sprawled itself willy-nilly out, not "restored," not dripping with flowers. When Jason was a boy on his bicycle, the view from St. Philip's had drawn and held him, had symbolized all the world to him, the world where boys played ball in the streets, and the fire hydrants weren't painted to look like toy soldiers, and the cars could drive at proper speed, not wary of canopied horse-drawn carriages and their resultant "mess" (as his mother fastidiously called the horseshit) in the streets. Bemused, Jason recollected the street cleaners coping with horseshit between the cobblestones on Chalmers. They never grumbled. They called out to each other in rich melodious voices, rich as the dark-brown horse manure, melodious as a production of *Porgy and Bess.*

Maybe one day they'd be "emancipated." Like Jessamine. Oh, brother.

Wryly Jason laughed and slipped through one of the panels of the tall carved doors of St. Philip's. Two tourist ladies in hats looked sternly askance at his ragtag attire. He grinned at them, and their frowns melted; flushed and flustered, they smiled back at him. It was blessedly cool inside. Jason glanced into the church where the dome caught, filtered, and cooled the sunlight into a golden peace. The stained-glass window over the altar glowed and beckoned. Jason's eyes wound up the spiral stairs to the pulpit, and he thought, I'll be preaching on Sunday. Lenni Lenape. I'll compose the sermon; I'll choose the hymns. He recalled again the hymns at Calvin's church in Pisgah, hymns like gospel rock, and he climbed the hall stairs and moved down the corridor to the rector's office, feet moving in rhythm to "Just a Closer Walk with Thee." Baptist rhythms out of sync in stately, elegant St. Philip's. Nashville rhythms. Nashville sound.

"Jason Baynard!" cried the funny little secretary, plump as a Carolina wren, who'd been there ever since he could remember. When he was a boy he'd thought she'd probably grow, but she never did. He hugged her now.

"Hi, baby doll."

"Jason, I virtually *promised* Rector you'd call on us before you left!"

Jason felt his eyes beam over his suppressed smile. She always called the rector "Rector," as if that were his name. "Oh, Rector!" she'd say when he teased her. "Rector, didn't I tell you?" he heard her now as she went through the door into the study. "Just look who's here!"

The rector came to the door. "Jason!" he said, his face full of light. I almost didn't come, Jason thought, ashamed. "Come in, Jason!"

They shook hands. They smiled at each other. The rector closed the door. "I was feeling blue," the rector said. "I was meditating on the Fourth Sunday after Pentecost. The Gospel's gloomy; the Epistle's Paul at his gloomiest. You know, Jason, every year I think, Well, this year I'm old enough to appreciate Saint Paul, but, by Saint Peter, Jason, I still can't stomach him!" The rector laughed. "Let's sit down."

Jason sat. The rector sat behind his big desk. The rector still pronounced "Saint" "S'n" in the old Anglican way. Jason wondered if he could get away with "S'n Peter," but he reckoned not. "God must have loved the sufferings of this present time," Jason parodied the Epistle, "for they are still with us."

The rector laughed. "A colleague." He let his pleasure show. The rector had finagled Jason's summer assignment, Jason knew, but the rector wouldn't mention it. If Jason presumed to thank him, he'd be embarrassed. He'd look at his hands, and Jason would know he was thinking, Let not the left hand know what the right hand is doing. Schizoid Christian hands. "Well, I had a letter from my old Presbyterian friend, Bill Daniels, at Vanderbilt." Bill Daniels was Jason's preaching professor. "Bill told me you're a cross between John Donne and Martin Luther King. That's a cross!"

"It sure is. It means I haven't shaken the Southern accent yet."

"Pah, who cares about an accent!" The rector rested his cheekbones in his hands and leaned his elbows on the desk. "Oh, my, I envy you, Jason, just starting out. I think you're right, you know, to go over to the Presbyterians, although please don't quote me. You'll have freedom; you can circumvent the lectionary; and just between us, the liturgy, beautiful as it is, gets on your nerves after a while. About once a year I find myself most wickedly and intentionally splitting that awful infinitive in the Thanksgiving. Rather than 'mercifully to accept,' I say, 'to mercifully accept,' and I swear I can hear God cheer!" Laughing, the rector leaned back in his chair and propped one foot on an open file drawer.

Jason, laughing too, felt his eyes fill with love. Years lay between him and the rector, years of counseling. When he was twelve—half his life ago—Jason had run away from a military school in Virginia, run away before he'd been there a week. His father was already dead; his mother simply couldn't handle him, or so she told everybody. At the military school, the older boys had called the new boys "rats." They would jump into their rooms after lights-out and growl "Rat!" in the darkness. Oh, it assaulted his eardrums, invaded his being; he slept with his hands clenched on the iron bar of his cot until a voice in his ear proclaimed, Enough. "I've had enough," Jason said mutinously to his mother, who was waiting at the railroad station—the school had called her; he felt hounded, run to earth. "Enough of being called a rat in the dark." (They'd also called him "Barnyard," but he didn't tell her that, because Baynard was her name too.)

That night late, Tradd had sneaked into his bedroom from the piazza. She was ten, wearing his cast-off pajamas. In the dark, her face floated, a white oval. Her hair was in the lopsided rag curlers Jessamine favored. Tradd was a tease. He was afraid she was going to call him "rat," and he didn't think he could bear it, not a girl's voice, not in the dark, but Tradd asked him softly, "Did they really call you 'rat'? Because Mother doesn't believe you. Mother says you hear things. Mother wants to send you to a psychiatrist. She's going to ask Great-grandmother Beau tomorrow."

Jason had stared at her in horror. Tradd's face was very solemn. Great-grandmother Beau's word was law.

The next day, her own connections all being in Princess Anne County in Virginia (where the military school was), Jason's mother had consulted his father's grandmother, who was ninety and sharp as the proverbial tack. She'd decreed that Jason should see the rector at St. Philip's. He was a distant cousin of her daughter-in-law's brother's son.

"Your mother," the rector had told Jason carefully that first time, "thinks you should see a psychiatrist. What do you think?"

"I think she's crazy," Jason had blurted, really meaning it, not trying to be funny, certainly not knowing he'd blundered on a standard psychiatrist joke. The rector had burst into startled laughter. He'd recommended public school. They'd become firm friends, remained so all through Jason's remarkably profligate (how else to tame them but by abstraction?) undergraduate years, and then something happened—what?—Athene plucking Achilles by the hair? A voice in the wilderness that told him he didn't like the way he was living? A thief in the night wielding a two-by-four? The rhetoric of conversion embarrassed Jason still, but then, when it happened, the rector had made even the language easy, had steered clear of the Road to Damascus, treated Jason with laughter and joy, and disguised his own eagerness to see him as son, follower, disciple.

"Your parish is called Lenni Lenape?" the rector asked him now, as if he'd had no hand in Jason's parish. "I think that's a name for the Delaware Indians," he said. "The Delaware were the only Indians up there friendly to the white man." He laughed shortly. "For all the good it did them. Sullivan's march up the Susquehanna in 1779 wiped them out; it was virtual genocide. One historian," he mused to Jason, "said Sullivan's march made Sherman's march to the sea look like a Sunday-school picnic. It's historic country you're going to, Jason." He smiled. "Have you found a place to live?"

Jason laughed. "I'm to have 'the manse.' "

The rector laughed out with delight. "The manse!"

Jason's vaguely photographic memory (spatially accurate, but selective and thus useless for serious study) started extrapolating phrases from the extraordinary letter he'd gotten from a Mrs. Helen Fanshawe, Clerk of the Session, Lenni Lenape, Pa. With a gushing lilt of parody, Jason recited, "A *divinely* rambling old manse, and at the manse landing, water lilies that do not fester and a fiberglass boat with a ten-horse-power Evinrude motor, the fastest allowed on Lake

Lenni Lenape." The rector laughed, filling the book-lined room with
the sound; and Jason, grinning, relaxed in his chair and went on, "I'm
to 'oversee' Sundays in the church and also to 'oversee' the teenagers
of the lake. Mrs. Fanshawe's command of parallel structure is amazing. She offers her daughter to play the harmonium"—Jason interrupted himself—"the church has a harmonium instead of an organ,
and Mrs. Fanshawe writes, 'Until you've heard "Rock of Ages" on a
harmonium, you haven't heard "Rock of Ages" at all. You could be in
Wales—wearing tweeds and carrying a walking stick.' " The rector
was smiling in perfect rhythm with Jason's words. His listening always seemed to warm your words as you said them.

"Her daughter for the harmonium, her table for Sunday dinner,"
Jason concluded with a flourish, "and her husband, a Shakespearean,
for conversation."

"A Shakespearean?"

"A Shakespearean."

"Good lord!" said the rector. Then he said, "I warn you, Jason,
against the daughter who plays the harmonium."

There was a discreet knock on the door of the study. "Not," the
rector said, standing up, "that I warn you against marriage. Despite
my own example, it is finally, I have come to believe in my heart, not
good for man to live alone. No matter what St. Paul says." He smiled.
"I prefer Adlai Stevenson, who said, 'I'd rather be married than President.' " Jason stood up too. They shook hands again. "Godspeed," the
rector said.

Then he laughed and said, "Godspeed your ten-horse-power
Evinrude motor!" They both laughed.

As Jason left the study, the little secretary bustled over. She put her
hands on her hips and looked up at him. "You write to Rector, Jason,
y'hear?"

TWO
Aaron's Rod
Sunday, June 23

1 MORNING

The *"Unter'n Linden Marsch"* blared through the morning air. "Aunt Chloe, watch out!" Pushed from behind, tangling arms with Abbie Barnes, flailing as she struggled to pivot around, Chloe Otway found herself observing the road from the leafy vantage of a mountain laurel bush. A round-faced man with a goatee nodded solemnly from the front window of a station wagon.

"Morning, Abbie," he said, keeping the car going at about two miles an hour. Chloe caught the faces of Liz and Betsy across the top of the station wagon. After "saving" her and Abbie, they'd sought refuge on the other side of the narrow dirt road.

"Good morning, Harold," Abbie Barnes said politely, as if she were not virtually impaled on the laurel bush. "Harold, this is—" Chloe stifled a laugh at the dishevelment of her prim, immaculate companion: petals of laurel had dropped into her carefully coiled fair hair, and dirt smudged a wavy line along her cheek.

"Hi, Mrs. Fanshawe," Liz was saying on the other side of the car. Both she and Betsy leaned, to reach for the door handles. "Hi, Olivia. Hi, V—"

The station wagon speeded up and passed on. Chloe and Abbie, Liz and Betsy emerged from their respective laurel bushes. "Don't offer us a ride!" Betsy shouted, glowering comically.

"Betsy, such vehemence!" Liz laughed. She shook a fist after the station wagon.

"Girls, this is *horrible,*" said Abbie with uncharacteristic animation. Chloe looked at Abbie with an interest that began as psychological and turned linguistic. Having gotten used to staid Boston vowels, she liked hearing the "horrible" of her childhood. "Hoorible," it was pronounced. She avoided the word herself, said "terrible" or "awful" instead, to escape the mimicry of colleagues and students, but it pleased her to hear it said thus. Sounded much more horrible really, that way. The station wagon disappeared around a bend in the road, splashing mud.

"It seemed like such a good idea," said Liz nostalgically.

"Yes, to stroll to church through the wildwood, communing with God and Nature—" Betsy melodramatized. She swept her arms up above her head, outlining the green arch of the trees over the road. She swooped around in a parabola and touched her toes. "Look at my feet," she moaned then. Her feet and Liz's, in thong sandals of woven leather, were clotted with mud. Three times they'd had (hyperbolically; well, they were all feeling hyperbolic) to dive for the underbrush, the girls most violently solicitous in shoving their elders from harm before they scrambled to save themselves.

"God, look at us," Chloe said. She started to laugh. Why, I'm giggling, she thought. She felt fourteen like Liz and Betsy, and no wonder; she was even wearing an outfit of Betsy's. They'd just about dressed her, the girls. "You didn't bring a single dress, Aunt Chloe? Not even a skirt?" They were delighted at her daring. "I hadn't planned on church," she'd retorted dryly. Now, traipsing along this road in full public view, Chloe felt her comeuppance for traveling light, doubtless looking like a clown in a raffish khaki affair: culottes and a jaunty little vest over a red shirt (the shirt was her own) gleefully "coordinated" by Betsy and Liz with a pair of frivolous red canvas sandals that tied around the ankles. She couldn't remember whose those were. "They're just a little bit loose, Aunt Chloe," they'd assured her, each tying one for her. She'd looked down on the two blond heads—Betsy's hair was short and curly, Liz's long and wavy— as they knelt in front of her like shoe salesmen, glowing faces tipping anxiously up to see how she was taking it, their dressing her. She'd hugged them suddenly.

She loved her nieces (great-nieces, to be precise), had loved them immediately, their chatter, their charm, their open, vulnerable, laughing faces. She'd been amazed how solemnly Abbie took her warm, lovely daughter.

"We mustn't forget Sam's *Times*," Abbie was saying now fretfully, walking along next to Chloe, having some trouble in high-heeled shoes. Abbie looked out of kilter with the rest of them, in an impeccable navy linen suit and pearls. At the last minute they'd been able to talk her out of white gloves.

"Uncle Sam," declared Betsy, "should get up and get his own *Times.*"

"How much farther?" Chloe looked at her watch. Five of.

"Not much. There's a shortcut." Liz gestured toward underbrush ahead where the woods cleared and the sun glinted golden.

Chloe thought of Sunday brunch in Cambridge, Bloody Marys at noon with lots of Tabasco and the Sunday papers spread out over the bed. She and Tony vied to read things aloud to each other. Now she was on a wild woodland lake road, bordered with mountain laurel and lush ferns, stumbling to church in red shoes while Tony slept warm, next to Sir Isaac in their corner room at the Barnes cottage. Sir Isaac had leaped into their bed as soon as Chloe vacated it. Men, it seemed, didn't go to church. Bill Wilson, Betsy's brother, was doing sit-ups in the living room. "Have fun," he huffed at them. Sam had shouted out of his bedroom window, "Abbie, don't forget my paper!"

"You'd think Harold and Helen would have given us a ride," Abbie was saying.

"All of us? Olivia's too fat."

"Liz."

"Well," Betsy hastened in, "it *is* mostly muscle, Liz." Abbie frowned at Betsy. "Bill says Olivia looks like a linebacker." The girls howled their delight into the trees. Chloe laughed out too. Even Abbie smiled a little.

"She plays the piano beautifully," she said then, as if to make up for smiling.

"She's going to play the harmonium in church," Liz said.

"Now, ladies and gentlemen," Betsy proclaimed, "silence all. Olivia Fanshawe is going to render us a selection. Oh, oh, the piano stool, the piano stool; excuse me, Miss Fanshawe seems to have had an accident. They don't make piano stools like they used to, do they, Miss Fanshawe?" In a different voice, she said, "V says the minister is *dreamy.* Oho, here's the shortcut."

Abbie and Chloe followed the girls into a narrow path cut through wild wheat higher than their heads. Trying to get her bearings, Chloe guessed they were somewhere on the southwest corner of the lake. The church, she recollected, commanded the southern end of the lake. They emerged, like magic, to the west of it. The graveyard was on the other side, she remembered; she and Tony were planning to inspect the graveyard. Planning rather gleefully to inspect it when the moon became full—probably tomorrow night. It's amazing, she thought then, what elicits glee on a vacation in the middle of nowhere: hot milk and honey for a nightcap, a deft crossruff at the bridge table. She'd been having a wonderful time. She couldn't believe it, had always thought work was necessary to her constitution, but they'd been here now, how long? since late Tuesday, and she felt marvelous, not at all bored, had great zest for tennis and cards and swimming, for the *company*, really, this incongruous, congenial sprawl of an extended family that broke down boundaries of who was one's contemporary, one's peer. She'd been too long among smug colleagues and obsequious graduate students, her mind trapped in the groove of scientific thought. Eschew scientific thought.

She and Abbie and the girls started walking faster; the door to the church was most ominously closed. A beautiful little church, white, with homely green shutters and a soaring, transcendent steeple, the lake glimmering behind through trees and crumbling old gravestones. Rusty wrought iron walled the graveyard. There were great maples in front, probably older than the church (was that a scientific thought? more an historical, Chloe decided), enormous, spreading maples with gnarled and ancient trunks. Wild roses climbed up the side of the stair railing. Sam's book, *The Thorns of Life*, flicked through Chloe's mind.

The four of them stood on the bottom step, looking up at the closed door. In Gothic letters, a sign said, "Lenni Lenape Presbyterian Church. Org., 1780. Erect., 1846." There was a large, open keyhole. Chloe resisted an impulse to peek through it. They could hear the wheezy, antique sound of a harmonium, the strains of "The Church's One Foundation."

"We could," Betsy offered, "go over to Esther's and have a hot-fudge sundae." She turned and waved her hand across the road.

"In the *morning?*" Chloe winced.

Then she saw Abbie's face, could catch the sympathetic gag in Abbie's throat. Abbie looks so strained, Chloe thought, not for the first time. At the table, Abbie barely ate, watching everyone else's plate, alert to proffer seconds. She started clearing too soon. She fretted over laundry and pillows. Abbie looked *afraid*, Chloe pieced it together, not liking the melodrama of "afraid," but finding it accurate. Afraid someone might notice her and, noticing, criticize. She spoke to both her husband and daughter in a soft, solemn voice that was always deferential, anxious to please. Her rhythms were off, Chloe thought. Abbie had lost herself. She never became properly exasperated. "Abbie, how old is this coffee?" Too quickly: "Sam, I'll make fresh." Sam takes terrible advantage, Chloe mused. I'd hit him. I may yet.

Now Abbie seemed unable to make the simple decision that fell automatically on her: should they go into the church late, or should they abandon the whole project? "Oh, let's go in," Liz said. "It's a long song. 'Jesus Christ, *her* Lord,'" she said. "When I was little I thought it meant Jesus had a wife."

"So did I," said Chloe. " 'From heaven he came and sought her to be his holy bride—' " She stopped, amazed. Where did the words come from? These steps must be the closest she'd come to a church (but for sightseeing, weddings, and funerals) in twenty-odd years, since she'd been a teenager about Liz's and Betsy's age and become a devout atheist. "There is no God," she'd once pointed out reasonably in junior high, before she learned it was bad manners. "Why do you keep pretending there is? *We are all there is.*"

Still the words of the hymn came back with an uncanny ease, and Chloe felt her scholar's mind selecting and concatenating now (wherever the material might come from—from reading? from Sam Barnes's casually dropped wisdom, the wisdom of the atheist who suspended disbelief about the symbol while he railed against what was symbolized?), her scholar's mind deciding that the hymn must refer to the Song of Solomon and Christ's love for the Church, "his holy bride." It was insidious and quite unconscious, this religious learning process. A menacing thought! Yet she'd been finding a lot of such material lurking about her mind lately, the infectious company of her nieces tending to catapult her back in time, make her pick up dropped threads and weave them makeshift through her life again.

Great-nieces, her mind corrected. She could have children older than this, had she wanted to have children. Up close, next to the girls' smooth faces, how grotesque, really, must appear her own weathered face, Chloe thought, juxtaposing it wryly, with its deepening etches of smile lines, the honed gauntness of the cheekbones, the harried forehead. She caught sight of her red sandals. "I must look like a parody of Moira Shearer in *The Red Shoes!*" she moaned suddenly.

"You don't at all, Aunt Chloe," Liz said. Liz was sweet.

"She had red hair," added Betsy. "But green eyes like you."

"You look marvelous, Chloe," said Abbie unexpectedly. "Sam says you get sexier every year." Chloe glanced quickly at Abbie, but if irony had been intended, Abbie had already covered its tracks.

"I'm for a sundae," said Betsy. But she stood there. They all stood there, on the bottom step, listening to the interminable verses drone on.

"That's the next to last verse," said Liz. "It's now or never." Before they could stop her, she pushed open the door and slipped in. Heads down, they all followed. Sidelong, out of the corner of her eye, Chloe saw a potbellied stove, a very little stove that looked like a toy. Blood must have been thicker in 1846, when the church was built. Chloe could feel heads turn, the singing voices converge on the four of them skulking down the side aisle. Her face felt scarlet. She followed Betsy into a pew. She heard Liz's voice (off-key, but Liz didn't seem to mind, maybe didn't know) pick up on "With the vision glorious her longing eyes are blessed." Betsy's pretty voice joined in. These girls must go to church, Chloe thought then. How quaint. She tried to look around her, but all she could see was Abbie on her right, Betsy on her left, Liz having grabbed space for maybe three people. Directly before her eyes was a large, flowered hat. She stole a look behind her, at the pew, with its neat striped cushion in dusty rose and cream. She looked up at a loppy chandelier in some wrought metal, bronze she thought. Out of the windows on the side, she could see the lake through the trees; in the rack before her a Bible and a hymnal. She touched the hymnal with a finger, but didn't take it out. She felt Abbie's elbow, saw her finger point; Chloe took out the hymnal and passed it along. Abbie opened and cradled the hymnal in her hand, leaning so Chloe could see too. Again Chloe felt transported back in time, transmogrified into a girl sharing a hymnal.

The harmonium wheezed to a close, and she could feel the air of the church still tremble a bit when the sound was gone, vibrating along her arms. The girl—Olivia?—wasn't bad, Chloe decided judiciously. She rather liked the effect of the harmonium, just as she'd rather liked the blaring German marches in the woods. Time dissolved, and space fragmented, stacked up its blocks anew, askew. A lovely sense of disorientation took her over. Where am I? When am I?

A man's voice filled the church: "The fool says in his heart, There is no God." Chloe leaned, went up on tiptoe, but she couldn't see. Around the flowered hat, her vision was blocked by the back of a huge, hulking man at least six feet six. "Their deeds are corrupt and vile," the congregation answered in a collective monotone. "There is no one good left." The first rich and living voice came back: "God is looking down from heaven at the sons and daughters of men, to see if a single one is wise; if a single one is seeking God. Let us pray."

There was general rustling. Consternation grew palpable in the air. Chloe was still wondering how the congregation had known what to say. "Aren't we supposed to kneel?" Betsy whispered past Chloe to Abbie. "Mother, there aren't any cushions," Liz whispered, as if it were Abbie's fault.

"It's a Presbyterian church," Abbie threw over Chloe to Betsy and Liz. "I do see a lot of Episcopalians, though, and Hans Strauss is Lutheran. There're some Catholics too. And Matt Bernstein."

"Bow your *heads*," said the voice. "Shut your *eyes*," and it became a human voice that wanted to laugh. Through the Lord's Prayer, Chloe tried to place the voice, its accent. Where was he from? A voice both hard and soft, a voice that could rasp, then soothe. A strangely seductive voice. "Can you see him?" Betsy demanded in her ear. Suddenly everyone sat down. Chloe found herself pressed between Abbie and Betsy; she couldn't move unless they did. "Anyone for sardines?" Betsy whispered.

It was during the Epistle that Chloe identified the accent. "I reckon that the sufferings of this present time are not worthy," the voice said, and "He's Southern," said Chloe to Betsy. It was the "reckon." "I'll bet he's Southern," and suddenly everyone stood up again. The harmonium strained forth. Was it "Rock of Ages"? Dear God, Chloe wanted to laugh. "Rock of Ages" on a harmonium. How authentic, how like that Welsh chapel they'd visited once with Tony's parents. Abbie and Betsy both extended hymnals in her direction. She found herself singing, elbows touching theirs, voices and bodies crowded, cozy. She began to like the singing. While everyone was sitting down again, Betsy said to her, "You've got a good voice, Aunt Chloe," and Chloe smiled with pleasure.

"From the fourteenth chapter of his Gospel, listen to St. John . . ." Chloe cocked her head. The "St." was almost British; it was how Tony said "St.," whenever she had heard him say it, which wasn't especially often. "S'n," a sly and irreverent pun, or one of those inexplicable English conflations like "Mary Maudlin." "S'n." Then she

tried to think of a context in which she might have heard Tony say
"St." They'd been married for almost twenty years, she and Tony;
they talked to each other all the time, were rather famous for it
among their bored married friends, but she could not, offhand, recol-
lect a single discussion of religion *per se*. Of course, in academic circles
where they'd met, agnosticism was assumed, as assumed as, say, liberal politics, enlightened sexual mores. . . .

Around her, Chloe could sense the congregation relaxing, settling
back. Evidently they were going to stay seated for a bit. Oh, God, the
sermon. In a stultifying pressure on her diaphragm, they all came
back, the dreary, plodding sermons of girlhood. Her ulcer protested
dully. She rummaged through her mind for something to think about.
Tony's perplexity over the unpredictable results of his polydentate
ligands? No, eschew scientific thought. Sam's and Abbie's difficulties?
Well, she could help out there, she would—

"There are many rooms in my father's house," the minister's voice
said. "If it were not so, I would have told you." A marvelous voice,
Chloe decided, letting it hook her again, drawn to its mysterious ori-
gins. He was a cultivated Southerner—her mind played with him—
educated at Oxford on a Fulbright or a Rhodes, acquiring along the
way a rakish, offbeat taste for Gospel hymns. "Passing the Peace is
out of fashion right now," the voice said suddenly, "but I'd like us
to." Chloe felt the congregation stir. "I want to see you up close. Why
should I talk to strangers?" A tall young man appeared in the center
aisle, shaking hands. He wore a tan suit; his hair curled wildly, all
silver and gold. The ascetic leanness of his face bespoke temperance;
but the curve of his lips as he smiled all around, reaching over people,
bespoke something else. "Ohhh," Betsy and Liz were sighing. Chloe
found herself delighted with the young man's audacious *poise*.

A poise born of sheer physical beauty and probably a lot of family
money, she defined it to herself then, trying to cultivate detachment.
She was, after all, a woman quite accustomed to young men. In her
department, despite her positive evangelism among promising undergraduate women, graduate students remained stubbornly male. The
young minister was a splendid specimen, she thought: handsome and
arrogant—dear heaven, when would she cease to find arrogance
charming? "A time must come in every woman's life," Tony had
teased her once after she'd had two of her graduate assistants to dinner and they stayed till three, "when she no longer finds irresistible

the strutting of the young male." She'd laughed. "They're *fun*. Besides, why do you think I married *you?*"

This young man had it, just as Tony had had it, and Sam Barnes still had it, the arrogance that unfailingly charmed her. Although she could see he was trying to moderate his stride ("Why should I speak to strangers?"—really!), he couldn't suppress a natural swagger. Walks were almost impossible to change after adolescence. The body became set. Chloe remembered how she had (inanely) cultivated her own droop about the shoulders, thinking it made her look poetic and intellectual; and by the time she wanted to change it, to stand up straight again, she couldn't.

The minister's hair looked like tarnished gold. He was going gray already, though he couldn't be more than twenty-five, Chloe discerned, interpreting the light tracery of lines around his eyes, the mere beginnings of furrows in the forehead. Then he smiled, so it seemed, directly at her. She found herself smiling back. She could feel Betsy and Liz in a kind of rapture on her left, and when the young man went back up the aisle, she found herself studying his stride, the long, beautiful line from haunch to knee. "Isn't he handsome?" Abbie whispered to her. Abbie's face was bright, animated. Chloe felt like laughing wildly. Why, I'm part of a mass feminine hysteria, she thought. Girls swooning over singers . . .

The exertion had relaxed his voice when the minister spoke again. "I'm Jason Baynard," he said conversationally, "and before I begin what a friend of mine calls 'sermonizing,' I ought to tell you my credentials. Or rather my lack of them. I'm a student. I'm not ordained. If you want communion, you'll have to travel. Yet I'm here before you, and, such as I am, I welcome you, all of you, if you want to stay here; and more of you, if you'll come back and bring somebody. A few more men would be welcome." The congregation laughed. "Let us fill this church, let us crowd it, let us welcome all denominations. We at Lenni Lenape are a community—transient, motley, summertime, this is true. But a community; and what is the gathering of any community of people together but a communion?

"There are more meals in the Gospels than the Last Supper; there's bread and fish without wine in the morning; there's bread and fish *and* wine in the evening. In the Gospels, any meal where people break bread together is a communion. I've been asked by Helen Fanshawe to announce that there'll be a covered-dish supper two weeks from next Saturday in the graveyard; and I'd like to invite all the young people of the lake to gather at ten o'clock this Thursday at Otto's ball diamond way up high, toward the river. In my father's house are many rivers, rooms, lawns, boathouses, cottages, and ball diamonds. There are loaves and fishes and a whole lot of wine . . . in my father's house.

"An adaptable phrase, that. One that settles comfortably in our ears. 'In my father's house are many rooms: if it were not so, I would have told you.' We all know those words. Yet I'd like you for the moment to perceive them afresh and originarily, as if you'd never heard them before. As if morning had broken like the first morning. *This is the first morning.* Listen to the candor, the charm, the absolute surety of Jesus—Why do you have to ask me this? 'If it were not so, I would have told you.' The King James places a stress on 'If *it were* not *so,*' a stress that echoes the rhythm of the same words in the Greek. 'If *it were* not *so,* I would have told you.' " The young minister paused. Then he said the phrase in Greek. Chloe, who'd had a year of Greek in college (at the insistence of her father) and could to her surprise remember the Greek letters and their sounds, leaned forward, her ears catching at the rhythms. Her eyes saw Greek letters.

"The magic of Jesus is in his rhythms; it is in his words, in his *poetry.* Oh, Jesus did a lot of tricks, drove out demons, scared swine, cured lepers, but the living magic of Jesus is in his *words*—'Follow me,' he said to Peter and Andrew, James and John, 'and I will make you fishers of men.' γενέσθαι—'I will make you, I will create you, I will give you birth as—fishers of men. Straightaway they left their nets and followed him.' Straightaway—εὐθὺς, from the Greek adjective that means 'straight.' Right away, for us; but *no choice*—there we go straight. Fishers of men, ἁλιεῖς ἀνθρώπων, we are for all time. What Jesus said was and still is."

Chloe found herself breathing a little hard; she tried to sense the reaction of the rest of the congregation, wondered if this intellectual approach would go over. How many of them could know Greek? Should it matter? How many philosophy? "Originarily" was one of Heidegger's terms; she'd groped to identify it. She hoped that Jason Baynard was getting through, she very much hoped so. She hadn't known church could be so stimulating.

"Are we not so accustomed to the words of the Last Supper that we take them entirely for granted? Are we not? I want you to listen to the words today *as if you'd never heard them before.* I want you to imagine yourself in a torchlit, ancient room, a large upper room in the home of Joseph of Arimathea in Jerusalem. You are eating the Passover dinner, the Seder, and the moment comes for the toasts. Jesus picks up a loaf of bread. *Pass over now. Listen.*

"Jesus says, 'Take, eat, this is my body, broken for you.' He holds the cup and says, 'This is my blood of the New Testament, which is shed for you and for many.' Do you, sitting close in loving conviviality, take this lightly? Are you casual? Do you eat and drink, thinking, Oh, you know how Jesus talks. Do you? *Do you?* It's not likely. Imagine the disciples, the sweat breaking, the fear, their awed looks at Jesus and each other. What is he saying? *What is he saying?* What bizarre, primitive thing, primitive even to them, those words—'Take, eat, this is my body.' Oh, they knew it was a metaphor, they were used to metaphors, but what a personal, *brutal* metaphor this was, a metaphor that was to inspire more schisms in the Christian Church than the virgin birth. And Jesus *knew;* he knew his words would shock the world; that's why Jesus said them. He needed drama, he needed an immediate, stunning, brutal metaphor; because, you see, he hadn't much time. . . ."

When the congregation stood for the recessional, Chloe found her head spinning, not in the unpleasant way that presages a faint, rather in the light, giddy way of too sudden a leap out of bed. The recessional hymn was spirited and unfamiliar, distorting her view of reality further. It is too much, Chloe thought, after the sweat-filled room in the house of Joseph of Arimethea, too much. I'm too old for church; it is much too jarring.

"Mother," Liz was saying to Abbie across Betsy and Chloe, "Betsy and I are going out the other side. The kids are waiting. We'll be at Otto's."

Betsy turned. "Liz, I want to shake hands with the minister," she said.

"You really should," Abbie said mildly to her daughter.

"Oh, Mother!" said Liz, as if her patience had been exhausted. "Bets, we'll meet the minister at the ball diamond Thursday. Okay?"

"Liz," Abbie said, "you be home at noon. You'll have to eat before you go to the airfield to pick up your cousin."

"That's *right,* " Betsy said. She looked a little alarmed.

"Betsy, let's go," Liz prodded. She led her reluctant cousin rather bumptiously through the people in their pew, but it didn't matter; the hymn had ended, and people were bumping into each other all over. These pews are too narrow, Chloe was thinking. People were evidently smaller in 1846. Vaguely she wondered about this impending cousin, Elise, a new niece for her—Sam's niece, to be precise—and then she hastened after Abbie, who, by slipping through the pew behind them, was negotiating a place in the glutted center aisle. Abbie'd be great at a popcorn counter, Chloe thought, amused, watching how subtly Abbie used her elbows.

Through the people in the center aisle, Chloe could catch glimpses of the young minister smiling broadly. Two women flanked him— wait, one was a girl, the girl who played the harmonium. She had an alert, interesting face that caught briefly at Chloe's imagination, but she was shaped just like her dumpy mother, poor thing, Chloe thought from the smug vantage of the ectomorph. The handsome young minister rose between the two of them like a god. "Abbie," she said suddenly. "Let's ask him to dinner."

Abbie wrinkled her forehead. Chloe could see her mind's eye start to go through the larder. "I think Helen Fanshawe has him for Sunday dinner."

"Not dinner today. Some night this week. Tony and I'll make shish kebob." She and Tony had learned an ambrosial shish kebob from an Armenian graduate student. Chloe remembered Garbis sitting importantly on a stool in their kitchen, issuing edicts: "Cut all the fat off the lambs, Doctors Otway. Don't leave any stems on the parsleys." All food being plural.

"Chloe, that would be wonderful," said Abbie. Poor Abbie, Chloe thought repentantly. All those meals! They were getting close to the front door. Through it, beyond, Chloe could see Liz and Betsy on the lawn with some young people, a girl in red overalls, another in shorts, many T-shirted boys in wildly assorted sizes. Up close she caught the minister's face. God, he looked elated, Chloe was struck, a trifle ironically. On top of the world. She knew how he felt, recognized the euphoria she might feel after having delivered an especially good lecture.

Abbie was shaking his hand. "And this is Mrs. Otway," she was saying. "Chloe, I'd like you to meet Helen Fanshawe and her daughter Olivia. We enjoyed the harmonium, Olivia."

Chloe shook the minister's hand. "A stunning sermon," she said. He grinned at her; she grinned back. "Listen, we want to ask you to dinner—"

"*We* have Jason for dinner," interjected Mrs. Fanshawe.

"For dinner on Wednesday," Chloe went on. "The Barnes cottage on the west side of the lake. The one with the little bridge."

"I've seen it," he said.

"Drinks at six," Chloe said. Mrs. Fanshawe frowned at her.

"I'd be pleased," said Jason Baynard. "I'll be there."

2 NOON

"We are all a lost generation," black-haired Zack Chandler lectured Liz and Betsy at Otto's. The sun was straight overhead in an indigo sky, and it was hot. "We have to stick together." Zack's eyebrows slanted dreamily up over his bright-blue eyes, and his tenor voice ran on effortless as a song. "We are, so long as school is out, expected to be children of nature. Our parents expect it; Otto expects it; even God expects it. You have quite ruined our morning, my dears, by going to church."

"Bullshit," muttered Fred Bunyan, on the ground near Betsy's feet. "Church is not *bad.*" There was genuine pain in his voice. Unlike Zack, Fred cared. He cared about everything; his friends and his foes, the behavior of dogs and grown-ups. He was a moralist. Next to Fred, Erich Strauss groaned in boredom, stretched his long body out on the ground, and pounded his fists. His white-gold hair looked like fleece on Otto's green, green grass. He was fifteen, six feet five, and still growing. Most of the girls were in love with him. His dachshund, Adolph, put his anxious little snout to Erich's face. Erich swatted him.

"Do you realize," Zack asked, standing over Erich, touching his foot lightly to Erich's shoulders, "next summer we'll have to *work?* We hover on the brink of adulthood."

"You could work this summer; you're sixteen, Zack." Long-haired Selina Thomas disengaged her lips from those of Charlie Scott and straightened up in the covered wagon next to Liz. Liz looked away fast. Selina's scanty red overalls had gone slightly askew. Charlie sighed heavily, both hands caught in the straps that buckled over her shoulders. "Besides, what were we going to do this morning? Otto won't let us use anything till noon. What did it cost us to wait at Esther's for church to be over? You didn't ruin anything." Selina smiled forgiveness on Liz and Betsy. "I think next Sunday I'll go to church too."

"God help us!" Zack called, exasperated, to the skies, his passionate tone belied, however, by the casual, lounging slump of his stance. The brilliant only child of the local police chief, Zack was never ruffled, seemed not to sweat, had smooth shiny white skin impervious to tan or burn; even jeans and a T-shirt hung on his body with a certain distinction, a natural elegance. It was through Zack that Liz (who knew him at school) and, about a week ago, Betsy had been tentatively admitted to this exclusive circle and sat now in the most capacious of Otto's seating arrangements, the covered wagon.

They sat gingerly and listened to Zack almost slavishly for cues about how to behave. A great Hemingway fan, he imposed a constant demand for grace-under-pressure on everyone. Both Liz and Betsy were being very careful to adjust to the style of the group, to be casually good at sports, recklessly daredevil in the water and the woods, not too girlishly enthusiastic about life. They had seen how most new young people simply skulked around the edges, pointedly ignored at Esther's soda fountain and left peering through the spruces that bordered the terraced lawns at Otto's. Although Otto Dolch's facilities were in theory (the sign said so) "FOR THE KINDER OF LENNI LENAPE," the basketball, volleyball, and tennis courts, the locked shed with all the equipment, the fantastic seats, all of Otto's belonged in fact to these particular *Kinder*—bright Zack, wild Selina, dour Fred, tall Erich, the whimsical MacNamara boys, and a few others— who, coming to Lenni Lenape since they were babies, had staked the proverbial claim. The Old Guard, Liz and Betsy called them privately. (They were reading *Gone with the Wind.*)

"*We* went to church," Denny Mac offered, looking over at Selina for approval. He was twelve. Kevin was fourteen, Brian eleven. They had the exhausted look of those who live in crowded quarters where no one knows who's baby-sitting. Between Kevin and Denny and after Brian, the Macs' mother had produced three girls, but (Liz and Betsy gathered) Selina didn't like them. The girls stayed home, waiting for Selina to grow up and move on. The Macs' mother positively *loathed* Selina.

"Leave my buckles alone, Charlie," Selina said.

"Early Mass," Zack said to Denny. "Before we were up. Besides, you'd go to hell if you didn't. Whereas these two"—he gestured at Liz and Betsy sitting cowed in the covered wagon—"these two—"

"Can it. You call them 'my dears' again, and I'll waste you." Erich Strauss started to stand up, a prodigious enterprise, a careful untangling of long, jumbled limbs. "You run at the mouth, Zack." He squinted one eye at the sun, brushed at his sun-bleached white-blond hair as if he'd just gotten out of bed, and turned towards Otto's little house, a house like something out of a German fairy tale squeezed between the dark, encroaching woods and Otto's Road that curved and joined the lake road, around the corner, out of sight. Liz, Betsy, and another girl, Wendy Bernstein, also a newcomer, a tall wistful brunette crammed into the wagon between Betsy and the oilcloth tarp that covered the side, all turned their heads and looked longingly, helplessly after him as Erich gangled off. He turned. "I'm going to ask Otto for a volleyball," he said. The girls relaxed.

"It must be noon," Fred said, frowning. He was restless and surly if not in motion. Before the advent of Charlie Scott, Selina had probably been his girlfriend, Liz and Betsy thought.

"The loudspeaker's still on," Selina interrupted another gluey kiss to say. "I can hear it humming." Every Sunday that wasn't a holiday, Otto stopped the loudspeaker exactly at noon. Through the loudspeaker (it stood, the better to be heard for miles, higher than Otto's house), they heard Erich's voice.

"Otto, may I have a volleyball, please?"

"*Gott!*" A terrible crackling began. The strains of the *"Petersburger Marsch"* roared through the air: *"Denkste Denn, Denkste Denn, Du Berliner Pflanze!"* It was horribly jarring. Erich threw himself on the ground and covered his ears. The three Macs leaped to their feet and broke into a spontaneous dance, swinging each other about by the elbows, kicking their feet in goose steps. Erich's dachshund and Fred's beagle joined the caper. Bing, the beagle, tried to mount Brian's leg, and Brian frantically kicked him off. "Ugh, look!" he cried. "That thing is coming out!"

"Brian," Selina said. "You're disgusting." Brian lowered his head and murmured an apology. Fred gently chastised Bing. Charlie buried his face in the hair at the nape of Selina's neck; she put her head back and smiled voluptuously. The straps of her red overalls were all twisted. Selina had a fey, elfin face and very long nut-brown hair; she had almost been born at the lake and somehow belonged to it, to its

woods, its ferns, its green waters. Both Liz and Betsy liked her tremendously, although they privately disapproved of just about everything about her: the way she dressed, her peculiar wild-eyed mother
and thirty-year-old half brother who owned a string of rental cottages
on the north shore (Charlie Scott's family was in one), most of all the
nerve-racking way Selina seemed always to be fastened onto Charlie.

From the sequestered path that led through the spruces to the terrace, Viola Fanshawe burst, still in the blazer and skirt she'd worn to
church. Her knee socks were covered with burrs. She was furious.
"Violent Viola," Zack commented. "What's up, V?" The others
looked at her curiously.

"I've been trying to find you for *hours,*" she gasped at them, out of
breath. "You're always saying we should stick together, Zack, but I
guess you don't mean me." A boy a little older than they were, a
stocky dark-haired boy, came diffidently behind Viola and stood to
the side of the covered wagon. His sneakers were brand-new.

"Who's he?" Zack inquired suspiciously.

Fred Bunyan eyed the interloper with hatred.

"I'm, uh, looking for Wendy Bernstein," the boy said. He had a
rumbly deep voice.

"She isn't here," Zack said. He motioned for Wendy to stay in the
covered wagon.

"Oh, shut up, Zack," Selina said. "He isn't blind." She had her
knees drawn up, her head on Charlie's shoulder.

Wendy peeked her head out of the wagon. "Hello, Joel," she said in
a resigned voice.

"Wendy, there you are!" said the boy. "Your mother sent me after
you. Everybody's waiting for you. Dinner's on the table." He laughed
nervously, looking around the hostile group.

"He helped me look," Viola said. The hostility relaxed a little. "I've
been looking all over for you," she continued. "I even went up to the
pipeline and yelled and yelled." She paused meaningfully. They all
looked at each other. No one went to the pipeline now. A week ago,
new to the group, Wendy Bernstein had told them in hushed tones
about a girl who'd been raped three years ago on the soft green path
through the woods called "the pipeline." "She was raped and left to
die. My father had to keep it quiet in his newspaper, but anyone who
goes there," Wendy had continued, "is just looking for trouble, my
father says. It would be *suicidal,*" she'd finished, looking sad and wise.

Zack hastily addressed the suicidal Viola. "Why, V, dear, we understood you were part of the minister's escort. You and Olivia. I really miss Olivia," he added. "I haven't seen her since Memorial Day."

"You only put up with me because of Olivia!" Viola seized the new grievance, bowed her mouse-colored, frizzly head, and started to cry.

"Remember how Olivia used to climb the loudspeaker?" Fred Bunyan asked huskily. There was a moment of silence. From the oral history that floated about, maddening and cryptic as a code, Liz and Betsy were gradually piecing together that, weird as it seemed, Olivia Fanshawe figured in the group as a legend, a daring leader, a sort of queen, with more power than either Zack or Selina.

"My father put me out of the car," Viola said, turning suddenly on Liz, "to give your mother and your aunt a ride. He just dropped me, and I couldn't find anybody, not even at the pipeline!"

Eyes turned to Liz. "I'm sorry," she said, apologizing for her mother and her aunt. Viola sat down on the grass, looking sulky but vindicated. She stripped off her knee socks.

"Joel," said Wendy, "why don't you tell them you couldn't find me?"

"Wendy, I can't do that!" Joel looked around him, wary of all the eyes on him now. The three Macs whispered to each other and laughed. "Wendy, my whole family came all the way from town—"

"Oh, all right!" Wendy wriggled out of the covered wagon. "Come on!" She disappeared through the opening in the spruces. Joel hastily followed. Viola took Wendy's place in the covered wagon.

"He's got *new sneakers,*" somebody said.

Selina leaned out of the wagon and made sure Wendy and Joel were gone. "He's the one," she said. "He's the only boy Wendy's parents will let her go out with. Wendy's afraid she'll have to marry him someday."

"But why?" Liz asked after a minute. Viola gave her a look of contempt.

"We don't like any kind of prejudice," Zack told Liz.

Liz blinked. "Neither do *we.*" Just then, Sir Isaac Newton bounded through the spruces. Adolph, the dachshund, and Bing, the beagle, groveled on the ground, acknowledging subservience to Sir Isaac's bumptious enormity. Sir Isaac ignored the little dogs; he ran straight for Liz and Betsy and put his big paws on their laps, tipping Selina on top of Charlie Scott, jostling them all to climb into the covered wagon. They all laughed. They pushed him out.

"He always does that," Betsy said, as Sir Isaac loped to the path, turned, and waited. "Look."

Liz and Betsy got up. "He's telling us to come home," Liz said.

"Hey," Erich said. "Can we swim from your dock this afternoon?" He grinned winsomely.

"Sure," said Liz. "Oh, wait—"

"We have to go get our cousin," Betsy said.

"*My* cousin," Liz said.

"Your cousin?" Viola asked Liz appraisingly. Zack raised an eyebrow. Fred frowned at them from under his dark brows. The Macs started to whisper.

"Oh, you'll like her," said Liz quickly. She and Betsy waved and started through the gap in the trees. Behind them, someone said, "We'd better."

"God damn it to hell," said Sam Barnes under his breath, concentrating his bile and adrenaline into savagely backing the Otways' Volkswagen onto the West Shore Road. The underbelly grated. Next to Sam, Chloe turned her head and rolled her eyes at Liz and Betsy in the back seat. "She knows I can't abide a little car." Grimly he ignored Abbie, fleetingly visible from Chloe's jolted vantage, Abbie lugging laundry bags and blankets to Sam's Buick, Abbie dispiritedly victorious, having appropriated Tony, Bill Wilson, and Sam's Buick for the trek to a distant Laundromat, a trek she had presented to Sam as "absolutely essential. Do you want poor Elise to sleep on dirty sheets, Sam? I don't suppose you asked her to bring some blankets."

"On a transatlantic telephone line?"

Now Sam muttered, "Claustrophobia. We'll all be killed. Look at how we hover over the road." Chloe started to laugh. In the back, Liz and Betsy were shaking with suppressed giggles. I wish Abbie'd laugh at him just once, Chloe thought. One laugh and she'd be saved. "Damned women," Sam said. Then Chloe saw his mustache twitch. As his smile won out, Chloe admired the gray hairs threaded through his mustache, a silvery reticulation repeated in his eyebrows, in the hair on his head, and even on his chest she'd noticed when he was wearing swim trunks. In her own hair, silver appeared at startled random, curly and wild. Her mind flicked to a woman friend of hers who'd remarked once, "The worst place to find a gray hair! Well, you know—" She must remember to check, Chloe thought, grinning at the imagined spectacle of herself seriously scrutinizing her pubic hair—

Abruptly Sam stopped the car at the stone arches that marked the West Shore Road. "Which way?" he asked them.

"Oh, for God's sake," Chloe said.

"He hasn't any sense of direction," Liz said.

"And he's proud of it," Betsy said.

"Mother always navigates," Liz said. "She marked the road map for me. Turn left, Daddy," she said in a resigned, encouraging tone. Sam ground the gears and turned the car left, past Esther's General Store, past the church. In front of Esther's, Chloe spotted Liz's and Betsy's friends, a straggling, lackadaisical group. That one extremely tall boy with the Viking hair languidly waved to them. Erich Strauss. Chloe heard ecstatic whispers behind her. She much preferred clever, witty Zack Chandler herself, but give Liz and Betsy time.

"How was church?" Sam asked ironically. He removed his right hand from the shift lever and pretended to cross himself. The gears ground. "Damn car. Demands total concentration."

"Church was *super*," said Chloe slyly.

"The minister was *darling*," Liz picked up her cue. Sam rolled his eyes in silent agony.

"But he was sort of, uh, intellectual," Betsy cut in, playing dumb to bait her Uncle Sam. Both of them, Chloe was wickedly enchanted to observe, went out of their way to try his patience.

"I think there was a lot of Greek in the sermon," said Liz in a casual but alert way.

Sam stopped the car at the main road. "Which way?" he asked.

"Right, Daddy." He turned.

"What do they mean intellectual?" Sam asked Chloe. "What do they mean Greek?"

"He quoted Jesus in Greek," Chloe said. "My father's house. Fishers of men. It was damned effective."

"That's a good trick," Sam said reflectively. "You know—"

Liz was laughing in the back seat. "Didn't I tell you, Bets?"

"You know," Sam went on to Chloe, "I always start out freshman English reading the first page of the *Iliad* in Greek."

"Show-off," Chloe said, but she was impressed.

"Precisely," Sam said. He heaved a decadent, world-weary sigh. "Showmanship. What else is there?" Chloe laughed. "How much farther is this godforsaken airstrip?"

Well, it was quite a lot farther, and the roads wound illogically, and they began to doubt the existence of the airstrip Jack Barnes had cabled them about. "Perhaps, like God," Sam mused, "the airstrip once existed and now no longer does. Or perhaps my brother Jack is pulling our legs. We'll probably get back, and he and Elise'll be sitting in the kitchen."

"How long since you've seen him, Sam?"

"God, I don't know. Years."

"I remember him," Liz said. "He gave me a five-dollar gold piece. He said, 'Hang on to this, baby doll' "—Liz, an excellent mimic, gave the line a Bogart twist—" 'and don't take any wooden nickles.' " Sam laughed.

"That's Mad Jack," he said.

"This must be the bridge," said Liz. "Yes! Turn right, Daddy."

Sam stopped the car. "Here?" he asked in disbelief. Liz thrust the road map over his shoulder. "Take that away," he ordered, cringing away from it. "Chloe, you look."

Chloe took the map. She followed Liz's finger to the tiny red plane Abbie had marked with an X. "It feels right," she said.

"Feels? Feels?" Sam started the car rumbling on the overgrown dirt road. "I swear, that much-touted 'sense of direction' is just some bastard offshoot of women's intuition."

The road was a masterpiece of zigzags and crosscut right-angle turns, unmarked. "Your Buick," Chloe remarked, "would have gone right off this road."

"The Buick is wonderful," Sam said. "Do we seem to you to be going up? I don't think they put airstrips on slopes," he said grimly. They were in deep woods by now, branches brushing the windows, swatting through the sunroof.

"They certainly don't put them in woods," said Chloe uneasily. Abruptly they came out of the woods, and before they noticed, the road had stopped, and they were moving aimlessly across an open field. They stopped at a weathered, weed-choked sign.

"Pee Wee's Airfield." Chloe deciphered the peeling paint. "Pee Wee's?"

"*That's* what the telegram meant," Sam said. "I thought it was one of Mad Jack's boyhood codes."

"Let's get out," Betsy said. "My legs are asleep." They all got out, the long-legged girls comically unwinding themselves from the cramped back seat. They both wore cut-off jeans, cut off very short, Chloe noticed, admiring their firm thighs as they staggered about the field, stamping their feet. Old milkweed pods and teasels made the field resemble something on another planet. Flowering Aaron's rods stylized the landscape with stiff vertical shafts of yellow and green.

"I'll bet that's a D. H. Lawrence flower," Sam said, confronting one of the tapering stems that stood as tall as he did. "It is positively obscene."

Liz regarded the same flower with suspicion. "It looks like something on Venus. Watch out, Daddy. It might start to walk."

"Observe," Chloe said, striking a haughty pose, pantomiming a lectern and a blackboard, "a splendid specimen of *Verbascum thapsus*. Aaron's rod, to the rabble, thought to have magical powers. With it, you can ward off wild beasts."

"I think I'd prefer a wild beast," Betsy said. She put her hands on her hips and scowled up at the flower.

"Aaron's rod," Sam said. "It *is* one of Lawrence's flowers." He stood smiling up at the tall shaft as if it were a person. Then he laughed. "How ridiculous," he said. "I'm standing here, congratulating myself because I recognized a flower I've only seen in words on a page. Finding literature in the real world. Still, it is quintessentially Lawrencian, isn't it?"

"You mean phallic," Liz undercut him.

Sam raised his eyebrows and parodied a shrug. "What can I do?" he asked the Aaron's rod. "She's an English professor's daughter."

"A plane!" They all listened. A small red Piper Cub materialized in the air. As they watched, it did a flip and dived precipitously for their heads. "Hey!" They scattered, ducking their heads, waving their hands as if hands could push away a plane.

"He's mad!" Chloe shouted. She pulled the girls to the ground with her, putting her arms around their shoulders, flattening them on their stomachs.

"Jack!" Sam was shouting, laughing, shaking his fist at the heavens. He seized the throat of a nearby Aaron's rod and heaved the whole plant out of the soil, roots and all. With both hands, he waved it over his head like a staff.

Chloe reached a hand into the big bathroom and switched on the light, then with stealth pushed open the door to the sleeping porch at the front of the cottage. A faint illumination came through the spooky trees from the almost full moon reflecting on the lake. She could hear the lake, smell it; the sleeping porch was screened on three sides and too chilly, Abbie thought, but the girls had prevailed. Chloe waited for her ears and eyes to adjust, caught first the whispery sound of breathing, then the dim outline of the three cots. The girls were all asleep, Liz flat on her back as if standing at attention, Betsy spread-eagled on her stomach, Elise semi-fetal, her hair veiling her face. At the foot of the cots, Sir Isaac raised his head and thumped his tail. Chloe put a finger to her lips. "Shh." Sir Isaac nuzzled his head back down between his front paws. All's well, Chloe thought, and then her mind commented skeptically, All's *well?* and she smiled into the darkness.

She closed the door and, in her short cotton nightgown, barefoot, walked quietly along the second-floor balcony that, on three sides, overlooked the dark living room of the cottage. The bathroom light made eerie shadows. At the first turn, near Abbie's and Sam's room, she met Tony coming up the stairs. "Oh!" they both whispered, pretending to be startled, and walked together to their room at the next corner. Inside, in the cozy lighted room, "Have a sandwich," Tony's voice said, sounding unnaturally loud. They sat down on the high double bed, and Chloe took a chicken sandwich, bit ravenously, chewed, swallowed, and said, "You know, Tony, what I found myself thinking when I checked the girls? I thought, All's well. Isn't it crazy the archaic clichés that rattle around our brains?"

Rafters ran up the slope of the roof. The walls were rough wood, the room small, square, holding just the bed, two nightstands, a curtained closet, and a bureau painted a bright, bilious green. On the bureau was a laundry basket full of folded clothes, the top heaped with balls of rolled socks. A few balls of socks were scattered about the room. "She made us roll the socks," Tony had reported. "Right at the launderette. Billy and I tried to lighten the mood a little by juggling them. Watch." A wavy mirror hung over the bureau and, on the wall to the left of it, a framed old newspaper photo of the Lindbergh baby. In Abbie's and Sam's room, there was a reproduction of Munch's *The Scream* over the bed. Sam found the decor of the cottage hilarious, spent much speculative ingenuity on the former inhabitants, their morbidity and their anal eroticism: "I mean, the toilets are truly inspired, those two in the big bathroom side by side. And who of us would dare use the open one in the kitchen? Have you? Have any of you?" No one would admit it.

Chloe and Tony ate their sandwiches sitting cross-legged on the bed. It was the first time they'd been alone together all day. "Did I tell you?" Chloe asked. "I invited the minister to dinner on Wednesday. You and I are to make shish kebob," she said, as if what a lark, hours of cutting up legs of lamb, and "Are we indeed?" Tony asked ironically. "Have you also invited Garbis?" Then he said more seriously, "I think you're right we ought to share the cooking, Chloe. It's all a bit much for poor Abbie. Work out a schedule for her, why don't you? And one for the girls. You're good at that."

Crisp committee meetings danced before her eyes. Chloe was a notoriously efficient department chairman. "Exploiting my administrative talents, you beast." She smiled at him.

"Right, love. Keep you out of trouble."

"Actually," she said, licking her fingers, "I've been thinking there's no earthly reason for her to do those huge breakfasts—as if we were ranch hands. And lunch! I'm never hungry. It's so damned autonomous." Tony laughed. Abbie insisted everybody gather at 12:30 for lunch. "How else can I get the kitchen cleared in time for dinner?" Abbie asked them in that soft, reasonable, humorless tone when any sensible person would be shouting and hurling the dirty crockery about. Now, at midnight, Chloe put her dirty dish on her nightstand and vowed, Tomorrow I'm going to wash all the dishes. She slid guiltless under the covers and with guilt felt the smooth luxury of clean sheets. Abbie must have changed their bed, oh, hell. . . .

Tony got under the covers too. "Well, now," he said, propping his head on an elbow, "tell me about your afternoon. Tell me about the acquisition of the Botticelli angel," the entire household being by this time thoroughly bedazzled by the presence of Elise. "Billy Wilson, you realize, Chloe, is quite head over heels. He talked at the dinner table, did you notice?" She had, she smiled to acknowledge, and indeed had been startled to hear her laconic nineteen-year-old nephew positively garrulous. Perhaps he wasn't laconic at all, only bored, bored speechless by the girls' chatter and the nonstop banter Sam, she, and Tony kept going—

"You say this lovely Elise arrived in a Piper Cub?" Tony prodded. Chloe sighed. After her lunatic plunge to the dirt, the scene at Pee Wee's Airfield had turned to rather a blur for her, and now, as she contemplated trying to recreate it for Tony, she couldn't think of any rendition that wouldn't come out stupidly farcical. Her own role was so undignified! At the dinner table, Tony had laughed out loud when Sam called her "a tigress protecting her cubs," and he was certainly going to roar with laughter at how Jack Barnes had kissed her. Sam had left that part out, but Chloe really owed Tony the story; they had this habit, long-cultivated, of bringing each other up to date after the briefest of separations.

"Chloe," said Tony rather plaintively, "I was folding clothes for three hours at the launderette. Tell me something. Tell me about Sam's mysterious brother. Chloe, tell me anything."

She laughed. "Tell you a story? Okay." She pulled her legs up under the covers, hunched her elbows over her knees, and embarked on her obligatory narrative. "Well, after I had hurled the girls to the earth, the plane landed quite decently, and when we had sheepishly gotten up, Sam and his brother were slapping each other on the backs, oblivious to the rest of us."

("You old Blackbeard!" Jack Barnes had boomed, leaping from the plane.

"You old barn burner!" Some inexplicable litany of brothers.)

"Then Jack Barnes came over to me," Chloe went on, "and he gave me this big, movie-star kiss." Tony grinned delightedly.

"I'll kill him," he joked.

"Naturally I was sort of stunned," Chloe said, looking down. Was Tony never really jealous, she wondered? "And all lost in his beard, and then he said, 'Abbie, you're looking marvelous—'"

"Oh, no!" Tony said. "Abbie's jealous enough of you already."

"Jealous? Why would that make Abbie jealous?" Chloe waved

Tony's bit of illogic away with her hand. "Well, anyhow, Sam of course thought that was the funniest thing he'd ever heard, and Jack kissed me again, even more passionately, and then he kissed the girls, and finally Liz asked him, 'Uncle Jack, where is Elise?'

" 'Oh my God!' Jack clapped a hand to his forehead, and I thought he's actually forgotten her, the madman, but then he muttered something about these English boarding schools, they teach girls to be so ladylike they don't even know how to open a door, they'd sit and starve to death just waiting, and he went over to the plane and opened the door. We were all of course watching as if it were a play, and Elise's face appeared, and I heard Betsy say, 'Oh, Liz, she's beautiful,' with a kind of despair, and Jack reached up and lifted Elise down."

(Chloe saw again, in her mind's eye, the floating auburn hair and a soft, graceful jump suit the color of pistachio ice cream, Jack Barnes lifting his daughter down, hands on her waist, light as a feather. "Here she is." He'd come forward grinning. "My best girl." In a kind of wonder, they'd all stared at her.)

"It was as if she were an angel, Tony, who'd flown in of her own volition to appear to us dusty mortals, Sam still holding that ridiculous Aaron's rod—did you see it? it was the centerpiece at dinner—and the girls and me absolutely speechless. Finally Sam broke the ice. 'Elise,' he said, 'you're the image of your mother,' and she smiled at him and said, 'Uncle Sam, I understand I met you as a baby,' and she held out her hand, paying no attention whatever to the fact that Jack had—I swear it, Tony—burst into tears. He was crying like a baby, not even trying to hide it. Then he blew his nose and he was laughing. 'Get her some decent clothes, Sam,' he said. 'Look at that designer outfit. Pamela took her down to Carnaby Street and bought her the kind of stuff you'd take to the Riviera. Dress her like these three here, get her some suntan, feed her up'—dear God," Chloe interrupted herself, "I hope nobody told Abbie that. She feels enough responsibility for my ulcer."

"Forget your ulcer," Tony advised. "So Sam's brother just handed his daughter over?"

"Well, yes, sort of." Chloe frowned, remembering. "It didn't seem at all odd at the time, or everything seemed odd, but she must have felt rather . . . abandoned. Deserted. Jack hugged her and went back to the plane and threw out some suitcases. 'I have to be getting back to New York,' he said. 'My bride is waiting.' And Elise just said, with the most exquisite irony, 'My best to Pamela, Daddy.' 'Jack, you'll come and have dinner, won't you, Jack?' Sam shouted frantically after him, but, no, Jack just got into the plane, and off he went. He waved good-bye with his wings." Chloe stared at the picture of the Lindbergh baby on the wall.

"And you all squeezed into the Volkswagen and came home," Tony said, after a bit. "Chloe?" With a finger, he traced the line of her cheek.

"Imagine just dropping her there like that, Tony." The trouble with recounting a day, Chloe thought, her eyes fixed on the chubby, jolly Lindbergh baby, the trouble was that you could completely change it. What had struck her at Pee Wee's Airfield as pure slapstick was fast turning to pathos. Dear God, she thought, the tigress is springing again, in some depressing, premenopausal pang—

"Chloe," said Tony, "she's going to love it here. She'll thrive. Just look what being here has done for you."

She turned her head. "What?" she asked him. "What do you mean?"

"Love, look at you; you're relaxed, you're sexy as hell."

"I *am?*" She felt her mouth curve into a little smile. She straightened out next to him under the covers, tangling her legs with his. She *felt* sexy as hell, she was startled to realize, no momentary defensive resistance, none of her usual sense of being somehow interrupted. "You feel good," she said, smiling. "You know something, Tony, I haven't felt my ulcer once today, or maybe just a tiny twinge in church—"

He kissed her.

"Isn't it menacing?" she murmured. He lifted his head, gave her a quizzical look. "I mean the psychosomatic dimension of the ulcer."

"Shut up, woman."

THREE
Bonding
Wednesday, June 26

At five-thirty on Wednesday afternoon Jason Baynard came lakeside out of his manse and stood with binoculars on his little deck. From the deck, a catwalk went vertiginously down, around, every which way, for sixty-seven steps through the trees till it joined his dock on the east shore of the lake. A drunken carpenter, Jason speculated, must have built it, or someone who worshiped trees, for the catwalk would skew madly at a tree, stop dead at a tree, veer around any tree: sumac, locust, spruce, oak, alive, dead, lightning-blasted, a home for angry bees. The manse woods. In 1783 the first pastor of the Lenni Lenape Presbyterian Church had been tortured by Indians in these woods, or so the historical marker in front of the manse said: "tortured and lived to tell the tale."

Jason liked the destiny he'd inherited. It smacked of heroism rather than martyrdom. He trained his binoculars on the lake, trying to spot the Barnes cottage, where he'd been invited for dinner half an hour hence. "The one with the little bridge," that stunning woman in the red shirt had said, and he was pretty sure that was the cottage with the big apple-green boathouse, although the view from the lake could be misleading. His own manse, a sedate, rose-trellised cottage from the main road, looked like a tree house lakeside. He batted down the fear of trespass Old Charleston had ground into him. So what if he tied up at the wrong dock? They'd hardly come out with a shotgun. He was hanged if he'd risk the bottom of his Triumph again on the West Shore Road when he could go straight across in his boat. He moved his binoculars slowly from the (presumed) Barnes boathouse and scanned the west shore. The posh and potholed West Shore Road petered out and stopped at an impenetrable stand of trees near the curve of the north shore. That was where he'd parted company with his muffler.

Jason moved the binoculars over the north shore. He grinned. The only person he'd met who might come out with a shotgun was that crazy Mrs. Thomas who owned those jerry-built rental cabins and public beach. He could make out people sprawled on the beach and playing in the water; he imagined raucous portable radios and careless beer cans. The north shore was to the west shore as Jamestown was to Williamsburg, Nashville to Charleston: cheap, shrill, pulsing with sleazy life. Had he not met Mrs. Thomas, Jason might have nurtured a perverse liking for the tawdry north shore. "For heaven's sake," she'd said Sunday at the church door, grating the air with her scratchy, high-pitched voice, "what was Matt Bernstein doing here?"

What indeed? Jason, who didn't know Matt Bernstein from Adam, was damned if he'd question the motives of any man who cared to attend his service, Christian, Jew, Mormon, headhunter, worshiper of Baal. "Anyone is welcome," he'd told her firmly, smiling, hemmed in by Helen Fanshawe on his right, her daughter Olivia on his left. "Good for you," Olivia had said. He'd smiled at her, surprised. He rather liked her. Apparently she'd failed to get into Harvard and absolutely refused to go anywhere else; her professor father was in despair over her stand. Jason admired her gallant perversity. And he'd been amused by the fierce look on her level-eyed face as she gamely worked out the stately "Church's One Foundation" on the harmonium. Still, he was put off by something too jutting, too encroaching about her body. Ah—

Unbidden, his sister Tradd's laughter came to his ears almost as a mocking sound in the air. He put down his binoculars on the railing and pictured Tradd the night he told her he was going to seminary. They were on the lower piazza at twilight, Tradd in the hammock, languid, lovely, fanning out her dark hair delicately to catch the breeze on the nape of her neck, Jason, standing, a hand lightly against a pillar, trying to carry off his announcement with wit, raising one of Robert's famous juleps "to the Rock of Ages." "Jason," Tradd drawled, a little drunk, "you'll have homely girls after you in droves. Considering your aesthetic proclivities, that'll be your biggest cross to bear, brother mine," pointing her cigarette at him, outlining him with it. "I'm drawing you in the twilight, Jason, drawing and quartering you in tongues of flame."

Tongues of flame, Jason thought, picking up the binoculars again: how the imagery is burned into all of us. "Tortured and lived to tell the tale." He veered the binoculars to the left and examined, as if for the first time, the steeple of his church. The late sun caught the cross on top of the steeple. "The spirit brooded over the waters," Jason heard in his ears, and he swept the waters, the whole lake, with his binoculars—the fat figure 8 of it, two miles long from north to south, the north shore about three quarters of a mile across, balancing the south shore which the church still commanded alone. The manse, erected two hundred years ago (the same year the first pastor was tortured), occupied a wooded tract halfway up the lake from the church at the belt of the 8. Half a mile, Jason reckoned, across the lake to the Barnes cottage on the other side. Five minutes by water, he estimated, dreading dinner with strangers. A congregation was one thing, individuals another. Jason rejected pondering the irony of that. What he wanted from the ministry, he rather helplessly knew, was not so much to be loved—that would cut too close—but beloved, another thing entirely. ("Don't be ashamed of a perfectly natural reaction to your family, Jason," the rector had rebuked him. "Don't be ashamed of wanting love that doesn't hurt. Nobody goes into this innocent of psychology. A call doesn't come as a package. The people will take a while to sort themselves out, but when they do, you'll see them as individual, unique, phenomenal. Every man an Adam. Every woman an Eve. Each one a Creation!") Jason shook his head to clear it of the rector's voice and looked across the lake again. Five minutes, if the motor started. It kept getting caught in the water lilies.

Jason started down the catwalk, letting his speed increase, veering left, right, around. It felt good to move, cooped up all day as he'd been, getting a start on his paper for the Luke-Acts prize. A decorous prestige accompanied the prize and possible publication; he had hopes, although his drift wasn't turning out exactly theological. Parenthetically he hoped his aged Adidas would pass muster for dinner with the Barneses or the Otways, he hadn't quite gotten the names straight and hadn't wanted to ask Helen, whose antipathy to the two women had been palpable. "Drinks at six," the woman in the red shirt had said slyly. She had amazing eyes, the color of green water over sand; he was pretty sure her name was Mrs. Otway. He'd liked her immediately, liked the way she deftly snubbed the formidable Helen Fanshawe.

Jason let the boat drift out a bit, clear of the water lilies. The water lilies that "do not fester," he remembered from Helen's letter, laughing a little. Three pulls sufficed to start the Evinrude, and he was about in the center of the lake dreamily watching the watery shadows of the trees with the sun behind and contemplating a distant water-skier who'd kicked off one ski and was doing pretty well on the other, when a large boat suddenly cut in front of him. It made a stiff circle around him, made waves rock him, slap against the boat, splash over the side. The large boat went around him again, going fast, faster than the legal ten-horsepower limit, he dizzily thought. The driver cut speed abruptly, and Jason saw an incredibly long-limbed tow-headed boy grinning at him from the stern, his hand on a green Mercury outboard. "Ten horsepower," a label on the Mercury clearly announced. Jason slowed his Evinrude to idle. The other boat was a beautiful polished wood grain with green trim and a windshield, Jason noticed enviously, feeling inferior in his pedestrian white fiberglass. Another boy about the same age, fifteen? sixteen? glowered at him furiously from the bow.

"Don't Evinrudes suck?" the blond boy asked conversationally. "Wanna race?" He grinned at Jason, squinting one eye into the lowering sun.

"Not right now," Jason said.

"Chickenshit," the boy in the bow said.

"Hey, just a minute," Jason started, but the blond boy said:

"Shut up, Fred." To Jason he said, "Another time?"

Jason regarded him coolly. "You get up early?"

"Sometimes," the blond boy said. The boy in the bow laughed sardonically.

"I'll race you," Jason said, "at seven tomorrow. If you'll do something for me afterward."

"What?"

"Don't do it, Erich," the boy in the bow said. Peripherally Jason wondered if he was practicing the evil eye.

"Come to the ball diamond at ten," Jason said to the blond boy.

"Hey!" The boy cocked his head and thought a minute. "Jesus Christ," he said. "You the minister?"

"Yeah," Jason said. "That's right."

"We were coming anyway," he said. "Olivia told us to. But you're on. For the race. Seven o'clock." He shoved the lever on the Mercury to fast and zoomed off northward, cutting in close to the water-skier on one ski. The skier boggled, the ski went scudding across the water, the skier's body comically collapsed in the middle, its hands let go the rope; and the large boat turned and came to sudden rest at a dock several cottages above the cottage where Jason was headed. "Strauss": his memory flashed a cedar sign on a tree into his head, from the day he'd explored the West Shore Road. The cottage had been walled like a feudal manor with Shaker shingles and yellow trim. Helen Fanshawe had mentioned the Strausses. "Construction," she'd said. "They're very tall. And very rich."

Jason tied up at the stone dock that abutted the apple-green boathouse. Up close, the boathouse did not appear to be for the harboring of boats, appeared rather to be fixed up as a cottage, with curtains on the little windows, the front boarded up, a faded Pennsylvania Dutch hex sign affixed to the boards; and there was no sign of boats, only a big wooden float in the water with old tires fastened to one side. On the dock scattered over chaise lounges were three beach towels embossed with signs of the zodiac: a yellow Aries, a green Gemini, and a red Sagittarius. Jason picked the towels up and started to climb the steep stone steps that led up the side of the boathouse to the wooded lawn in front of the cottage, a big cottage, apple-green like the boathouse, with two screened porches along the front, one over the other. Mountain laurel bordered the lower porch, and tall maples and oaks rose above the roof. A low door in the back of the boathouse opened, and a big man with a mustache ducked out.

"Hello," he said to Jason. He raised one eyebrow and asked, "Are you the Lenni Lenape towel thief?"

Jason looked at the towels over his arm and laughed. "I was going to take them up. The price of towels is above rubies. I keep losing mine."

The man had a broad, hearty face, dark hair shot with gray, and warm, witty hazel eyes. His teeth flashed white under his mustache. "Above rubies," he repeated, nodding. "I'm Sam Barnes. What can I do for you?"

"Jason Baynard." Jason held out his hand. They shook hands, the towels waving between them on Jason's arm.

"My niece brought those from England," Sam Barnes said. He took the towels from Jason. They walked together up the lawn. "Say," Sam Barnes said, "who *are* you?" He smiled as if it didn't matter especially.

"Uh, Mrs. Otway invited me—" Jason began.

"Oh, yes, *Chloe*, well then, of course, come on up. They're all around back. You'll never guess what they're doing. My women have taken leave of their senses. They're waiting"—Sam Barnes did ironic tricks with his eyebrows—"for the *minister*. I've been hiding out in the boathouse."

Beginning to feel like a character in a Shakespearean comedy of errors, Jason laughed. "Yes, well, laugh," Sam Barnes said. "You'll have to put up with him too. Nothing," he went on, "spoils my appetite like *grace*."

"Hmm," said Jason, "perhaps he'll arrive by water. You know, walk across it."

Sam Barnes threw his head back and laughed. Then he stopped. "Wait a minute," he said. He slung the towels over his shoulder and stood appraising Jason. "You're the minister, aren't you?" Jason allowed he was. "Oh, Christ!" Sam Barnes said.

"Not quite," Jason said. They locked eyes a minute.

"Come on in," Sam Barnes invited, beckoning. "Let's play a trick on them."

He led Jason fast through the cottage into a long cluttered kitchen at the back. Drying herbs hung from the rafters, and fresh vegetables in wire baskets. There were plants on the window ledges, shading the kitchen from the lowering sun. Balanced across the sink were myriad skewers of shish kebob: great chunks of meat, whole peppers, tomatoes, onions, big mushrooms. Jason looked at the skewers with a sudden, ravenous longing. He'd forgotten to eat lunch again. Then he found himself regarding a, yes it was, a toilet, fastened to the floor and completely exposed between the sink and the stove.

"No," he said to Sam Barnes then, seeing the writing on the wall in the gleam of the man's eyes, "I'm *not* going to sit on the toilet."

"Okay," Barnes said. He started to laugh, shoulders shaking, the laugh rising from his diaphragm in small explosions. "It would have been funny, though."

"The spirit brooded over the waters," Jason suddenly intoned, fluttering a hand over the toilet. Clown, his mind rebuked him, but Barnes gave a startled hoot of laughter.

"Not bad." He nodded judiciously. "You can sit at the table," he said graciously then. Jason sat down at the butcher-block kitchen table. In the center of the table, pushed into a wide-mouthed beer bottle, was the worst-looking plant he had ever seen. It looked like some kind of exotic dildo, studded with green pods that opened at random into yellow flowers. What kind of stage set had he wandered onto? Where were the other people? Barnes was taking something out of the refrigerator, a martini pitcher it turned out. "Ice?" he asked.

"Please." Barnes poured two martinis into large wineglasses, added more gin from a bottle of Beefeater on the counter, plopped in ice cubes and lemon peel, and sat down across the table from Jason.

"Chloe!" he suddenly bellowed. In a normal voice, he confided to Jason, "I love to shout the name 'Chloe.' "

The back door opened a crack. "Sam, what is it?" a woman's husky voice asked. "You come out here. Where have you been hiding? Have you seen Elise?" The door burst open wide, and a huge Old English sheep dog bounded into the kitchen. It raced around the room and paused noisily to drink out of the toilet.

"Sir Isaac, stop that," Sam Barnes said. "Chloe!" he bellowed again.

The woman Jason remembered came through the door. She wore khaki trousers and an olive-green shirt. "Sam, the toilet's probably cleaner than the dog dish," she said. She put down the lid of the toilet. Then she caught sight of Jason sipping his martini at the table. A grin spread across her striking face, lighting it with pleasure and a spare, fine-boned beauty. She put her hands on her slim hips. "Well, hi," she said. "We thought you'd stood us up."

Within minutes, Jason was surrounded by laughing people, Barnes and Chloe Otway squabbling amiably over who was to introduce him, and he met again tense, slender Abbie Barnes, who'd been at church Sunday, was introduced to Chloe Otway's husband, Tony, a lean, friendly man with an English accent, and some sort of nephew, a broad-shouldered boy named Bill Wilson with a face like an Indian brave and muscles that suggested he worked out, and two pretty young girls, one a Barnes, the other a Wilson, both blond and tanned and chattering like magpies, demanding finally to know, "What do we call him?"

"You call him Jason," said Jason, and around him people repeated "Jason," as if they'd never heard the name before but quite liked it; and before he knew it, he'd been propelled into the living room and was sitting on a soft and rumpled sailcloth couch near the center of the room, his feet on a big coffee table in front of a fieldstone fireplace. Chloe Otway's husband was saying, "The coals are just right," as he and Chloe arranged the shish kebob on a grill in the big fireplace, and Sam Barnes was putting gin, vermouth, and a wooden ice bucket on the coffee table. Jason settled back in helpless comfort, gave himself up to it, and looked around him. The room was large and square, rimmed above on three sides by a wooden balcony onto which, presumably, the bedrooms opened. Under the balcony, next to the cantilevered stairs that went up, there was an enormous picnic table painted yellow, set with fine china and crystal goblets and a big bouquet of field daisies in the center.

"Elise did a beautiful job on the table," Abbie Barnes said, as she slipped napkins under the silver. "Look at the centerpiece."

"It took her forever to do the daisies," one of the girls said. "Daisies keep turning their heads up, just like people toward the sun, and she wanted to get them just right." The girl tossed her hair. "Say, Bets," she said to the other girl—Jason was beginning vaguely to differentiate them; one was long-haired and hazel-eyed, the daughter of Sam and Abbie, the other short-haired and blue-eyed (and the sister of the Indian brave?); one was Liz, the other Betsy—"where'd Elise go?"

"Did she go off with that Fanshawe girl?" Chloe Otway asked. She was doing ballet kicks, one hand braced against the mantel. To Jason she said, "That girl who plays the harmonium was around, drumming up kids to meet you at the ball diamond tomorrow."

"She was?" asked Jason, remembering the boys in the boat and thinking, For God's sake . . .

"Elise didn't go with Olivia," the young man named Bill volunteered. He was drinking a can of beer, one shoulder hunched against the fireplace as he avoided Chloe Otway's brisk kicks.

"Who'd go with *Ollie?*" Betsy asked, rolling her eyes.

"Ollie, the golliwog," said Liz Barnes. She giggled. So did Betsy. Sam Barnes, sitting next to Jason now on the couch, said:

"These two have a highly sophisticated vocabulary. 'Golliwog,' " he pronounced. Then he clapped his hands. "All right, everybody, what's a golliwog?"

"Oh, Daddy."

People stopped what they were doing. Tony Otway straightened up, and Chloe Otway stopped kicking.

"A gutteral German polliwog," Tony Otway tried, as if to get it over with quickly. Sam Barnes groaned.

"The alter ego of a goshwog," Chloe Otway said.

"We've got to do better than that," Sam Barnes said. "I have one." He frowned and brought out slowly: "A benevolent British colonel admonishing a native."

"Sam, that's awful! It's too complicated. It's even *racist.*"

"You." Sam turned suddenly and pointed to Jason. "What's a golliwog?"

"Hellfire!" Jason, startled, said, and everyone laughed. Sam's finger, however, pointed inexorably. "A golliwog is," Jason mulled it over aloud, "something grotesque that perches on a . . . gillyflower."

Sam Barnes laughed out with surprised delight.

"Hey, he's good," Chloe Otway said. "Did you notice, Sam, he listened to the sound of the word? He didn't focus on definition the way you always do," and "I love the way he swears," Betsy Wilson said. "Hellfire." Jason found eyes on him, found himself the center of much warm admiration, as if he'd passed a test, and all at once he felt at home, a part of the rather manic nonsense. He was also beginning to feel the martini on his empty stomach. "All right," Sam was saying, "now we have to define a gillyflower. It has just got to be something dirty." Jason let the groans and the refusals, the banter eddy about him, leaned his head back, and on the balcony above him, pat as in a movie, a girl's face appeared, an achingly beautiful face, big-eyed and haunting. Ephemeral as a candle flame. She leaned over the railing, and her long auburn hair hung down. She wore a white robe with big sleeves. She and Jason looked at each other for a moment, and then she looked away. "Liz!" she stage-whispered urgently. "Betsy!"

The young man, Bill, looked up. "Elise," he said, stepping backward, his face glowing. "Come on down."

"Elise, what's the matter?" Both Liz and Betsy ran up the stairs. The Old English sheep dog went too. They were very young, these girls, Jason was belatedly realizing. Only young girls had that open concern for each other, that trust. There was a whispered consultation over his head. "I'm awfully *early,*" the girl was saying. Abruptly they all disappeared, and a door shut with a bang.

"Isn't she lovely?" Sam Barnes asked Jason. "She's my brother's child."

"She's breathtaking," Chloe Otway said, sitting on the couch the other side of Jason. Her da Vinci eyes caught his. "It's like having a

great work of art in the house. How's the shish kebob coming,
Tony?"

"Splendid, love," Tony Otway said, stooping to turn the skewers.
"We've done Garbis proud." He straightened up and called, "Abbie,
you come back in here!" He turned to Chloe. "Chloe, I'm afraid she's
putting together the salad!" Chloe got up and hastened to the kitchen.
"Abbie." They could hear her. "You stop that."

Abbie Barnes came into the room. She clutched a big black cardi-
gan sweater around her. She sat on the couch next to Jason. Tony
made her a martini. "Thanks," she said. She sighed a little, sat back,
then forward. "Sam," she said across Jason with the air of someone
making a shameful confession, "I had to throw out that awful
flower." She wrinkled her nose.

"You did what?" Sam leaned forward. "You threw it *out?*"

"It was giving off an awful stench," she said. "Like sulphur. I'm
sorry, Sam."

"My Aaron's rod," Sam lamented. "Abbie, that's almost like castra-
tion!" At the fireplace, Tony started to laugh.

Bill Wilson said fondly, "Nobody talks like you, Uncle Sam." Sam
smiled, as at a compliment.

Liz appeared on the balcony. They all looked up. "Mother," she
said. "We need you."

Abbie put her martini on the table and went up the stairs.

"The women seem to be gathering in the big bathroom," Sam
Barnes commented.

"Somebody's *early,*" Bill Wilson said.

"Oho," said Sam. "We live," he said to Jason, "in a circle of pet-
ticoats." He got up and poured new martinis for himself, Jason, and
Tony Otway. Bill Wilson held out his beer can. "No, no!" Sam said.
"It's bad enough you're drinking beer. He's from New York," he said
to Jason. "They let them drink at nineteen there." He sat back down
on the couch. "Well, tell me, Jason," he said, "what do seminarians at
Vanderbilt study? Chloe tells me you're rather impressive on languages," he remarked ironically, and then he asked, "Tony, who muffled the telephone?" The old-fashioned telephone on the wall near the
fireplace was making feeble noises. Bill Wilson reached over and removed a folded cigarette pack from between the bells on the box. The
phone rang angrily, bells knocking together, the crank on the side
turning.

"These rural phones seem to follow you," Jason said. "If that were my ring, I could answer here."

"I listen in sometimes," Sam said. "What's your ring?"

"Four shorts," Jason said. "Wait a minute—"

"I don't really listen," Sam said.

"He does so," Bill said. "Hey, what's our ring?"

"I don't know," Sam said. "I never recognize it." To Jason he said, "My brother tried for ten hours to get us from England, and we sat here all day long with it ringing over and over. Helen Fanshawe finally came over and told us." He snorted. "Damned efficient woman, Helen."

Chloe Otway called from the kitchen, "I think that's our ring."

Sam shrugged with elaborate incredulity and picked up the receiver. He stooped to put his mouth to the mouthpiece. "Hello?" he said. "Who? Why, yes." A smile of amazement came over his face. "It's for Chloe," he said. With his hand, he covered the receiver, not the mouthpiece, Jason noted, amused. He bellowed, "Chloe! For you! Long-distance. Somebody with a foreign accent." To the others, he said, "The guy sounds like he's *crying.*"

Chloe came in from the kitchen, put a big wooden salad bowl on the table, and took the old-fashioned receiver from Sam. "Hello?" she hollered into the mouthpiece. She shook the receiver, frowning. "Hello? . . . Yes, *Krishna.*" She mouthed, "It's Krishna," to Tony as if he couldn't hear. "Krishna, what's the matter? . . . Krishna, stop crying . . . Oh, they have? How'd that happen? . . . Krishna, stop crying this minute. Of course it wasn't your fault. They'd outlived their allotted span anyway . . . I said they'd outlived—never mind. No, I don't blame you. Honestly . . . Yes, Krishna, I still like you. How's the *Ficus?*

"Well, good . . . Yes, Sir Isaac's fine. Yes, Tony's fine . . . Krishna, God damn it, it's all right!"

"What on earth?" Sam asked when Chloe finally put down the phone.

"Tony, I knew we should have brought the nasturtiums. They're dead," she said dolefully, and then she started to laugh. "You should have heard Krishna. He was howling, 'They have died, they have died, the nasturtiums have died.' Say," she interrupted herself, "where is everybody? I'm starving. Oh, don't they smell marvelous?" She smiled at Tony over the coffee table, and a door opened on the balcony, releasing chatter and clatter, darting figures like ghosts, and another door slammed. Wide-eyed groundlings in the pit, they all looked up. Abbie Barnes came along the balcony and down the stairs.

"A little girl trouble," Abbie said, whirling her hand lightly at the wrist. The men all looked down, embarrassed.

"The menstrual taboo is alive and well," Chloe said to Abbie, grinning mischievously. "Look at them. They're all blushing."

Sam let go one sheepish burst of laughter. "Say, Chloe," he said, cocking thumb and forefinger at her, "how's your ulcer?"

Whether it was the menstrual taboo (do angels have periods? a flip question in Jason's ear) or just that he met her officially on his own level, the lovely Elise had to his relief resumed human proportions when, a few minutes later, she, Liz, and Betsy joined the rest of the party, three flower-faced laughing figures. Easily everyone took places at the table, Jason himself directed and almost seated by Chloe Otway's quick hands on his shoulders, and they all started passing the salad without ceremony (Jason had anticipated some mocking prayer from Sam) and dove into the shish kebob, the skewers deftly stripped onto plates of pilaf by Chloe and Tony. "We thank not God, but Chloe and Tony," Sam Barnes did declaim then, his mouth full, and Chloe said, "We really should thank Garbis Garbooshian," and then she laughed and added, "and thank God Garbis isn't here."

From the conversation that bounced lightly about the table, casually, without anyone explaining anything, out of the mad middle of things—the demise of distant nasturtiums, the persistence of menstrual taboos, exotic names like Krishna and Garbis, vehement curses of William Blake, and mysterious references to 'ligands,' whatever they were—Jason gradually extrapolated and pieced together that Sam Barnes was an English professor, Tony Otway a chemist, and Chloe another scientist, but a scientist on leave, a scientist with an ulcer, a scientist plied with milk, while Bill Wilson, a much-teased but good-natured scholarship quarterback, kept drinking it for her.

As the meal progressed and the laughter grew general, Jason became conscious of a feeling of incredible luck, as if he'd encountered movie stars in a beat-up diner or a famous senator on a bus: what a wonderful company to stumble upon unawares and even reluctantly, for he usually loathed social events, cherished his solitude, and Sunday dinner at the Fanshawes' had been, well, he could acknowledge to himself, deadly. Now he could hear the rector saying, "Wait, Jason, till you see the people God will give you!" and, over sweet, warm watermelon, beginning to feel his Spartan manse across the lake as a patch of cold, he was inordinately pleased to be assigned a chore to perform. Then a little later, companionably drying dishes between Bill Wilson, who washed them, and Tony Otway, who put them away, Jason found out what a ligand was.

"Uncle Tony," Bill asked, "what exactly is a ligand again?"

"Ah, Billy, it's a recalcitrant little bastard. I've got fourteen of them I'm dashed fond of that get on well together but won't attach to anything. What a ligand technically *is* is an atom or molecule attached to a central atom in a complex bonding; but the thing is my ligands are so complex themselves it's all rather a production. Were I not so disheartened by the whole project, Billy, I'd show you in the spectrometer."

Bill put a soapy hand on Tony's shoulder. "That's okay, Uncle Tony. I think I'm a history major anyhow."

Watching them grin at each other, Jason remarked, "I never saw a family who liked each other so much."

Tony cocked his head, interested. "Well, actually," he said, letting Jason pile plates in his hands, "it's rather a bogus family. The bondings are off."

"Bondings?" Bill asked. "What do you mean?"

"I mean," Tony tried again, "we're not exactly 'related' in the classical sense." He leaned against the counter, arms weighted down with dishes. "I'm trying to get a picture of the pattern in my mind. Let's see, Chloe is Abbie's aunt, and Sam and I are just tacked on, by way of marriage, and Bets and Billy are Abbie's niece and nephew." Tony stacked the plates in a cabinet. "So that makes Abbie the nucleus, or would it be Liz? I think Liz is related by blood to more people than anyone else, because, you see, Elise is Sam's brother's daughter." Jason's head spun as if he were listening to a great-aunt explain some Byzantine Southern kinship system; he shook it.

Tony smiled apologetically, as he started taking silverware now, for a drawer. "What I mean to say is that we're more an accident than a family, and we are bound together by fortuitous affinity rather than blood. We do like each other; you're quite right to notice that."

"What is more"—Chloe Otway stood behind them smiling—"we like *you*, Jason. We like you very much. You've done beautifully," she said, "thrown to the wolves. Tony, wouldn't you hate to meet Sam for the first time now? He can be so merciless," she said, but fondly.

"Sam *is* a bit wild," Tony agreed. "It's this Blake business. He spends all morning in the boathouse shouting poetry aloud and talking to me, which fortunately I don't mind, but I really do think he ought to chuck it. It isn't good for him. He hasn't got the temperament for Blake, would you say?" he asked Jason.

"How would he know, Tony?" Chloe asked, although Jason was ready to agree, having been idly wondering how such an evangelical atheist as Sam Barnes came to be working on the maddening and mystical William Blake, but Chloe said, "Come on, hurry up, we're going to play hearts. You do play hearts, don't you?" she asked Jason as if this were to be a sudden final testing, and Jason allowed that, yes, he did.

A few minutes later, gliding his legs over the picnic bench again, Jason heard Elise warn him softly on his left, "They play really cutthroat hearts," and he looked into her face and felt a dizzying sensation from long ago. "Don't!" came the voice in his ear, and he mumbled something, reached to catch at cards already skittering like molecules across the table.

There were eight of them playing, Bill Wilson having begged off, nonetheless watching the action from behind Elise, and the play went fast, and Jason found himself winning hand after hand. What on earth? he was thinking; he'd never seen such bad hearts players in his life. He stuck Betsy with the ace of hearts and maneuvered the queen of spades to Sam and, peripherally, became aware of increasing hostility about him. Sore losers? No, more as if he were doing something wrong, and he wondered what it could be, and suddenly he realized. "Why, you're all shooting the moon."

"Of course," Sam Barnes growled. "What else is there?"

Elise was laughing next to Jason, a light, delicious laugh. "They did the same thing to me," she said. "They hate it if you ruin it for anyone. But they won't tell you first. You have to find it out for yourself."

"What a den of thieves," said Jason, laughing. "I will mend my ways. I will shoot the moon."

"It's after eleven," Abbie Barnes announced. The girls groaned rhetorically. "And, Billy, you have to be up at quarter of six." The table emptied rapidly, and motion resumed at the foot of the stairs.

"I get Sir Isaac next to my bed."

"I get the horoscope book. Jason, what sign are you?"

"You have *Gone with the Wind.*"

"Go, go!" Sam said, shooing them off, shuffling the cards. "Everyone under thirty go to bed," and then he grinned at Jason. "Company excepted. You know," he said to the rest of them, "this here preacher's no more than a *boy.* Say, do you play bridge?" Jason's head was already light from hours of hearts, but not for nothing had he lived in the Beta House all his undergraduate years at U. Va. He played bridge. But then Chloe Otway said:

"Oh, Sam, that's enough cards. I've gotten so I see them in my sleep."

"Do you?" Sam asked, diverted. "While I'm typing something, I always dream I'm typing, the most boring dream imaginable. Right now, I dream I'm reading Blake, a total nightmare." He glowered.

"I'm going up too," Abbie said, standing behind Sam. Sam waved a hand backward at her.

"Good night."

"It's time I went home," said Jason, getting up, but Sam said, "No, it isn't. Abbie always goes to bed early. The rest of us are night owls. Stick around. We're getting sick to death of each other," and Chloe and Tony joined in, "Yes, stay, we haven't had a chance to talk to you properly," and soon Jason found himself on the couch again while Tony built up the fire and Sam, at the other end of the couch, tamped a pipe and Chloe brought out crackers and cheese and beer.

"Besides, as long as you're here," she said, "they won't make me drink hot milk. Beer is just as good, Tony," she said defiantly to his wry headshake. "High in calories and helps me sleep." She turned to Sam. "You know, I'm finding Emily Dickinson a little too stimulating for bedtime reading. Recommend something else."

"Wordsworth's *Prelude,*" Sam said. "Puts me to sleep in seconds."

"Try Freud," Jason suggested. "He always makes me want to dream." Everyone laughed.

"I'm too old for Freudian dreams," said Chloe, clowning. "I think I'd prefer a good mystery."

"The boathouse is crammed with mysteries," Tony said. "Sam reads them on the sly."

"The girls are reading *Gone with the Wind,*" Chloe said. "At least one of them always has it. I'm beginning to feel the most awful nostalgic longing to read it again, if I can steal it sometime. I think it's become one of those menacing rites of passage for girlhood. Hey!"—she touched Jason's arm as she passed him the cheese and crackers— "where are you from? I've been wanting to ask you ever since church, but this household frowns on small talk, as you may have noticed, at least of the conventional variety." She put the cheese and crackers back on the table and smiled at him. "Nobody ever says, Where are you from or what do you do? it simply isn't done, but I do think you're Southern, am I right?"

"I'm from Charleston," Jason admitted, picturing, for some reason, the pillared bandstand in Battery Park.

"Tell me," Sam Barnes said, "do you hate the South?"

Jason thought a minute. "Like Quentin Compson," he said slowly, "I want to, but I can't. Or I don't want to, but I can't help it. If that makes sense."

Sam sat forward, interested. "That's not bad," he said. He pointed his pipe. "Do you know, you're the first Southerner I've met, outside the profession, who knows Faulkner." He nodded approval at Jason.

"The profession being," Chloe said ironically, "*his.*"

Jason made himself her ally; it was irresistible. "Oh," he tossed sidelong to Sam, "religion's not all that different as a discipline."

"You must be kidding," Sam Barnes demurred. He leaned his head back against the couch cushions and contemplated Jason.

"No," Jason said. "You use the same techniques of interpretation." He saw Sam's face assume an expression of skeptical outrage, as if in preparation for being baited, and Jason grinned. "Really," he said, laughing a little. "I'm working right now on a paper on Luke-Acts, and I'm calling it 'The Narrative Continuity of Luke-Acts.'"

"Narrative continuity . . ." A smile spread across Sam's face. "Say," he said, "I'd like to take a look at it."

"Anything to get away from Blake," Tony said. He and Chloe sat on the floor by the hearth, close, touching.

"I'm not too crazy about Blake myself," offered Chloe. "There is nothing symmetrical about a tiger."

"Blake!" said Sam histrionically. "Spare me Blake. I ban the word!

You know," he said then in a quieter voice, "I once tried to teach the Gospels." He tipped his head as if pulling in memory from a certain current of air. "I taught it as a novel from four points of view, and I found the experience quite . . . unsettling. Even disturbing. I was out of my depth. Reading the Gospels is like being in another kind of mind, human, but somehow, I don't know, deficient in free will. Afraid of imagination, and then Jesus comes along, and he has a new kind of mind, a new language. He's not afraid. He's *awake*. Jesus emerges as a poet amid automata." He frowned. "I'm not putting this very well—"

"I wish you'd heard Jason's sermon," said Chloe, giving Jason a warm smile, like a gift. "It was about Jesus's language."

"Oh?" Sam looked at Jason speculatively. Then, "Oh, no you don't," he said to Chloe. "Nobody gets me to church. It isn't *right*; I don't believe in *God*. You know what I do in church? I get sneezing fits. I'm allergic to church."

"Chloe, wouldn't you love to hear Sam on his deathbed?" Tony asked, laughing. "Summoning the priests. The Recantation of Samuel Coleridge Barnes." He ruffled Chloe's dark hair, hugging her.

"Never," Sam said. "I will leave stiff-necked and unshrived. I do not go gentle."

Jason leaned forward, his elbows on his knees, and asked Sam, "Is your middle name *Coleridge?*"

"Well, what's wrong with that?" Sam asked, pompously aggrieved. "What's your middle name?" he countered. "I suppose it's John or something dumb. Francis. I hope it's Francis."

Laughing, Jason shook his head. "Mine's cornier than yours," he avowed. "Beauregard."

"Beauregard?" Sam stared. Chloe laughed out with glee. "Oh, that is *perfect*," Sam proclaimed. "Jason Beauregard Baynard. What's your number? You must have a number."

"Third." Jason grinned sideways at Sam.

"Well, Jason Beauregard Baynard the Third," Sam said, "welcome to our midst. Now I know," he added slyly, "why you hate the South." Everyone laughed, as at a private joke, and Sam said, "That paper of yours. Bring it over sometime. I'd like to take a look at it," and Jason felt something he couldn't remember ever feeling before, pleasure, of course, that he'd be invited back, but, truth to tell and corny as hell, the sense of belonging to a family.

FOUR
Ligands
Thursday, June 27

1 ELISE

On Thursday morning, Elise woke up, sat bolt upright, felt the light horizontal leverage of a smile on her face—had she slept with it there? On the sleeping porch, the early morning sunshine dappled through trees and screens on the apple-green wall that separated outdoors from indoors. On the apple-green wall, the speckled sun was straight ahead, meaning early. Folding her knees to shield her stomach, Elise lay down again, had shut her eyes before she thought to wonder what had awakened her, then caught grunted stirrings from Betsy and Liz. She opened her eyes a little, enough to see, but not enough to commit herself to being awake, and saw Betsy reach out a hand and wrench her pillow over an exposed eye and ear, Liz blindly reach out both hands for the scalloped black satin sleeping mask Pamela had so thoughtfully included in Elise's luggage: "You'll find this an invaluable little garment, dear."

"Good God, Pamela, she's only sixteen," Jack ranted, as he had when he mistook the curling iron for a vibrator, whatever exactly that was.

"Mad Jack, it's not a bra," patient Pamela had murmured, tucking the fluffy black object lovingly into a shoe. "Bras have a contour. This is a sleeping mask."

"A sleeping mask!" Liz had dangled it aloft and appropriated it, even though it did make her wake up rather frightened—"Oh, God, where am I?"—and her masked face had certainly frightened Betsy and Elise the first time they saw it. With idle irony, Elise pictured Jack waking to a masked Pamela, turned and curled her body to resume sleeping, wondered who had let Sir Isaac out. . . .

She heard something. An alien noise. She slid out from under the covers and knelt on her cot to look out through the screens at the lake. A white motorboat rippled the waters. From the table next to her bed, she took her binoculars (more invaluable than the mask or the curling iron, Pamela) and focused them through the trees, on the lake. Oh, it was *he*. Him, her mind corrected with the appropriate American colloquialism. Even Uncle Sam, she'd noticed, said, "It's me," the objective case giving a tender possession of one's self to oneself. Through the binoculars, she looked at *him*, Jason Baynard, the handsome minister. Greedily she looked at his face, the face she'd thought last night she'd like to sculpt, digging the heels of her hands into the hollows of the cheekbones, mashing out declivities with her thumbs for the eye sockets. He's him, she thought; he's *mine*. John the Baptist had looked like that, she fancied. A head on a platter. His boat turned out of sight, up the lake. Morning prayers?

She felt a burning sensation between her legs, remembered with alarm her profuse and premature period and the extra-large tampon she had been supplied with, actually rather horrified with, accustomed as she was to the old-fashioned gauze sanitary napkins that St. Catherine's issued along with sheets and towels and cotton knickers. "Super," it had said on the box Betsy brought her. "We both use super," Liz said, noting Elise's hesitant, vague fingers on the cardboard cartridge. "It's all we've got. Mother and Aunt Chloe use it too." "Superwomen!" Betsy proclaimed, and they'd laughed; then Elise sneaked a look at the pictured instructions, gritted her teeth, and managed the ordeal, while Liz summoned Aunt Abbie to deal with Elise's bloody clothes and the towel she'd stained. She got gingerly out of bed now, not wanting to soil Aunt Abbie's sheets, hiked up Betsy's pajamas, flowered cotton flannel with an elastic waist like a little girl's pajamas, pulled open the door into the cottage, and entered the balcony.

At either end, the doors were closed, but across the pit of the living room, opposite her on the balcony, Bill Wilson's door stood open; he had gone; he worked all day building a road, getting darker and darker, ruddy and gleaming, like an Indian. Then she felt a gush and hastened to the bathroom, dropping her pants, watching through her legs the blood fall into the water of the white toilet, coil and swirl, mingling with the toilet water, rather pretty, like wine. She pulled out the sodden tampon, a bloody firecracker, wiped herself, filled the water glass at the magenta sink, and let the water splash over her in an intimate cold rush. She wiped herself again and selected another tampon from the big box that rested unabashedly open on the back of the magenta toilet that was right next to the white one: a peculiar, low-slung toilet, the magenta, the sensation of sitting on it rather like, as Elise had demonstrated with slapstick flourishes, for Liz's and Betsy's amusement, riding on her father's Harley-Hogg.

Frowning a little, she inserted the tampon, tried standing, found it all right. Will not impair virginity, the circular said. Must however whittle out at least an awareness of such an impairment, Elise thought, clenching muscles tentatively. She could feel the tampon, was conscious of its bulk inside her as she pulled on fancy bikini knickers (Pamela thumbed her nose at St. Catherine's cottons) and zipped up an old pair of denims (jeans, they called them here). She chose a big army shirt from the arsenal of clothing Liz and Betsy had thoughtfully pooled, being grateful for a share in the booty from Pamela. Pamela had bought Elise masses and masses of clothes; she, Liz, and Betsy had, while unpacking, tried them on in the big bathroom, emerging on the balcony as in a play, the three of them floating down the stairs in caftans and string bikinis to Aunt Chloe's great amusement. Elise had given Chloe a caftan, a soft, muted cashmere woven of earth colors, clay and wheat and umber, like a biblical cloak. The umber matched her warm/cool eyes. Elise had instantly adored Aunt Chloe; when Jack had kissed her at the airfield she had had a sudden fantasy, fleeting and fierce: "Why couldn't he marry someone like *that?*"

Tying the tails of the army shirt, Elise returned to the sleeping porch, stared hard, but elicited no reaction from the black mask and the twisted pillow. She located her sneakers under her bed. The sneakers, selected for stripes and labels by Pamela's eagle coordinating eye, were now stripped of labels and had been dipped in mud by Betsy, who had an eagle eye of her own and a sense of style every bit as relentless as Pamela's. "You know they're good sneakers; why brag to the world?" Admiring their scruffiness, Elise put the sneakers on and sat cross-legged on the bed to plait her hair (braid, they called it here), her eyes fixed idly and fondly on the pillow that covered Betsy's head. Betsy tore labels out of blazers, cut Levi's tags off bum pockets of jeans, little alligators off shirts, had even been caught, by Aunt Chloe, who'd laughed, with a cigarette, not smoking it but burning a little hole with it in a new tweed hacking jacket. "Betsy, you are too much!" she'd said. "Here, let me finish it," taking the cigarette, although she wasn't supposed to smoke. Aunt Chloe was extremely rebellious about the state of her health.

Yet she seemed as healthy as they did, Elise mused, braiding efficiently without aid of mirror, pulling each braid over a shoulder. Aunt Chloe did everything she, Liz, and Betsy did—played tennis with them, swam with them when Uncle Tony was working with Uncle Sam in the low-ceilinged boathouse where Sam had a desk and typewriter and Tony had appropriated the rest of the space for test tubes, beakers, some mysterious "instruments" rented from his department. Actually "working" was a generous . . . euphemism for what they did (Elise groped for the word, her vocabulary stimulated by the company she'd been thrust into, a company that relished language above all, and talked, talked, talked. She'd never heard so much talking in her life). On the float, having been cautioned not to disturb "the men" who were "working" (Aunt Abbie had cautioned), she, Betsy, Aunt Chloe, and Liz—being quiet, even splashing gingerly— heard loud voices and sporadic bursts of laughter from the boathouse. "They're probably telling dirty jokes," Aunt Chloe said, and the four of them had exchanged indulgent smiles.

Hair in proper braids, Elise left the sleeping porch again. She went down the stairs to the living room and checked the mantel clock. Seven-twenty. She saw a book open on the coffee table in front of the fireplace. Was it *Gone with the Wind*, that greatly desirable object? Aunt Chloe had threatened to steal it from the sleeping porch, but in her mind's eye, Elise could see *Gone with the Wind*, fat and gray and old—a legacy from Aunt Abbie's mother—still on Betsy's bed table. She, Elise, was next in line, Liz having already read it, Liz now doggedly struggling with *Ulysses*, because it was the only book Uncle Sam had ever discouraged her from trying. Liz had pinched it from the boathouse; the thick spine said ULYS SES in red, like two words. The book on the table was neither of these. Hearing the motorboat again, Elise bent quickly to look and saw it was a Bible, open to Acts.

Jason Baynard, she thought, Jason Baynard. As she stood erect, a flush, like a fit of temper, seemed to rise from her chest into her face. What was under his shirt connected to the two chains she could follow only to the collarbone? Bloody hell, she thought, *I want him*, and whatever that meant, she grinned at the arrogance of it. It was a bold thought. She felt again that physical, visceral warmth and roil from last night when she'd encountered his eyes from the balcony. . . .

She pressed a hand flat and hard against her stomach and felt a beating flutter. Ah, she'd been sheltered, Betsy and Liz kindly told her, and this was new, this feeling, quite embarrassingly out of the compass of her experience. Jack and his wives circumscribed that, and the few boys she'd met through friends at school. They were pink-cheeked cheerful boys, these brothers of friends, and said, "Awfully jolly meeting you, Elise. I say, shall we write?" She had the feeling that in America, whatever it might be, it wouldn't be "jolly." Bill Wilson had a strong, brooding face like an Indian; Elise knew he "liked" her, yet in such a bedeviled way he couldn't come close to her; it was as if he preferred to suffer. He became morose whenever Liz and Betsy talked about the boy they'd picked out for her—Zack, his name was, Zack Chandler. She quite liked his name. Well, she'd meet Zack Chandler at the ball diamond this morning, and Jason . . . Jason was of course "unsuitable," unsuitable in reality, although available for a crush. A man and not a boy. It would be perfectly all right, she gleaned, for her to join her voice to the rhapsodies of Liz and Betsy, crying, "Oh, he is so gorgeous," shrieking, "Hellfire!" as Betsy had a hundred times last night, sighing a parody of rapture when they'd heard, after two, his motorboat skulk across the quiet waters; but it would not be all right for her seriously to, well, *covet* him.

Still, he wasn't very old. Elise let last night come back in its warm and noisy totality. She'd felt an instant identification with Jason Baynard, had circumspectly watched him, another outsider floundering a little before his rhythms adjusted to the restless, demanding spirit of the group and its high standards of verbal wit. Then rather breathlessly, she'd watched him pulled in as she had been pulled in. The group, the "family," reached out and selected people—I'll take you and you—and carried on with the newcomer, adjusting its outline accordingly, like that complexing agent—was that the word?— Uncle Tony had shown her under the microscope, which would select some ions to assimilate and ignore others. The ions blurred in her mind; Elise looked up at the balcony where she'd stood bleeding last night: what had Jason seen? felt? how to get behind those deep-set eyes? Elise clenched her fists and closed her eyes. It's a crush, she told herself, a crush.

A roar of motorboats interrupted her passionate stasis. She hastened out of the cottage onto the lawn and saw two boats speeding madly down the lake, turning in tandem, speeding back up. The sun glinted on Jason Baynard's old-gold hair and on the white-gold hair of Erich Strauss. Elise made her eyes avoid Jason as if he might feel them, deflected her thoughts from him as if he might read them, and fixed with jolly irrelevance on Erich Strauss. Liz and Betsy both "liked" Erich, were reticent about him (reticence being proof of seriousness), had simply told Elise, "You're too old for him." Elise started down to the dock to watch the boats (an innocent pastime, surely, to watch the boats), smiling to think of herself as an "older woman." Actually she hadn't liked Erich Strauss much—too full of himself, he was—had perversely rather preferred Fred Bunyan, his grim, glowering friend; but Fred Bunyan, Elise recollected with a tinge of parody, "liked" Betsy but Betsy knew Viola Fanshawe "liked" him so Betsy was trying not to encourage him. Elise hadn't met Viola (V, they called her), but had met her older sister, Olivia, yesterday when she came to the cottage to urge their presence at the ball diamond.

"Jason says ten o'clock," the girl had said, possessive about "Jason." Elise had been rather a long time with her, for Aunt Chloe had left her to entertain Olivia alone, sitting on the railing of the deck in back of the cottage, a long enough time for her to decide that Olivia was, although Liz and Betsy apparently didn't find her so, somebody to reckon with. In a mysterious way, Olivia was . . . imposing, that was it, although why or how, Elise couldn't quite figure out. Guardedly she'd glanced once, sidelong on the rail, and found Olivia openly appraising her. Olivia was short-legged and round; her body looked as if it would be firm and hard to the touch, but her body wasn't what imposed, it was rather her way of cutting herself down which disarmed you and then manipulated you into a position of unfair advantage. Elise worked this out in a burst, settling herself on the steps next to the boathouse.

Yes, that was it. "Your hair is beautiful," Olivia had said, touching her own nondescript brown hair with wry fingers, and Elise had found herself having a sudden thought to cut her hair, it was showoffy so to flaunt it, then had thought, How ridiculous! but scissors gleamed, an image in her mind. Elise saw them now, keen barber's shears superimposed on the green of the lake. "Your hair's as long as Selina's," Olivia had said. "Have you met Selina Thomas?" Elise, who hadn't, said so and, with Olivia's startled "Oh?" began to wonder why Liz and Betsy were introducing her so gradually to the young people; she felt like a bride being gently broken in to her husband's hostile family.

"We could go to the Thomas's now," Olivia offered. "You could meet her."

"Oh, I can't; I'm frightfully sorry; we're having company," Elise had apologized, her voice sounding gushy and insincere in the extreme under Olivia's level gaze. At least she'd had the sense not to say the "company" was Jason!

Olivia jumped heavily from the rail. "Okay," she said, sweetly reasonable. Elise got down too. They shook hands. "I'll see you tomorrow," Olivia said. "Ten o'clock."

We shook hands like a business deal, Elise thought now. Olivia's level, fearless gaze recurred to her like a threat. Ah, but Wendy Bernstein had been nice enough; Elise selected the tall shy girl as a comparatively reassuring figure, the girl who'd come the other night to the cottage with her father, a friend of Uncle Sam's. Mr. Bernstein— "Matt"—was a newspaper editor, Elise was told, and he'd come to meet the daughter of Mad Jack Barnes, a hero of his, he'd confided warmly to Elise: "Your dad's one of the best prose stylists in the business. His Central American stuff was superb. What's he working on now?"

"He says he's going to write his memoirs," said Elise, smiling. "But he can't think of a title."

"His memoirs! That'll be something," Uncle Sam had said. "He's on his fifth wife, Matt; can you believe it?" and Uncle Sam had led Matt Bernstein away, leaving long-legged, awkward Wendy to the tender mercies of Liz and Betsy, who didn't seem to know her very well, and Elise, who didn't know her at all.

"Let's go up to the sleeping porch," Liz had suggested, and once they were up there, after some wandering about and exclaiming over the view and settling on beds, Liz and Betsy had managed to draw Wendy into conversation, a conversation that eventually left Elise at sea, about "Selina" and "the Macs" and universal wistful eyes about "Erich"; and finally Wendy had turned and asked quickly, "Elise, how old are you?" as if to surprise her into telling the truth.

"Sixteen."

"Oh, well," said Wendy to Liz and Betsy, "she's just perfect for Zack."

"We thought so too."

"Selina has been wanting to meet Elise," Wendy sat erect to say, and Elise noticed what large breasts Wendy had, full and low, an encumbrance.

"Oh, yes, well, soon," Liz and Betsy had seemed to carol in unison. "We've been so busy since she got here!" letting emphasis rather than reason carry the weight of their apology.

Across the dreamy, preoccupied line of Elise's vision, the two boats suddenly zipped out from around the curve of the west shore, Erich Strauss's dark-wood boat and Jason's white boat, moving in an intricate pattern. What a strange thing for a minister to be doing, she thought suddenly as the scattered evidence of her eyes came together. Morning prayers indeed. They were definitely racing. Elise fixed her eyes on Jason Baynard's head, his wild and blowing hair. She wished she'd brought her binoculars.

Jason, exhilarated by the motorboat races with Erich Strauss and
sheepishly recollecting the fierce erotic dream he'd had the night before (curious how the celibate body takes care of itself: undignified
but efficient), made coffee on the gas stove in his small, immaculate
manse kitchen and gradually perceived his ring on the telephone. It
was the quavery kind of ring people cranked themselves, not the operator's ring. He listened to the four jagged shorts twice more
through before he answered and heard, "Jason, it's Olivia. I didn't
wake you, did I?" Her voice was anxious. "Jason, you didn't forget
about the ball diamond, did you?"

Vaguely irked (too large a chapter in his life this ball diamond!),
Jason was nonetheless polite, no, he hadn't forgotten, and where was
the ball diamond again? and with an audible sigh of relief, Olivia
volunteered her services as chauffeur. "I'll pick you up at twenty of;
I'm picking up some others too," and as he drank his coffee he heard
the dogged ring of the phone, presumably Olivia calling other riders,
whoever they might be. He tipped his chair back and put his legs on
the scrubbed deal table, letting the edge slide into the backs of his
knees. His eyes lit on the red-painted trapdoor in the ceiling. (The
ladder-back chairs and other random items throughout the manse
were painted the same odd red—almost the color of blood.) Looking
at the trapdoor, Jason felt his Old Charleston sensibility stir, that god-
awful sense of the past ground into him against his will, but irresistible. "If you've historical as well as religious predilections, Jason,"
Helen Fanshawe had fluted, "the old church records are up there, safe
from antiquers who *will* break into the church," waving one hand up
at the ceiling while the other hand opened the refrigerator door.
"There! You shouldn't have to defrost for the rest of the summer."
He'd looked up at the trapdoor, then into the gleaming refrigerator,
physically trapped in one of Helen's skewed parallels. "Who put

them there?" he'd asked, meaning the church records, but she said, "Oh, Olivia and I thought you'd need milk and mushrooms and eggs. It was no trouble. Olivia made the torte. She learned in Germany."

Now, waiting for Olivia, Jason looked at the trapdoor, half closing his eyes to make it blur. The pillared bandstand in Battery Park came unbidden to his eyes again, like a mock-up of his house of origin (more so than the Meeting Street house); and his memory ranged over the Battery monuments as if he were riding his bicycle among them: myriad monuments to military heroes and pirates (violently against pirates, actually, the plague of the seacoast), cryptic symbols of continuity and adventure, blood driven into the soil on which we stand. He saw the tallest trees of the manse woods from the windows that lined three walls of his kitchen like a bus; he felt the earth slant beneath. At night he pulled the red-and-white-checkered curtains against whatever ghosts lurked in the woods below him, where the first pastor was "tortured and lived to tell the tale." Was the tale told behind the red trapdoor?

Material up there maybe for a sermon; material maybe for a paper on American church history. He'd like to try a paper from original sources. And, speaking of papers: Luke-Acts. Luke, the promoter. Luke, the wheeling, dealing advance man for Jesus and Paul. Jason began to feel the coffee start his system jumping. He lit a cigarette, thinking vaguely he should be eating something, but then he got looking at his Luke-Acts introduction, frowning at the hubris of it. Wasn't "narrative continuity" rather a big mouthful? He was amused to realize that he would have more qualms about showing a final product to Sam Barnes than sending it to the august committee that decided the Luke-Acts prize. Funny thing to try for, really. Ah, try for anything. Shoot the moon.

He was mucking about with the wording and fretting over colons (the word "pretentious!" kept invading his ears in Sam Barnes's voice), when he heard Olivia's honk outside; and when he went out, he saw the back of the station wagon crammed with bodies: Erich Strauss vertical, his head resting against the back window; other people perpendicular, their heads resting on Erich, feet up on the side windows. A boy and girl were kissing. Except for the writhing girl, the rest in the back were boys: three freckled Irish faces and that evil-eye boy he'd seen in the boat with Erich yesterday.

"Jason." Olivia's face leaned from the driver's side as he opened the door, a face lit with a little smile. Her round sunglasses were sliding down her nose, her brown hair was mussed, and she looked rather appealing. He got in next to her, turned to say something to the kids in back, and found himself eye-to-eye with evil-eye. Jason retracted his head a little. "That's Fred," Olivia said. "Don't mind Fred. My father calls him our resident Thersites," she told Jason, getting the station wagon moving. "That's from *Troilus and Cressida*," she footnoted. "The railer. Our conscience. Now we'll get Zack Chandler, whom you'll like. Wendy has to come with her boyfriend."

"Her awful boyfriend," a girl's lazy voice wafted the words from the back. "His family has rented the cottage next to the Bernsteins'. His father's a psychiatrist. He's going to be one too."

"That's what you could use, Fred," said Olivia over her shoulder.

Jason heard a growl directly behind his left ear, remembered his own youthful dread of psychiatrists, edged his head to see how Fred was taking this, and was amazed to see that Fred was laughing.

"Welcome back, Olivia," said Fred sardonically.

"Fuck you," Olivia said cheerily to Fred, turning the station wagon sharply down a steep dirt road. Jason stared at Olivia. "I should have made Zack come up to the road," she told him sweetly. "I think you'll like Zack, Jason." She raised her voice. "Unlike the rest of these shitheads, Zack has a brain." She stopped the car short, throwing the intricate grid of bodies in the back into a slide.

"Hey!"

Olivia honked the horn. A boy came out the side door of the bright-pink cottage and made his way through jimcrack birdbaths and plastic animals to the car. Jason started to get out, to put him in the middle, but the black-haired, blue-eyed boy said, "No, you sit next to Olivia." Jason hunched his legs up on the hump in the middle of the floor.

"Fred," the boy said, turning to the back. "It's good to see your smiling face." He nodded affably across at Olivia. "I knew you hadn't outgrown us, Olivia, no matter what your mother said," he told her. Then to Jason he said, "You must be the clergyman who's setting all our mothers' hearts ablaze."

Jason looked at him, then started to laugh. He could hear his startled laughter bounce on the roof of the station wagon. Zack laughed, and so did the kids in the back. "I told you he was all right," Jason heard Erich Strauss say.

"Do you know everyone?" Zack asked him. "No, I'll bet you don't. Olivia's so *rude*. You know Olivia. Another heart ablaze." Zack poked Jason in the ribs.

Light-headed and giddy and feeling like a kid, Jason was thinking, Where am I? He'd expected deference, a barrier to chip through by being casual with these kids, but they were taking him over, treating him like one of them. I should get my hair cut, he thought dizzily. "The copulating couple," Zack was saying, "are Selina Thomas and Charlie Scott. Charlie never talks; he only kisses. Selina talks too much."

"Shut up, Zack," came the girl's lazy voice.

"Our golden boy," Zack continued, "Erich Strauss, the Lenni Lenape heartthrob, enough inches of him for three girls—" Raucous laughter greeted this riposte. "If he isn't torn to pieces in the process by the love-starved creatures. Speaking of which, where's Wendy?"

"She's coming with Joel." The girl's voice made the name into two syllables.

"Oh, my God!" Zack clapped a hand to his forehead. "Him again!" He turned around. "Erich, you've got to do something."

"I don't like Wendy," said Erich.

"Erich likes Liz Barnes," Olivia remarked to Jason. "I don't care for her myself. She came on the scene when I wasn't looking."

"*I* like Liz Barnes," Zack protested.

"She doesn't like *you*." A slender hand with long pointed fingernails crept between Jason and Zack. Jason felt a sudden, hot memory, as if from another life (well, it *was* another life): a girl from Sweet Briar with nails like that, painted and pointed, a girl who liked to scratch, liked her loving hard. . . . Zack grabbed this hand.

"Selina, love, send Charlie Scott home. All is forgiven."

"The new girl is for you, Zack," Selina said soothingly. Another hand crept around Zack's head and stroked his cheek.

Olivia was nodding briskly over the steering wheel. "Yes," she said. "Good. Her name is Elise," she told Zack.

"I don't even know her," Zack complained. "Why are Liz and Betsy keeping her such a state secret? I haven't seen them in days."

"Because she's a knockout." Fred's grim voice.

"Really?" Selina's petulant voice.

"Her hair's as long as yours," Olivia threw over her shoulder.

"Longer." Fred's voice. "And shinier. The color of horse chestnuts."

At this unexpected poetry, Jason turned but found Fred's face as dour, as refractory as ever. Still he took the image from him to mull as the station wagon grew silent, focused Elise on the balcony last night, thought of opening a prickly green horse chestnut, of cracking it, and finding the warm smooth russet within, new and shining to the eye, the fingertips; and then Olivia lurched the clumsy station wagon through the arches onto the West Shore Road and, past the side of the church, jolted it up a side road, above Otto's, to the ball diamond at the top of the hill where the mountains higher in the distance hazed off, dim purple darkening to indigo, toward the Susquehanna.

"Move your asses!" Olivia broke the spell of the moving station wagon as she braked it. Jason looked out and saw people waiting near the backstop that flanked the woods, people of all sizes, saw Liz and Betsy and, with them, Elise, her hair in braids, looking like a white child who'd been captured by Indians.

3 CHLOE

Through the spruces at Otto's in search of a tennis partner Chloe
came at noon with Sir Isaac at her heels. "You are dogging my footsteps," she said to him, as he bumped into her from behind. "Wish
you could play tennis." She'd listened hopefully at the boathouse
door, but Tony and Sam were quiet, meaning really working. Although tempted to seduce Tony into becoming a full-time playmate
for her, she staunchly resisted, knowing he'd abandon his ligands in a
trice and never, never reproach her for it. Which was why she
couldn't do it. And, really, it was only in the mornings that the terrible panic of infinite leisure seized her, churning her stomach, agitating her ulcer. . . .

The terraced lawns were empty, the grass freshly cropped and
bright, gleaming green, its sweet smell suggesting Otto was somewhere about on his funny lawnmower. Chloe put the tennis rackets
and canister of balls in the covered wagon and sat down on the grass
to wait. Sir Isaac sat beside her like a person. From far away, through
the thick woods above the basketball court, she could hear shouts at
the ball diamond where the girls were. She hoped Elise's initiation
into that rather brutal band of young people was going all right; she
very much hoped so. There was a fragility about Elise, perhaps just
an accident of physiognomy actually, which caused Chloe to watch
her with caught breath, and she winced a little, picturing Elise next
to that strapping Erich Strauss, that mean-faced Fred Bunyan, that
amoral wood sprite, Selina Thomas—

Chloe laughed out loud and rocked back in the soft grass, her arms
around her knees. Amoral wood sprite! How astringent a judgment!
Poor Selina was cursed with a truly dreadful mother, a witch of a
woman who'd, the other day at Esther's, wrangled with Abbie over
the last Bermuda onion in the bin, still clawing for it after Abbie had
the onion cupped in her hand. "You stop that," Chloe had said to Mrs.

Thomas, surprised at herself. Despite her embarrassing mother, however, Selina Thomas, give the girl credit, had status in that random group of young people Liz and Betsy so inexplicably yearned after. That wild and wily group: Chloe tried out the epithet tentatively, a preliminary sketch, while she sorted her impressions of the kids. They were like Indians, she thought. They lurked. They wandered. They migrated and, like a pack, hung together. Their bodies moved, but their faces didn't seem to. Even Zack Chandler, for all his easy banter, had a languid face. Chloe had noticed that after Liz and Betsy had been with them for any length of time, it took a while for their faces to regain natural animation.

Leaning back on her elbows in the grass, listening to Sir Isaac snore, Chloe began to be intrigued, in an idle, scholarly way, by the dominant young people at the lake. Who decreed this territory belonged to Selina and Zack, Fred Bunyan and Erich Strauss? Why did *they* set the style? for style it was, that wary, exclusive arrogance. Why did Liz and Betsy, both bright and independent girls, find them so irresistible? In a sociological sense, it was all rather fascinating, Chloe decided, if one happened to cleave to a *Lord of the Flies* school of sociology: *we are all animals.* Maybe the woods dictate the leadership, she brooded, chewing on a tender blade of grass, or the simple fact it's so dark at night. She and Tony had walked up to Otto's night before last, smelling the strong smell, sweet and fungoid, of the woods at evening, and they had gradually become aware of other people, voices in the covered wagon and the oriental chaise, hushed laughter, a sense of breathing all around.

Were the girls there? Chloe hadn't known, but Tony had put his arm around her as against something alien and frightening. The young people were playing a game that involved a shouted, feral, vaguely Indian catchword, as they seized each other and then fought fiercely to escape from the covered wagon, fleeing for the dark woods. The woods were full of them. She and Tony had left quickly, laughing at their nervousness. Tony'd said, "I think the graveyard was friendlier."

"*I don't,*" Chloe'd returned, shivering. The night before, they'd both been spooked by the graveyard in the light of the full moon. The walled portion was sedate enough, all its marble and granite gravestones dated after 1846, when the church was erected; and persevering in exploration, she and Tony had followed the outlet to the lake.

"An estuary!" Chloe had stage-whispered, then demanded, Sam Barnes-style, "What's an estuary?"

"It's a new month between January and February," Tony had come back, and they were both still laughing when, close to the lakeside where the soil was loamy and dark, they'd stepped into a circle of makeshift sandstone tombstones, fourteen in all, none of them labeled. In the center, shaped like an uncircumcised penis, a small, rather sly-looking obelisk, also of sandstone (which, they learned later, hadn't been used for tombstones since the eighteenth century because it crumbled), sported simply a date: 1783. There was such an air of atavistic menace about the maverick graveyard, such a primal sucking noise around their feet, that she and Tony had barely discussed it, beyond looking up sandstone in a book about old burial grounds that belonged to Abbie. "Yes," Tony had matter-of-factly reported, "the date on the obelisk is probably authentic."

Now Chloe shivered again and focused resolutely on Otto's playground in the daytime, which was lovely. She smiled at the thought of squat Otto with his broad ruddy face and far-apart blue eyes, his gruff German voice belied by his enchanting smile. "I like the children," he'd told her. "You are a child too," he'd said, raising a finger. "I can always see it in the eyes." She'd been delighted. Sitting up impatiently now, pummeling Sir Isaac to wake him, Chloe began to wonder if Otto'd play tennis with her, but then she heard voices in the woods, coming down the path from the ball diamond.

She stood up and saw blurred color and motion at the parting in the trees. Elise emerged on the volleyball court, braids aswirl, circled around by Zack Chandler and the three MacNamara boys. Ah, good, Chloe thought. Liz followed with tall, tall Erich Strauss (a coup, that, Chloe knew); then Matt Bernstein's daughter and Betsy and Viola Fanshawe in a cluster around Fred Bunyan; next, that entwined centaur of a couple, one of which was Selina; a lot of straggled-out people Chloe didn't know; and bringing up the rear, Jason Baynard, carrying bats with the girl who played the harmonium in church. There were shouts of laughter as they all leaped at random from the high top terrace. So much for lack of animation, Chloe wryly thought, as she scrapped the sociology notes in her head.

"Aunt Chloe." The girls surrounded her, and Zack Chandler said, "Hi, Mrs. Otway, we're going swimming from your dock. I hope it's okay," and a group of about eight detached itself from the swarm and headed through the spruces toward the Barnes cottage. Those remaining looked around, uncomfortable.

"Hey, aren't you all coming too?" Jason Baynard asked them, but it was too late; they scattered like Tony's recalcitrant ligands in the spectrometer, walking off in different directions. "Well, see you next week," Jason called after them. "Hello, Chloe," he said to her, smiling warmly. "You know Olivia Fanshawe, don't you?" Chloe and Olivia both nodded. "Olivia," said Jason, "thanks for everything. Why don't you go along down for a swim? I'll take care of the equipment." Olivia didn't want to go at all, Chloe could see and felt a swift rush of sympathy, but what the hell?

"You'll come down when you're finished, Jason?" the girl asked. Her voice was sweet, musical, and serious.

"Right down," he said. He sounded deliciously Southern. Olivia went slowly through the spruces.

"Heartbreaker," Chloe said to Jason.

He laughed a short little laugh. "You ought to hear her with those kids. She's amazing. She orders them around like a drill sergeant, swearing like a trooper, and they love it. It breaks them up."

"That girl?" Chloe couldn't believe it. "That harmonium girl?"

Jason laughed, spreading his hands helplessly, dropping bats. "What can I say? She's two people."

"Well, aren't we all," Chloe returned, thinking, Look at you. She loved how he'd dropped all the bats just for the sake of a *gesture*—how gloriously cavalier! "Say, do you play tennis? Unless you want to go swimming." He did look a little hot, his hair all wild and curly, some lovely color softening that gaunt face.

"One set," he said. "I swear I've had more sporting activity this morning than in all the rest of my life. You'll slaughter me."

"How was the softball?" Chloe asked, helping him pick up the scattered bats. "How'd Elise do?" They stashed bats and balls in Otto's equipment shed.

"Elise," Jason said. He snapped the padlock on the shed. "Well," he said, "she turned out to be a devilishly subtle pitcher." Raising one eyebrow, he feigned the rackety patter of a sportscaster: "The boys were mightily impressed that Elise could throw a curve. And once she stopped holding the bat like a hockey stick, she was three for five." In a different voice, he said, "Listen, I know what you mean. I have worked with hostile black kids in the Nashville ghetto, and yet in the station wagon with those kids this morning, I was damned rattled. That's a tough bunch."

"I'd be afraid of them," Chloe said. "I'm glad I'm not that age again. When that Fred Bunyan looks at me, I go zero at the bone, I mean it."

"Ah, Fred's a fraud. I've suspicions a poet's soul lurks behind the evil eye." Jason grinned at her. "Fred's a lot less intimidating than your Sam Barnes, I might say."

"Sam?" Chloe burst out laughing. Sam, at the breakfast table, had said, "Let's get Jason over here again. I want to ask him about the Road to Damascus. Besides, we need some new blood." "Vampire," she'd retorted. Now she said, "Sam liked you a lot, Jason. He really did. I mean, Jason, he was up half the night reading Acts. He kept muttering he didn't know why he'd never read it before." She saw pleasure spread across Jason's face like sunshine. "Come on," she said then, feeling a little beckoning smile tilt the corner of her mouth. "Let's see you on the tennis court."

They played a fast set on Otto's immaculate clay court, Sir Isaac watching the ball like a parody of a tennis gallery, and Jason won easily, six games to two, to Chloe's chagrin. Why did winning really matter to her? "I don't know now," she told him, sweaty, panting, "whether Tony lets me win or not. Just as I don't know if I really try. It's hell," she said, hamming it up, "being a woman."

"I reckon it is," Jason said, and she was enchanted with the "reckon"; he took her racket from her to carry it for her, and she smiled up at him, feeling young and attractive and rather wanton. The medals around his neck had come loose from under his shirt; she wanted to look at them but didn't dare; she lowered her eyes and pivoted around.

"Come for a swim," she invited, and they walked through the spruces and across the road, over the little wooden footbridge that spanned the grade from the road to the deck at the back of the Barnes cottage. Around the side of the cottage, near the vegetable garden, they could hear shouting from the dock, and Chloe, repentant, thought of Tony and Sam in the boathouse (had she been the sanction for the invasion?), felt trebly repentant as Abbie emerged from the cottage with a basket of sandwiches; but Abbie was smiling. She wore shorts, and her blond hair was loose. Chloe resisted taking a sandwich from the heaped basket. She was starving.

"The girls are having a wonderful time," Abbie said. "I really like that Zack. Hi, Jason," she said, smiling a bit flirtatiously, Chloe thought, and she and Jason and Sir Isaac followed Abbie and her sandwiches down the lawn, toward the dock.

Sam came out of the boathouse door. "Abbie, what's all this racket?" he asked. "Hi, Jason."

"Shut up, Sam," said Abbie airily and went on down to the dock. Chloe felt like cheering.

Sir Isaac jumped up on Sam. "Get thee behind me, Cerberus!" Sam ranted. He staggered backward, pushing Sir Isaac off.

"Sam!" Chloe reproached him. "Don't call him Cerberus." She patted Sir Isaac's maligned, shaggy head. Abbie went by them again, dragging a garbage bag up the lawn. Sir Isaac followed her.

A grin took over Sam's face as he watched Sir Isaac's retreat. "Chloe, the damnedest thing. Blake hated Sir Isaac Newton." At Chloe's look, he put his hand on Jason's shoulder. "Honest to God, Chloe; I swear on the preacher. Blake made Newton the principal head in his *Cerberus*. The other two heads were Bacon and Locke, and the central head was Newton's. Sir Isaac Newton was for Blake the very devil."

"Why on earth?"

"Maybe he didn't like him dropping apples," remarked Jason.

Sam guffawed appreciatively. "That's possible. Blake was a consummate madman. He and his wife used to sit around naked in the garden when people came to call on them, probably just waiting for the proverbial apple, which they never got. No children. Oh, wait a minute, Chloe, speaking of sex, I've got a poem to read you. A Blake poem. I read Blake all morning. Wait, wait." Sam ducked into the boathouse. Tony stepped out.

"Hi, love. I'll be out directly."

Chloe kissed him. He looked harried. Sam crowded by, bumping his head on the doorjamb. "Damned door." He opened a book and, pausing, raising his head haughtily, read with unctuous sibilance:

> "To Chloe's breast young Cupid slily stole
> But he crept in at Myra's pocket hole."

"Sam, that's dirty!" Chloe broke away from the three laughing masculine figures, flamboyantly shucking her clothes as she ran down the steps to the dock. Under her clothes, she wore a bathing suit of course —they all did, like underwear—still she knew the *effect*. From the rippling green water, Zack Chandler whistled appreciatively. Chloe felt herself blush; the act had *not* been for the kids. She dove, letting the cool water draw the ruddy temper from her face.

After a positively adolescent romp in the water, Zack and Erich and *Sam* stealthily grabbing any vulnerable ankle, the "adults" repaired to the woven chaises on the dock while the "kids" collapsed suddenly, as if by tropism, in neat, torpid rows on the float. Dreamily, from the dock, her eyes half shut, Chloe admired the composition of the weathered wooden float against the green water, enjoyed the vivid stripes of color: Fred Bunyan's Indian-bronze back, Betsy's yellow bikini, the orange towel Zack Chandler had whimsically draped over his entire body, Olivia Fanshawe's matronly purple suit. Someone should make that girl get a bikini, Chloe mused a trifle irritably, recollecting how in her own youth she'd been made to feel self-conscious about being slim and boyish. Whatever is the matter today, she wondered, with being short-legged and solid like Olivia? Someone has made that girl embarrassed about her body.

Sam rooted noisily through the sandwiches Abbie had left for them in the picnic basket. "Tony, you like tuna fish, I distinctly remember," he cajoled, trying to press an already unwrapped, evidently rejected sandwich into Tony's resistant hand. "Well, it's better than peanut butter and jelly." Tony kept his hand clenched stubbornly shut, like a little boy.

"I'll eat the tuna fish," offered Jason. "Unless you want it, Tony?"

"No, no," Tony demurred. "I hate tuna fish. I find peanut butter and jam most consoling. It's like nursery tea."

"Did you have an awful morning, darling?" Chloe asked and, listening to her own sympathetic tone, had the odd sense she was play-acting the loving wife for an audience. For Sam and Jason. Sam or Jason. Whyever? To set them straight, she considered saying in a voice more like her own, Oh, Tony, why don't you let the ligands stew and take a week off? but she didn't. She had, after all, plenty of company. I'm lying here almost naked with three men—the thought came unexpectedly. Jason had a beautiful body, she'd noted sidelong.

Had also noted he'd taken off his chains to swim. Tony was looking at her from his chaise. She looked away.

Sam inspected the cooler. "It's all soda pop," he complained. "Why didn't she bring down any beer?" Chloe shaded her eyes against the sun and watched Sam look up at the cottage as if he might actually holler, Abbie! His mustache twitched, and then his better nature triumphed. "I'll go get some beer," he grumbled. He started up the steps.

Tony tossed Chloe a sandwich. "Chloe, get this roast beef before Sam finds it." Smiling, Chloe peeled the tacky plastic off the sandwich and found rare roast beef on rye with horseradish and a slice of tomato: the grit of the horseradish and the slickness of the tomato celebrated the texture of the beef. As she slowly ate, Chloe watched the float, her eyes working on angles now, not colors: the vertical trees on the other shore, the low horizontal relief of the ripples. Elise's long hair dangled over the side of the float like a banner. One of Erich Strauss's surrealistically attenuated legs slanted across the line of the prone bodies like a vector. Liz, on her stomach, bent both legs upward at the knee, sinuously rotating her ankles; Olivia's breasts jutted —my! Yes, someone should definitely get that girl a bikini.

"Chloe, you're eating my sandwich! Abbie just described that sandwich to me!" Sam was back. Chloe grinned up at him and chewed voluptuously. She heard Tony and Jason laugh. "I shall drink my lunch!" Sam proclaimed. Chloe heard the sucking sound of a flipped beer cap. Then another. "Say, Jason," bargained Sam, "I'll give you a beer if you'll tell me how a certain really slipshod discrepancy got into Acts. I was so shocked about it I couldn't sleep all night. How something like that got in the Bible!" Chloe could hear Jason laughing. "Ah, no, Tony, don't go! You make me feel guilty. Have a beer."

"No beer for me, Sam." Tony sighed loudly. "My ligands!" He lurched his body up as if his ligands were touchy internal organs or something he'd left boiling on the stove.

"Good luck, darling," said Chloe.

"Thank you." From a pile of rumpled clothing on the dock, Tony extrapolated his tattersall shirt and put it on, frowning over the buttons. He squared his shoulders and, glancing back once longingly, ducked into the boathouse. His legs were awfully white, Chloe observed critically, looking down the chaise at her own, sleek and

brown with one knee crooked, her toenails painted for the first time
in her life.

Sam settled into Tony's chaise next to her. The green of his
Heineken bottle glinted in the sunlight as he drank. "Well, Jason," he
said, "are you ready? Are you ready for Acts? Words are very well,
but acts matter. I've taught too many years to let anyone off the
hook."

Chloe giggled. As a teacher, she too remembered her own unan-
swered questions forever. She occasionally threw them at former students on the M.T.A.

"It's on the Road to Damascus, right?" Jason's voice asked.

"Great God, it *is*." Sam turned to Chloe and said, *sotto voce*, "I'm
impressed. Acts is full of shipwrecks and annoying point-of-view
shifts and magical escapes from jail; but he knows where the most
egregious discrepancy is." Chloe felt Sam's voice shift away from her.
"Jason, I have got to allow that the Bible is, unlike, say, the *Book of
Mormon*, on which I am an unlikely expert, a great work of literature.
But for this blatant inconsistency to have become canonical is unconscionable—"

"Not to mention polysyllabic," murmured Chloe.

Sam laughed. "That too," he said. "But listen. The narrator of Acts,
whoever the hell he is, Luke I believe legend has it, tells us early on
that when Paul was attacked by Jesus—"

"Attacked? That's too much," Jason protested.

"All right, all right, let's say accosted. I mean it was hardly a gentle
meeting. When Paul, then called Saul, was accosted by Jesus on the
Road to Damascus, the narrator remarks that the men with Paul *heard*
the voice of Jesus but *saw no one*. Later, when Paul tells the story, he
reverses the senses—testifies that his companions saw the light that
was Jesus but *did not hear the voice*. Jason, whoever claims the Bible, be
it philosophy, literature, or religion, has got to demand that such a
paradox be reconciled or at least acknowledged. We have thesis, an-
tithesis, where's the synthesis? Jason, this is the *Bible*."

"Tell you what," said Jason, his voice easy. "I'll do a sermon on it.
If you'll come to church to hear it."

Sam howled to the heavens, "God damn it!" Then he sneezed. "Yes,
I'll come, I'll come. I'll sneeze you to kingdom come!" He sneezed
again. Chloe sat up and clenched a comic fist in the air.

"Right on, Jason," she said. Jason got up from his chaise, laughing and shaking his head. His gold and silver hair made a kinetic aura around his head. He raised his fist like hers.

"See you in church," he called and dived into the water. Sam sneezed. Chloe laughed. Jason swam fast toward the float. Chloe saw the kids move, disperse, rearrange themselves in preparation for his invasion of their territory. Olivia sat up and tugged at the top of her purple bathing suit; Elise also lifted up, on her elbows, giving her long hair a shake. The younger girls, Chloe noted, idly at first, didn't revise their bodies (which simply were their bodies as yet, of course, not stage properties to pose and dispose. Her mind wandered ahead to old age: would one's awful self-consciousness erode and one return to childhood when the world flooded the senses with no ego in the way? *Vanitas, vanitas*). Then she saw Erich Strauss give Jason a hearty hand up, and as soon as Jason stood on the float, all the boys came to standing position, while all the girls remained supine. What the hell? Chloe wondered, alert now. They *did* resemble some kind of biochemical structure, those kids.

"Y'know, Sam," she remarked, "those kids are like ligands."

Melodramatically Sam groaned. "Spare me ligands. Spare me your cruel, transcendental, scientific jokes."

"Sam, it's a metaphor. Alone, or in twos or threes, the kids are people. They respond as individuals. All together, they're absorbed into some sort of structure, a pattern. Even Liz, Sam."

Sam mocked a frown at her. He passed her a Heineken. Undaunted, she took the green bottle and sketched a diagram with it in the air. "Look. The kids form a hybrid orbital around some nucleus, like, oh, say the float. When an alien but friendly atom like Jason moves in on them, they regroup to accept him. An alien atom they don't like—that boy, Joel, for example, whom they drove away from the ball diamond this morning, Jason said—they expel by mutual repulsion." With the bottle, she dotted a serrated circle and placed another dot outside to represent Joel.

"Chloe, I think you're all crazy."

"All women, you mean?" she asked Sam, miffed. She wrapped her arms around her knees, holding the cold bottle against them.

"No, not all women, woman! All scientists. Do you know what Tony did all morning? I was going to spare you, but now I see you're as crazy as he is." Sam leaned out of his chaise and glared at her.

Chloe grinned. "Sam, what did you do all morning besides watch what Tony did all morning?"

Sam ignored her question. He leaned closer as if he might be overheard. "Tony took about twenty little pieces of paper and folded them in half. Then he scribbled things, not words, mind you, *things*— marks, runes, shapes, hieroglyphs—on one side of each folded slip of paper; and then he turned them all over so the scribbles didn't show and jotted more things on the other half. When he finished, he stared out the window as if he were praying. Then he opened the papers one by one and intensely *scrutinized the scribblings,* which of course had to be random." Sam lay back on the chaise. "Now you come up with Jason swimming to the float like a friendly sperm. I, the last of the flesh and blood intellectuals, am set about by crazy scientists."

"Poor Tony!" said Chloe. "D'you know what he was doing, Sam? That's the way Linus Pauling discovered the alpha-helix. He was sick in bed with a bad cold and he took to scribbling bondings on folded paper, just like Tony, and one of them replicated itself. *Voilà!* The alpha-helix!"

Sam shifted impatiently. "Chloe, why the blue hell was a Nobel Prize winner like Linus Pauling scribbling things on folded paper?"

"To find a new way of *seeing,* idiot! For an educated man, you do have the narrowest mind. I'll bet you don't even know what the alpha-helix *is.*" Chloe suppressed a grin as, from under her lashes, she watched Sam try to muster a retort. Actually, she was thinking, the fact that Tony's ligands wouldn't "behave" hinted at one of those fortuitous breaches of scientific etiquette that signifies discovery: Tony might just be onto something. She crossed her fingers. "Okay, Sam," she prodded, "what's an alpha-helix?"

Sam let loose a sheepish, reluctant laugh. It exploded twice, agitating the grizzled hair on his chest. "Chloe, I am praying for a *deus ex machina* to get me out of this!" They both laughed. "You know, Chloe, you look—"

A scream came from the float. Startled, Chloe registered a revision of the orbital: a scattering of heads in the water, diagonal bodies on the float, Jason and Liz standing upright. Jason's hand was raised, and Liz was screaming. "What'd he do to her?" Sam grimly muttered, all father of teen-age daughter. He and Chloe both rose as Liz and Jason dove into the water and swam fast toward the dock.

"Sam, she probably got stung by a bee," Chloe tried to reason with him. Jason climbed out of the water and headed up the steps to the lawn. Chloe and Sam knelt to catch Liz's first gulped words. Her mouth was full of water.

"Daddy," she gasped. "Daddy, the *Mormons!*" She flailed her arm out of the water to point.

Slowly Sam's head turned to follow the angle of her arm. "Oh, God!" he exclaimed, clapping a hand to his forehead. He turned back to Liz. "Little girl," he said, eyes twinkling, "didn't I teach you never to scream unless you're being raped?"

Chloe turned and saw on the lawn, like a triptych, two crew-cut young men in dark suits framing a third man almost a head taller: black and handsome, wearing blue jeans and a faded work shirt. "Well, what do you know?" Sam asked her and Liz. He lay back on the dock like an exhausted crucifix. "The prophet Moroni is *black.*"

Jason joined the three on the lawn, and the triptych fragmented, as he and the young black man caught hands in a soul shake. The detached dark suits came down the boathouse stairs.

"Mr. Barnes," the Mormons said in solemn unison, holding out their hands. "We're so glad we found you again."

Sam raised his head and said fast to Chloe, "An alpha-helix just won the Grand Prix at Watkins Glen." Then he banged his head back on the stone dock and howled.

FIVE
Schisms
Fourth of July
Weekend

1 SATURDAY EVENING

"But Calvin you must have realized such groups existed. For God's sake, what'd you think *Paul* was talking about?" Jason heard some of Sam Barnes's extravagant exasperation in his own voice and was amused. Tried not to let Calvin see it, however. Laughing a bad idea. Clearly. It had taken him from Thursday night till just about two minutes ago to coax out of Calvin what had happened on Mount Pisgah to send him so abruptly packing; and when he found out what had happened on Pisgah, Jason had laughed. He couldn't help it. "Is that *all?*" he'd asked. "Calvin, are you shining me on?"

Calvin had taken a swing at him.

Now standing up, Jason leaned his elbow on the refrigerator, the better seriously to confront this affronted stranger, this parody of a shiftless, drunken Southern black on fight-night. Jason felt his elbow encounter something thickly sticky and tried to ignore it. Seated, Calvin pulled Jason's typewriter in front of him, as if Jason might attack, and knocked a pile of pencils to the floor. You could hear them roll. Variegated clothing hung from the ladder-back chairs in Jason's kitchen; dishes filled the sink; the gas stove was—for no reason—alight; the refrigerator door was smudged with fingerprints and food and slightly ajar. With his heel, Jason kicked it shut. Things weren't too tidy in the manse kitchen. Carbon paper had been ground into the linoleum, spaghetti sauce had been spilt on the typewriter, and the window on the door that led to the deck had been broken. Higher on the Great Chain of Being, Calvin Cunningham, once an urbane and witty Upper West Side New Yorker who just happened to be black, had found his "roots" on Mount Pisgah, Tennessee, and didn't like them, didn't like them at all. Not that the kitchen was Calvin's fault. It wasn't. But Calvin had altered in the kitchen; under the blood-red trapdoor, Calvin now slumped behind the typewriter as sullen as Robert after a reprimand.

With his fist Jason pushed the typewriter to one side and pointed a finger at Calvin. "Though I speak with the tongues of men and of angels—that ain't just a metaphor, man." Jason mimicked Calvin's own funky style, which was itself a mimic. "That ain't just whistling 'Dixie.' That's glossolalia, or speaking in *tongues,* man, a fine old tradition."

Calvin looked hurt. "Don't you make fun of how I talk," he reproached. "You been jiving me ever since you knew me, Jason? You think I come out of some ghetto church where people roll around in the dust? You know where I go to church at home? The Riverside Church, you know the Riverside Church? That's William Sloane Coffin's church. Don't you fake saying 'ain't' to me like that's my language."

Jason jammed his tongue in his cheek and made a sucking noise. He sat down opposite Calvin and let out his breath. His chair was wet, he registered peripherally. Calvin had once again, he noted head on, lost his sense of humor. Jason almost preferred him bellicose. He had never, in the two years they'd shared a Nashville apartment, adjusted to Calvin's quick shifts from jive to whine; and now he frowned to himself about a country that could program the defense mechanisms of inferiority even into Calvin, born to modest privilege, blessed with intelligence and a face like the young Harry Belafonte. Happy Fourth of July! Leaning back in his chair, Jason kept his head high and tipped back, as he regarded Calvin, his best friend.

When did it happen? a voice prodded in his ear. When did Calvin first feel someone look down on him? Buying candy? On a jungle gym in the park? Hearing *Little Black Sambo* in school—when did they stop reading that? What did black parents *tell* their children when they asked, "Mama, Daddy, what's wrong with us?" Ah, this was no time to ask. Calvin's face was (as Jessamine might say) "snarled up" into a pout.

"Didn't you ever read Baldwin, man?" asked Jason, instantly sorry about the "man," but Calvin let it pass. "Didn't you ever read *Go Tell It on the Mountain?* That's ghetto storefront, and that's charismatic, and it's your roots. It's also a brilliant book."

"I read Baldwin's *Another Country,*" Calvin countered, suddenly grinning. "Sexy book. Oh, that black singer-girl! And I read *The Fire Next Time,* which charts the revolution that will not come so long as blacks are slaves to this kind of soul rot. That jive on Pisgah, it's a way of getting *off*, man. You ought to see their faces. But do they fuck? Do they get honestly off? No, they don't fuck. They ain't *suppose* to fuck. I'm telling you, Jason, this is genocide, just like heroin."

"Elder Mathews, you can't do that!" Jason and Calvin looked warily up as the two Mormons raced into the kitchen from the big and only bathroom at the foot of the stairs, both clad in baggy white boxer undershorts and flicking each other with wet towels. The towels were the sort that came with the manse, blood red to match the trapdoor, the ladder-back chairs, the shower stall, the bedstead in Jason's room, and the mailbox. Heel-heavy, the Mormons circled the table. Jason could hear the pencils roll. The smell of Right Guard filled the air like a call to arms. The kitchen, stilted and additional to the manse like the deck, shook. The red-and-white-checkered curtains on the windows fluttered, and the floorboards groaned. The dishes in the sink rattled. Jason reached over and turned off the gas from all four burners of the stove. At the refrigerator, the dark-haired Mormon turned around like a bullfighter and rebuked, "Ow, you got me, Elder Olson!"

"Mighty nice of you to put us up, Reverend Baynard," the blond one called as he chased his friend out of the kitchen. "We sure do love your hot water!" He hurled his wet towel. It landed in the sink on top of the dishes.

Jason caught Calvin's eye and laughed. "What can we do?" He'd drawn the Mormons as houseguests through Sam Barnes's vicarious largesse. ("Listen, boys, Abbie and I'd love to put you up here, but look around you—all these tempting young girls. Not to mention Chloe here"—raising his eyebrows and picking up the teasing where Calvin had left off. "But across the lake, the Reverend Jason Beauregard Baynard III operates an exclusively male establishment, sober and celibate as the grave, I assure you.") Jason had good-naturedly offered to board the Mormons while they canvassed the area, twelve hours a day, six days a week, in their black woolen suits. Enough to make your head spin, their hours, till you knew what they did with the other twelve. Day before yesterday, the Mormons had broken Calvin up. They were the funniest things he'd seen in shoe leather. At the Barnes dock, using manic Richard Pryor gestures, Calvin had entertained not only Jason and the kids, but also Sam and Chloe: "The perils of hitchhiking from Tennessee were considerable, until I met up with these two handsome, well-dressed, and sexy dudes"—

wickedly indicating the two hot, flustered Mormons. Now Calvin
didn't laugh at the Mormons's antics, although Jason went to the
unprecedented extreme of trying to prod him into laughing.
"They're so deprived of stimuli, they get high on hot water," Jason
joked.

Calvin stared morosely at the table. "The Mormons are slobs," he
said. "Maybe all religion is like heroin." His long-fingered hands
stroked the sides of Jason's typewriter, the hands of a natural, intuitive sculptor. Give Calvin a scrap of metal and he would hammer it;
give him a hunk of wood (from, say, the woodpile) and he would
carve it. Jason wore around his neck a cross Calvin had hammered on
demand out of a can that had held pork and beans; he kept Calvin's
unbelievably erotic bas-relief woodcarving of Mary Magdalene on the
lakeside windowsill of his bedroom. She looked a lot like the girl
who'd given him the Alpha-Omega medal. Yet tell Calvin he was an
artist and Calvin would say Jason was jiving him. If he handed him a
hammer and chisel, Calvin would say, Don't treat me like a kid. You
think pounding can handle my shame?

Calvin indulged, but trivialized his gift of hands—what would he
have done with the gift of tongues? Calvin ran the heels of his gifted
hands around the spaghetti-spattered metal contours of the typewriter and said softly, "Jason, I think I've lost my faith."

"Lost your faith? A week on a mountaintop in the Bible Belt has
made you lose your faith? That form of religion isn't your style, Calvin, just as, say, Mormonism isn't your style. You don't think Joseph
Smith's treasure is buried at Spanish Hill, do you? They do. They'll
go and look for it, if we're lucky. Do they offend you? Do they challenge your faith? Of course they don't. They amuse you. Can't you
get the same perspective on the charismatics?"

"The Mormons are *white*, " Calvin said. After a second he grinned a
little. "And I taught them how to hitchhike. They'd been walking
alongside the road for two days in those monkey suits—you could
smell them across the Susquehanna. They'd been to see the place
where Joseph Smith and Oliver Crowder were baptized by John the
Baptist. John the Baptist in the Susquehanna! They'd plunged in, and
now they smelled of wet wool and river in addition to the natural
sweat of a ninety-degree day.

"So they were walking along the river in search of Sam Barnes, and
it never occurred to them, never even crossed their minds they should

thumb a ride. Couple of babes in the woods looking for a man who didn't want to be found. Muttering among themselves, 'Well, I saw John the Baptist, didn't you?' 'Well, Elder Mathews, I'm not exactly sure. There's a certain more solid aspect about someone like Mr. Barnes, I would say.' 'Mr. Barnes is harder to find than John the Baptist.' You were mighty hard to find too, Jason," Calvin added then, as if he suspected Jason of hiding from him. "Oh, hey, I forgot till just this minute another lost soul, another babe in the woods, looking for you. When I stopped off in Nashville, your sister called the apartment."

"Tradd?" Jason frowned. He conjured again his mother's vignette of Tradd and Jessamine among the cut flowers at the corner of Meeting and Broad on Memorial Day. Hadn't he written Tradd since before Memorial Day? "Tradd and Mother must not be speaking again," he mused aloud. "What did she want?"

"She has left her husband." As Jason stared, Calvin flopped his hands sideways. "What can I tell you, man? It's what she said. I said, 'Sugar, I am sorry,' and she said, 'Sugar, don't be.' She a smart-ass like you?"

Jason caught his breath, relieved at Tradd's spirit. A tough lady, his sister. "I think you might call her that," he allowed. "So she left Whit." Jason whistled. "Not even six months." He leaned his head to look down the hall (it was glutted with suitcases) as if Tradd might be standing there, the logical and inevitable completion of his bizarre new household. Ah, give her time, he thought. Whatever this manse was going to be, it wasn't going to be lonely.

"How can they do it, Jason?" Calvin suddenly moaned. "It's like a mockery of Africa or Haiti; it is downright barbaric; they have tambourines; they even have a *drum.*"

"Calvin, there are thousands of white charismatic groups. This is not a black aberration!"

Calvin eyed him cagily. "Do the white groups have *drums?*"

"How should I know if they have drums? What the hell difference does a drum make?"

Calvin leaned forward and pounded his fist on the typewriter. Its bell rang like a sound effect. "The drum is what sucks you in, if you're black. If I had stayed there for one more week, I'd've been just like them, feeling the spirit descend, my eyes rolling back, babbling like a baby or a bell. I'd've lost *me* and found not God, but madness: I'd be part of their funky primitive circle!"

2 SUNDAY MORNING

Next day, in the middle of his sermon on Jesus and the disciples, striding about as he'd discovered he was wont to do (God help him if he were ever confined to pulpit and microphone), pausing at a lakeside, open window and gesturing out of it to refer to the Sea of Galilee as the medium for their friendship (Jesus and his disciples, both male and female), an idea he'd gotten from Tony Otway's bondings, developed from observation of the kids at the ball diamond, and suddenly grasped and forged last night from Calvin's tale of woe, Jason was rattled when a flashbulb popped. He went on talking, but the monolithic congregation blacked out in a circle; and when vision returned with dancing sparks, he found his eyes focused on Erich Strauss's blond head looming between Zack Chandler and Fred Bunyan.

So they'd turned out, the kids, for church. As had the Barnes-Otway contingent with the exception of Sam Barnes, who had refused to darken the solid oak door of the church until "his" sermon was on. Calvin hadn't come either; he'd be "too conspicuous," he kept saying, to Jason's eventual disgust. But there were the two Mormons in the back—ah! As Jason caught himself counting the house, he pulled up and retreated into his sermon: he saw, as if by firelight, Calvin's funky circle; dimly and behind, he saw Paul and the early Christians on a bare stage stripped back to absolute openness: just us there. This is the catacombs, he thought, and for an instant felt the congregation as a body held together by him. Well, not by *him*—"We are bonded together," he wound it down, "a small circle of believers, by a lake and by the living water of words, which survive like nothing else. Jesus's metaphors live; they are all around us, casual blessings. Let us all be fishers of men."

After the service, as the too fast and frantic world came back, the long-haired, long-nailed Selina Thomas was the first to shake his hand. "The Macs wanted to come too," she said, "but their mom wouldn't let them. I promised to tell you," she carefully explained, "that it's a mortal sin for Catholics to go to a Protestant church."

Jason almost laughed. "Tell them they are a great infield anyway," he said, feeling Selina's nails rasp his palm as they disengaged. (Was it really a mortal sin? A mortal sin?) Selina smiled up at him. Jason's body relaxed; the world billowed and steadied, and he became part of it, damn it, ready for people again.

Chloe Otway's slim hand had a pulse, Jason discovered, near the thumb joint; she was nervous, he observed with some surprise; she couldn't quite hit his eyes with her eyes, veered them off, lowered them. Her husband, Tony, took over for her. "We were just saying, weren't we, Chloe? that you'd be a splendid teacher. We're all in a fine state of mystification about what happened on the Road to Damascus, by the way, because Sam has all of us reading Acts. Hasn't he, Chloe?" Jason watched Chloe try to laugh but not quite bring it off and found himself linked with Tony against her inexplicable loss of poise. She looked . . . vulnerable, Jason thought. The word spun around in his head; she could be—

"Jason, I want you to meet someone important!"

Helen Fanshawe brought forth a bright-eyed, enthusiastic man with a beard who said, "Excuse the flash in there; it was too good a shot to miss."

"This is Matt Bernstein," said Helen, bowing out with visible reluctance. "We'll expect you at noon, Jason." She waved a sprightly hand.

Matt Bernstein, it turned out, was a newspaperman. "I watched you last week," he said. "I came to scoff but didn't. You're damned good. Also, my daughter Wendy has been singing your praises. I don't know how you got through to that bunch of young ruffians, but you evidently did. They scare the hell out of me," he confided in a mock whisper, laughing. "Especially that young fellow with the scowl. Anyway," he continued, while casually, in one hand, he hoisted an expensive camera as if it were a dumbbell, "I'd like to do, with your permission of course, a feature on your church," and Bernstein explained that since he'd seen Jason the previous week, he'd been scouting out a series on rural churches. "I'm a Jew, you see; this whole scene is fascinating, almost exotic for me." He hung the camera around his neck, letting it settle between the lapels of his madras plaid jacket. "And if you don't mind I'll kick the series off with Lenni Lenape, as that's my summer home base, so to speak," and offhandedly scribbling in a spiral notebook, he went on to ask Jason a few shrewd questions, the last of which was, "Are you going into politics?"

"Ah, no!" Jason demurred, startled.

"Well, you're young; we'll see." Bernstein winked. "Don't protest too much. Or too soon." He palmed the notebook around him into a back pocket, gave Jason a beatific smile, and shook his hand with warm exuberance. "I'll start sending you the *Bugle*. Compliments of the house. 'The Manse,' that right? An address out of another century. Well, Vicar, Naomi and I'll have to get you over for dinner real soon, maybe some Shabbat. Great meeting you." He tapped Jason on the shoulder and went jauntily down the church steps, across the lawn toward Esther's General Store, whistling, Jason could hear him, "He Who Would Valiant Be," the recessional hymn.

Later, his ears jamming from the drive in his as yet unmuffled Triumph—where the blazes could he get it fixed?—Jason returned from Sunday dinner at the Fanshawes' claustrophobic and wanting to tear off his clothes, rend his garments. No one was at home to sympathize, neither the Mormons nor Calvin. Every clergyman, Jason thought, wrenching off his tie and throwing it on the littered kitchen table, ought to be allowed a primal scream among friends after a service. The adrenaline!

Instead: arch small talk about the Church of England with a Shakespearean scholar who thought the "turn of the century" happened when 1599 turned to 1600; mashed potatoes and gravy in the ninety-degree heat; a regular *lecture* from Helen on "The Deleterious Effects of Bilinguality," a lecture that seemed inexplicable to the point of being downright hallucinatory until it emerged that Helen had, with a stunning twist of logic, decided to blame Olivia's fluent German ("Speak some German to Jason later, darling") for the Harvard rejection. "After a year in Germany to learn the language, of course it would take the poor girl some time to get her English back for the Scholastic Aptitude Tests!" While Jason nodded bemused agreement, Olivia had suddenly shouted, "Shut up! Shut up! I can't take any-

more!" and left the table. "Don't you see?" Helen had asked, shaking
her head sadly. "Olivia's English is *eroded.*"

In short, over the Fanshawes' Sunday dinner table, Jason's sermon
—both its substance and its exhilaration—had vanished much more
swiftly than the lingering fumes from the overcooked cauliflower.
Had the sermon been good? He'd thought so, but Harold and Helen
hadn't even mentioned it. Not once. God forbid anyone should mention a sermon outside of church. Ah! Shuddering a little, Jason pulled
on damp swim trunks (the Mormons must have gone swimming after
church; the Mormons borrowed any clothes that weren't being worn
at the moment, then threw them on the floor), shoved open the back
door, and headed down the catwalk for the boat: there was still time
for spray on his face, still time to retrieve some of the exaltation of
church. Someone was on his dock. Jason slowed his pace and saw it
was Fred Bunyan, sitting patient and immobile and impassive, his
red-orange kayak pulled up next to him, his hands clenching the
double kayak paddle so that it pinioned his raised knees.

"Fred," Jason said.

Fred didn't look at Jason. He kept his brooding blue eyes fixed on
the lake, but he spoke as if in the middle of a conversation. "I've been
thinking about what you said this morning."

Jason sat down next to Fred. He found himself assuming the same
position, trapping his knees with his wrists, flexing his hands around
an imaginary paddle. Fred's (actual) paddle was wrapped with adhe-
sive tape. Must be sticky, Jason thought idly.

"We used to be like that," Fred said. Jason waited. There were
motorboats tearing about the lake, but he and Fred seemed wrapped
in a small pocket of quiet. Jason could see people on the Barnes dock
across the way and indistinguishable, androgynous figures diving
from the float.

"You know how you said it was Galilee that bound those different
people together? The lake used to be like that," Fred said. "We were
all from different places, but—" He looked at Jason, then looked
away, at the lake again, eyes grim and pained under dark brows. "Up
here, we were together."

Jason waited.

"I'm nobody at school," Fred said. "Up here, I belonged." He got
up. Jason watched his profile against the sky. Fred had a hawk nose;
his head pointed a little at the top, the back of it flat to his shoulders.

He stood for a moment, a figure from another century, holding his paddle in one hand like a spear; and then he turned to Jason. "It was nice talking to you," he said. He lifted his kayak into the water and climbed into it. Jason watched him slice at the water with the paddle, catching lily pads as he made ready to move away from the dock.

"Come again," Jason said.

Fred turned his head. "I will," he said.

3 SUNDAY AFTERNOON

On the Barnes dock across the lake, wet and sweat and the hot air of tumid, testy conversation combined to form a sticky suspension in the humid air: Chloe Otway saw the elements take shape as a bloated pink sponge. She shifted fretfully about on a chaise lounge, watched Olivia Fanshawe swim out to join the girls on the float, and tried to ignore Harold Fanshawe, who, with Olivia, had just turned up, Harold gloating, "Didn't see you in church, Sam," and now nattering away about department politics: "If Hudson doesn't get that interminable Thackeray book published, he is out."

"Damn it, Harold, he's a good teacher," Sam snapped.

"We're all good teachers," said Harold archly. "That's a given." Chloe stole a look at Harold. His goatee wobbled in place like a hairy insect. Chloe could imagine him teaching. Why weren't universities more stringent about Ph.D. orals? People taught who couldn't *talk*— or, worse yet, talked like Harold.

Sam laughed. "All good teachers! Hear that, Clo? Chloe's a department head too, did you know that, Harold?" Harold glanced at Chloe, startled, his eyes taking in her pinstriped bikini (actually Betsy's; Betsy had cast it off as too scanty for serious swimming, sports rather than sex seeming to obsess the young people as yet, thank heaven). Harold turned his head away fast. He thinks Sam's putting him on, Chloe realized, amused. Usually in such situations she said something cutting and brilliant, but it didn't seem worth the effort. Not for Harold. And what kind of department chairman, come to think of it, would twit a colleague about not being in *church*? Sam ought to clear out of that reactionary college posthaste!

"If you'd come in to the campus once in a while, Sam," Harold went on, his tone waspish now, "instead of lotus-eating out here . . ." Chloe began to feel trapped by Harold's prissy voice. "By the way, how's the Blake volume coming? My own rule is five pages a day. Time's not important. Pages are." Harold sat down on the steps that led to the lawn, effectively blocking escape by land. Speculatively Chloe eyed the water. On the float, Selina Thomas was teaching Elise to do a racing jump; the two slender, long-haired beauties hit the water in perfect splits.

"You shut up, Liz!" On the float proper, Olivia, feet planted stolid as an angry Amazon's, stood. Liz and Betsy faced her. Olivia feinted left, then pushed Liz hard into the water. Quick as Liz's sprawled and unwilling splash, Selina reached out of the water, grabbed Olivia's ankle, and yanked her from the float. Olivia and Selina fought in the water. "Stop that!" Chloe wanted to shout, but then she remembered that Olivia was eighteen and could hardly be ordered about like a child.

"Hey, take it easy," Sam called from the steps where he now sat with Harold. Gradually the splashing subsided, and Olivia swam in, a ponderous and furious crawl, and climbed grim-faced up on the dock. She sat down next to Chloe's chaise and pulled her knees together with her arms; Chloe found herself actually shrinking away a little from the hunched, unhappy figure. Really she should ask the girl what on earth was wrong, but she couldn't. She couldn't bring herself to want to know what had brought on such ugly—well, what else call it?—violence. "Mrs. Otway," Olivia said almost inaudibly. In self-defense (no exit now), pretending not to hear the low voice, Chloe detached the strap of Elise's powerful binoculars from the arm of the chaise and looked across (as she'd been doing desultorily) at Jason Baynard's rickety dock. The binoculars transported her from her own strained setting. She watched Fred Bunyan's scarlet kayak move away from the dock, then watched Jason get into his white motor-boat. That sermon! Something settled like gold dust, and Chloe's body relaxed; she began to feel loose and dreamy, thought she might go up to the cottage and tempt Tony into a "nap," Tony having defected at the arrival of Harold Fanshawe, and no wonder. Bill Wilson had actually said he'd promised to help Aunt Abbie with the potato salad. Chloe giggled. Dicing potatoes *would* be distinctly preferable.

"You can't break the contract, Sam!" Harold Fanshawe's voice looped into a higher register. "We've already announced the Blake volume."

"So unannounce it." Sam's voice was testy.

"You listen here, *Thorns of Life* was witty and stylish, but not exactly *substantial.* It's popular, and that's gone to your head, which of course simply will not do. You're making enemies. You don't want to spend the rest of your life being the bad boy of the department, do you? You're forty-one, Sam—"

"No shit."

"Do you hear yourself? That's what I'm talking about. I'm your friend, and you're talking to me like that. You should be a full professor by now, but it's that kind of no-shit attitude that's kept you from making it."

"You know God damned well that it's a case of the prophet being without honor on his own turf, Harold. On *Thorns* alone I could demand a full professorship at any college in the country, and you know it, Harold. I can write my own ticket."

Why doesn't he? Chloe wondered, shocked Sam wasn't a full professor yet. Both she and Tony had achieved the dubious honor under thirty-five, but perhaps it was easier in science. Less subjective, she suspected, anyway. She wondered if Abbie was keeping Sam from leaving. Quite the hometown girl, Abbie. A different wife—

"If I just knew where I wanted to write the ticket to," Sam went on, his voice uncharacteristically dreamy. "You'll be the first to know, Harold."

"That's a childish threat. Why do you purposely cut your own throat?"

Sam started to whistle. After a second, Chloe identified the tune: the Beatles' "Ticket to Ride." He's got a ticket to ride; he's got a ticket to ride. She laughed as, through the binoculars, she watched Jason Baynard, his arm a visual staccato, start his motor with three quick pulls. She saw he was laughing, just as she was. The wind caught his hair. Next to her, Olivia asked, "May I see the binoculars?" Reluctantly Chloe handed them over and, thrown back on her own optical system, felt her vision shift dizzily as Jason's boat, tiny now, took off up the lake toward the church.

As dusk turned to absolute dark (with savage abruptness, about nine o'clock), Elise warily watched Olivia in Otto's canopied oriental chaise while rather enjoying the weight of Zack Chandler's hand on her own shoulder. They sat on the grass. Elise couldn't quite feel his arm, which made (she knew) a loose V across her back without, however, touching her. His arm was not "around her," in Liz's and Betsy's language, but it was close. And Zack was, for Zack, awfully quiet —Elise expected he wasn't much more used to this intimacy than she was, and that was a relief.

Aunt Abbie had given the suddenly ravenous family homemade dill pickles, potato salad, and lovely rare hamburgers on homemade buns for Sunday supper; and while Elise and Bill Wilson washed up, Bill had quietly asked her if she wanted to go to the "movies." Uncle Tony would let them take the Volkswagen, Bill said. It had sounded scary—to be all alone with him in a car. What if he suddenly started behaving like Charlie Scott, who was also nineteen? She thought she would rather try her hand (or foot or lips or whatever such things called for) at the kids first. But Otto's was unexpectedly spooky at night. The air smelled dark green, heavy, and expectant; insects droned and peeped from the moat that surrounded Otto's basketball court behind the tennis courts. The place seemed . . . fecund, whatever that exactly meant; and Olivia was—well, awfully *there*, Elise thought, as in the dim light that came from Otto's tiny windows, she apprehended again the girl's palpable anger. It seemed to hover in the air like impending acid rain over London. Olivia's face made Zack's hand incidental for the moment.

Olivia was still mad at Liz for what had happened that afternoon on the float. Elise hadn't exactly witnessed it, and Liz would only say she had probably been "a bit high-handed" (Liz's vocabulary often made her seem older than fourteen); but Betsy had related the scene

to Elise as they both, in the big bathroom, changed to jeans before
going to Otto's. "All Liz said," Betsy exclaimed, standing on a toilet
to check out the fit of her jeans in the mirror, "was that she'd asked
Uncle Sam what one should do—she actually said 'one,' not 'you'—if
one didn't get into a certain college. She didn't even say Olivia's name.
She didn't even say Harvard! Uncle Sam said, well, *one* could go to
another college, get straight A's, and transfer next year. That is all
Liz said to Olivia, and then Olivia jumped up screaming and pushed.
I thought she was going to push me too, and I hadn't said a word the
whole time."

Elise had looked at Betsy's indignant, pretty face in the mirror and
wanted to say, "Olivia's awfully defensive," but she didn't, for Olivia
was so visibly aggressive Betsy would scoff. Betsy wasn't much on
paradox. Olivia reminded Elise of Sister Tekakwitha, the hockey mistress at St. Catherine's, who had once, during a frightfully important
match, hit a referee with a hockey stick and then burst into tears.
Sister Tekakwitha had taken her saint's name from an American Indian princess and fancied herself fearless; but there had been behind
her violence a soft-eyed panic. . . .

"Wendy, come here a minute." Olivia's sweetly reasonable voice
broke into Elise's revery. She saw Olivia's arm beckon, dim white
against the darkness. Her imagination placed a hockey stick in
Olivia's hand. Wendy Bernstein moved from wistful proximity to Liz
and Erich Strauss to kneel by the side of the exotic chaise where
Olivia sat. Erich immediately put his arm around Liz's shoulders.

Selina Thomas and Charlie Scott were three spruces away, prone
in the shiny-topped covered wagon, but Selina's lazy voice drawled,
"Don't listen to her, Wendy." Elise heard Liz giggle.

"Shut up," said Olivia, her voice a little desperate. Selina's voice
laughed. Fred Bunyan, on the grass between Betsy and Viola Fanshawe but not touching either of them, suddenly said:

"The minister is the greatest guy. I was over at the manse today,
and—"

"Fred's in love," Olivia jeered.

Liz leaned forward, pulling Erich's arm with her. "I think Jason's
great too, Fred," she told him. A wayward smile lighted Fred's face.
"I'm impressed you dared go talk to him."

"What do you want, Liz?" called Olivia, her voice sleek. "You've
taken over Erich, and now you want Fred." In the dim light, Liz's

profile lurched into disbelief. "She wants all the guys," Olivia continued, her voice carrying. One of Otto's spotlights came on.

"She probably even wants Otto!" said Wendy. Somebody laughed.

"I think Liz is probably a nymphomaniac," Viola offered, her voice hard.

Shaking off Erich's encircling arm, Liz jumped up. "You're horrible!" she cried. "This is *primitive*, like a . . . shunning. An ostracism!" She sounded very literary, and Elise felt for a wild moment as if she were at a play.

"Hey, what'd she say?" Viola's voice asked ironically.

"Liz should learn to keep her mouth shut," Elise, stunned, heard Zack whisper.

Liz's posture crumpled. So did her elegant diction. "You're golliwogs!" she accused, her voice breaking. Elise saw the silly word hang in the air, but nobody laughed.

"Well, honey, if I'm one of those things, then you're a nymphomaniac," countered Olivia. "Listen, don't go away mad," she said in a reasonable tone.

"*Just go away,* " Viola and Wendy finished in unison. Liz stared a minute, then turned, scaled the high terrace in one motion, and ran across the volleyball court toward the hidden path to the ball diamond. You could get to the pipeline from the ball diamond. Elise had never been to the pipeline, but a girl had been raped on the pipeline three years ago, Wendy had most plaintively told her. Raped and left to die. Wendy's father had not been allowed to report it in his newspaper. Getting up fast, Elise went after Liz. She didn't want her running on the pipeline at night. The hard-packed narrow path wound through the woods, and she could hear someone running just behind her, but didn't take time to look—it was Erich, probably, or Betsy. When they reached Liz, faces leached gray in the moonlight that seemed to flood the ball diamond where the sky was wide open, Elise saw that her companion was Fred. He was carrying a large box, which must have slowed him down. Artillery? She grinned at him, feeling a welcome camaraderie. Fred put the box gingerly down on the dirt of the ball diamond, dirt that still smelled reassuringly of baseball from last Thursday. Liz had tears streaming down her face, but she smiled at Elise and Fred.

"Thanks," she said, and then looked toward the path that emerged just to the right of the backstop. Checkered in the moonlight, the backstop was higher than the trees and looked like a web they'd escaped from. Selina appeared, her hair disheveled. The silver studs that bordered the seams of her jeans glowed in the eerie light as she moved to join them.

"I'm with you, Liz." Selina's voice had a thrill in it. "Do you realize Olivia is eighteen? What's she doing, hanging out with us? She ought to be working, or at least married."

"Where is *Erich?*" Liz asked. They all looked at the path, but nothing happened.

"Don't feel badly, Liz," said Selina. "Guys!" she appended disdainfully. "Erich's always been really tight with Olivia. She taught him to French kiss when he was twelve. Remember that, Fred? She was fifteen. Wasn't that *sick?*"

"She taught me too," Fred laconically remarked.

"Oh, gross!" Selina cried. "She didn't teach *me.*"

"Nine or ten guys did."

"No, I knew all along. Or I learned like you're supposed to— Never mind! Oh, shut up, Fred. Do you think you're my conscience, or something?"

"I don't know what to do," said Liz. "Nobody ever hated me before."

"Oh, Liz," Selina said, "don't worry. We're with you. You saw how they turned on you, right? Well, we turn *away* from them. We don't speak to Olivia, Viola, or Wendy, even if we're in the same place with them. Even if we're at the soda fountain or in church or playing baseball next Thursday. They're invisible. For a day or two, we'll speak very coolly to Zack and Erich, because maybe they'll change their minds. If they don't, well, so much for them." Selina looked toward the backstop. "I was wondering if she would come." Betsy burst out of the woods above the path and came around the backstop.

"I got lost!" she cried. "I forgot where the path was! I got caught in that little cemetery where Otto buries his dogs!" She brushed rust and dirt from her jeans. Liz drew her into their tight circle.

"Fred, do you remember how we burned Richie Goldman at the stake because he was slow coming to help us?" asked Selina. She darted her slant-eyes around the circle. "So much for Charlie Scott. Let him stay in the covered wagon and talk to Olivia! He goes home Wednesday anyhow. Fred, you grabbed all his firecrackers, didn't you? I saw you do it!" Fred gestured at the box he'd brought as if, Oh,

it was nothing. "Charlie will have a *fit*," Selina declared gleefully. "He bought them in South Carolina. Come on, let's declare war right now." She knelt on the hard dirt of the ball diamond to open the box of firecrackers. The studs on her jeans formed a right angle.

A decorous cushion apart on the sailcloth couch, lulled by books and the Sunday *Times* and ice melting in the Dewar's and Mozart piano trios on the stereo and, despite all the lulling, beset by dis-ease, Chloe and Sam sat up late by the superfluous fire on Sunday night. Chloe wore a diminutive ruffled cotton nightshirt; Sam wore lurid purple paisley pajamas. Chloe, who'd fallen asleep earlier in the rope hammock on the back deck, had been so brutally awakened by a thousand firecrackers set off at the ball diamond she thought she might never sleep again. From a modified lotus position (modified because of the diminutive nightshirt), she stared into the fire. Sam was reading (the Bible again; heaven help us all!), but he fidgeted nervously, like Sir Isaac having a nightmare. Well, she wouldn't stroke his flank as she would Sir Isaac's. Sam's last remark had been, "There's this guy sleeping with his *stepmother*. First-century Corinth was sin city; did you know that, Clo?"

Questions! Question marks fretted the air like barbed wire. Chloe had been, she could finally admit to herself, although of course she couldn't admit it to *Sam*, jolted by Jason Baynard's sermon that morning, had all day felt her perception . . . what? altered, opened, shot through with scarlet flares, firecrackers, tongues of flame. A silver-tongued devil! Rhetoric! She was trying to convince herself she'd been manipulated.

After a fanciful quotation from Jesus about Galilee, Jason had begun innocently enough: "The Sea of Galilee is about seven times the size of Lenni Lenape, and it's the same shape." Chloe had relaxed. As a scientist, she found facts comforting. "Where's the Sea of Galilee?" Jason went casually on. "Well, everyone knows the Sea of Galilee is not a fiction; it has a latitude and a longitude, and it's still there in Israel, blue as the sky, despite threats from over the border. More important, the Sea of Galilee is still there in the Gospels. Each Gospel begins in the lakeside, sunlit air of Galilee, and each Gospel ends with a reference to Galilee. 'I am going before you into Galilee,' the risen Jesus promises in Matthew and Mark. The Gospel of John ends by the lake, with the risen Lord barbecuing fishes over a charcoal fire for his bereft disciples." Lit-crit structuralism, Chloe had thought, fretting a little on the pew next to Tony, but still facts. Well, fictional facts.

What had unnerved her about the phrase "risen Lord"?

It was that *Jason believed it,* she realized now. She had heard it in his voice. The "risen Lord" existed for Jason just as people existed for her. *This was no game.* (How could it not be a game? She was beginning to realize she not only hadn't believed in God, she hadn't believed in belief.) "The area around this lake—for we would call it a lake—was Jesus's old stamping grounds." Folksy, Chloe had thought, but it was her last critical thought before she was caught up in some mysterious flow. "Lights still flicker dimly today from Capernaum, Bethsaida, and Magdala, towns around the lake where Jesus found his disciples. From Capernaum, Jesus called a hothead named Peter, from Bethsaida a couple of cultivated gentlemen named Philip and Nathanael, from Magdala a brave and beautiful woman named Mary, who was willing, literally, to go with him to the grave."

Was it the inclusion of the woman, Chloe wondered now, that had hooked her? Was it possible she was an atheist simply because no one had ever given her a figure to identify with before? After Mary Magdalene, she'd identified right and left today, identified even with those who were healed beside the lake, those who were fed beside the lake. "Well," Jason had so easily explained such identification, "we'd all like to be healed, and we'd all like to be fed. But what about the other thing that happened at the lakeside? What about the call to discipleship? Do we all want *that* call?

" 'Come with me,' Jesus says to Peter and Andrew, 'and I will make you fishers of men.' 'Is this the ground of your faith,' Jesus wittily asks Nathanael, 'that I told you I saw you under the fig tree? You shall see greater things than that.' We don't know how he called Mary of Magdala, but we do know he drove seven demons out of her; we know she is, according to John, the first person Jesus speaks to after he is risen. 'Why are you weeping? Who is it you are looking for?' He is gentle with her sadness; he doesn't frighten her. They are all being called to discipleship. He speaks to each of them in the emotional

language they understand. That's how he speaks to us, and that's how
we should learn to speak to each other."

Chloe covered her eyes with her hands and rocked back and forth—
like Mary Magdalene, she realized after a minute! Oh! Jason's voice
came back again; she couldn't stop it. "There was water in the Sea of
Galilee that chemically bonded Jesus and his disciples together. 'I am
going before you into Galilee' was his promise of the living water
that lives forever. Where is *our* Sea of Galilee? Where is the living
water we all thirst for, whether we know it or not? How do we
channel all our deflected desires back to God? How do we take our
part in the Creation—which, translated, means, How do we make our
world what it could and should be? We don't know, because we don't
see what's right before our eyes. We don't see the living metaphors all
around us; we don't see that the task of discipleship is simply to pick
up the connections that naturally exist to bond us together—connections we have *dropped*. We are chemically meant to be bonded together. Friendship, we call it—or, more simply, love.

"Our Sea of Galilee is right here—the lake—a living metaphor. Our
living water is here at our docks and the docks of our neighbors. Our
lake is a circle that connects us and tries to pull us together, to make
us all disciples, all fishers of men. For where the fishers of men are,
the risen Jesus is also."

Chloe unwound her legs and jammed her bare feet against the edge
of the coffee table, fixing her heels, digging in. Her personal geogra-
phy had been invaded by something alien—an undiscovered element,
say, or an elegantly simple, hitherto unnoticed scientific law. "We are
all fishers of men," she thought. "We all want living water," she
thought. Oh, *hell*, she thought then: why do these words strike
chords? Where are those unseen, unheard piano keys, smooth as
ivory, and ready? In church she'd had a catch in her throat as if she
were on the edge of a new kind of breathing. Now she put her tongue
in her cheek, feeling the filmy tissue on the inside of her mouth. A
new kind of breathing? she mocked herself. What new kind? I
breathe; I'm alive; I'm more alive than most people. "Vibrant," my
student evaluations say. "She brings herself with her." I can light up
a lecture hall. I'm a teacher—isn't that a fisher of men? No!

Like a flashbulb, anger illuminated her mind: why am I so disoriented by the catapulting of a mythic figure (for Jesus is mythic, he is)
into my life? Yes, it *is* life, what I have: this real life of human beings

and passion and mess and trying to do one's work. I am happy, she told herself firmly. I was happy. Even if there's a greater ecstasy, *I don't want it.* I like it here, where it's too warm by the fire, and I can go up and nudge Tony to make love to me, so I can sleep. What's living water to me?

Do you hear yourself? she asked herself then. What you're really saying is, There's a God, but I don't believe in him. I will go on as stubborn as Sam, looking neither left nor right, and certainly not up.

The record player switched itself off, exposing expectant silence. There isn't a God. Just ask Sam.

"Say, Chloe." Sam cleared his throat. "Did you ever cheat?"

Chloe turned. What a wild question! She was delighted at the diversion. She wrapped her arms around her knees and tilted her head against the back of the couch. "Sam," she asked him demurely, "are you sure that's a proper question?"

Sam snorted. Then he laughed. He threw back his head and clutched a sofa pillow to his chest to muffle the resonance. "Chloe," he managed between explosions of laughter, "I hadn't realized propriety was one of our goals!"

"Shhh." Chloe was laughing too. Sam moved closer to her on the couch, rustling the *Times* as he sat on it, and beckoned with his finger. She leaned her head toward him.

"Well, did you?" he whispered loudly.

"Sam, is this a proposition?"

"Oh!" he shouted, the sound rising to the rafters. Uneasily they both looked up at the balcony (how absurd if this scene should be misconstrued!) and, with tacit agreement, guiltily repaired to opposite ends of the couch, legs crossed away from each other.

After a minute, Chloe stole a sly look sideways. Sam was stroking his mustache. "You didn't answer my question," he said self-righteously, not looking at her.

"You didn't answer *mine.*" She'd been kidding when she asked, but now, What were you up to, you bastard? she wondered. "Was it? Was it a proposition?"

Sam grinned wickedly at her, then stretched and yawned extravagantly. "None of your business," he finally said. Chloe laughed, and, laughing, felt her world settle around her again. I mean, she asked herself, did Jesus ever laugh? The sound of a firecracker across the lake made her laugh again. What fisher of men was setting off fire-crackers on Jason's dock at three o'clock in the morning?

6 MONDAY MORNING

Early Monday morning, a couple of hours after the crazy, patriotic Mormons had exhausted their arsenal of firecrackers and retired at long last, Fred was on Jason's dock again. When Jason went down to him, Fred continued his train of thought as if no time had elapsed since yesterday afternoon. "I've figured out why it's gone bad," he said.

Jason sat down on the bottom step of the catwalk.

"It's *sex*," Fred said. "We used to be all alike. There was Olivia and Erich and Selina and Zack and the Macs and V, and it didn't matter that some of them were girls. Now it does. The Macs' mom won't let them go around with us because of Selina and Charlie Scott. We were all alike. Now we're not." Fred looked at Jason. "Don't get me wrong, Jason," he said. "I like girls as much as the next guy."

SIX
The Lion of Lake Lenni Lenape

Wednesday, July 17

1 THE MANSE

About two and a half weeks hence, in the morning, Jason was rousted out of bed by his ring on the telephone. The strident four shorts, repeated over and over, drilled into his sleep, leaving aural perforations that made him cover his ears. Naked, he crawled out of bed and blearily tried to gauge time by the fact that the Mormons (who'd appropriated his alarm clock) had already left—it had to be after seven. Calvin's door was closed, but Calvin slept all the time; Jason hoped he'd sleep off his depression. Hoping this, Jason almost fell down the stairs over a heap of clothes at the top (fast becoming reminiscent of his undergraduate Beta House, the manse!), jammed his toe on a suitcase at the foot of the stairs, hollered, finally reached the kitchen, and, as he grabbed for the still angrily ringing phone, glanced out the back windows down at the dock; and there was Fred. At least nine o'clock. Patiently every morning Fred would wait for Jason to wave him up.

Jason hadn't even said hello when the receiver guffawed in his ear. "Young preacher, wake up!"

"Who's this?"

It was Sam Barnes, laughter juggling his voice. "I made the operator ring you and wouldn't let her stop. She was mad as hell. Go out and get your newspaper. And if you can shake the Elders Olson and Mathews, bring Calvin and come to dinner tonight. Come about four. Or three. The cocktail hour here gets longer and longer. *I*, by the way, am making dinner tonight in celebration of *you*. Chloe says we should get to you before you become an insufferable social lion." Chloe Otway's husky protest carried to the phone, and Jason found his head leaning toward it. "All right, Chloe, I will take the credit—*I* made up the title 'The Lion of Lake Lenni Lenape.'" Sam laughed richly at himself. "Like Byron, Baynard woke up and found himself famous. I didn't know Matt had it in him!"

"Sam, what are you talking about?" Jason was laughing too, though he knew not why. He sat on the edge of the table—naked, an awful, sticky mistake. He and Calvin washed up after their meals, but the Mormons ate after seven when they got back at night, ate night and morning boxed cereals and canned variations on tomato sauce: Cheerios, SpaghettiOs, Beefaroni, Armour Texas Chili. Jason suspected he was sitting in Armour Texas Chili. Patiently he waited for Sam Barnes's hilarity to subside.

"Go get your newspaper!" Sam finally roared. "Come to dinner, but no Mormons! I don't like the way they look at my gin, and I don't like the way they look at my daughter!"

"Okay, okay." Jason wrestled with a pair of jeans a Mormon had left on the kitchen floor, the leather belt still laced through, and accepted the dinner invitation. "The Mormons don't like you anyway, Sam. They really thought you were a live prospect. Why the hell did you read *The Book of Mormon?*" His shoulder holding the old-fashioned horn-shaped receiver on his ear, Jason fumbled with the zipper on his jeans.

"*The Book of Mormon* is not a bad effort for a seventeen-year-old boy with imagination," Sam judiciously proclaimed, "and Joe Smith surely had imagination all his short, happy life. Who else could have put over polygamy in the nineteenth century? Do you know he had at least fifty wives? Besides, I'll read anything. What's the matter, Chloe? Oh, oh, yes! I'll read anything, even the *Bugle*. Jason, go get your newspaper!"

Jason rang off and went down the hall and through the front door of the manse. His grass needed cutting. His rambler roses needed tying back so he didn't have to duck, going off the porch. Maybe Fred? His Triumph needed a new muffler. In the blood-red manse mailbox, he found a postcard, a letter from his mother scented with lemon verbena, and Matt Bernstein's *Bugle*, a newspaper he'd been noting had considerable circulation in this part of Pennsylvania as he watched, surreptitiously, nearly three weeks now, for the promised article. Suddenly wary of the newspaper, shy almost, Jason stood at the mailbox for a minute, letting the ripe yellow scent from his mother's letter invade these northern woods. He caught the newspaper against his side with his elbow and looked at the postcard, turning it from a gaudy rendition of the Nashville Parthenon to a cryptic message: "Brother mine, make me a pallet on the floor, hear? Tradd." The postcard had been around, having no zip code, but the postmark was Nashville. Tradd was supposed to live in Savannah, where Whit had joined his father's law firm and restored an eighteenth-century town house in the historic district. Jason shook his head to think of moving from one historic district to another. Talk about living in the past! With a home of his own, he'd be hard-pressed to suffer even an antique. In his mind's eye he saw Tradd in the slick little Mercedes 300 SL that Whit had given her for a wedding present traveling steadily northward. Any day now. Maybe Tradd could figure out some way to rid his house of Mormons.

What an unchristian thought! Jason suppressed the unchristian thought, stashed postcard and letter in his back pocket, and leafed through the newspaper. On the front page of the second section, he had a sudden view of his own pictured face. Hellfire! his mind shouted. He felt his face flush, saw the ruddy color spread to his bare chest, realized he was standing nearly naked on the main road next to the historical marker, folded the newspaper, and headed back into the (relative) privacy of the manse. Calvin's door remained closed; Fred still waited on the dock, with Selina now, Jason saw, also saw that Calvin had replaced the glass in the door to the deck. At the kitchen table, he opened the paper again, standing back a little as if it might explode.

"YOUNG PREACHER SPELLBINDS AT LENNI LENAPE," the headline read. A large photo of him dominated the upper left-hand corner. Jason was amused, fascinated, horrified all at once. The photograph was egregiously flattering, catching him with his head framed against a window, a hand up in a graceful, casual gesture. Both head and hand were haloed. Jason was startled at how dramatic the accidental, natural lighting appeared. A skillful photographer, Bernstein.

Below were smaller photographs, one of the church, one of him on his dock with Fred, Zack, and Erich Strauss, Erich lying down. Did Bernstein prowl the lake with his camera? Wryly Jason remembered the third photograph. At the ball diamond the first week Wendy Bernstein had suddenly cried, "Cheese," and snapped him with Elise, Olivia, and Selina. He was holding a softball as if he'd just clapped his hands around it and grinning nonchalantly at their upturned faces.

Jason looked again at the dock photo, bit his lip, and frowned. That had been taken before the boys had been absorbed into whatever

crazy feud had split the girls into hostile forces. Nobody would tell
him what had happened, but he thought it was a damned shame. He
remembered the day all three boys had been on his dock; they had
really talked, Erich about feeling guilty he had so *much*—money,
height, girls after him. "I'm a simple guy," he'd said, "but I don't look
like a simple guy, so people imagine I'm special. I'm *not.*" "Most simple guys don't know that they are simple guys," Jason had said offhand, leaving that to work on Erich, who was no simple guy. Zack,
too, was embarrassed about excess—a regular lesson in Puritanism
these boys were for Jason, raised on Southern largesse and hidden
pride. Zack was ashamed of his mother, a nice but silly woman, and
had fantasied as a child he'd been switched with a prince. They'd all
laughed at that, Zack most of all. But he got these great grades without trying—why? He had this *taste*—should he? He had this *wit*—
from where? And Fred—oh, Fred broke the heart: "I wish I could be a
likable person," he'd said, so open, so vulnerable, so exposed that
Jason's eyes burned. "*I* like you, Fred," he'd said, his voice husky.
"You see what I am," Fred had told him.
Someone had snapped a picture of that. Jason felt for a moment like a
primitive who thought a camera stole his soul. Was this newspaper
article an exercise in vanity? Had he inadvertently exploited the kids?
Should he have turned Matt Bernstein down flat? As he read the
article through, feeling pleasure, feeling pain, both sensations keeping heat in his face, he wished he could talk to the rector about it. "A
seminarian not yet ordained is nonetheless packing them in at Lenni
Lenape." *Packing them in.* By next week he would indeed be packing
them in, Jason foresaw. The church would not feel the same; space
would alter, muffling his voice, inhibiting his movements. His sermon would have to be *terrific.* "The lake itself serves as his personal
Sea of Galilee." Jason groaned out loud. "A faithful band of young
followers of all faiths . . ." "Next week: A Miracle up the Road."
With grim amusement Jason wondered what that would be. Should
pack 'em in.
He laughed. He put the newspaper away. He put on a plaid shirt
that hung over a chair—his, he thought. He picked up a King James
from the stack of Bibles he kept on the narrow counter that served
him as "library," sat down at the kitchen table that served him as
"desk," and started reading Acts from the beginning. Since Sam
Barnes's challenge he'd become fascinated with the Road to Damas-

cus, had chucked his too grandiose idea about "narrative continuity," and concocted a new thesis, tentatively titled "Synesthesia in Acts." Gradually settling into the archaic style of the King James, he read, "Let his habitation be desolate, and let no man dwell within; and his bishoprick let another take," and got laughing. His mind flippantly conjectured the title, "Dirty Puns in the King James," and conjured the shocked faces of the Luke-Acts committee. He heard Sam Barnes clap his hands: "All right, everybody, what's a bishoprick?" He was still laughing when he glanced up from the book and saw Fred and Selina shyly looking in at him from the back door. "Ah, come in," he called, repentant. He'd completely forgotten them.

They came in, Fred with his head down nonetheless giving off an energy, an excitement. He wore an army shirt with a flap that said "Bunyan" on the breast pocket. Selina's sloe eyes were shining. She wore very short white shorts and an odd knit affair, lavender, with a design of mirrors across the chest; and despite her extraordinary attire, had a certain winsome, tawdry beauty. A wood sprite, Chloe Otway called her. A gilded wood sprite, Jason amended, in his mind seeing slim, green-eyed Chloe as the genuine article. "What'd you *think?*" Selina asked Jason. Ah, the newspaper.

"I don't know," he said honestly. "What did you?"

"I thought it was wonderful! I couldn't believe I was actually in church that famous day! It was a little weird, though, seeing my picture with *O-liv-i-a.*" Selina said the polysyllabic name with great scorn, and Jason made a mental note to try to get to the bottom of this fierce, childish rift. Of course Olivia was eighteen, and he should probably confront her first, but, hell, he didn't want to.

"What'd you think of the article, Fred?" Jason asked him carefully, a little apprehensive. Did he really expect Fred to castigate him for vanity? Did he really look on the fifteen-year-old boy as his conscience? Selina moved, and her mirror design temporarily drew his eyes from Fred.

"I thought it was great," said Fred. "I never had my picture in the paper before. My mom already sent a copy to my dad. I mailed it for her." Fred's parents were divorced, and Fred, Jason gathered, did not see his father very often. Still he said "my dad" with guarded love. Fred put some stones on the table in front of Jason: two arrowheads, a perfect spearhead, and a small weathered rectangle with a groove.

Jason laughed. "Are you declaring war?" He glanced up at Fred

and caught the "Bunyan" on his army shirt. He laughed again, but
the kids just looked baffled. "These are real, aren't they? Where'd you
get them?"

"Oh, we just picked them up while we were waiting for you to
emerge," Selina said airily. She was prowling about the kitchen.
"This place is an awful *mess,*" she said, more with objective wonder
than censure. "There's tomato sauce all over everything."

"You picked all these up this morning?"

"The manse woods are full of Indian stuff," said Fred.

"What's this one?" Jason picked up the rectangle, running his
thumb over its carved groove. Fred sat down at the table.

"That's a canoe anchor. Hey, they really work too. I always carry
one. I've got about twenty. You can keep this one."

Selina had turned on the tap. "Don't bother with those, Selina."

"It's no bother," she caroled, twirling with a flash of her mirrors.
Her chest left Jason a little dazed. He turned back to Fred.

"You mean all these Indian relics can just be picked up underneath
my house?"

"Well, yeah." Fred scowled all of a sudden. "Not only *things,* either."

"What do you mean?"

"I found something else once." Fred's deep-set dark-blue eyes went
evasive. Selina danced around the kitchen, gathering dishes. She wore
purple sneakers.

"What is it?" she asked Fred. "Come on, Freddy love, don't be
secretive. Aw, honey boy, tell mama." She ran a lavender fingernail
down his nose and let it rest on his chin.

"A human jawbone," Fred said, flinching away. He looked from
Selina to Jason. "I kind of wonder what went on down there sometimes," he continued. "You know, when the guy was tortured, the
guy on the marker."

Selina had sat down hard at the table, her eyes alight and staring.
"You found a jawbone! You found a human mandible! That means
there are bones in the woods! Skeletons!" She lilted her voice into
another rhythm. "Flesh still clung to some of the bones. The bodies
were literally covered with gold and jewels. One of the skeletons
wore a golden crown. The head wearing the crown had almost completely crumbled to dust."

Jason and Fred stared at her as she went through a radiant, singsong recitation. When she paused, Fred asked critically, "Why are you talking that weird way?"

"I was *quoting,*" she retorted, miffed. Then her slant eyes went dreamy again. "The wall paintings show youths wandering through the meadows, gathering saffron flowers, and maidens—"

"Selina, stop it!" Fred glowered at her. "She's okay, Jason. She just gets a little carried away sometimes."

Selina laughed: a fey note of pure joy. Jason laughed with her. "What were you quoting?"

"Archaeology!" Smiling, she got up. "I'm going to be an archaeologist." Humming something sprightly and classical, she went back to the sink.

"They're all crazy," declared Fred like a misogynist in a movie from the fifties. Jason laughed.

"All archaeologists, you mean?"

"No, all *women.*" Jason laughed again, but Fred went doggedly on: "They start fights by calling each other names; they never hit each other, so it can never be over; it's damn scary." Selina kept singing at the sink. Suddenly she cried out:

"Fred!"

"What? What?"

Selina sprang around, favoring both of them with her mirrors. Dramatically she spread her arms and gripped the sink with her hands. "Let's have a dig!"

"Huh?"

Jason caught his chin in his hand, speculatively. He juggled two disparate thoughts: Was he living on top of a graveyard? And wouldn't a crazy project like this be just the thing to get the kids talking to each other again? A third thought bounced in and settled the dilemma: Wouldn't it be *fun* . . . ?

Fred's dour face flickered with an interest he tried to convert into suspicion. "You mean," he asked Selina, who still held her rapt pose at the sink, "like at Pompeii or Troy?"

Selina clapped her hands. "Yes!" Jason had the dazzled thought her mirrors might be hypnotizing both of them.

Fred turned to him. "What do you think?"

Jason took a deep breath. He disengaged himself from fears about living over a graveyard. "Well, if you'll promise we'll give anything valuable to an Indian museum, and if Mrs. Fanshawe doesn't mind—"

Helen Fanshawe virtually constituted the Session at Lenni Lenape. Why should she mind? She'd probably be impressed. Jason shrugged. What the hell? "My woods are your woods," he told Fred and Selina. Effusively Selina kissed his cheek.

"We can get shovels from Erich's dad," Fred was saying.

"No!" cried Selina. "Not shovels, *rakes*. We don't want to rape the land, and we don't want to destroy precious artifacts and potsherds!"

"Huh?"

"She's right, Fred. Wait a minute. Wait a minute. Sit back down, Fred. Sit down, Selina." Jason was remembering excavations along the Battery that had unearthed an amazing number of buttons—both Confederate and Union. Quite young, on his bicycle, he remembered picturing the entire Civil War as a button-throwing contest. "Selina, you know archaeology, so you must know you have to start with a concept. They found Troy because they were looking for Troy. What was here? What might have happened on this piece of land to give us a clue to why all those Indian relics are down there?"

"The guy was tortured and lived to tell the tale!" exclaimed Fred.

"What was the tale? What else do you know about him?"

"Nothing." Fred frowned. So did Selina. Casually Jason swung his arm upward.

"Y'know what's up there?" They looked up at the blood-red trapdoor. "All the surviving church records are up there. That means a record of the manse and the pastors who lived here, including, if we're lucky, your guy who was tortured." Fred and Selina looked confused. Jason tried again. "Those church records will give you historical sanction for what you're doing. They may even tell you what to look for. You don't want to go at this blind. That would be"—he nodded at Selina—"raping the land, as Selina says." Selina beamed. "Whose were those arrowheads? Whose was"—he swallowed—"the jawbone? Even, and this is what you'll probably come up with more of, Whose were those old beer cans and green-glass Coke bottles? The actual manse has been changed any number of times, but it has always been *here*, right here since 1783."

"We can figure out the whole saga of the manse!" Selina rhapsodized. "We'll go down, layer by layer, culture by culture. It'll be just like *The Source* by James Michener!"

"Well, not quite," said Jason, hiding a smile. "We don't go back that far, and earth doesn't preserve things like sand does. But we'll go back two centuries. All right!" He assumed his fast-talking ball-diamond voice: "I got work to do! I got a paper to write and a sermon to make up. That's hard work, and I ain't just whistling 'Dixie.' " Fred and Selina grinned. Unlike Calvin, the kids appreciated his accents. "Fred, why don't you get up there and start bringing the stuff down? Neatly. And, Selina—" Why not? "You can be getting the kitchen clean so we don't get any valuable records dirty." Jason felt a pang of conscience. "Or, Selina, you can go up there, and Fred can clean the kitchen—"

Fred grabbed a chair and put it on the table in front of Jason. Jason sat back and started figuring, yeah, he could move his stuff into the "parlor," the one inviolate room in the manse, inviolate mainly because it harbored antiques that reminded him of Old Charleston. There was a little Queen Anne desk— With great vigor, Selina went about washing the dishes. Soapsuds flew. Fred pulled himself up monkey-style through the trapdoor. Dust and dead moths and mouse droppings fell like a plague of locusts on the table.

"Oh, gross!" Selina cried, but it was rhetorical.

Jason picked up his Bible and called out from the doorway, "Right on, team. I'll be in the front room if you need me." Fred thumped comprehension on the ceiling slightly to the left of the trapdoor.

"Jason, there's even tomato sauce on the *typewriter*," he heard Selina report as he went down the hall. Laughing, Jason escaped back into the threatened bishoprick in the King James.

"Hey, man, how can you read on that little bitty sofa?" Hunched sideways on one of the two hump-backed love seats that, along with the spindly Queen Anne desk, a rosewood melodeon which wouldn't play, and a wing chair covered with a pale-blue fabric that turned out to be simultaneously slippery and sticky (Jason had tried it), made up the furnishings of the pretty little manse "parlor," Jason came out of Acts as if out of deep water. What an uncanny effect Luke's shifts from the third to the first person had on the shipwreck scene; how the rhythms drew a reader in! The alternating "they's" and "we's" could make you seasick. Jason was suddenly certain that Luke had known exactly what he was doing when he confused eyes and ears in the Road to Damascus passages. Luke's Gospel proved he could write a straight narrative *if he wanted to*. Luke was a "modern" novelist; Acts was experimental! Stunned at this unexpected and unsought epiphany—a literary rather than a religious insight, after all—Jason stared at Calvin until Calvin asked with real concern, "Hey, man, you okay?"

"Yeah, yeah." Jason unfolded his cramped legs and put his feet stiffly on the floor, rucking up the aged (and probably priceless) oriental rug that exactly centered the small room. Its ambers, golds, and blues had paled to the ghosts of colors. As Calvin sat gingerly down in the wing chair and laced his fingers together in his lap, Jason couldn't help laughing at the prim look his face assumed; the manse parlor did things to one! He had his own legs crossed at the ankles.

"Damn thing itches." Calvin got up out of the wing chair. "Jason, let's get out of here. This is a room for old ladies. Besides," he went on as Jason got up from the love seat, "wait till you see what those two kids have found in the attic." Calvin and Jason together wove through the suitcases in the hall to the kitchen. "I like those kids. The little gal is the funkiest dresser," Calvin confided in a loud whisper. "And when Fred came down from that hole in the ceiling, he said, 'Yikes!' just like somebody in a comic strip. I'm going to let them tell you what he found."

In the kitchen, seated side by side at the table like two kids sharing a school desk a century ago, Fred and Selina were conferring earnestly over an open book. The kitchen was clean; it smelled of ammonia. The scrubbed deal table looked scrubbed again; the typewriter gleamed from the shelf where Jason kept his books. Fred and Selina looked up, with wide, solemn eyes, at Jason's face. "Tell him how you found it," prodded Selina without taking her eyes off Jason's face.

"I was looking through old books for slips of paper," Fred slowly began. His blue eyes, embarrassed at the limelight, shunned Jason's and focused on something outside the window. "My dad says that's how you find the real stuff—even money sometimes. People use dollar bills for bookmarks. They put five-dollar bills in Gideon Bibles in motel rooms— What's the matter, Selina?" Selina was tapping his shoulder with a finger.

"Why are you looking out the window? Look at people when you talk to them."

Fred shifted his eyes back into the kitchen and settled them on the refrigerator. It had been polished, Jason noted. "My dad collects old lawbooks," Fred went on, "and I don't know if I told you, but he found a note from a courtier to Henry VIII in a sixteenth-century book, and another time he found a newspaper clipping about John Brown's raid—"

"Look, Jason," interrupted Selina, losing patience. "Look at this." Her lavender-tipped finger pointed at the book. "Isn't it the wildest thing you ever saw!" she exulted. Fred trapped her hand with his and covered up the page.

"*I* found it," he said.

"I know you found it! Don't you want him to see it? If we wait for you, it'll have disintegrated like the woman in *She* by H. Rider Haggard!" Selina stood up to give Jason space, and his eyes confronted the lavender jersey and the mirrors again. He leaned to look at the quarto volume open on the table. He could feel Calvin's anticipation. What the hell . . . ? The book was Dante's *Inferno* with the Doré engravings. Fred's finger pointed. On a torn piece of old parchment, caught in the binding next to Doré's engraving of Paolo and Francesca, was a line drawing of a woman who turned Doré's nude Francesca vapid and unreal. The woman on parchment, drawn in ink that had faded to reddish-brown, was naked (as opposed to nude), naked but for a feathered headdress and an intricately detailed necklace: woven beads and an attached cross that touched the erect nipple of her left breast. Her belly was distended. In one hand, she cradled the blade of a tomahawk, its shaft resting against her arm like a baby. The breasts, belly, and scrawled dark thatch of pubic hair were drawn with obscene beauty, a hatred.

Jason heard himself let his breath out. Fred's eyes finally engaged his eyes. "It's Queen Esther," said Fred dispassionately.

"Queen Esther?"

"Hey, tell him, Fred," said Calvin. "Wait'll you hear this, Jase!"

"Yeah, Fred, we haven't got all day, Fred!" Selina heaved an exaggerated sigh, crossed her arms over her mirrors, and leaned against the refrigerator.

"Queen Esther," Fred related, "was our Esther's great-great-great-grandmother. You know Esther Montour who owns Esther's General Store, don't you?" Jason nodded, mentally juxtaposing that stocky redheaded woman with the brazen warrior queen on the parchment. "Queen Esther's last name was Montour too. After her son was killed, she tomahawked fourteen men after the Wyoming Massacre. She made all fourteen stand in a circle on a rock overlooking the Susquehanna, and then she tomahawked them one at a time, all by

herself. That isn't easy," Fred grimly said, "when you think about it."
Calvin whistled. "Then," Fred continued, "she scalped all fourteen,
which isn't easy either, and then she put on all the clothes she owned
under a scarlet riding cloak, stole a horse, and rode away from the
bloody rock, waving the fourteen scalps all strung together from her
hand like a banner."

"Why fourteen?" Jason's ear was teased by the number Fred had
repeated like a refrain.

"It takes fourteen commoners to make up for a prince. Esther was a
queen avenging her son," said Fred matter-of-factly.

"That is some bitch," Calvin commented with admiration. "I'd like
to carve her." Selina gave out a little squeal. Calvin grinned at her. "I
mean in *wood,*" he told her. "I'm going to look for a hunk of cherry
wood in Jason's woodpile and see if I can reproduce this red lady. You
know," he said then, tipping his head and twisting his mouth with
light irony, "when you were talking, Fred, about the scarlet cape—
you know what I thought of? I thought of when I was a kid at school
and we read the story 'Little Red Riding Hood.' You kids know the
story of Little Red Riding Hood?" Fred and Selina nodded in unison,
watching Calvin's face as if they were five instead of fifteen.

"Well, there I was, a little black kid who didn't quite know I was
black yet. Or I knew I was black, but I wasn't sure what was wrong
with it yet. I just sure knew all the stuff we were studying in school
was *white.* And here we were about to read a story about a little chick
named Red Riding Hood. Well, great! I thought—an Indian girl. She
ain't black, but she sure ain't white either. Then we read the story,
and on the last page there was a picture of Little Red, and I yelled out
at the teacher, who was, of course, a white lady, 'Hey, that's a *white*
girl!' You know what she said? These were the days of women's liberation. I was seven years old, but she said to me as if I was thirty years
old, 'At least she's female. One out of two ain't bad.' End of story."

Jason and Selina laughed. "What's funny?" asked Fred, a trace of
his evil-eye glower coming on his face. Laughter, Jason had noticed,
alarmed Fred.

"Women are another oppressed minority," Selina impatiently explained. "Just like blacks and Indians and the poor and the deaf. I'm
going to have to teach you a thing or two about women's liberation,
Fred." Jason sat down at the table, leaned his chin on his hand, and
thought, I just learned more about Calvin than I learned in two years

of living with him. Is this why people have children? Children draw
things out. Children remind us. It was Fred and Selina who pulled
that story out of Calvin.

"I'm glad *I* didn't live in the days of women's liberation," Fred
averred. Jason covered his mouth with his hand not to laugh, and
Calvin, shoulders shaking, turned away. Selina just rolled her eyes.
"About Queen Esther," Fred went single-mindedly on, "how did a
picture of her get here, if she wasn't ever here? Esther went north, to
New York State. She was last seen at Cayuga Lake in 1783."

"*I* never believed that was Esther!" Selina argued. "I never liked
the way they described her as always drunk and sleeping on porches.
Esther wouldn't do that; she was a *queen*. I bet Queen Esther *was* here,
and that was somebody else, also named Esther, at Cayuga Lake."

"How are you two so sure this is Queen Esther?" Jason asked them.
He looked at the shadowed face in the drawing. It was turned almost
to profile toward the arm that held the tomahawk. Feathers touched
the exposed cheekbone. "You can't even make out her features."

Fred and Selina looked affronted. "We've read all of Esther's
books!" Selina contended. "We know Queen Esther when we see
her!"

"It's the necklace," explained Fred, his level voice turning Selina's
into an obbligato. Fred ran his finger across the woman's necklace,
fastidiously avoiding her breasts. "Esther's necklace is mentioned
twice by people she captured."

" 'Queen Esther wore a necklace of pure white beads,' " Selina
chimed in with her rapt "quoting" voice, " 'from which hung a cross
of stone or silver. It was carved from a whitish stone, polished by
long use—' "

"Selina, you're right," said Jason. Carefully he detached the parchment drawing from the binding of Dante's *Inferno* and passed it to
Calvin. Calvin looked at it a long time.

"You can't make out her face," he remarked, "but the body's so real
it's almost flesh. You can almost touch the necklace. I got to carve this,
if I can find a piece of wood with just the right ruddy tinge. I don't
know why, but I got to."

Selina's voice resumed. " 'Queen Esther had not the bend of the

squaw; she had not the Indian mode of turning her toes in. Her skirt
was with brooches of silver as were the warriors' clothes.' "

"Jason," Calvin bent to ask him, "what is that crazy little chick
doing?"

"She's quoting, Calvin," replied Jason, keeping his face straight.

2 THE BARNES COTTAGE

Elise grated a great triangular chunk of Parmesan onto the cutting board; the crumbled cheese piled up in little mounds like gold dust or Indian cornmeal. The cutting board was one of the few things in the kitchen that wasn't spackled by the spaghetti sauce Uncle Sam had exuberantly thrown together, then abandoned to take a swim. Sam looked like the reddleman in *The Return of the Native*, Elise had told him, and he'd laughed. He loved references to books. "From a newspaper celebrity, that's high praise," he'd said. Now his sauce bubbled on the stove—spattering, but he had very firmly told Aunt Abbie not to turn it down: "It's better with the slight *frisson* of a burn." Aunt Chloe had rolled her eyes on that one.

"Abbie, are you muttering an imprecation?" Aunt Chloe, on a tall wooden stool, washing mountains of fresh and very gritty spinach at the sink, stopped spinning the salad spinner to ask now. Elise glanced at Aunt Abbie, curious. Abbie, who was very neatly cutting stalks of celery on the slant, colored. She gave an embarrassed little laugh. "I wouldn't blame you," Chloe went on. "He's a grown man. He ought to be able to clean up after himself. 'A *frisson* of a burn,'" she added, laughing. "Sam would be the lousiest scientist. D'you suppose that's the basic difference between science and art? That science hasn't the luxury of paradox? Never mind. I'll ask Sam later. Were you cursing him out, Abbie?" Aunt Chloe twined her bare feet in the rungs of the stool; she had absolutely smashing legs.

"I was counting," Aunt Abbie said.

"Counting?"

"I find myself doing it all the time. I count slices of celery; I count slices of carrots and onions; I count slices of potatoes; I don't know what's the matter with me!" Aunt Abbie put down her paring knife and covered her eyes with her hands. "It doesn't matter how many slices there are!"

"Abbie." Chloe set the salad spinner down on the closed toilet seat and went over to Abbie. She touched her shoulder. Abbie pulled away a little. "Abbie, I want you to leave the rest of dinner to us. Go for a swim. Not a shower; a lovely, luxurious *swim.*" Aunt Chloe turned to Elise. "Elise, go find your cousins. I heard them sneak upstairs with Sir Isaac. Liz made some of this mess anyway dipping all that bread into the sauce." Little scraps of bread all over the counter next to the stove mutely testified to Liz's enthusiastic samplings. Elise looked at them. "We'll all finish the salad, and then Liz and Betsy can clean this place up. Go on, Elise. Come on, Abbie." Aunt Chloe untied Aunt Abbie's apron, let it drop to the floor, gave Aunt Abbie a little push, and within a few minutes, almost without a break, the kitchen resumed activity with the energetic (and apologetic) addition of the truant Liz and Betsy.

"We got to reading, Aunt Chloe."

"Betsy's in the middle of the burning of Atlanta chapter, and you know how gripping that is. We're sorry, Aunt Chloe."

For some reason no one minded helping now that Aunt Chloe was in charge, although she was much bossier than Aunt Abbie, setting Betsy to finish the celery ("Do it on the slant the way your Aunt Abbie was doing it—no strings"), Liz to slice the mushrooms "symmetrically," and Elise to continue grating the Parmesan. "Elise, you've been at that for *hours.* As long as I've been at this stupid spinach." Aunt Chloe returned to her stool and her spinner and her sinkful of spinach.

"There's tomato sauce on the floor. Yuk." Liz shifted her bare feet as she chopped. Betsy hummed the movie theme from *Gone with the Wind* over the celery. Diligently applying herself to the slow process of grating, Elise found a mischievous image before her eyes: a red, white, and green container of already-grated Parmesan cheese. It being received opinion in Britain that all Americans were addicted to convenience foods, Elise had been surprised to find that natural, organic food ruled this household in ways it most certainly did not rule Jack's flat, St. Catherine's, or any of the homes of her school friends— even those with servants. Why, Aunt Abbie even made the pasta on a little machine.

"This spinach. It tastes," Aunt Chloe said thoughtfully, "just like the spinach you can buy wrapped in cellophane. There isn't a particle of difference." They all turned to see Aunt Chloe frowning as she chewed a spinach leaf. "Imagine washing all this stuff when you can buy it already washed!"

"Mother washes the kind you buy in packages too," Liz remarked.

"You're *supposed* to; you *have* to wash it," Betsy declared, her blue eyes shocked. "You could poison somebody!" She raised her paring knife in the air with murderous emphasis. "How do you know *who* put the spinach in the packages?"

"Betsy, such vehemence!" said Liz sidelong, laughing.

Aunt Chloe stared at Betsy in bemused disbelief. Elise smiled at the look on her face. Aunt Chloe caught her eye and grinned. She lolled her head back and laughed. "All these years," she murmured to the ceiling, "I've been poisoning Tony with dirty spinach. For God's sake, Liz, don't tell your mother. She'd ban me from the kitchen."

"This looks like my kitchen." Jason Baynard came into the kitchen with Uncle Sam. His "kitchen" jibed exactly with Aunt Chloe's "kitchen," as if they'd planned to say the word at the same moment. "Early tomato sauce, Calvin calls it. Sam, you ought to see what your Mormons have done to my kitchen." Elise, turning toward Jason, caught everyone else turning too. She knew she was standing a different way from how she would stand if Uncle Sam had come in alone.

"*My* Mormons! Ho, ho," chortled Uncle Sam. Elise saw that Aunt Chloe had sat up straighter on her stool, hugging the salad spinner; Elise then saw Jason glance at Aunt Chloe's legs wound gracefully around. She willed him to look at her, Elise, but he didn't. "Hello, Chloe," he said warmly. He had his thumbs hitched into the back pockets of his grass-stained white jeans. Elise was surprised to see Aunt Chloe's green eyes swerve, her face color: Aunt Chloe was usually so poised.

"Hi," Aunt Chloe said. "Welcome." Her voice sounded out of breath. Uncle Sam was grabbing up bottles and glasses and the ice bucket. Elise found her eyes focused on the little red polo player embroidered on Jason's tan shirt. Betsy, for some reason, did not disparage the little polo players as she did most labels: polo players did not go the way of feckless little alligators. The knit shirt stretched over Jason's shoulders. Elise raised her eyes to his face and caught him looking at her.

"Hi, baby doll," he said. Her insides seemed to melt.

"Come on, Jason," said Uncle Sam impatiently. He stood at the door that led to the back deck where they had all taken to gathering before dinner, sometimes catching the sunset over Otto's woods. A big rope hammock extended from an old oak tree and hooked onto the cottage. There were three old-fashioned rocking chairs painted red, white, and green, like a container of Parmesan cheese. A little bridge ran over the steep pitch that separated the Barnes cottage from the West Shore Road. From the deck, the girls could sit and rock and unobtrusively watch the road—cars struggling over potholes and rocks and mud, people walking and jogging. Bill Wilson liked to guess how long each car's muffler would last. Liz and Betsy had, with hushed anguish the past two weeks or so, watched Olivia, Wendy, and Viola stride by, ostentatiously and often, with Erich and Zack.

By now, Elise was just about as weary of that silly row as she was of grating Parmesan cheese. She wished Bill Wilson would come home from work, for he seemed so refreshingly adult now. He had shoulders like Jason's. Sister Diana, the biology mistress, always told them not to look at men's bodies. "Sight is the gift of Satan—don't look! Listen to their voices; listen to their *minds.*" Still Elise caught herself speculating again what it might feel like to have a man's arms around her, close and tight. Hard and hot. Really she spent too much time thinking about this! She ought to stop it. The thought would dart into her head and spin around at times most inappropriate—in church, watching Jason move about; in the upstairs hall, catching Bill damp and rosy in a terry cloth robe after a shower.

Zack Chandler left her quite cold now, the way he was conducting himself in this puerile row. He was sixteen—as she, Elise, was—too old for such rubbish! Elise had tried and tried to identify with whatever facet of arrested development had made Olivia Fanshawe instigate hostilities in the first place, but she couldn't. She moved the grater vigorously on what was left of the cheese, as if the cheese were Olivia, and a chunk broke off. Surreptitiously Elise slipped the renegade bit of Parmesan into a pocket of her shorts, banished it from her mind, and proclaimed, "Finished!" Liz yelled, "Yay!" With a flourish, Elise picked up the cutting board and, with a knife, slid the mounds of grated cheese into two bowls Aunt Abbie had supplied. The bowls said, "Cheese," like Wendy Bernstein taking a picture.

"Oh!" Aunt Chloe was viewing with hatred the washed spinach that inched up in the wooden salad bowl. "Elise, I want you to vow right now that when you get married you'll buy your Parmesan grated and your spinach washed. D'you know how long we've *been* here? Forever! Look at that sink; it spews dirty spinach." Aunt Chloe whirled around on her stool. With her hands she started scooping up spinach and throwing it behind her like a bride throwing a lot of bouquets. Elise caught a leaf by the stalk. Errant green leaves settled about the kitchen. Liz and Betsy, now mechanically scrubbing tomato sauce from counter tops, turned, startled. Elise was laughing.

"Well," Aunt Chloe said, slapping her hands briskly together, "that finishes the spinach. Now we shall get on better." She got down from her stool. "Elise, let's join the men."

On the deck Elise perched herself on the rail near the bridge, the better to watch both the road for Bill Wilson's arrival and handsome Jason Baynard lying in the big rope hammock. Jason was turned toward Uncle Sam, his head resting on his outstretched arm. Uncle Sam was sitting in the green rocker, smoking his pipe and frowning as he rocked. "You're on the level that you have a sensory perception? Which sense?"

"I'd say it comes mostly through the ears," Jason said. "But it's phenomenological. A mind blow. Hi, ladies." He tipped his head to catch the eyes of both Elise and Chloe.

"Sensory apprehension of God!" Uncle Sam suddenly exploded. "Hogwash! There is no God." He got up from the rocker and started mixing drinks fast on the picnic bench painted blue that served them for a bar. Jason, laughing, reached out his hand for a glass. "Somehow I've been tricked," Uncle Sam went on, "into talking about God as if there were a God! No more tricks, Jason. I ban the word. You know the word I ban." Sir Isaac pushed open the screen door and came out. Absently Uncle Sam handed Elise a martini. She giggled and passed it to Aunt Chloe, who'd sat down in Uncle Sam's green rocker close to the hammock.

"You look beatifically comfortable," Elise heard her say to Jason. Her voice was husky. Jealously Sir Isaac sat down and pushed his woolly head at Aunt Chloe's hand. Aunt Chloe stroked him.

"An intelligent man," Uncle Sam was muttering distractedly to Elise, "a man to reckon with, and he hears the voice of God. The voice of God! How do we explain it? Crazy, that's what he has to be. Crazy." Uncle Sam smiled at Elise as if that settled everything.

"My kind of hammock," Jason was lazily telling Aunt Chloe. He'd let his voice go Southern, Elise noted with delight. "They make these here fancy rope hammocks for the rich folks on a haunted island just off the Carolina coast."

Liz and Betsy came through the screen door onto the deck. "Daddy," Liz balefully said, "you ought to be *shot.*" Uncle Sam mimed wide-eyed innocence. "And, Aunt Chloe, there was even spinach in the sauce on the stove." Aunt Chloe laughed. Liz and Betsy sat on the rail with Elise. Betsy covered her eyes.

"See no evil," she said.

"Hear no evil," Liz said, covering her ears.

"Wait!" called Uncle Sam from the bench before Elise could say, "Speak no evil." "Listen, Jason. I've got you, Jason. See no God. Hear no God. Ergo—there is no God!" Uncle Sam looked very proud of himself.

"Sam, that is the most garbled bit of logic I've ever heard," said Jason, laughing. He clasped his hands together and put them behind his head. Aunt Chloe inclined her head toward him, and Elise heard her say, "Jason, there's something I've been wanting to ask you." She sounded serious. Elise listened.

"Shoot," said Jason.

"Did Jesus ever laugh?"

Jason laughed. "Of course!" he said. Then he took a hand from behind his head and touched Aunt Chloe's hands, which were folded in her lap. "Everything all right?" he asked. She laughed a slightly nervous laugh and nodded. Uncle Tony came through the screen door from the kitchen. Fast, Aunt Chloe got out of the green rocking chair and went over to the bench. The chair kept rocking without her. In her cut-off jeans and gauzy embroidered shirt she looked like a girl, Elise thought. She wondered if it was the exercises Aunt Chloe did every night with ankle weights, or the fact she had a career instead of children. Golly, she had marvelous legs!

"Here, darling." Aunt Chloe handed Uncle Tony a drink.

"Such solicitude," Uncle Tony remarked, raising his eyebrows. He sat down in the rocker nearest the kitchen door—the red one. The red of the rocker as he leaned his head back against it accentuated the pallor of his face. His ligands must not be behaving, Elise thought sympathetically. They must be either scattering or holding still. "I missed your bombast in the boathouse today, Sam," Uncle Tony said. "My ligands, damn their eyes, were inert around the new ion." Uncle

Sam sat down in the green rocker near Jason. Aunt Chloe sat down in the white rocker next to Uncle Tony's rocker.

"You should hear voices; they'd keep you company," said Uncle Sam to Uncle Tony. "Jason hears voices."

"Not voices," Jason good-humoredly protested. "Words."

"I can hear my father's voice sometimes," said Aunt Chloe. "And his laugh. Most of all, his laugh. He's been dead twenty years, and his laugh still makes me smile."

"He was a politician," Uncle Tony said. "His laugh was worth votes." Aunt Chloe looked down. "I say, I'm sorry, love. I never knew your father, just your stories. I hear voices too, Sam. Don't you ever hear voices? I think that's rather sad—as sad as having never seen a visual image. It's a kind of sensory deprivation, don't you know? Almost a retardation."

"Do I hear voices?" Uncle Sam asked himself out loud. Liz heaved an impatient sigh and went into the cottage. On the rail next to her Elise could feel Betsy fidgeting with boredom, but she, Elise, watched Uncle Sam's face. She loved watching him run his emotional gamuts; he was so like her father. Gradually a look of wonder informed his features. "Why, I guess I do hear voices in a way, not exactly 'hearing' them." He scratched his head. "I 'hear' quotations. Well, for example" —Uncle Sam rocked his chair back and held it—"every time I approach the boathouse where all those stones are piled to keep it out of the water, I think a line from *The Waste Land:* 'These fragments I have shored against my ruins,' and every time I think the line, I feel silly, but . . . reassured. Isn't it crazy, the human mind? Isn't it complex beyond all reason? The quotation's not exactly heard aloud, but I don't see the printed words either. It's more as if I've just read it and it's in the process of being transformed into whatever kind of perception *reading* is. Hearing and double seeing—seeing the words and seeing the image the words conjure. It's voiceless sound, the quotation, or maybe soundless voice . . ."

"Synesthesia," Jason supplied. He was lying back in the hammock, one grass-stained knee up.

"Exactly!" said Sam, rocking excitedly. "Can you believe I'd forgotten the word? You know, Jason, it's a damned shame literature had to lose you to God." He said it so ruefully everyone laughed, and Elise leaned forward, hoping the conversation wouldn't dissolve with the laughter. This was the kind of talk she'd more or less expected from the intellectual brother Jack had described. Uncle Sam's habitual banter was fun, and it was certainly challenging; but it seemed to skip along the surface of what was important, to avoid the core of things almost on purpose. Was that perhaps "intellectual"?

"Christ, Sam!" Uncle Tony said. "Literary criticism's the most effete discipline going! Let the young beware."

"Lit'ry criticism," Uncle Sam said prissily. He made a limp-wristed gesture. "Ligands!" Uncle Tony laughed.

"Mother's asleep," Liz came out through the kitchen door and reported. She carried three Pepsis in tall, frosty glasses and had to hold the screen door with one bare foot in order to get out. The screen door banged.

"Shhh, let's not wake Abbie," said Aunt Chloe. "She needs a nap." Taking a Pepsi from Liz, Elise imagined Aunt Abbie curled up on her bed under that scary picture of Munch's called *The Scream.*

"Sometimes you can hear a picture," said Elise, venturing a trifle diffidently into the adult conversation. Everyone looked at her. "The one over your bed, Uncle Sam," she continued, feeling her face flush.

"Ah!" Uncle Sam gave her a startled smile. "Of course!" He nodded his head. "My own visual sense is so commonplace I'd never have noticed that on my own, Elise. In fact, if I had a keener eye, I'd probably be a poet today instead of just the world's least effete literary critic!" Everyone laughed. "But, of course! The artist was drawing a *sound.* Elise is talking about Munch's *The Scream,*" Sam told Jason. "Sound made visible—the thing reeks with sound waves. The figure is even holding its ears. God, what a thing to sleep under. But you've taught me something, Elise." Uncle Sam looked at her with speculative approval, lifting his eyebrows. "And here I told Mad Jack he was out of his mind to put you in that Anglican convent."

Jason had raised up in the hammock on his elbows. His eyes congratulated Elise. "Do you paint?" he asked her.

"No," she said, engaging his eyes as an equal—how bold! "I like to use my hands more. I sculpt." She pictured the freeform clay triptych she'd done of herself and Daphne and Jane in a niche of the grand staircase at St. Catherine's.

"Ah, she's a biologist, Chloe," said Uncle Tony. "Not a chemist." They both laughed—one of their private jokes.

"You should see what Calvin's doing," Jason told Elise. "Calvin sculpts too; he pounds stuff out of metal"—Jason's hand went to the neck of his shirt—"and carves things out of wood." He turned his head to include the whole company. "In fact, that's why he's not here. He found a big hunk of cherry wood in my woodpile, and all afternoon he's been at it with hammer and chisel, carving this rather frightening Indian queen he wants to make 'so real she speaks.' Calvin has the same kind of graphic, tactile, well, synesthetic imagination you have, Elise." Elise basked in the accolade, as Jason collapsed back into the hammock. "You all wouldn't believe what a madhouse the manse is—Calvin carving on the kitchen table, Fred and Selina digging up the woods, Sam's Mormons throwing things—"

"Sam's Mormons!" Uncle Sam laughed.

"Fred and Selina are doing *what?*" asked Betsy, seizing on the topic with audible glee.

"Oh, say," Jason lazily said, "I meant to tell you kids." His hand swept the three of them, and Elise fell resentfully back into place as "kid." "Under the manse, there's a whole storehouse of Indian relics just there for the taking—arrowheads, spearheads, canoe anchors, amulets, what have you." Jason waved his hand. "And Selina, who is a budding archaeologist, just as, say, Elise is a budding sculptor and aesthetician"—Elise watched Jason grin as he warmed to the subject —"and Liz will probably be a writer and Betsy an actress and Fred— well, Fred could be—I don't know." Jason had a little smile at the corner of his mouth as he said that about Fred. "A pilgrim maybe. A modern Bunyan."

"But what are Fred and Selina *doing?*" Liz asked.

"Oh," said Jason. "Well, I want you all over at the manse early tomorrow to help with *the dig.*"

"The dig!" exclaimed Liz. "Like *The Source!*"

"Michener," grumbled Sam. "Liz, I thought I taught you to stay away from trash. Especially trash over a thousand pages!"

"Daddy, you know you read *The Source* too. It was overdue at the library."

"What should we *wear?*" Betsy asked Jason. Jason laughed.

"Mirrors," he said.

"I'd like to come too," Aunt Chloe said. She had one leg hooked over an arm of the rocker. "May I come too?" Uncle Tony looked at her.

"The conversation has definitely lagged since synesthesia," declared Uncle Sam. Liz and Betsy groaned. "No, wait a minute." He held up one hand. "Every once in a while, a great line of literature will knock your eyes and ears into a cocked hat. I'm thinking about Henry James's introduction to *The Turn of the Screw*, where handwriting turns to sound: 'Douglas had begun to read with a fine clearness that was like a rendering to the ear the beauty of his author's hand.' " Uncle Sam's voice as he quoted was both passionate and precise. Elise wondered, not for the first time, why he wasn't an actor. It would certainly be more fun than being an English professor!

"What an exquisite tonal sense," said Aunt Chloe. "James doesn't circumscribe the senses. He's saying you should read, or listen, with all of yourself."

"His father was a Swedenborgian," said Jason.

"And his brother was William James," pointed out Uncle Tony.

"That kind of biographical rinky-dink has nothing to do with his literature," objected Uncle Sam.

"Bullshit. Jason and Tony are right, Sam," argued Aunt Chloe. "No wonder Henry James was so alert to the varieties of perception. Artists are here to break down rules like yours, Sam."

Uncle Sam rocked fitfully. "I can't abide mishmashing the disciplines and bringing in the *family*. Whose brother was who is irrelevant. I'm getting very uncomfortable with this conversation."

"So am *I,*" Liz interjected. Betsy giggled.

"Why are you uncomfortable, Sam?" Aunt Chloe jumped up and confronted Sam in his rocker. "What do you suppose literature *is?* Empty words? Words without philosophy, psychology, religion, *science?* Was Henry James as ignorant of what his father and brother were doing as *you* are ignorant of what Tony is doing? What Jason is doing? What I am usually doing? We've all read literature, but you're scared to death of religion and science. I mean, what kind of close-minded person"—Aunt Chloe laughed her low, chuckling laugh— "bans words? God!" she called defiantly. "Ligand!" She raised her arms to the skies and held them there. Elise watched Uncle Sam's shoulders shake with a silent laughter that rocked his chair. Then Aunt Chloe moved her head to look beyond the girls, up the road.

The girls turned. A dark-haired young woman was walking slowly along, pregnant, wearing a long red and blue peasant dress Elise recognized from shopping with Pamela as a Liberty print. She had red sandals on her bare feet and a soft red shawl clutched about her shoulders. She was beautiful. She looked like someone who belonged in another world.

"Extraordinary!" said Uncle Sam, who'd turned his rocker around. The young woman paused to examine the name on the Laceys' mailbox next door, then continued her graceful progress toward the Barnes's wooden footbridge.

"She's looking for someone," whispered Betsy loudly.

"The father of her child," Uncle Sam conjectured.

" 'Don't git up. Ah'm only paessin' throo,' " drawled Liz, who could mimic anyone. Uncle Sam passed her a quick grin and said, "*Streetcar.*" Jason, however, gave a whoop and almost fell out of the hammock.

"Fire and brimstone, Liz!" he said. "That was an authentic Southern accent. You sounded like a voice out of my checkered past."

Uncle Sam laughed heartily. "The only clergyman I could ever stomach, and he has to be one with a checkered past."

Betsy said, a little shyly for her, "I love the way you swear, Jason. 'Fire and brimstone.' It's so imaginative."

"Hellfire, Miss Betsy," drawled Jason, parodying himself. "That ain't *swearin'*, that there's *sermonizin'.*" He struggled to sit up in the hammock and looked, with the rest of them, at the young woman on the road. "Hell*fire!*" he said again. He jumped up and moved fast by the girls across the little footbridge toward her.

"Jason!" the young woman cried and flung her arms around his neck. On the Barnes deck, eyes sought each other with wonder and shock. Uncle Sam looked at Elise and said:

"There's an abstraction made visible, Elise. Feast your eyes on a *checkered past.*"

"Flower-sprigged," Elise started to murmur in honor of the lovely Liberty print, but then Jason called from over the bridge, "She's my sister, Sam!" Whose brother is who *is* relevant, Elise thought with sudden relief. Jason wasn't married after all. Uncle Sam laughed.

"Why, how unchivalrous, Jason!" the girl said ironically. Her voice carried, as if she were on a stage. "Whatever would Mother say?" She had the same smile as Jason's as she took his arm and let him help her across the little footbridge. "Of course I do reckon you have to consider your position," she rattled on lightly in a truly Southern accent, Elise heard with fascination. "I arrived here quite at sea, or rather at *lake*, and at that General Store across from the church—where for all

I knew you might *live,* you being such a changed character and all—
there were newspaper clippings of you." As she and Jason arrived at
the now standing group on the deck, she raised a light hand to include everyone in her recital. "Newspaper clippings of my brother
Jason splashed all over the store window, and Jason, you must have
become the regular *lion* of this lake, for that redheaded woman with
the mean look in her eye actually knew where you were. He's not at
the manse, he's having dinner with the Barneses, she said, and directed me most gruffly here, thank heaven warning me about this
deplorable road so I didn't lose the muffler on my car, my car being
the last remnant of my marriage, well, the last but for *this.* Just don't
worry about it, Jason. It does happen, you know." She placed her
hand lightly on the mound that gracefully swelled the pretty Liberty
print of her dress.

"My sister Tradd," Jason began. Elise could see he was upset but
trying not to show it. "T-R-A-D-D. Oh, babe, are you okay?" He
looked down at Tradd; she looked back up. She was just awfully beautiful, even though pregnant; her coloring was not anything like
Jason's, but her smile was. She had black hair that hung just right and
smoky blue eyes, and there was a hint of cleavage at the scalloped
neckline of her dress. Tradd looked away from Jason and held out her
hand first to Uncle Sam, who, visibly enchanted, didn't take his eyes
off her, as, spattering words lightly, she shook everyone's hand.

"I'm Tradd Baynard. Yes, I am, Jason, or I will be soon as the
divorce papers give me free will again. I'm sorry but I've been Mrs.
Whitney Pratt DuVal III quite long enough, thank you, living in a
veritable fishbowl. Whit put the house on the Savannah *tour,* can you
imagine?" Jason threw his head back and laughed. The laugh rose to
the trees and seemed to cheer Jason up. He turned to tell Aunt Chloe
something. She laughed. "Mrs. Whitney Pratt DuVal III," Tradd repeated. "Have you ever heard such a mouthful?" She grimaced prettily at Liz.

"You're just like Scarlett O'Hara!" blurted Betsy, her eyes round as
saucers. Tradd laughed.

"I intend to be," she said, veiling her eyes with her lashes. "Oh,
aren't you beautiful?" she asked Elise with what seemed honest admiration, but as Elise colored she couldn't help wondering if the compliment was designed to fluster her. "You were in the newspaper too. I
thought, There's Jason, surrounded by girls again." Tradd's hand, as

Elise shook it, proved as narrow as her own; it also proved to be rather cool and perfunctory. "Why, that's a Pawley's Island hammock!" Tradd cried. "Do you all know about the ghost of Theodosia Burr that haunts Pawley's Island?"

"No, but we'd love to!"

"It's just like *The Turn of the Screw,*" Uncle Sam chortled. "She's got us all mesmerized!"

Within minutes (Elise could not quite follow the choreography), the entire back deck was rearranged at the sudden, energetic instigation of Uncle Sam, who pulled the red rocker to where Tradd could sit easily down in it. It matched her red-sprigged dark-blue dress and her red sandals that peeked out from under it. Her shawl draped prettily over her arms. Sir Isaac lay at her feet like a rug. Liz and Betsy sat sideways in the hammock facing her. Uncle Tony sat in the white rocker and Uncle Sam in the green, both of them also facing Tradd. It was the first time Elise had ever seen Uncle Sam willingly forgo being center stage.

Elise herself, perched on the rail, conscious of being a bit uncharitable, wondered why Jason hadn't the same cloying accent and why he didn't talk so frightfully much as Tradd; thank heaven he didn't. Then, from behind, she felt Bill Wilson come over the little footbridge and sit next to her. He didn't say a word, just very nicely sat there, wearing his work clothes and smelling of perspiration and dust, like the ball diamond, pleasant; he simply sat next to Elise on the rail and listened with the rest of them to Tradd Baynard, who was telling a ghost story about Pawley's Island, South Carolina, where, so it seemed, their hammock had come from. Betsy and Liz sat in the hammock as wide-eyed and solemn as if they'd been transported in it to the Southern island where the ghost could still be seen on stormy nights.

"She was perfectly lovely, and she walked the plank without ever faltering, without ever crying out, with her arms outstretched as if death were welcome to her." "She," Elise gradually learned, was Theodosia Burr Alston, the daughter of Aaron Burr, the famous American traitor who shot Alexander Hamilton. Jason called out:

"Hamilton deserved it. I've always liked Aaron Burr, and so do you, Tradd."

"Hush up! It makes a better story like this."

"So much for history," Jason commented to Aunt Chloe. "God," he said then. "She's pregnant."

Tossing her dark hair, Tradd resumed. "Although Burr, a feminist before his time, and I reckon we have to admire him for that, educated his daughter just as if she were his son, and although she was the beautiful toast of New York City, still Aaron Burr persuaded her, at age seventeen, to marry a wealthy planter from South Carolina. This even though she was deeply in love with a wonderful young painter by the name of John Vanderlyn." Elise almost giggled at the look of outrage on Betsy's face. "And John Vanderlyn loved her deeply too. You can tell by the perfectly exquisite portraits he painted of her.

"But Theodosia made the best of things in South Carolina, which both Jason and I will tell you can be seductive for a short stretch of time, and she settled into the Alston family at The Oaks on the Waccamaw River, and I reckon she wasn't too unhappy. Not at first. Then, the same year her father shot Hamilton and became an outcast, Theodosia gave birth to a baby boy she named Aaron Burr Alston. Think how mixed her feelings must have been! After her father left the country in disgrace, she'd've been heartbroken. She'd have poured all her thwarted, lonely love into that little boy. Then in June of 1812, just when Aaron Burr was to return to New York City, little Aaron Burr Alston died." At that point, Betsy started to cry.

Tradd gave her a sad little smile and continued, " 'There is no more joy for me,' " Theodosia wrote to her father. " 'The world is blank.' " On her way to her father in New York, her ship captured by pirates she must have welcomed, Theodosia was forced with all the people on board to walk the plank in an awful, horrid storm. Oh, the storms on the coast are something fierce, aren't they, Jason?

"Natives still claim to hear Theodosia on the beach at Pawley's Island, sobbing and calling for her little son," Tradd went on with a little catch in her voice, "and in a crude island cabin some fifty-seven years later, a visiting doctor found a painting of Theodosia Burr hanging on the wall. It was a Vanderlyn. Don't you see?" Tradd asked them excitedly. "Theodosia was leaving her husband. Else why not leave the painting at The Oaks where it'd be safe? You don't take a valuable painting on a *visit*. Oh, that poor little boy!" Tradd began to cry. She cried hard, her whole body convulsed. Jason, his face shocked, got up and went to her. Kneeling on the deck, he put his arms around her.

"Honey, honey," he crooned, "this isn't like you."

"Oh, Jason," she said, as if they were alone, "don't you know what I almost did? Can't you guess? I almost had an abortion, Jason. I went home to talk to Mother, and who the blue, screaming blazes can talk to Mother, I ask you? So then I talked to Jessamine, and guess what *she* did! She made me an appointment with an abortionist! Can you believe it? Jessamine! Nobody's going to take care of my baby but me, Jason, I mean that!" She wept against his shoulder. No one on the deck knew what to do; they all just sat watching as if this scene were part of the ghost story. After a minute, Tradd raised her swollen face. "I am most awfully sorry," she said. "I'm behaving like trash. Please forgive me!"

"Tradd, it doesn't matter," said Jason. "These are friends." Aunt Chloe stood up. Elise sighed with relief. Aunt Chloe always did the right thing.

"Jason, let's persuade Tradd to lie down for a while before dinner. You can sit with her. She's driven a long way all alone, and then to meet this boisterous crew . . . !" Aunt Chloe waved a cavalier hand at the assembly on the deck, who never, in Elise's memory, had been so *un*boisterous. "She can lie down in Tony's and my room." Aunt Chloe and Jason helped Tradd out of the rocking chair. They each put an arm around her. Their arms touched in the back.

"Wait'll you taste Sam's spaghetti, Tradd," improvised Aunt Chloe. "It's a pregnant lady's dream. I threw spinach in the sauce, and Elise stashed the Parmesan in her pocket." Tradd laughed, a little tremulously, at Aunt Chloe. Elise hastened to open the door for them. Uncle Tony suddenly moved past her.

"I'd best get that Lindbergh baby off the wall, don't you think, Elise?"

"I like the Otways and Sam Barnes," Tradd told Jason on their slow motorboat ride across the lake in the eerie light of a waxing gibbous moon. "I'm glad you've not become a recluse, brother mine. You were showing every sign of it back aways." She laughed. "That Sam is funny; isn't he funny? You know, Jason, I think Daddy might have been like that if he didn't drink so damn-fool much—just witty and outrageous! Don't you ever wonder what Daddy would have been like? He called me baby doll. Course Daddy did marry Mother, which doesn't speak particularly well for his taste, but then Sam Barnes married that drab, drab lady. Does she ever talk?

"Oh, my, I'm hoping I look as good as Chloe Otway when I'm that old. Her eyes are almost as unusual as mine with dark hair." Tradd combed her fingers through her hair. "How old is she, Jason? She must be over thirty to be head of her department. Oh, bleeding Jesus, why didn't I finish at Hollins? Course I can always go back to school now, if Whit gives me some money. I hear at universities in the North girls breast-feed their babies right in the classroom nowadays. Gracious, wouldn't Mother just *die?*" Propped against two motorboat cushions, Tradd let her hair fly back. The black water shimmered silver in their wake. "What a glorious evening, Jason. I am so glad I came. I almost didn't. I almost just set up residence in your apartment in Nashville. My, it was fun vamping your landlord into giving me the key. I'm sure he thinks I'm some discarded mistress of yours, Jason."

"You seem to have recovered your spirits," Jason remarked, speeding up the motor to get the ride over with. How the hell could he get pregnant, volatile Tradd up sixty-seven steps?

"I wasn't very nice to Elise, was I, Jason?"

"No, you weren't. What made you pick on her?"

"I was *jealous!* Why in hell do you think? She's beautiful; she is *free;* she's not pregnant; she's in love with my brother!"

"She's also only sixteen, Tradd. It's a crush."

"Oh, my soul!" Tradd sat forward. The pupils of her slate-blue eyes were as dilated in the haunted light as if she were on drugs. "Jason, I didn't know she was so young. I honestly didn't know!"

Jason shrugged and slowed the boat for the water lilies.

"Jason, you are just too God damned good for words, aren't you, Jason?"

Hearing her breath come fast about halfway up the dizzying catwalk, alarmed (Tradd pregnant!), Jason lifted her firmly, an arm under her knees, the hand of the other arm that went around her waist touching her stomach and cringing comically back, like a claw in the air. "It's all right, silly," said Tradd, snuggling her head on his shoulder. "He's alive, and he is strong as a little wrestler. Sometimes I can see his feet kick." Jason let his hand rest gingerly on the potentially explosive mound. A nephew?

Holding Tradd, sensing with all his body how much softer and more acquiescent she'd become, Tradd who'd always been prickly about being touched, evasive about the gentler emotions, Tradd who (perhaps taking her lead from him, Jason, when he was younger) had seemed to choose her young men for sex rather than affection, Jason felt a surge of love. His childhood ally, after all. He shouldn't have rebuked her, even tacitly, for her small display of Southern belle bitchery. He was pretty sure she'd make it up to Elise, who'd handled the left-handed flattery well, actually—watching, deflecting, and absorbing. Throughout Tradd's performance, she'd had her tongue in her cheek, had Elise. As had Chloe Otway. Chloe, in fact, put her tongue quite literally in her cheek: you could see it. Jason laughed. He heard Tradd giggle quietly against him. Panting as he reached the deck and the lighted kitchen, Jason kicked open the kitchen door and beheld Calvin, hammer poised in midair, ready to whack the chisel into the already altered hunk of cherry wood.

"You must be Tradd," said Calvin with a big smile. "Hiya, sugar." Jason set down Tradd. Calvin set down the hammer and chisel.

"Hi *you,* sugar," Tradd said prettily to Calvin. "Hell, I was hoping everybody'd think I was one of Jason's by-blows."

"The whole *lake* knows about you, sugar. I went to Esther's for some beer, beer being somehow necessary to my creative process, and there was a whole crowd of little kids hanging out round this funky little Mercedes SL with a Georgia license plate. Then mean old Esther told me I had just better purchase some milk too, as the manse was about to be invaded by a young lady in the family way."

"Did she really say 'in the family way'?" asked Tradd, delighted.

"Calvin!" Jason held the rough part of the cherry wood in his hands. A wood sculpture was emerging from the top, like a baby. Queen Esther's almost life-sized head was completed to the shoulders, and what a head! "Calvin, this is the spitting image of Olivia Fanshawe!"

"Aw, that little pussycat don't spit at *me*. 'You got a face I would like to sculpt'—it's the best line in the world. And she actually did have such a face. Selina left me a description of Queen Esther; she wrote it down, all out of her own crazy little quoting head. And then half an hour after she and Fred left, what should appear at the front door over a coconut cake but Queen Esther's head. I couldn't believe my eyes. Her body was all wrong though. Too squat. Too ashamed."

Jason ran his hands lightly over the replica of Olivia's plain, strong, alert features. In deference to Queen Esther's Indian headdress, Calvin had feathered the wood over one eyebrow, but the eyes—direct, level, and unafraid—were Olivia's. He'd even caught her suppressed anger in the tension of the muscles around the full mouth.

"It's superb," Tradd murmured. "You're *good.*" She had sat down in one of the red ladder-back chairs at the table.

"A glass of milk for the little lady?" Calvin asked.

"And a piece of coconut cake," said Jason. "Calvin, where is my coconut cake?" Calvin got laughing.

"Jason, I ate it *all*, ate it without thinking, washing it down with the beer while I was carving, and then I thought, Well, Jason doesn't know a thing about the cake, so I just won't mention it, and here I mention it first thing. At least the Mormons didn't get it, Jason." Calvin took a carton of milk from the refrigerator.

"That doesn't exactly console me, Calvin," said Jason, passing him a glass from the cupboard over the sink. "The Mormons probably can't eat coconut. I'm sure it's too stimulating. It would stimulate *me* right now."

Tradd stood up to take the glass of milk from Calvin. "Who are the Mormons?" she wanted to know.

"Oh, just a couple more of my houseguests," said Jason. "Southern hospitality—you know what it's like. They occupy the—what color is their room, Calvin? I don't dare look in."

"The Mormons occupy the yellow room," Calvin said absently. "We can put Tradd in that ruffly pink room at the foot of the stairs we keep the sheets and towels in." He was looking Tradd up and down. His eyes fixed on her middle. "Jason, I've got it!" He pounded his fist on the table. "I know what was wrong! I know why I couldn't figure out Queen Esther's body from that two-dimensional drawing!"

Jason and Tradd looked at each other and shrugged. As if he were holding a basketball, Calvin reached out both hands and let them outline Tradd's belly.

"Queen Esther was *pregnant*. Our wild red lady was with *child*, Jason! Wait'll the kids hear that!"

SEVEN
The Lord of the Dance

Weekend of July 20

1 SATURDAY AFTERNOON

Fearlessly negotiating a snappy, exceedingly dangerous U-turn (the main road curved just ahead toward the Lake Lenni Lenape Inn), Chloe maneuvered her Volkswagen onto a patch of land worn barren (presumably by sightseers) near the historical marker in front of the pretty little green-shuttered manse. She found it hard to recognize. From their cottage across the lake, the manse resembled an aerie perched on treetops. "I've come to see the dig," she said out loud to herself. "I've come to see the dig": a mantra. "I've come to see why the girls come home every afternoon so dirty and so mysterious. That's why I'm here. I've come to see the dig."

Still talking to a hypothetical spectator, Chloe got out of the Volkswagen. Oh, she hardly knew herself these days! Her motivations were an utter mystery to her: she was breathless, restless, sleepless. Her heart pounded at erratic times. She felt caught in a flow she didn't understand—was it water, air, or fire? Who else was caught there? She couldn't tell. She didn't care. She was driving Tony crazy. Poor Tony!

Chloe paused to read the historical marker as one who'd come to see the dig would surely do. The first pastor was "tortured and lived to tell the tale." The tale was evidently too terrible to be told on the marker, but a kinetic image surfaced from her subconscious like a thirty-second spot: the first young pastor, tattered collar askew, running the gauntlet. Burning ropes held his wrists behind him. Blood splashed as tomahawks hacked at his head, his arms, the bones of his shins—

Whenever had violence invaded her sensibility? This wasn't like her, not at all. On the top shelf of the bookcase in her entry at home, she'd propped only the comic muse, Thalia, next to a basket of dried heather. No tragedy in *her* life. Was that why she'd decided not to have children—to ensure that?

A softly shouted "Hi!" interrupted her brooding. She assumed it
was "Hi"; it sounded more like "Hah." On the steps of the spindly
pillared manse porch sat Tradd Baynard, framed by pink rambler
roses that had overgrown their fan-shaped trellis. Tradd wore a
sleeveless pink smock, perhaps contrived to match the roses, perhaps
not. Her smooth, lightly tanned legs, tented to the knee, supported a
paperback book. Dr. Spock. Were first-time mothers still reading Dr.
Spock? Natural childbirth is ecstasy; just keep your feet in the stir-
rups and don't fight the leather bonds on your wrists. And don't, for
God's sake, *yell.* Tradd's feet were bare. Dr. Spock would like that.

"I've come to see the dig," Chloe told her.

"That's fine. So long as you haven't come to see Jason. I'm a senti-
nel. Calvin's guarding the back door, and I am guarding the front
door so my poor brother can write his sermon for tomorrow without
his cast of thousands disturbing him. D'you know, those two untidy
Mormons didn't decamp, even after they saw me? Sit down with me a
minute, Chloe. I'm dying for someone to talk to. Calvin's been chas-
ing the kids back down the catwalk into the woods all afternoon, but
you're *my* first interloper. I'm getting lonesome." Tradd patted a
place on the top step next to her. Chloe sat down. The roses smelled
like heaven. "Chloe, can I fetch you a lemonade? Or better yet a julep.
I do make the meanest julep."

"Too early," protested Chloe. All she needed now was to become a
lush! "Even Sam's cocktail hour doesn't start until four."

"Well, yes." Tradd leaned back against a fluted pillar. "Actually I
shouldn't drink, I suppose. You're so *slim,* " she moaned then, in a
different voice. Chloe looked down at her own admirably (well, she
worked at it) flat middle exposed between a denim halter and cut-off
jeans. "You didn't have children, did you, Chloe? Did you know your
name means 'a blooming green herb'? I've been looking at books of
names. A Chloe was also a friend of Paul's in 1 Corinthians, Jason
tells me. Oh, I know you didn't have children; I asked Jason. Was it on
purpose you didn't have them? I'm sorry to be asking such a rude
question, but here you are, happily married, says Jason, and having
no children; and here am I, miserably married and about to bring a
child into the world. I can just hear Great-grandmother Beau saying,
'Poor little baby coming into this cruel world.' Course she said that
every time a baby was born, probably even Jason and me."

"On purpose." Chloe acknowledged the "rude" question, although

she was beginning to know enough about Southern belles to realize
Tradd had given her an out. Several outs, in fact. She could have
linked in anywhere and continued the conversation without a hitch.
"Tony was ambitious, and so was I. It didn't seem fair to a baby. So
when we quit medical school together because it was altogether too
mindless and cozy, we vowed it would be just the two of us and
science."

"Science," murmured Tradd. "I was of course brought up to be
utterly useless, which is maybe why I married Whitney out of a
purely financial infatuation. Am I saying this? Am I actually saying
this? Can this be delicately nurtured me? I slept around like crazy
before I got married, but I wouldn't sleep with Whit till our wedding
night. Oh, my, it was disappointing! I sure do wish I'd tried him out
first so I'd know whether it was marriage to blame, or him. But it
made me pregnant."

Chloe leaned back against the pillar on her side of the steps, making
them a pair of sentinels. Looking at Tradd's rounded belly, she
laughed. "It did do that!" They both laughed. "What does Jason say,
Tradd? Do you know, if I were a pregnant wife fleeing her husband,
I'd steer clear of ministers. Don't they have to send you back to your
husband even if he beats you?"

"Oh, not Jason. Jason didn't like Whit. Jason didn't think he had a
thing behind his pretty, drunken face. I'm giving Jason hell right now
for never telling me not to marry Whit. For even agreeing to be
Whit's best man. Oh, yes, I am refusing to forgive Jason."

"Tradd, how unfair," Chloe murmured.

"Well, of course it's unfair. But it's bringing Jason back. It's getting
him so he's talking to me again, getting mad, expressing opinions, and
being a human being again. D'you know—oh, how could you know?
—that my brother Jason was the biggest lady-killer on the whole
U. Va. campus at Charlottesville when he was an undergraduate?
When I visited, Jason'd get me dates with young men exactly like
Whit DuVal, and Jason's girls'd try to suck up to me. I was still in
high school, but they'd tell me all the stuff he'd do in bed, as if I could
interpret it. 'If he lets me do this or that, does it mean he loves me?' 'If
he goes down on me, does it mean he loves me?' Oh, it was an education! And all the time, even though I was so young, I knew he was
just dating them so as to sleep with them. None of them ever got to
him; and then when *God* got to him, I began to be afraid no woman

ever would. He is so holier than thou, Jason! Would you believe he's been celibate for two years? Celibate! Jason! I love making him mad and making him swear and driving him into a corner. Calvin's getting mighty good at it too."

Chloe, despite herself avidly recording all Tradd said (although she shouldn't know it, it was none of her business), was both relieved and sorry when a big station wagon tried to replicate her daring U-turn and knocked the manse mailbox from its post. The mailbox rolled onto the lawn.

"Hey!" hollered Tradd. She stood up. The paperback Dr. Spock fell down the stairs. The station wagon parked down the road. Olivia Fanshawe got out and headed up the road toward the manse. She wore blue jeans and a T-shirt with a big yellow happy face on it, and she looked mad as hell.

"That mailbox sticks out at least a foot beyond the postal regulations. Besides, if Jason showed up when he was supposed to show up, I wouldn't have been in such a rush!" Olivia stormed up the walk. Seated, Chloe looked up at the still standing Tradd and saw Tradd was grinning. Her grin was just like Jason's.

"You're Calvin's model!" Tradd said to Olivia. "I'd know you any-place. Gosh almighty, you even look as mad as Queen Esther. Though why you should be mad at innocent us when you just knocked over our mailbox is beyond me."

Olivia halted on the walk and regarded Tradd with suspicion. Chloe hastened to intervene. "This is Jason's sister, Tradd. Olivia Fanshawe, Tradd Baynard. Olivia's your brother's"—what was Bach called?—"church musician, Tradd." Olivia looked startled.

"Oh," said Tradd respectfully, just a tiny glint of irony in her dusky blue eyes. "Like Bach."

Olivia refused the bait. "Can you help me?" she asked Tradd. "Jason hasn't given me the final hymn, and I've got a date tonight. Do you know where he is?"

"He is writing his sermon," Tradd said. She plucked a rose and put it in her dark hair. "He is not to be disturbed. So long as he has chosen this disreputable profession, he is going to do it well, so far as I and Calvin are concerned. But I will relay your message to him. You need to know what is the last hymn, is that right?" Tradd winked at Chloe. Chloe hid a smile. Olivia merely nodded. Tradd went into the manse. Olivia sat down on the steps.

"Have you seen the dig?" Chloe asked her.

"No. Have you?"

"Not yet. But I'm dying to. Want to come?"

Olivia's face vacillated. She bowed her head. "No, I can't. I have to practice."

"It's a really silly feud, Olivia."

"I know." Olivia's gaze caught Chloe's head on. She had reached Olivia, she saw; but then Tradd came back out on the porch, carrying an open hymnal. She handed it to Olivia.

"I've never even heard this," Olivia complained. "I'll have to learn it." She hummed a rollicking measure. "A Shaker hymn? Didn't the Shakers die out because they wouldn't fuck?"

Tradd's arched eyebrows went up a jot. Chloe giggled. Had Olivia said that on purpose to shock them? Why on earth? Tradd seemed to decide it was all right to laugh, and laughed. She leaned to look over Olivia's shoulder. The rose fell from her hair onto the open hymnal, like an offering, a frivolous blessing. "That's a wonderful hymn," Tradd declared. "It's Jason's favorite. And the rector's."

As both Chloe and Olivia looked up at her, she went on, "The rector of St. Philip's in Charleston has been like a daddy to Jason ever since Jason was so-high. He thinks religion should be a thing of joy. He's the one," she continued with an exasperation light as air, "who seduced Jason into the seminary. I was going to see the rector on Memorial Day," she mused, "but I reckoned, just like you, Chloe, that he'd send me back to Whit fast as Pastor Manders sent Mrs. Alving in *Ghosts* back to that syphilitic husband of hers. I was a theater major, did I tell you? I was a wonderful Blanche DuBois. Anyhow, Olivia, I do think you are going to enjoy playing this hymn." Tradd sat down on the top step again, hugging her knees tight so the pink smock entrapped her.

Olivia (probably sensibly, thought Chloe) did not allow herself to be diverted into the intriguing clutter of Tradd's recital. Chloe herself was retrospectively amazed that fourteen-year-old Liz had caught Tradd's Blanche DuBois persona at first glance. But Olivia stood up, keeping the rose balanced on the hymnal. "Tell Jason I'll try it. It looks too fast for that harmonium, which is a real bitch to play, but Jason does have a flair for what a service should be. A flair for 'theater,' like you, Tradd, honey." The hymnal against her hip, Olivia walked across the lawn and picked up the (dented) red mailbox. One-handed, she fastened it back on the post. "Mighty sorry 'bout that," she called in a parody of a Southern accent. "See y'all in church." She flung the rose hard in their direction and headed for her station wagon.

Tradd breathed, "Talk about a flair for theater! What the blue blazes is wrong with her?"

"Tradd," Chloe asked her, "did I hear you say something about a julep?"

Around the side of the manse, the lawn gave way quickly to woods and underbrush, and the incline was steep, about forty-five degrees. Chloe, a bit muzzy from two of Tradd's devastating mint juleps ("I learned from Robert. Hasn't Jason mentioned Robert? You mean he hasn't even mentioned Jessamine? What the hell does Jason *talk* about all the time—the stupid Bible?"), clung to the stilts that held up the back of the manse on her precipitous journey down. Sticks, stones, inexplicably alarming large pinecones—where had she read that captive apes were scared to death of pinecones?—avalanched before her as her sandaled feet slid on pine needles and damp black earth. After the sunlight of the rose-covered porch, the woods were dim as Otto's at twilight. She could hear voices, but saw no one. What a place to be tortured! The close-growing trees, punctuated here and there by enormous, protruding rocks, were gauntlet enough. Why hadn't she worn proper clothes?

"Yikes!" Chloe careened into Fred Bunyan running out from under the manse. They fell together, wrapping arms around each other and landing in a sprawl that was comically intimate, Fred on top. High above them, over Fred's shoulder, Chloe could see the beginning of Jason's catwalk. Sun glinted through the steps.

"I'm sorry," Chloe said, disengaging her legs from Fred's and pulling herself out from under him. They'd landed on a large flat rock, carpeted with blue-green lichens. Chloe stood up. Lord, she was dirty! Standing up too, Fred glowered at her angrily. "I didn't realize you were digging under the manse," she apologized. "I was expecting the dig to be in the other direction."

His blue eyes touched hers, then retreated sidelong. "It's okay," he mumbled. Then he eyed her halter and shorts critically. "You're going to get eaten alive," he commented. "There're spiders the size of pinecones in these woods." Involuntarily Chloe shuddered. She hugged herself like a timorous ape newly released from captivity. "Selina!" called Fred. "Emergency!"

"Yes, Fred!" Selina Thomas crawled around one of the gouged posts that supported the catwalk and climbed gracefully to stand with Chloe and Fred on the rock. She wore a white turtleneck, white pants flared at the hips and pegged at the ankles, and little white boots. Dazzled, Chloe stared at her, as at an apparition. How on earth did she stay clean?

"The spray!" Selina caroled, slithering down past the post again and disappearing into the underbrush. Within seconds, she returned with a large spray can of Off, which she pointed purposefully at Chloe.

"I'll do it," said Chloe hastily, taking the can. The insect repellent stung on skinned elbows and knees. She could feel a very large bite hotly swelling the back of one thigh. A spider?

"You should have come down the catwalk. It was very silly of you to come that way, Mrs. Otway!" Selina chastised, somehow inoffensively. "Come! Come see the site of our dig!" Chloe followed bright-white Selina, sliding around the post on her backside, twisting to crawl through thick, brambly bushes. From behind her, Fred, the rear guard, growled, "Where's Jason, Mrs. Otway? When's he coming down?"

"His sister says he's working like a fiend and smoking like a chimney," Chloe flung over her shoulder, both amused and irked at this unseemly demand for conversation while crawling. The brambles were tearing at her flesh.

"He has to work sometimes, Fred!" Selina sang back. "You always get too possessive about people, Fred!"

"He smokes too much," Fred grumbled. Following Selina, they emerged in an area of tall trees where they could stand. No more underbrush. It was another world. Feeling for one wild second as if she'd been kidnapped by guerrillas and led into their hidden camp, Chloe looked about her in wonder. It was like finding Egyptian slaves still busy in the interior of a pyramid or opening an anthill: all this bustling activity going on almost underground. Amid tree trunks spaced decently apart, on ground that remained slanted at an angle of forty-five degrees, Liz and Elise, in jeans and tartan flannel shirts, assiduously raked, eyes fixed on the ground. Zack Chandler carefully sliced at the earth with a flat shovel, and Erich Strauss pushed a wheelbarrow. Betsy, sitting Indian-fashion on a protruding rock with a pail between her knees, scrubbing something, did look up. "Aunt Chloe!" she cried. Liz and Elise raised dazed eyes. "Come see, everybody!" Betsy called. "Wait till you see this!"

Adjusting her feet to the incline as Selina and Fred did, Chloe edged her way with them to where Betsy sat. Betsy wore a khaki safari suit. There was even a white helmet on the rock, Chloe noted, trying not to laugh. Shovels propped, rakes dropped, wheelbarrow abandoned, everyone converged on Betsy's rock. Arrayed next to her was an impressive collection of Indian artifacts: arrowheads and amulets and even a very nicely preserved mortar and pestle. Chloe touched the mortar and pestle reverently with a finger. You could still use it for basil or garlic.

"How wonderful that you could find both pieces," she said.

"I found the mortar," said Selina.

"I found the pestle," said Liz.

"Fred found most of the bones," said Elise. She waved a hand to the other side of Betsy. On an adjacent rock, all clean and seeming to gleam, arranged like a Rorschach or a squared-off double helix, were bones. Offhand, Chloe spotted one human tibia, three human phalanges, and several sections of human vertebrae. The rest were animal— from chipmunk to deer. Without a word, Betsy hefted a huge bone from her pail onto the rock. Her wrist buckled.

"A thighbone?" asked Elise.

"A human femur!" cried Selina. Chloe laughed.

"Selina, look at it," she said. "Hold it up to your leg. Better yet, let's hold it up to Erich's leg." Grinning a bit foolishly, Erich submitted to the measuring process as Selina and Elise together held the bone up to his long thigh.

"To be bigger than Erich, it would have to be a monster," Liz snidely remarked. She and Erich exchanged hostile glances. Oh, for heaven's sake, thought Chloe. Liz is as stubborn as her father. Or Olivia. About time this feud got cracked wide open.

"I was talking to Olivia Fanshawe earlier," Chloe remarked to Selina, who struck her as both commanding and uncommonly good-natured, "and I think she'd really like to work with you on this dig."

"Oh, that snake in the grass!" hissed Selina. "Do you know who Olivia's going out with tonight, Mrs. Otway?" Selina's long brown hair swirled as she confronted Chloe like a contemporary.

"No," said Chloe, startled. "Who?"

"Charlie Scott!" Selina returned. "Back to work, everyone!" Chloe, glancing around for enlightenment, caught Fred Bunyan's glare.

"What kind of thighbone *is* it, Mrs. Otway?" he asked.

Chloe laughed. "A plow horse," she said. Fred tipped his head and whistled.

"Well, I'll be damned!" he said. "Imagine toting a dead plow horse down here." His rusty laugh bounced roughly through the manse trees and floated upward, high above them, to where Jason's catwalk charted a crooked line of light.

"Well, you see, Elise, I started out playing football in high school because of girls, but it turned out that the girls who liked me because I played football I didn't like, and the girls I did like thought I was just some macho jock even though I got good grades, so I gave up on girls."

"Why didn't you just chuck football?"

"What?"

Elise waved her hand as if to say, Never mind, relieved the gaudy Country and Western group in the dim-lit, enchantingly rustic Lake Lenni Lenape Inn was wandering back to the small stage. She'd tried to talk about the dig, hadn't she?—to tell the story of Erich and the thighbone of the plow horse—but Bill Wilson had treated that subject as too wet for words. At the film they'd gone to, a Neil Simon "comedy," he'd laughed his head off, almost patriotically offended when she asked him, after, if all American comedy consisted of one-line quips with no genuine comic rhythm.

"Chuck football?" he asked her now. "I wish I dared order a beer." He twirled the ice in his Coke with distaste. The tables were shiny black; Elise could see him double.

"We're gonna play for all you beautiful folks here at the no-to-ri-ous Lake Lenni Lenape Inn," the lead guitarist began; and people sitting in the other booths and standing at the bar laughed uproariously. Elise laughed a little too, she wasn't sure why. "An old favorite by Waylon Jennings called 'I'm Glad That I'm Crazy 'Cause It's Kept Me from Going Insane.'" Now *that* was funny. Leaning her head back against the dark-stained booth, feeling her long hair soft as feathers on her bare shoulders, Elise laughed out loud.

"What's so funny?" Bill, across the table, looked hurt. You didn't laugh at the film, she could feel him thinking.

"Did you hear the title of that song, Bill?" Elise leaned across the

table and lightly touched his hand. He smiled. "I love it! Shh. Listen."
Across the waxed dance floor, the band started to play. People got up
to dance, the women wearing polyester trouser suits if they were old
or blue jeans if they were young. Nobody was dressed as she was,
Elise noted: she wore a pretty crocheted camisole and bright-orange
trousers that were tight at the ankles. She also wore wedge-heeled
espadrilles that belonged to Aunt Chloe and made her feel quite tall
and glamorous. The vocalist, a short, curly-haired young man with a
mustache and a fringed waistcoat who also played what Bill had told
her was rhythm guitar, stepped up to the microphone and sang, "I'm
Glad That I'm Crazy 'Cause It's Kept Me from Going Insane" with
incongruous poignancy, a kind of moan that missed all the wit and
irony of the lyrics. Or did he do it on purpose? Elise thought she saw
him wink. She laughed.

"Elise, you can't *like* this music. If we were in New York, I'd take
you—"

"Well, it's new to me isn't it? Bill, let's dance."

Across the table Bill Wilson's Indian-brave face went chicken. Or
chickenshit, as Fred Bunyan would say. Oh, damn. Elise let her eyes
wander around the place from the fake saloon doors at the entry to
the brass rail at the bar, finally to the view of the lake where lights
flickered dimly as in that wonderful sermon of Jason's about the Sea
of Galilee. Her nose inhaled the beer smell. Her bare shoulders enjoyed the varnished booth. Wishing for new company, she looked
back at the saloon doors and saw her wish granted like magic, as
Tradd Baynard entered in her Liberty print dress, with Jason and
Calvin in tow, all of them talking, laughing, arguing. Bill turned and
followed the trajectory of her eyes. "Oh, oh," he said. In the hush that
came over the room for a second, Elise suddenly saw the motley trio
objectively: a black man, a pregnant white woman, and a minister.
Impulsively she stood up.

"Tradd," she called. "Jason. Calvin. Over here."

Calvin slid in the booth fast next to Bill. Jason squeezed next to
him.

"Over there, Tradd, over there!" They both waved her away with
their hands.

Laughing, Tradd sat next to Elise. Looking at the three tall broad-
shouldered men compressed into the high-backed, high-armed bench,
Elise giggled. "They're *scared*," Tradd said to her, really friendly this

time, Elise was relieved to see. "Can you believe these big strong men
are scared?"

"Sugar, this is the worst-looking place I have ever seen. Look at all
the rednecks. That bar is one big fat ugly redneck!" Calvin whispered
urgently. "And look at that band. They are going to break into a
chorus of 'Nigger, Don't Fuck with Our Women.' "

"Is there actually such a song?" Elise asked, shocked. Calvin
laughed.

"Oh, probably, sugar, probably. Tradd, how the hell we going to
get *out* of here?" Next to Calvin, Jason was laughing so hard he almost
had his head on Calvin's shoulder. "Quit that, Jason!" Calvin pushed
at him. "They'll be singing 'Nigger, Don't Fuck with Our *Men*' next."
Elise burst out laughing. Bill Wilson's face looked as if he were having an REM nightmare.

"You may be black, Calvin," drawled Tradd, "but your liver is lily-
white!" Jason collapsed on the tabletop laughing. Calvin gave him a
mock shove.

"Jason, go over the other side. There ain't room for you." Tradd
moved nearer Elise. Jason, still laughing, sat on the end next to
Tradd. He collapsed on that side of the table.

"You see, Jason," said Tradd, "you're as punchy as a butted-out
billy goat. Admit to me you needed this break."

Jason propped his elbow on the table, his cheek in his hand. He
started to say something to Tradd, then just laughed. "Elise," he said.
"Bill. I've been kidnapped. I am the victim of a kidnapping. I had my
sermon by heart, and I was all ready to go to sleep and get it firmly set
in my mind, when these two came right into my room and dragged
me out. They kept me locked up all day, and when I'd finally adjusted, they flung the doors wide open."

"Jason, if I had known where Tradd was going to bring you, I
wouldn't have conspired."

"Let's have beer," said Tradd blithely, ignoring them. "This is
most assuredly a beer place. Call the waiter, Jason."

"Call him yourself. I'm the *minister*, Tradd."

"Don't look at me, sugar. I'm the *nigger.*"

"I'm only nineteen," Bill Wilson said. "I'm the *kid.*" He was grinning. Elise was pleased he'd finally relaxed.

"Well, Mother'd scream till you heard her at Fort Sumter if she
knew you were making me do this. Here goes. Waiter!" Tradd called

without looking. She beckoned her hand in the air. A hefty young waitress wearing a feather in an Indian headband materialized. Calvin did a double take. The waitress looked at him in a bored manner. Then she looked at them all in a bored manner.

"What'll you have?"

Perplexed, Tradd frowned. "A pitcher of beer?" The waitress nodded. She was chewing gum. She asked:

"What kind?"

"What's that beer in the pretty green bottles Sam Barnes drinks?" Tradd asked the table.

"Only one kind of beer comes in the pitchers," the waitress said. "Genny."

"Well, I reckon we'll have Genny then," said Tradd.

When the waitress had gone, "Did you *hear* that?" Calvin asked in a loud whisper. "Why do you suppose she asked what kind if there's only one kind? It's a metaphor. *Only one kind.* Hear how she said it? She said it 'cause of *me.*"

Groaning with laughter, Jason collapsed on the table again.

The frosty pitcher of beer, when it came, came with five tall curvy glasses, and Elise felt deliciously sophisticated drinking it in such dazzling company; the beer was yeasty, cold going down and warm when it hit; she leaned comfortably on her elbow and listened to Jason, who'd revived through laughter, so it seemed, regale her and Bill with the "psychological abuse" being visited on him by Tradd and Calvin. "One at a time, I could have taken them. Don't ever introduce your roommate to your sister, Bill. Oh, no! Calvin, that wasn't racist; it wasn't. Marry my sister, Calvin." Jason mock-groaned. "Do you see where they've gotten me, you two? I'm brainwashed."

Elise looked back and forth between Tradd and Calvin, who were grinning at each other. Did they want to get married?

"What Calvin is blaming me for," Jason continued, "I have finally figured out. I never told Calvin he was black. I never came right out and said, Calvin, you're black. No matter that he knew it already. Have either of you ever seen anyone so conscious of being black? Have you? But I never told him." The waitress came with another pitcher of beer. Jason paid her.

"Just walking into the kitchen at the manse is like wandering into a vicious group therapy session when you think you're going to have breakfast. All of a sudden, the other people turn on you. You're the pillow they punch. Tradd tells me that if I had told her not to marry Whit DuVal, she wouldn't have. I never even saw Whit DuVal till the night before the wedding when he asked me to be his best man because his roommate didn't show. *I fit the tux.* That's why Whit asked me. Tradd has twisted that around so that I was Whit's best friend. What really happened is that my sister came up to see me in Nashville flaunting an heirloom emerald on her finger. My sister is only two years younger than I am, but I'm supposed to tell her, Don't. She tells me she's going to live in a restored town house in Savannah. She tells me Whit's going to give her a Mercedes for a wedding present. She was throwing all this material stuff in my face, because she knows I hate it. My sister has a contempt for the ministry that you wouldn't *believe.* She once told me she'd prefer I be a criminal. If I told her not to get married, she would have kicked me in the shins."

"Ah, Tradd can kick higher than that," said Calvin. Jason, Tradd, Bill, and Calvin all laughed. Elise had to think a minute, but then she flushed and giggled.

"Elise," said Jason, "yes, honey, that's the proper reaction. A blush. Don't you dare leave, you two. They'll go for me again."

Elise looked at him. She'd not seen him like this before, except with Uncle Sam and Aunt Chloe. He seemed . . . accessible. The band struck up a song with a cool and pretty keyboard introduction.

"Oh, I love this song," said Tradd with a sigh. "Can pregnant ladies dance?"

"No!" said Jason and Calvin together.

"Shit," said Tradd. "Well, somebody dance. Elise, you and Bill." Elise was catching some of the words to the song: "Don't it make my brown eyes blue?" Country and Western music was much wittier than Neil Simon, she decided.

"He's already declined, Tradd."

"That's a synesthetic song," commented Jason.

"That's a racist song," countered Calvin.

"Calvin, nobody's *blue.* Besides, blacks invented the blues."

Everyone groaned.

"Dance with Jason, Elise," Tradd urged. "He's a wonderful dancer. All his girls used to tell me."

"All right," Elise said, feeling bold. Jason grinned and shrugged.

He, Tradd, and Elise all stood up, and Jason led Elise to the dance floor. She was glad of Aunt Chloe's shoes. She put her hand on Jason's shoulder—broad and bony—felt his hand take her hand, the other hand go around her waist.

"How's the dig coming, baby doll?" Jason asked in her ear. She let one leg touch his leg at the top, held it. What an extraordinary feeling!

"Splendidly," she responded, British schoolgirl-style. Tentatively she leaned her hips in toward him. Oh. She felt a shifting motion, almost a circle, and then Jason pulled back.

"Honeybunch," he said, laughing a little. "Watch it." He stayed back, touching her only lightly at the chest, but it was all over. Everything fell into place for her; she'd felt the motion; she'd felt the involuntary thickening. A pulse beat in her ears; her eyes went wide, then heavy. She wondered if actual loss of virginity could bring any more knowledge than this.

"At the dig today," she said primly, as if nothing had happened, "we found a very large thighbone that Selina thought was human. Fortunately Aunt Chloe was there, and she had us hold the bone up to Erich's thigh, and it was double the size of Erich's. Aunt Chloe identified it as the thighbone of a plow horse."

"Like the jawbone of an ass," Jason said, laughing. Holding her waist tight, he swung her sideways, and they walked together, dancing. Some other people stopped dancing to watch them. "When was Chloe there?"

"Oh, late afternoon. Didn't you see her?" Jason pulled her back to face him, keeping his distance. She could *feel* him keep his distance. A sense of power washed over her.

"I didn't see Chloe. I was working on my sermon for tomorrow, guarded by Calvin and Tradd. They shut me in the parlor. My only communication with the outside world was to send 'The Lord of the Dance' out to Olivia Fanshawe, who probably pitched a fit."

" 'Lord of the Dance'! How super. In England they play that on the radio right along with the Stones. Just as they do a Blake poem that Uncle Sam abhors, called 'Jerusalem.' It almost became the national anthem in the First World War, our history mistress told us." Elise sang:

"Bring me my bow of burning gold
Bring me my arrows of desire . . ."

It sounded suggestive; she broke off. "D'you know, in England, religion is much more a part of *life* than it is here. Uncle Sam says it's because people still believe in ghosts there."

Jason put his head back and laughed. With the laugh, Elise felt his body trace hers lightly before he pulled back again. When the song wound down and he led her back to the booth, Elise felt that something irrevocable had happened to her.

"Never *mind*, Elise," Bill Wilson said to her in the Volkswagen. "Let me take you home."

Chloe couldn't sleep. There was nothing for it; she simply couldn't. She sat in the dark in the living room, wide-awake. Despite perfunctory lovemaking (Tony, bushed from having worked all day, just rolled off), an agitating attempt at meditation (her mantra was DON'T THINK, DON'T THINK), and quite a lot of scotch, Chloe could not turn off her hundred-mile-an-hour nattering head. She was shocked at how recklessly Tony had begun shifting his central positive ion—Tony was usually so patient! Painstakingly shift your ligands first: a rule. Exchange them, not the ion! How could he have faith in a circle of ligands without a nucleus to bond them? "Chloe, I *know* the ligands are right, damn it! You haven't been following this. You're over your head, you know."

DON'T THINK about ligands. DON'T THINK about God. DON'T THINK how the sky seems to be sliding open just a jot, threatening to burn like a laser through the cozy security of your existential world. DON'T THINK how you're afraid you're falling in love with a very young man. Chloe sighed out loud. She had not thought *that* before. Not in words. So much for mantras! You're not falling in love. You need some attention. And some sleep.

Wearing just wispy bikini underpants and a *M*A*S*H* T-shirt she'd donned after Tony rolled off (Tony, who was usually so patient!), Chloe wandered from the couch in the dark living room to the screened front porch. The moon was full again. She pictured herself and Tony in the arcane little graveyard behind the church at the last full moon: a circle of stones like ligands. Fourteen sandstone ligands held together by a mystery. Oh, hell, she couldn't even remember how many ligands Tony had become attached to in his perverse and daring speculations. She *was* over her head. She pulled the big *M*A*S*H* T-shirt straight. Tony had given it to her for her birthday: "For mucking about with your placentas. Also, it matches your matchless eyes!" Placental dissections *were* the goriest things, quite like a scene out of *M*A*S*H*. Her lab coats would not wash clean.

Eschew scientific thought. DON'T THINK about that intriguing little quirk in the left ovary of Sally, the rhesus monkey, who twice had seemed to conceive immaculately. She did hope Mark, her assistant, was keeping a good eye on Sally. One could never be sure that some sentimental student wouldn't just decide that Sally needed company once in a while. Sally did plead so! Chloe sat down in the cushioned swing that hung from the rafters of the porch. Abbie loved the swing. The only time of day Chloe saw her look really happy was when she curled up there in the morning with her coffee. The swing squeaked. Conscious of the girls on the sleeping porch just above, Chloe fixed her feet. Well, two of the girls. An hour ago Sam had expressed concern that Elise and Bill weren't in yet and, at Chloe's scoff, turned on her: "Chloe, stick with the extended family and be all buddy-buddy with everybody. You don't know what it's like to be *in loco parentis,* or be a parent either!"

Stupid to sit in a swing without swinging. She should find herself something to read. That was, after all, what she'd come down for. "The boathouse is crammed with mysteries," Tony had said. "Read Wordsworth's *Prelude,* " Sam had said. "Read Freud," had said Jason. Jason! Chloe left the porch and walked down the lawn toward the boathouse. The grass was dewy. The kitchen of the manse across the lake was dark. For a change. The full moon cut a diagonal swathe through the lake: like God's laser, searching. She heard the insinuating coo of a mourning dove. She shivered. She ducked into the boathouse and switched on the light, closed the door. It was cozy, the ceiling comfortingly low, the walls lined with books. Tony's makeshift lab tables were a mess! Diagrams and scribbles all over the place. Chloe heard the mourning dove again—perhaps it had a nest nearby? Mourning doves were famous for their slovenly nests, she remembered. Perhaps Tony had been influenced. Why, he'd even left a chart in the spectrometer. She turned on the little light and peered at it. An octahedron? What the hell . . . ?

Ah, she should have been keeping up with what he was doing!

She moved to Sam's desk. Blake and volumes of eighteenth-century and romantic criticism occupied the shelf immediately above, but on the desk proper was *The Midnight Raymond Chandler.* She laughed. Through the window between the shelves she saw a light go on in the manse kitchen. On impulse she sought out "F" on Sam's meticulously alphabetized shelves and found a generous sampling of Freud. Retroactively she altered her attack on Sam's narrow mind: "The only other discipline you'll accept is Freudian psychology, for you're all a bunch of sex maniacs!" Not altogether untrue, she expected. At her university, the affairs of the English department put Hollywood to shame. Oho, there was a copy of Freud's letters to Karl Abraham. She remembered when they had come out, in the sixties. She'd been a graduate student, too poor to afford lunch, much less books outside *her* discipline. But she'd been intrigued. Rather a scandal. Susan Sontag (a hero of hers at the time) had protested the fact the letters had been censored. With an intellectual glee that had survived almost twenty years, Chloe took the volume out, sat down at Sam's desk, and, pushing *The Midnight Raymond Chandler* aside, started to look through the Freud-Abraham letters, aware in a way almost tactile of the kitchen light across the lake. She much preferred warm human lights to, say . . . moonlight.

She found herself smiling as Carl Jung, whom she adored, began sporadically to stroll across the scenes of the letters—to Freud's mixed pleasure and consternation. Quite the ladies' man, wasn't Jung? "The Randy Goat of Zurich," didn't people call him? *Be nice to Jung,* Freud counseled Abraham. *We need him.*

> . . . on the whole it is easier for us Jews as we lack the mystical bent . . . you are closer to my intellectual constitution because of racial kinship, while Jung as a Christian and a pastor's son finds his way to me only against great inner resistances. His association with us is the more valuable for that. I nearly said that it was only by his appearance on the scene that psychoanalysis escaped the danger of becoming a Jewish national affair.

Fresh from Acts and the stunning speed with which the once recalcitrant Paul cut through the inbred and exclusive Mosaic law, Chloe picked up a pencil and jotted in the margin of the book, "Jung, the Paul figure." Yes. Rather good, that. Had it not been for Paul, so would Christianity have become "a Jewish national affair." It was Paul's "appearance on the scene" that knocked out the irksome dietary and circumcision laws; it was Paul who opened Christianity to the Gentiles and thus the world. What Jung did for early psychoanalysis, Paul did for early Christianity. Pleased with the symmetry of her discovery, Chloe gazed out the window. The moonlight on the lake had brightened perceptibly. She heard the dove again, close—could it have a nest in the rickety eaves of the boathouse? Slovenly indeed.

Science pierced theology. Or vice versa. Feeling her heart beat fast, Chloe wrote down a simple, devastating equation:

$$JUNG : FREUD = PAUL : ?$$

My God, thought Chloe, there was no Freud to mastermind what Paul did! The simple, white-hot, unavoidable *fact* was that no one on earth could have plotted the strategy for extending Christianity to the Gentiles. *No one on earth.* No one even wanted to. Certainly not Saul of Tarsus. What "happened" on the Road to Damascus must have happened!

$$JUNG : FREUD = PAUL : THE RISEN JESUS$$

There is a God. There is a "risen Lord." Suddenly terrified, Chloe pushed Sam's big chair back and, banging her head, stumbling, fled the boathouse. She had to tell someone. She had to tell someone straightaway! She ran through the wet grass, up the stairs to the porch, and, in the doorway to the living room, ran smack into Sam. He was big, he was human, he was here, he was warm like flesh and firelight, a refuge from where it was cold as moonlight and searing as a laser; and he put his arms around her.

"Chloe?" he asked in her ear. "Was it you in the boathouse? You left the light on. I couldn't sleep either. Chloe, what are we going to do about this?" Chloe leaned her head back to look at him, to tell him—! "Oh, my God, Chloe, you look beautiful. Your eyes are incandescent." He kissed her, deliberate and deep; she held on, feeling his tongue probe, his body stir against hers, melt hers; and she thought, No, no; but she was too boneless and vulnerable and open to resist. Sam's hands moved down her back to hold her buttocks; she fought a little, but the resultant tension felt like play, a feigned tease, an antic dance. "God, you feel good!" he uttered when he finally pulled his mouth away.

"So do you," she said honestly, then went on in words that seemed to come from someone else, "but it's not important."

She felt Sam's helpless laugh joggle against her before he put his hands on her shoulders and pushed her back, to look at her. "Not important? My God, woman, if this isn't important, what is?"

She looked up at him, standing there so human and comforting in his pajamas. She could still feel his erection, like an imprint on her body. "I don't know, Sam," she started to say; and then a light switched on in the living room. Automatically she and Sam took a step away from each other.

"Oh!" Elise, looking lovely but a bit tear-stained, regarded them. "What are you doing in the dark?" Outside, Chloe heard her own Volkswagen drive away, heedless of muffler, grating on the West Shore Road.

"Where's Bill?" asked Sam.

"He said he wanted to go off and scream someplace," Elise said, half-ironic, half-woebegone. "I'm afraid I wasn't very nice to him."

Sam leaned back against the doorjamb. "I used to do that," he reminisced, "when girls drove me crazy. Never yell at a girl, I was taught. I'd take the maddening creature home, then sit in my car in the middle of nowhere, and scream my head off." He heaved a comic sigh. He gave Chloe a quizzical, humorous look. "Had I the youthful energy, I'd do that right now!" Chloe laughed; she couldn't help it. Whatever must Elise think?

Elise gave both of them a smile of uncomprehending indulgence. She yawned. "Well, don't stay up too late, you two." She started to climb the stairs, wobbling a little on Chloe's shoes. "Church tomorrow. There's to be an absolutely smashing recessional hymn."

Taking advantage of Elise's own recession, Chloe hastily followed.

"Abbie, we're going to be so awfully late!" Desperately Chloe scrubbed at Elise's mattress protector, tossing it impatiently into the bathtub with pajamas, sheets, a fleecy gold blanket, and even a pillow, to soak in cold water and salt. In the middle of the night, Elise had gotten her copious but right-on-time period (observe the full moon!), slept on, awakened in a welter of blood, wept, apologized, been "forgiven," and sent on her way with the girls and the boys, the girls wearing skirts and the boys shirts with collars. To church. Church! Chloe could not believe that on the day after the turning that already promised to be the single most drastic act of her life (there was a God, there was! She'd been shoved, and a door had closed behind her), she was kneeling by the bathtub with Abbie in service to her fellow woman, when, where, all, only she wanted to be in church.

Con-vert. At the crack of dawn, she'd looked it up. It meant "to change into another form"; it was almost scientific. I am changed into another form. "Abbie!" she cried.

"Those clots will set if we don't scrub them off right now," said Abbie grimly, "and I don't want to drag bloody sheets to the Laundromat." But she stood up, rolling down the sleeves of her silk shirt. "We'd better drive, if you're in such a hurry."

An apologetic note on the refrigerator from Bill Wilson told them the Volkswagen was out of gas up at the ball diamond, and they had to hunt frantically through Sam's trouser pockets to find the keys to the Buick. Sam grumbled on the bed under Munch's *The Scream.* Chloe was terrified Tony would wake too; she didn't want him with her today. Maybe later. The German "march" that assailed the West Shore Road from Otto's loudspeaker as she and Abbie left the cottage was disorientingly romantic: Marlene Dietrich singing "Lili Marlene." The husky tones lilted through the open windows of the Buick.

Very late, out of breath and disheveled, Chloe and Abbie entered the church at the beginning of a prayer:

> Thou shalt make me hear of joy and gladness, that
> the bones that thou hast broken may rejoice.

Chloe and Abbie slid into a pew on the side. The church was packed. Chloe heard Jason's voice slide out of scripture into himself. "Lord, today we've had enough of worry and intellect and fear; Lord, today give us joy. Joy without reason, joy without reservation, without fear for the punishment of tomorrow. You don't punish us for joy—let us know that. Let us know that laughter is the language of praise, that we laugh because we live, and laughter is our expression of life, our sign of life. And let us boldly say to you now, laughing as we say it, filling our lungs with air and spirit and breath, Our Father who art in heaven . . ."

Chloe bowed her head. I can't say this, she thought. I can believe, but I can't say this with all these other people. But she said it.

The text for the sermon was human and dramatic as a play:

> "And he entered Jericho and was passing through it. And behold, there was a man called Zacchaeus, and he was a chief tax collector, and he was rich. And he was trying to see which one was Jesus and could not see him from the crowd, because he was short of stature. So he ran on ahead and climbed a sycamore tree so that he could see him, because he was going to pass by it. And as he came to the place Jesus looked up and said to him: Zacchaeus, hurry and come down, for I must stay in your house today. And he hastened and came down, and welcomed him with joy.

"A friend of mine," Jason began, "asked me the other day if Jesus ever laughed. Well, conventionally since medieval times, we men of little faith, we men with the weight of the world on our shoulders, we preachers, we say no. Who could ever laugh at the human condition? We who 'understand' know that it's serious, it's grim; and salvation is no laughing matter. I mean, we're all in *trouble*.

"Still I, victim of, say, *Jesus Christ Superstar*, which presents a laughing Jesus so believably as to cause an audience to dance with joy, I said to my friend, 'Well, of *course.*'

"Jesus laughed.

"Although I believed it, I went home and checked my Greek New Testament. Not one. There's not one laugh. The word γελάω, which means laugh, does not even appear in the New Testament. Jesus weeps, but he doesn't laugh. The Son of Man comes eating and drinking, but not laughing. It can't be! I decided. No one could have attracted the following Jesus attracted without laughing. I started to look for laughter *built into* the Gospels. I found this little guy in a tree. All right, here's Jesus looking up at a little man in a sycamore tree:

"Zacchaeus, hurry and come down, for I must stay in your house today."

Gesturing with his right hand, Jason delivered the line sternly. The entire congregation looked up. "Will that *work?* Will it theatrically, dramatically, humanly *work?* Think of the Zacchaeus within us, the little man who so daringly, this once, exposes himself to ridicule. Will decorous sobriety and a stern command speak to that brave little man in us?

"Would decorous sobriety and a stern command understand the real Zacchaeus in the sycamore tree? Would it know him? Let's try it another way. Zacchaeus!" Jason called, laughing, raising his left hand this time,

"Zacchaeus, hurry and come down, for I must stay in your house today.

"Was Jesus not charmed by Zacchaeus; was he not delighted? Was he not *amused?* Why else *stay at his house?* Look at the texture of the act. Hear the implicit laughter. See Zacchaeus's reaction. He isn't embarrassed; he isn't shamed; he doesn't climb down the tree clumsily; no, 'he welcomed him with rejoicing,' χαίρων, rejoicing, a word that does appear again and again in the New Testament. By the grace of his gesture, Jesus makes Zacchaeus rejoice. . . ."

As Jason went on with examples of Jesus's wit and laughter—the prodigal son, the needle's eye, the numbered hairs of the head, the wonderful line "Martha, Martha, you are worried and troubled over much!" when Martha frets about dirty dishes while her sister Mary sits with the men and talks to Jesus—Chloe caught her breath and, as if through glass, absorbed that the sermon was for *her*. She was the friend who'd asked if Jesus ever laughed; she had inspired this; and it was too much, it was too *soon*. She didn't deserve it. She started to cry. She'd been to church maybe three times, how many times? God should not be called upon to look at her as if she'd climbed a tree!

"Could the risen Jesus have allowed doubting Thomas to poke his wounds with a straight face? Do you listen to the Gospels? Do you hear the wit and humor? Do you realize how funny it must have been for Jesus to ride in triumph into Jerusalem on a *colt?* A grown man, thirty-three years old, on a colt? Was he solemn during that comedy that precedes the greatest tragedy of all time? Hell, no, he must have laughed. Just as he must have laughed at little Zacchaeus in the sycamore tree. Jesus loved him, as he loves the Zacchaeus in us who doesn't mind being laughed at, doesn't mind climbing a tree to see him.

"If we've that courage, he makes us his own. He gives us comic relief, the laughter that wards off tragedy, the laughter that defines the life of joy we are supposed to have. We're supposed to be happy; we're supposed to have it all. The Kingdom is right here, if we can find it. Joy is the substance of Jesus's life, of what he is to us and what we are to him, if we dare risk our dignity to climb a tree. When Jesus tells the people in Matthew 5, 'We played for you, but you did not dance,' he announces himself as the piper, the man who laughs, who leads the dance. So be it. So be the dance!"

The harmonium wheezed into life with a wild and lilting melody. As Abbie fumbled with the hymnal, Chloe felt the rhythm take over the church—heads and shoulders and hymnals were moving. The little church rollicked. The little church rocked.

> I danced for the fishermen, for James and John—
> They came with me, and the dance went on.
> Dance then, wherever you may be,
> I am the Lord of the Dance, said he,
> And I'll lead you all wherever you may be,
> I'll lead you all in the dance, said he.

Chloe was crying so hard she could see only colors and motion. She let the whirling music invade her, simply living now, caught up in a flow. "I am the dance and I still go on." How to tell the dancer from the dance, the noun from the verb? What was human from what was God?

> They cut me down and I leap up high—
> I am the life that'll never, never die;
> I'll live in you if you'll live in me—
> I am the Lord of the Dance, said he.

Tears still streamed down Chloe's face as she and Abbie joined the laughing crowd on the way out of church; tears streamed, but Abbie, usually so alert to the moods of others, didn't notice, just chattered on. "I'm going right over to Esther's and buy a whole pile of paper plates, Chloe. I remember she had some pretty ones. I'm not going to fret over dishes like Martha anymore. That sermon could have been for me!"

They reached Jason at the door. Chloe lowered her head. Still blithely talking, Abbie breezed through. "Jason, I think you changed my life. Next time you come over we'll use paper plates and those nice blue plastic glasses, and I'll get to talk to you too. I'll be one of the boys like Chloe. Ta, ta!" Abbie blended into the crowd on the lawn headed toward Esther's for newspapers and hot-fudge sundaes. Jason took Chloe's hand. He wouldn't let go. They had a comic struggle, and then she laughed a little, still held by his hand.

"That's better," Jason said. Chloe could feel people piling up next to her. "The sermon was supposed to make you laugh. I was afraid you weren't going to make it." His eyes held her eyes. She could almost feel them. "Oh," he said, as if he'd read something. He smiled. In the sunlight she saw crinkles at the corners of his eyes, the rowdy silver in his hair. "It's not the end of the world," he said. "It's the beginning. Believe me. We'll talk," he said, finally releasing her hand. "Soon." He turned to take on Selina Thomas's dotty, carping mother. "Yes, Mrs. Thomas, I know exactly what you're going to say. I shouldn't have said, 'Hell, no'; I was sorry the minute it came out of my mouth."

Chloe, moving down the church steps, suddenly laughed out loud. She felt like skipping.

EIGHT
A Miracle up the Road
Monday, July 22

Intently having watched from the porch swing a golden dawn slowly heave forth a hot ruddy sun over the manse across the lake, Chloe, in her *M*A*S*H* T-shirt again, moved to the kitchen for the coffee Bill Wilson always thoughtfully made before he went to work. Hans Strauss, Erich's father, had picked Bill up at six-fifteen, his polite honk having served to sanction Chloe's sleeplessness; she'd been downstairs before the truck disappeared. Now she took her cup and repaired, humming "The Lord of the Dance," to the vegetable garden on the side of the cottage, bare feet aware, as she walked, of boards worn to a patina on deck and steps, the stony tilt of the land, the soft, dark texture of the topsoil Abbie had, with Otto's help, hauled in to structure a verdant garden on rock. It was a charming, old-fashioned garden, propped, twined, and pinned on aged cucumber frames, tomato stakes, and bean trellises Abbie had resurrected from under the cottage; and in a manner unwontedly fanciful, she'd alternated the vegetables in a symmetrical pattern through which viny zucchini twisted and tall garlic wove, making each tomato plant, each frame of cucumber, each trellis of bean a work of art.

Fragrant basil punctuated, thyme and dill fluttered, and splashes of parsley bordered the stone-edged octagon in lacy scallops. Harold Fanshawe, his pedant's eyes agleam, had dubbed the whole "An Elizabethan Botanical Fantasy." "A Vegetable Sonnet," Sam had one-upped him, deadpan. "Let's hope it produces," Abbie'd murmured, embarrassed by all the lyrical hyperbole.

Lyrical or not, the garden was producing. Weeds too, Chloe's own biologist's eyes noted critically. She put down her coffee cup on a rock and began efficiently to yank dandelions, crabgrass, a sly milkweed mimicking a tomato plant. A small Aaron's rod had pushed its way up next to a plumy carrot. Had it come from Otto's lush topsoil or from the grim, hard earth beneath? Aaron's rod spent one year as a

fleecy ground tissue called "Adam's blanket," Chloe recollected, before it burst into full phallic glory. She'd never seen the blanket except in pictures, indeed most people hadn't as it sheltered beneath
taller plants, but last year, somewhere, an Adam's blanket had pre-
pared the way for this small but resiliently flowering Aaron's rod.
Chloe decided to let it be. In Europe, people cultivated *Verbascum
thapsus* for its vertical counterpoint to softer, meeker flowers; she
would allow it to center the swirling carrots. Probably, she speculated, softening the dirt around the velvety leaves that protected the
stem, American puritans uncomfortable about sex had relegated Aaron's rod to the weed patch. Or the schoolroom!

Tony came out of the front door of the cottage, down the stairs
from the porch, carrying a stack of periodicals and his thermos of
coffee. Chloe stood up and waved, but he didn't look in her direction,
just moved straight and purposeful down the lawn to the boathouse.
God damn it! Didn't he wonder what had become of her at this hour
of the morning? Just spatially, as a mere wandering woman, didn't he
wonder what had become of her? A wandering woman up for grabs,
come to think of it. Here she'd been groped by Sam (well, she could
handle Sam), plucked by the hair or pulled down from a tree by *God*—
ah, the metaphor didn't matter, didn't explain. The experience was
beyond metaphor, or, rather, she pondered it, before metaphor: the
motive for metaphor.

Without metaphor, how to explain it? Oh, she was sure Tony was
not going to handle her headlong leap into belief in a way that would
satisfy her! Good show, darling! would not work.

Abbie's octagonal garden suddenly blurred to replicate the vibrant
spectrum of the octahedron she'd seen night before last in Tony's
spectrometer. Her response to that wouldn't satisfy *him*. Poor Tony.
Automatically Chloe waited for her ulcer to protest the unresolved
internal battle. It didn't protest. Not a twinge. Gingerly she touched
her middle, seeing in her mind's eye like an X ray the horseshoe of
her duodenum behind the peritoneum: clean as a whistle, healed. She
caught her breath. DON'T THINK. She hunkered down by a cucumber frame, letting her mind's eye shift to the inner structure of a
cucumber leaf, the air spaces surrounding the mesophilic cells—such
an elegant confection of air, water, and tissue, the cucumber!

Would Abbie make these cucumbers into pickles? Would she can
the tomatoes? Chloe and Tony had once been to a most peculiar party

at the home of one of Tony's graduate students in exurban Boston, a
rural place called Ayer, where each woman entering announced how
many quarts of tomatoes she had just canned. It was obviously un-
rehearsed, yet became as predictable as a stylized absurdist play. And
these women were young! Chloe and Tony had laughed later, but at
the party—it had culminated in a vinyard with vats of raw red wine
—were rather taken by the young wives' devotion to the obsolete
domestic arts. Now Chloe thought she might actually enjoy helping
Abbie can the tomatoes. Oh, this wasn't her! She was Mary, not
Martha. She had already defined herself. Chloe Otway neither canned
nor baked, didn't sew. She was a scientist, a teacher, an atheist. She
was Tony's wife. How dared she change her definition at this late
date? It was too much to ask of Tony. If he were condescending, she'd
never forgive him!

A roaring noise on the West Shore Road interrupted her musing.
She frowned. Was it one of those illicit motorcycles they were supposed to call the police about? No, it was louder. She stood up and
saw the very old gray Triumph convertible turn into the space across
the road they used for parking. Her innards lurched (but painlessly)
as Jason Baynard, looking awfully spiffy in a tan corduroy jacket and
blue shirt, got out and came toward her. He was smiling. His old-gold
hair looked wild and newly washed. His white jeans were still grass-
stained. Chloe smiled back. "Want to go to Wappasenink?" Jason
asked her.

She laughed. "What's Wappasenink?"

He clapped a hand to his forehead. "Too early! Ah, let's see, Wappasenink is what Olson and Mathews clogged my sink with this
morning."

"In that case, I'd love to go to Wappasenink," said Chloe demurely.

"Well, go get some clothes on, ma'am," drawled Jason. "I don't
know that $M*A*S*H$ has made it to Wappasenink yet." Chloe looked
down at the black stenciled letters and big red cross on her T-shirt.

"What does one wear to Wappasenink?"

Jason tipped his head and considered. "Wappasenink," he said.
"Population four thousand. About fifty miles northeast of here, on
Route Six. Its principal attraction at the moment is a service station
called Dolly's that'll replace the muffler I've been missing for a
month. Dolly has a very tough sexy voice, and her grammar slips
once in a while. I would say that one should wear something pretty.

Preferably green." Looking as patiently expectant as a suitor, Jason sat down on the rock next to Chloe's coffee cup.

Inside the cottage, wearing just bikini underpants, Chloe raided the girls' closet in the big bathroom for a sundress she'd been coveting that belonged to Elise, dark green with delicate pale-green flowers and narrow strips of lace. She slipped it on. At the mirror over the two sinks carefully she tied the drawstrings that held the dress at top and waist. Oh, it was lovely, perfect!

In the hall she paused near Sam's and Abbie's door, thinking to tell Abbie where she was going—odd, almost unprecedented that Abbie wasn't up yet. It was nearly nine o'clock. Through the door she heard Sam's rumbly mumble, and then she heard Abbie laugh. A laugh with a guttural edge. Chloe felt an amazed smile spread across her face. How marvelous! How perfectly marvelous. Not that she thought that they *didn't*, she reasoned to herself, but wasn't it nice that they *did?* From her own room (where Tony had made the bed), she collected her favorite sandals, then let Sir Isaac off the sleeping porch where the girls were still asleep, fed him in the kitchen, put him out, and composed a breezy note to put on the refrigerator: "Gone to Wapassink (?) with Jason to get the muffler on his Triumph replaced." The details (especially the misspelling and the question mark) ought nicely to obscure the subject (understood) and the vague infinitive of the sentence. Outside she found Sir Isaac and Jason sitting side-by-side on the rock. Jason was drinking her cold coffee.

Over the roar of the crippled exhaust system, Chloe and Jason could hardly talk on the way to Wappasenink, could only laugh in the way of two people who like each other tremendously but don't speak each other's language, a kind of right-brain laughter, Chloe decided it was, then wondered if perhaps all laughter wasn't on the right side of the brain, for wasn't laughter (when you came down to it) a defiance of logic; wasn't all comedy somehow at the expense of logic, like a belief in God? It was one of the ways God *got to you,* making you question your own obeisance to logic. Who was to say, Chloe's mind stormed about, that Chloe Otway's career was any more important than Abbie Barnes's garden? That Tony Otway's ligands mattered more than Otto Dolch's ditches, where the water lilies weren't holding like they should? Logic had become a *god.*

Chloe contemplated telling all this to Jason, but it was too complicated. It could wait for quiet and a little less nervousness on her part.
She wanted to ask him how to tell Tony, how to change her life, how
to go about learning—there was so much to learn! But she could stay
herself a while longer today, so she watched the midsummer landscape, watched the hills pitch steeper, rocks stud the land, the soil
turn red, the tree trunks blacken against the green as they approached
the Susquehanna and smooth, guard-railed Route 6. The rough mac-
adam road from Lenni Lenape roller-coasted, then dipped straight
down, and the noisy little Triumph crossed the Susquehanna River at
an ugly factory town called Laceyville. The town was named after
ancestors of their next-door neighbors at the lake, Chloe recalled.
How ignominious! They headed west now on Route 6, seeing signs
for a truck stop in Wappasenink, hearing nothing but the roar of the
Triumph at sixty; and about twenty miles along Jason suddenly
turned from breathtaking craggy bluffs above the Susquehanna up a
dirt road marked only by a faded billboard that advertised

DOLLY'S SERVICE
DOES EVERYTHING
FOR WHEEL OR HOOF

Chloe did a double take, looked at Jason, and they both laughed
uproariously as they wound up a steep, wooded road with a gorge on
the left, past a precarious farm on the right, then into a small eyesore
of a service station. Chloe was reminded of Pee Wee's Airfield. A sign
on the decrepit building said "Blacksmith" in gilt letters. Numerous
fragments of automobiles in varying degrees of decomposition littered the grounds as far as the eye could see. A shiny, waxed Coupe
de Ville near the pumps appeared to be the sole operative vehicle.
From under the maroon Cadillac, a strong-faced woman of about
fifty, her black hair wound in braids around her head, slowly
emerged, headfirst. She wore black overalls. Jason got out of the Triumph, and Chloe, her ears still in shock from the ride, leaned back in
the leather seat, closed her eyes against the rusty wasteland, and listened to the sound of water rushing through the gorge on the other
side of the road. Slowly the two voices intruded.

"You're the man who called. I been wondering about you ever
since. Kept thinking, Where have I heard that voice before?"

"That's the Triumph I told you about on the phone. The muffler's
gone. You're sure you can find a muffler to fit a Triumph that old?"

"I can find anything. Give me an MG TF, and I can reconstruct her. Give me a '64 Volvo, and I can cure her ills. Give me a '69 Firebird, my very favorite car, and I can make her hum. I never throw a thing away, that's the secret. I'm supposing you don't mind a second-hand muffler." She cocked a canny eye at Jason.

"Not if it works."

Chloe got out of the Triumph, wondering if the woman extrapolated her spare parts from the rusted wrecks that filled the adjacent field. Despite herself, she'd been rather impressed by the shrewd rationale for all this squalor. Then a breeze swirled her skirt, and Chloe felt oddly superimposed on the derelict setting, flimsy. "You must be Dolly," she guessed, holding out her hand. Startled, the woman shook it.

"I'm Dolly," she affirmed. She frowned sidelong in Jason's direction. "Can't be Robert Redford," she muttered. "Robert Redford has blue eyes. Don't tell me," she cautioned Chloe. "It'll come to me."

Jason caught Chloe's eye, grinned, and shrugged. Oh, he did look impossibly handsome! "How long do you think you'll take, ah, Dolly?" he asked the woman. "We thought we'd explore the town if we can find it."

"Back down the road you just come up, past my farm, my Iris Rose, my Violet Rose, and my Billy Rose, then you can cut across the gorge on the wooden bridge, and there, right before your eyes, you'll find Scully's Hangover, Wappasenink, and the church." Dolly lay down flat on her back in the dirt and stuck her head under the Triumph. She coughed. "Be about three hours for this here cream puff," she estimated. "You didn't tell me the exhaust was gone too. Angus!" she suddenly bellowed, still lying flat on the ground. A big, ungainly man came out of the little building. He had a lurching gait—an artificial leg, Chloe thought. "These here two folks are going to explore Wappasenink while we fix up this pretty little car. Oscar can just wait for his Caddy. This Triumph's an antique. Run along now," she prodded Chloe and Jason from her prone position. Jason winked at Chloe. As they started obediently down the road, they could hear Dolly stage-whisper to Angus, "Where've we seen them before? Do you think it's TV or the movies?"

"Oh, Jason, look. Goats!" Around a turn in the road that mercifully blotted out Dolly's wrecks, a small red barn appeared and, in a pen, two white goats. Clean as cats, they looked expectantly through the rail fence at Chloe and Jason. Chloe grabbed a handful of tall grasses and approached the pen. In the bushes on the other side of the fence, she saw two very young human heads bob up, then down. "Hi," she called to the heads, as she held out her offering to the smaller goat.

"Hi!" called a shrill, disembodied voice. "That's Violet Rose. Billy's gonna be mighty jealous."

Jason, also holding grass, came up next to Chloe. "Here, Billy Goat," he said. Chloe giggled.

"Not Billy Goat, Billy Rose!" Two little girls' heads popped up from the bushes. "Because roses are Dolly's favorite flowers."

"Don't goats have extraordinary faces?" Chloe asked Jason. "What a sense of humor God must have to create a goat!" As she heard herself she couldn't believe her ears. The line seemed to have been fed to her by some offstage prompter. Chloe felt her face flush.

Jason was looking at her, a little smile at the corner of his mouth. "I thought the same thing when I saw Sir Isaac come out the door this morning. Are you ready to talk?"

Chloe took a deep breath. She leaned back against the fence. She felt afraid, at a disadvantage. "In a bit," she said.

Jason leaned back against the fence with her. He crossed his arms like hers. "Chickenshit," he said casually. Chloe laughed. Then the fence shook. Chloe and Jason moved away fast. A scream came from the bushes, and the two little girls burst out.

"Iris Rose! Iris Rose!"

Ferociously another white goat was butting the fence. Shocked, Chloe and Jason looked at her. The children hastily grabbed grass and pressed it on Jason, who handed it to Chloe. The savage butts seemed to shake the earth under their feet. Surely the small goat would knock herself out. Gingerly Chloe poked the grass, the timothy, and wild wheat toward the furious, butting little creature, who gradually, albeit balefully, subsided and began to eat the grass from Chloe's hand.

"Iris Rose has got a mean temper," one little girl confided to Chloe. "You're *brave*."

Jason laughed out loud as, over the little girl's head, Chloe mouthed the word "Chickenshit" at him.

Later, after awful cheeseburgers and sublime french fries at Scully's Hangover (it literally hung over the gorge), talking desultorily and laughing a lot, Chloe and Jason wandered down the pretty Main Street of Wappasenink, Pennsylvania, till it wasn't pretty anymore. Still, as the hanging fuchsias set in sphagnum dwindled and the bright, trailing window boxes were replaced by utilitarian clothes-lines slung across cluttered porches, Chloe noted that a certain electricity began to quicken the air like wind. Why were so many people walking in such an unattractive area of so small a town? Lunch hour? A lot of unemployment? But there were children too, families incongruously dressed up for summertime—little girls in fancy dresses, little boys in suits. That was Route 6 at the base of the hill, Chloe saw; had there perhaps been an accident? No, the glee—for there was glee —was muted, quietly expectant.

"Jason, what do you suppose is going on?" Chloe plucked at his sleeve, then took her hand away. She'd never touched him except to shake hands. He offered her his arm. She shook her head.

"No?" Jason put his hands in his pockets. Still walking, he looked around him, alert, curious. "There's something damned strange in the air," he said. "Like too much oxygen. Let's find out." They followed the crowd. Route Six became a street with sidewalks and trees as it passed through Wappasenink, but the billboards continued. Chloe and Jason laughed at one:

DOLLY'S SERVICE
GO BACK
YOU MISSED IT, SUCKER

At a traffic light, everyone turned to cross Route Six. People were leaving a tree-shaded little building on the other side.

"It's a church, Jason. Look, it's just a little church."

Next to them on the crosswalk, a woman in a red dress was telling a woman in a blue dress, "It's a miracle. This is the first time I ever drove anyplace by myself without George, and I got here. A hundred miles! It's like I was led right here."

"No 'like' about it, honey. You *were* led right here."

From the crosscurrent of the people leaving the church (a really tacky little church, Chloe registered, nowhere near as nice as the one at Lenni Lenape) came exultant fragments. "I saw the Blessed Virgin." "Everybody sees her, stupid. I saw St. Francis and two little lambs." "That was St. Joseph, *stupid*." "I saw the face of our Lord!

You didn't see a thing, did you?" "Clouds. I saw clouds." "Why can't I have a rosary, Daddy? *Why can't I?*"

Jason took hold of Chloe's hand. She could feel a pulse between them. "I know what it is," said Jason. "It's Matt Bernstein's 'miracle.' I'll bet that's what it is."

Matt Bernstein's "miracle" rang a bell. Chloe stopped walking to think, got jostled from behind by the woman in the red dress, then pulled from before by Jason's hand. She remembered. She remembered the cryptic little teaser at the end of Matt Bernstein's article about Jason: "Next week, A Miracle up the Road."

"It's packing them in, Jason, just like you," she said to him, a bit breathless as the collective pace quickened; and she heard Jason's startled laugh cut through the hubbub around them. On a decorous wave, no running, just fast walking, they were borne up the steps of the church, then halted at the door.

"What is this?" Jason asked a broadly smiling man with a camera who officiously guarded the door. "What's going on?"

"It's our *miracle,*" the man almost shouted. "Father's gonna get it authenticated. Look at the tabernacle veil. You can't miss it, Reverend Baynard. Ah, I saw you in last week's *Bugle*—that's how I know who you are. Wait'll you see the spread we're gonna get this week!"

Inside all was filtered daylight, quiet. The ceiling was pale blue trimmed with gold; the stained-glass windows were primitive, with bold primary colors delineating mangers, people on donkeys, women at wells, children. As she and Jason waited for an usher, Chloe saw rosaries and little knotted-together squares of felt piled willy-nilly on a long table. A lot of money had also been strewn carelessly on the table; she spotted a hundred-dollar bill. She touched Jason's arm and showed him. "If they actually have this authenticated," he whispered, "people will tear this little church to shreds." A solemn usher appeared before them. "What *station?* Ah, the . . . eleventh. All right, Chloe?" Wide-eyed, Chloe shrugged. Jason shrugged back. As they followed the usher's black back, he whispered, "I always feel so ignorant in Catholic churches. One of these days, I'll learn the Stations of the Cross."

Down the aisle, the usher made Chloe go into the pew first, although she tried to hang back. "Good seats," a man already in the pew commented sidelong to her. He was kneeling. Chloe knelt. She didn't know what else to do.

"I'm glad we got the aisle," whispered Jason from her other side. He was kneeling too. "What we're supposed to look at is that veil just ahead." Chloe looked and, between the heads in front of her, saw an amorphous shape tented in filmy white and gold lace. The shape was on an altar. Candles flanked it; a gold cross was on top of it; a scalloped tablecloth was under it. Above it, in an alcove, was a statue of a slender madonna holding a slender child. After a bit, the gold cross usurped Chloe's eyes. Slowly, almost imperceptibly, it replicated itself under the veil and became a tiny gold figure who danced. It was hypnotic.

Dimly, within the veil, Chloe began to make out the face of a young man, sculpted as if in white marble, bearded, earnest, talking, obviously talking. The eyes gradually took on life, and the young man laughed. Then his expression turned to anguish . . . his eyes became shadowy sockets . . . his head tipped back . . . and he seemed to scream. The colors turned to sepia tints, ruddy hues. Chloe saw a muscular arm raised, a hammer strike. A cross angled itself across the kinetic scene. A mushroom-shaped cloud eclipsed everything. Chloe felt Jason get up on her left, but her legs wouldn't obey her impulse to follow. She wanted to see what was going to happen.

The colors changed again. Everything swirled together, dark, dusky. Soft and hard. As if it were happening for the first time, Chloe remembered an image she'd envisioned as a child, an image that had lured her into her own career, the image of Marie Curie's storehouse of pitchblende which, after years of mess and labor and sacrifice and help from her brilliant husband, Pierre, had become radium. In her child's eye, pitchblende had looked just like this soft-brown darkness. The distillation to radium had seemed both magical and logical, like this, this . . . Out of the darkness, in deep brown with a golden sheen, two heads appeared, like bronze, but flesh, dark and shadowy. Two heads, a man and a woman, who appeared to be kissing and indeed were kissing, Chloe made out, but they were also eating an apple. A golden apple, but a real apple, pulpy and juicy. They were eating it together.

Suddenly terrified to be alone, Chloe stood up, catching her feet in the kneeler. Her knees felt bruised. Quickly she went up the aisle of the church, out the door into the lowering golden sunlight. How much time had passed? "Some photos of the experience?"

"No, thank you." Chloe turned her head and saw the awful man with the camera who'd recognized Jason. Where was Jason?

"Free, no charge. Come on, take them!" The man pressed a small yellow packet on her; she slid it into her shoulder bag. Then she saw Jason standing by a maple tree on the sidewalk, smoking a cigarette. She felt her face break into a smile.

"What *happened?*" she asked him. "Why'd you *leave?*"

All around them, milling people were talking about what they'd seen in the veil: "Then it all went into a blur." "But St. Augustine came back, right?" "Looked like clouds to me." "St. Teresa had blond hair." "The blonde was the Blessed Virgin!" "Nothing but clouds. You're all crazy."

Jason ground out his cigarette on the sidewalk. "Chloe, did you hear anything in there?" He flicked his thumb at the church.

"Hear? No. It was all visual. Kinetic." Nonplussed and disoriented, Chloe hurried to keep up with him, crossing Route Six again. "What time is it?"

"Four forty-two."

"I was in there for—"

"Three hours, yes. You didn't hear anything?"

"Jason, tell me what happened to you."

He took a deep breath, glanced at her once, then looked straight ahead, not slowing his pace. His tone was steady, almost a monotone. "According to accounts I overheard while I was waiting for you, my perception was pretty straightforward at first, although I didn't see any saints. I saw people in the veil, biblical figures maybe, but I didn't know who they were. Kneeling in there, I began to wonder if a vision like this appears to the church rather than to the individual—was I, a Protestant, simply not recognizing saints any Catholic schoolchild would know? Then something happened. Vision stopped. Except for this crazy couple who kept praying through everything, all I saw were lights." Under the maples they walked fast along Route Six toward the road that would take them to Dolly's. "But what I *heard* was enough to send me screaming. Metaphorically, that is. Chloe, please don't stop listening to me. I feel all broken down. I mean it, Chloe."

Chloe looked at Jason. He was still walking, still looking straight ahead. She grabbed for his hand, amazed that he trusted her. "Jason, why?" She watched his profile, the strained temple muscles, the splendid zygomatic arch, as they walked.

"I heard, there was a point where I heard, quite simply, the apocalypse. Lights started flashing. I began to hear this pounding, this clanging pounding. Then I heard a god-awful scream that went on forever and turned into an explosion that jammed my ears. When it finally stopped, there was this awful hum, almost too high a frequency to hear, but it wouldn't stop, and I had to get out of there." They'd reached the wooden bridge over the gorge. Chloe took hold of the railing and pulled at Jason's hand till he stopped trying to walk. Stopped, he looked down at their comically struggling hands and laughed. "I'm acting like a little kid!" he said. Water tossed restlessly under the bridge. The gorge was all in shadow.

"You're scared," said Chloe coolly, respectful of his vulnerability. No glib comfort now! No easy soothing. He needed company, not condescension, just as she would need it in his place. "Probably I should be scared too," she slowly began, "because I saw what you heard. I was the eyes while you were the ears. If you're crazy, I'm crazy. If it's the apocalypse, it's the apocalypse. One or the other." Chloe let go of his hand. She caught her breath.

Jason leaned his flanks back against the railing of the bridge, folded his arms across his chest, and looked at her. "You were the eyes while I was the ears. Okay, tell me what you saw," he said, like a challenge. His head tilted arrogantly against the bruised and mottled backdrop of the gorge.

Tipping her head back like his, Chloe sorted through her shimmering, hazing, rapidly fading memory for the relevant action. She leaned back against the railing too and folded her arms. She knew she had seen relevant action (what kind of term was "relevant action"?), but the vision thereof had already become so ephemeral she felt as if she were making something up. Perhaps it *had* been all clouds, as the man said. "I saw—I guess it was the Crucifixion. Oh, it's so hard to describe without interpreting! What I saw was a head thrown back in agony, then an arm raise up with a hammer and pound. On the diagonal, a cross fell, slanted, appeared, I don't know, and then everything vanished like Hiroshima. A mushroom-shaped cloud." Jason let out his breath in a long whoosh. She could see the tension leave him, his face, his body, even his hands. Then he whistled.

"Hiroshima. That's when I left?"

"About then. Jason, this is so hard to remember!"

"You saw all the evil in the world that nailed him to the cross. Weren't you scared?"

"I was fascinated. I wanted to see what was going to happen after." Hadn't she been scared after? After . . . ? Suddenly she realized she *couldn't remember* what had happened after.

Jason's laugh told her that his memory of the "experience"—what else to call it?—was fading too. His eyes warmed and softened. He wouldn't think to ask her what had happened after. "That kid with the goats was right, Chloe. You're brave."

Chloe saw the imagery on the periphery of her mind brighten, just as everything evaporated from the core. "I just thought the silliest thing, Jason. I just thought this line from *Gone with the Wind*. What a warren of nonsequiturs the memory is! It's when Atlanta is burning, and Scarlett says to Rhett, 'Of course I'm scared, and if you had the sense of a goat, you'd be scared too.' " They grinned at each other, and then, "Jason, there's a God!" Chloe heard herself exclaim. "It's true. It's really true!" She laughed and he laughed, and their laughter seemed to blend like music. It echoed in the gorge. Chloe felt pierced by a joy so wild and sweet she could have died that minute.

NINE
A Wild Mad Night
Thursday, August 1

1 THE SLEEPING PORCH

"Aiee!"

"No! No!"

"You got the little red bastard!"

"Doubled *and* vulnerable!" Mingled cries of triumph and chagrin rose from the front porch of the Barnes cottage to the screened sleeping porch above.

"Aunt Chloe must have made her grand slam."

"Or else she got set. I think the cry of triumph was Daddy's." A tall, pink-shaded lamp on the table between their cots shed light on the fat, open books of both Liz and Betsy. Elise's cot, farthest from the door, was still neatly hospital-cornered, although Liz and Betsy had borrowed her pillows. She wouldn't mind, they had glumly agreed. *She* had a date. *They* had decided to go to bed early and read.

"It's so hot. I wish we had a slave like at Tara to fan us." Giggles. The August night was hot and close, and the girls, propped on pillows against the frame of the screens, idly shifted about in their baby-doll pajamas, kicking off blankets, rucking up sheets, in search of a fugitive breeze. A pink dab of Clearasil decorated each face. Liz's was on her cheek, Betsy's right between the eyes.

"There'll be a thunderstorm. There's always a thunderstorm when Sir Isaac won't come up the stairs. I hope it won't wash away the dig."

"How'd you like to be at a drive-in when there's a thunderstorm?"

"Betsy, I wouldn't mind being at that drive-in tonight if there were a tornado."

"You know Elise is with *Zack*, Liz. What're you worried about?"

"Elise is with Zack and Erich."

"*And* Olivia."

"That's what I'm worried about."

"You're worried about *Olivia?*" Betsy sat up on her cot and turned to look at Liz.

Liz didn't look up from her book. "Olivia taught Erich to French kiss."

"Oh, *ugh!*" Betsy gagged. "How do you know? Who told you?"

"Selina." For a second Liz looked as if she wanted to cry.

Betsy leaned back against her pillows and the one she'd pilfered from Elise. She bit her lip thoughtfully. "Maybe Olivia was better-looking when she was young."

"What do you suppose she's up to?"

"You mean, asking Elise to go with them? Picking her up first in the station wagon so your father wouldn't ask questions? I think Olivia's trying to split the three of us up and get Elise on her side. I don't think Elise should have gone."

"Elise thinks the whole fight is pretty childish."

"Elise didn't get called a nymphomaniac like you did!"

"Oh, that." Liz waved the fighting word away with her hand and sat up Indian-fashion. Her pillows toppled behind her. "Bets, you know what I think? I think Olivia is trying to make up with us and just doesn't know how to go about it. I think that's why she asked Elise, who's the oldest and most sensible, to go with them. I think it was probably a nice gesture."

"Oh, Liz, sometimes you're so charitable you remind me of 'that mealy-mouthed ninny,' *Melanie!*" Betsy tapped her fat gray book meaningfully.

"Shit," said Liz. She leaned back where her pillows had been and banged her head on the windowsill. She and Betsy laughed. Liz retrieved her pillows from the floor, picked up her book, and they both went back to reading. Betsy's fat book was (still) *Gone with the Wind,* enthusiastically recommended to her by Liz. On the table between their cots, Betsy kept her Webster's Collegiate Dictionary that had her name, "Betsy Wilson," stamped in gold on its blue cover. Both she and Liz consulted it dutifully whenever they encountered an unfamiliar word ("fornication" was Betsy's favorite thus far), but lately Liz had been having trouble even finding words from her fat book in the dictionary. There were a lot of foreign words. Liz sighed often. She was reading James Joyce's *Ulysses,* specifically because it had been *not* recommended by her father. Understanding about one fourth of what she read and appreciating perhaps a fourth of that, Liz had by tonight nonetheless blundered stubbornly through to ("Let's hear it for the little lady!" Betsy cheered) the last section.

Lightning flashed occasionally. Distant thunder rumbled. Laughter floated up from the four adults on the porch below. "Have you noticed how much later Mother's been staying up lately?" Liz idly asked Betsy, but Betsy's blue eyes were now glued to her book. "I think I'll read something easy after this," Liz went on. "I think I might even read the Anne of Green Gables books again." Getting no response from her cousin, Liz sighed and dipped back into Joyce.

"Liz!" suddenly exclaimed Betsy. "Rhett's carrying her up the stairs! He is! She's putting her arms around his neck!" Betsy's breath came faster; she gripped her book and sat on the edge of her cot. "Oh, *shit!*"

"What's the matter?" Liz put her finger on her place on the page and looked at Betsy, eyes slightly glazed.

"They skip the night—why do they always do that? Oh, Liz, don't you hate it when they skip the night? Look at this!" Betsy tried to make Liz look at her book, but Liz wouldn't.

"This part of my book has no punctuation," she explained. "I keep losing my place. Besides, Bets, I already read that wild mad night thing." Liz flopped over on her stomach and resumed reading, pointing with her index finger. Betsy hunched up her knees, the better to hold the heavy first-edition *Gone with the Wind*. Concentration thickened. Lightning forked. Emotions steamed from the books. Betsy wept a little about Scarlett's miscarriage—so much for "wild mad nights." Liz's eyes doggedly followed her finger, word by word. All of a sudden she shrieked. Betsy jumped.

"What? What is it?"

"Oh, my *God*. Listen to this, Betsy, listen to this. They don't skip the night here. Or maybe it's the afternoon. Who cares? Listen." Liz turned over, sat up, and read:

"yes, when I lit the lamp yes because he must have come 3 or 4 times with that tremendous big red brute of a thing he has I thought the vein or whatever the dickens they call it was going to burst though his nose is not so big after I took off all my things with the blinds down after my hours dressing and perfuming it like iron or some kind of thick crowbar standing all the time . . . ."

Liz read aloud well—her father had taught her how to breathe and project and be patient—and she even caught the lilt of Molly Bloom's brogue; but, without punctuation, the junctures gave her trouble, so it took Betsy a minute to grasp what the salient "it" was. When she did, "You're making it up, Liz!" she cried. She slackened her shoulders, let her body go limp, fell back against the pillows, and stared at Liz. Liz was laughing.

"Making it up? How could I make up something like that, Betsy? I can't even figure out where the legs go!"

"Well, *go on.*"

Liz resumed, occasional incredulous gasps punctuating her reading:

"no I never in all my life felt anyone had one the size of that to make you feel all full up he must have eaten a whole sheep after whats the idea of making us like that with a big hole in the middle of us like a stallion driving it up into you because that's all they want out of you . . ."

"Let me see; oh, let me see!" Betsy jumped up from her cot and came over to Liz's. She sat next to Liz. They leaned back against the pillows and looked at *Ulysses* together. "Oh, that crowbar! I like that the best, but I don't know why. How come she starts talking about something else?"

"Her mind is skipping around. I think she was maybe asleep and wakes up in the middle of the night."

"You think? Why doesn't it just say so?"

Liz said drily, "If Daddy hadn't forbidden me to read it, I'd ask him."

"No *wonder* he didn't want you to read it!" Betsy stared glassily into space for a minute, then asked, "Liz?"

"Hmmm?"

"Do you understand the crowbar?"

"I understand that. It's the legs I don't understand. Where are the women supposed to put their legs, I wonder? But that's an erection. The man's, uh, penis stiffens. A lot of blood rushes into it, or something. We learned in biology. Erectile tissue. Like our nipples."

"Our nipples?"

"Yes, you know how when you're cold or you touch them—"

"Touch them?"

"Betsy, you must have touched your nipples."

"I might have, but I don't remember. What happens?"

"They get stiff. They get all wrinkly. Look." Liz pulled her pajama top off over her head, exposing pale, shy, beautiful breasts. With her thumb, she flicked one pink nipple. It stiffened. Betsy squealed. Betsy took off her pajama top. Liz reached out and touched Betsy's left nipple. They watched it become erect. Betsy squealed again. She touched Liz's other nipple. They touched back and forth like a game, till they were lightly pinching. They laughed. There was a knock on the door of the sleeping porch. There was no lock on the door. The girls grabbed frantically for Liz's rumpled sheet to cover their chests. "Come in," called Liz.

Liz's father put his head in the door. "Is Elise back yet?"

"No, Daddy. She won't be back for hours."

"What're you two doing?"

"Just talking."

"All right. But don't squeal so. You scare me." Liz's father went out, closing the door.

Liz and Betsy were stifling giggles. "Hurry," said Liz. "Get your top back on! He'll send Mother up. He is such a chicken." Fumbling, they helped each other with their pajama tops. Liz's had buttons shaped like hearts. Then they sat up very straight and prim against the pillows on Liz's bed, pulling her sheet over them again. Another knock came at the door, and without waiting for anyone to say, Come in, Liz's mother came in.

"Have you got your pajamas on?"

"Huh?" said Liz and Betsy together. They pulled off the sheet and looked down at themselves.

"Sorry," Liz's mother said. She shook her head and laughed a little. "Come on, Betsy, get in your own bed. It's too hot to be doubling up." Betsy got up and got into her own bed. Her pajama top was on backward. Liz's mother smiled at them from the doorway. "Night," she said.

The girls waited till a hoot of disbelief from the front porch told them that Liz's mother was downstairs. Then they allowed themselves to become convulsed with laughter. "Have you got your pajamas on?" Betsy mimicked her Aunt Abbie. Their laughter lost itself in the ribald laughter from below.

"Bets, your top is on backward!"

"Yours is buttoned up all wrong!"

"You know the funniest thing, Bets?"

"What?"

"Daddy must think he had an incest fantasy!"

Oh, it was awful, horrid, beastly! Betsy had been right on the mark that one couldn't trust Olivia, right on the mark! At the drive-in, while they'd watched not one but two films about a heavy-breathing, bloodthirsty, faceless murderer, Olivia had slyly, almost without Elise's noticing it, goaded the boys into consuming so much beer that now, on the road back to the lake, Erich had declared himself ready to kill anyone within reach, and Zack, who just a few minutes before had been toasting "depravity, debauchery, and damnation," was almost comatose. Regretting she'd worn a pretty challis skirt no one had even seen, now so wrinkled it would never look the same, Elise sat gingerly in the backseat with Zack and, with alarm, saw Olivia in the driver's seat suddenly turn the wheel and pull the station wagon to a stop on the side of the main road near the Lake Lenni Lenape Inn. "Why are you stopping?" Elise called, hearing her voice desperate. "Olivia, let's take these poor boys *home.*"

Olivia ignored Elise. Elise had a momentary scary fancy she might have become inaudible. "There's going to be a thunderstorm," Olivia finally turned to tell her, after she'd set the emergency brake. Her tone was supercilious. "I don't like to drive in thunderstorms. Erich," she crooned then, "have I got something for you."

From the backseat, Erich's big head was briefly visible as it flopped over in Olivia's direction. "Olivia, I love you. Honest to God." He sounded so exactly like a drunk in the movies, Elise couldn't help giggling. "You're not pretty as Liz," Erich went on, "but you're understanding, by Christ."

"Zack, wake up," Olivia said seductively over the seat. "Erich, stop that! That tickles. And *that hurts.* Don't bite." Olivia flaunted a bottle over the seat. "Zack, wake up." Then Olivia and the bottle disappeared.

Elise called out, "Olivia, why are you doing this to them? We were having such a good time till you started getting them drunk." Olivia's head reappeared. Her eyes consulted Elise's with interest. Elise couldn't help asking, "Are you intentionally destructive?"

"I think I might be," Olivia allowed, giving Elise a little nod of approval. "That's very well put."

"Whiskoo!" Erich suddenly howled. "Whiskoo, Zack." His head surfaced for a second, then fell with a thud. Olivia turned to attend to him. "Livia's got us some whiskoo," his voice came faintly.

"Whiskoo," Zack sleepily echoed, his tenor voice making it sound like a song. "Whiskoo." He fell asleep again, across Elise's lap this time. Elise tried to push him upright. There was lightning in the sky over the inn. An awful clap of thunder came very soon. "One thousand, two thousand, three thousand, four thousand," she heard Zack count. "Four miles away. We'll all be killed," he mumbled, laughing.

"Close windows," called Olivia. Elise crawled to close the back windows and immediately felt trapped. Erich's big arm swung the whiskey bottle over the seat. Elise ducked. Zack sat up like a shot, tilted the bottle, and took a swig. Elise could smell it as it spilled down his face and splashed into her hair. Oh! She could feel the warm whiskey run down her neck.

She moved as far away from Zack as she could. For a clever boy he really was behaving like an ass, she decided, feeling tears sting her eyes. They'd had such a nice conversation at the drive-in too—had gotten excited about how the unkillable villain in the film reminded them both, at the same moment, of Rasputin. Zack even remembered how much poison and how many bullets it had taken to bring the resilient Russian down. "Resilient Russian," that's what Zack had called Rasputin. A clever boy, Zack. Elise felt his head encroach her shoulder and didn't push him away. Back at the drive-in, Rasputin had led them to archetypes: could a real, historical figure be an archetype? By some quirky path, the conversation had then veered to Jung, whom Zack had precociously read. Zack was awfully interested in how Jung thought, in the Book of Job, that God was morally inferior to Job. Now, letting Zack sleep against her shoulder, Elise wondered what Jason would say about that interpretation of Job. Perhaps if she asked him cleverly enough, he'd do a sermon for her, just as he had done the one on laughter for Aunt Chloe. Elise smiled a little to think of telling Daphne and Jane back at St. Catherine's, "A minister preached a sermon for me." It would be almost as super a coup as having Mick Jagger or Greg Lake write a song for her!

"I hate the fucking Indians," complained Erich from the front seat. Elise wondered how the Indians had come up. "I don't like Fred's fucking dig, Livia. I won't work on Freddy's dig no more. I won't let Selina boss me round no more. I'm sick of the lake, Livia, and I'm sick of school. I wish I was old enough to go in the Navy, or home enough to go to bed."

"You're drunk," said Olivia fondly. "Erich, I think it's time for the special treat now. No, not that one, Erich. Stop that!"

"Special treat!" demanded Erich.

"Special treat," echoed Zack from Elise's shoulder.

"Olivia, let's take them home," Elise implored.

"After the special treat," said Olivia. "You'll like it too, Elise. Charlie Scott got it for me." Getting up on her knees and leaning over the front seat, Olivia showed Elise a slender, molded meerschaum pipe. Elise's father had one like it.

"Charlie gave you a pipe?"

Olivia laughed. "No," she said, "I got that in Germany. Here's what Charlie got for me." Olivia took a small plastic bag from her pocketbook. Carefully she edged some of its contents into the bowl of her pipe. "Did you ever smoke marijuana, Elise?"

"No," Elise said. She watched Olivia's fingers deftly tamp the pipe. Olivia lit a match and sucked on the pipe. A sweet smell filled the station wagon, making it feel cozy, a refuge from the lightning.

"It's a peace pipe," said Olivia softly. "I want us to be friends, Elise. I've been wanting a woman friend." Olivia sounded as if she meant it, Elise thought, rather flattered to be called a "woman." She took the pipe when Olivia passed it to her. She put it in her mouth and tentatively breathed. The embers in the bowl brightened. "Hold it, Elise. Don't blow it out yet." Elise held, enjoyed, and finally let the smoke out. Oh. The station wagon turned warm and red. Olivia's eyes over the pipe looked soft. Elise felt her center shift, making her comfortable in the backseat. Zack's head felt nice on her shoulder.

"Whiskoo," called Erich softly, like a dove. Elise laughed.

"Try the pipe," Olivia urged Erich.

"Hate the Indians. Whiskoo."

Olivia passed Elise the pipe again. The air in the station wagon was wispy and soft with smoke. Elise drew on the pipe long, holding as much as she could. "Is Zack still asleep, Elise?" she heard Olivia ask. I think so, she started to say, but forgot.

"Erich, you go in the back with Elise. Send Zack up here so I can wake him up. I miss his brain." Elise was jostled by the changing of the guard. Buckingham Palace. Leaning from the front seat, Erich picked Zack up under the arms and cajoled him into the front seat. Elise took another long drag on the pipe before she passed it back to Olivia. Olivia smiled at her. Olivia's eyes were warm. Elise giggled as Erich came over from the front seat and sprawled on top of her. Her skirt pushed up. Erich put his mouth on her mouth, and he kissed her. His mouth tasted of whiskoo.

"More grass, Elise?" Olivia's voice came faintly from the front seat. It was starting to rain outside the windows. The rain streamed down the windows like . . . rain.

"No, thank you," Elise dreamily replied. Her mind seemed to have moved from her head to where Erich was fumbling with her skirt. Then she felt something warm and blunt and unpleasant fall against her bare thigh. Oh, *God!* She felt Erich's big hand move her hand toward that spooky, unwieldy thing. Oh, God. Elise sat up and tried to cry out, but no sound came. It was like a nightmare.

"Livia," Erich complained, "she won't do me. You promised you'd do me." His knee ground into Elise's thigh as he tried to climb into the front seat. She could feel a bruise start to form, black and blue and mottled.

"I'll do you, Erich," said Olivia soothingly from the front seat. "Come on . . ."

When Erich's weight completely left her, Elise said politely, "I think I'll get out now." She reached for the door handle, rather surprised that the door opened. The station wagon had not become a cage. "I'm going home now, Olivia." Putting out her leg, she saw that her challis skirt had been ripped right through the hem on both sides. Erich had big hands. "Good night, Olivia."

"Don't go away mad," Elise heard drift from the front seat as she plunged into the thunderstorm.

"I'll just go away," she said out loud, as she headed up the road away from the inn, feeling the driving rain wash her clean of beer and smoke and whiskoo.

3 THE MANSE

Before any visible, audible signs of one's impending, in fact while the sun was still shining hotly in a pallid blue sky, Jason anticipated the thunderstorm; he always did. He should have been a weatherman. There was going to be a beaut of a thunderstorm. A couple of hours after dark he was sipping bourbon over ice, waiting for something, anything. He sprawled back in one of the parlor love seats, his feet in the wing chair. His eyes gazed at its pale-blue shimmer. The ashtray at his elbow was full. At the other end of his pacing route (he'd been pacing intermittently for some time), he'd left a can of beer and another full ashtray on the kitchen table. Left them near Calvin's sculpture of Queen Esther, which was almost finished and scary as hell. Left them also next to his recalcitrant typewriter, which had balked at continuing "Synesthesia in Acts." Acts speak louder than words. Jason wanted to shout. He wanted to shout the name Chloe as loud as Sam Barnes did. Wanted to shout, and she would come.

He had the manse to himself for the first time in weeks, Jason had, and there was going to be a thunderstorm, and maybe Chloe Otway would come and be caught and stay all night. That lithe body next to his, the silky dark hair, those eyes . . . romantic dreams. But he'd made it clear to her—had he not?—last night at the Barneses' despite the mob scene there, Tradd and Calvin included, that he'd be alone tonight, that Olson and Mathews had departed last week (unfortunately without all of their luggage) to Palmyra, New York, for the Hill Cumorah Pageant. He and Sam had joked about it. "How many kitchens do you suppose they'll devastate in New York?" And he'd told Abbie Barnes within earshot of Chloe ("Here, Jason," Abbie ordered, "you husk the corn") where Tradd and Calvin were going, that Tradd had clamored and pleaded ("Are you actually so heartless, Calvin Cunningham, as to let my poor baby perhaps be born all alone in a strange place?") till Calvin had agreed to accompany her to the

Corning Summer Theatre, a good hundred miles away, to see a re-
vival of LeRoi Jones's *Dutchman.*

"She'll probably knife me on the way home just like the sexy white
lady in the play," Calvin had added, eying his paring knife as if he
meant it, then resumed chopping the homegrown cucumbers to put
in the sour cream sauce Elise was so flamboyantly concocting with a
whisk. Jason kept ducking. Sour cream flew about the kitchen like
rumors. Abbie Barnes, bright-eyed, interested, talkative, showing off
delft-patterned paper plates with matching napkins, questioned Calvin severely about *Dutchman.*

(Jason had seen *Dutchman* performed at the University of Virginia
when he was an undergraduate. Although he was a Southerner, he
had not known before that, in his gut, how deep lay the black hatred
of whites.)

"Wouldn't you call the play racist, Calvin?" Abbie asked. "Oh, I
don't mean what the white woman does; I mean what the playwright
has done to the white woman. You must admit the play certainly
pillories white women. I'm getting so sick of race," Abbie ran on with
uncharacteristic vehemence. "I'm beginning to think even ethnicity
is pernicious. You can't imagine, Calvin Cunningham, you raised on
Baldwin and LeRoi Jones, excuse me, Amiri Baraka, what it's like to
grow up a WASP in this country. Nobody likes us, we don't like each
other, and, unlike other groups, we haven't even any cute little tribal
customs to be proud of."

"Hear, hear!" Sam passing by with garlic bread for the oven had
cheered; and all the while Jason was conscious of Chloe at the
butcher-block table, her amazing legs propped on a high kitchen
stool, arguing amiably with Bill Wilson, who was cracking ice cube
trays. "You can't be conservative about science at your age, Bill!"
Chloe raised her hands from her knees. Her ankles were crossed. The
line of her legs was— "Einstein kicked himself for being cautious
when he was young. The new physics is the only physics now. It is
the *youth* of science." She flung one hand back.

"Really!" said Bill.

"See how I've learned to delegate, Jason." Abbie's voice pulled him
from his contemplation of Chloe, and he went dutifully at the corn
again, a big pile of corn, being careful with the silk, as Jessamine had
taught him. "Martha should have delegated. Let Jesus wash the
dishes." Abbie flourished her hands at the kitchen like a conductor.

"Everyone but Chloe. Ah, well, Chloe pays her way like Mary of Bethany, with her wit. And her legs." Mary of Bethany? Jason's eyes had flicked again to the supple, tanned legs. Chloe's legs. The part for the whole, he thought now, slightly drunk in his parlor. No, no, no. His mind rejected the inadvertent, indecent pun. He really had intended a decorous figure of speech, and there did exist such a figure of speech. He was sure of it. Some polysyllabic word like "synesthesia" he couldn't pronounce right now to save his life.

Jason took another long pull on the dark smoky bourbon in his glass. My father died of this, he thought with customary resentment; and then something happened. He thought the words "my dad," like Fred Bunyan said them. He tried the words. In the Meeting Street house, which *my dad* had inherited from three generations of Baynards, with a beautiful, but cold, dissatisfied wife and two children, aged six and eight, *my dad* had too much of this soothing liquid. . . . That's all. Once I was crying, and I remember him coming to my room from the piazza, looking desperate, as if he'd escaped from something, and I said, "Dad, I didn't mean to cause trouble, but I was crying because I wanted you to come even though Mother said you spoil us."

He said, "Whatever trouble there was was worth it."

"My dad." That was the name for my dad.

"Synecdoche." That was the name for the part-for-the-whole.

With the highfalutin figure of speech, the manse parlor condensed around Jason like a mock-up of the generations of bloodless Southern rhetoric he trailed behind him, the unnumbered girls he'd . . . To get on with my life, he thought impatiently now, riding roughshod over the past, Chloe Otway, the woman I love, has been adequately though indirectly informed that tonight the Mormons are in Palmyra, Tradd and Calvin at a distant theater watching *Dutchman.* She could get free; she could, she could. Tony Otway didn't even show up last night. Of course she and Sam were thick as thieves; Sam was always hanging around her. Come to think of it, he, Jason, never got to talk to Chloe alone at the Barnes cottage anymore. Since Wappasenink, their most intimate encounters had been once when she trounced him at tennis with Sam watching and another time on the Barnes dock amid a clutter of very noisy others. Ah, she'd been so poised, he'd felt like a kid. Reading the New Testament for the first time (he gathered), Chloe had treated him to a charming diatribe

against Paul and Peter for putting the early Christian women down,
when Jesus had clearly wanted them equal. "Acts doesn't even mention that the *women* were first at the tomb. You'd think Jesus might
have said something about that on the Road to Damascus! While he
was about it!"

Sprawled in adjacent chaise lounges, Chloe and Jason had laughed.
For Jason, their laughter still seemed to reel in the air over the lake,
caught for all time. Chloe's relationship with a God she had just met
enchanted Jason. She was so feisty. Quite a coup for God she was,
he'd thought, that day on the dock. Quite a coup in that bikini.

"Oh, *God!*" Jason heard himself say out loud. Could you pray for
something you weren't supposed to have and still expect the promise
to hold? "What do you want me to do for you?" "Master, let me
receive my sight." "Master, *I want her.*" Lightning flashed outside the
windows. Ah, at last. Jason got up from the love seat and paced once
around the parlor, then reversed his pattern and sat down in the
slippery wing chair, putting his feet on the love seat. Closing his eyes,
he went back, as he often did, to that glittering day in Wappasenink:
the goats and the gorge and the miracle.

He'd been scared shitless of the miracle. Never been so scared in
his life, as vulnerable as he'd ever be. Had he acted like a boy? Jason
wondered about that a lot now. He couldn't bear to think that Chloe
had been mothering him. Reflecting on it all once again, he decided
once again that she hadn't been mothering him. She'd assumed their
equality; her tact had been perfect. I am like you, her marvelous green
eyes touching his, filling his had signaled. And then she'd presented
her gift, that excited, wonderful, eccentric belief, with total trust that
he could handle such a revelation.

Because he was her pastor.

And that moment he had fallen in love.

Jason groaned. Because he was her pastor, he was not allowed to
fall in love with her. It was very simple. And, thank God, the pastor-
ing had come easy—his joy in her joy, his fascination with the imaginative, mad ways that God worked (the Freud-Jung connection was a
stroke of skewed genius; Chloe was convinced her belief had come
through her intellect and would not have accepted it otherwise), the
way his heart had leapt when she'd admitted that, yes, at first, "I
thought I might be falling for you, Jason," and yet he'd been able
merely to counter, "Yes, it's a little like falling in love, isn't it?"

"Not exactly like," she'd discriminated. "There doesn't seem to be any metaphor for it. It isn't like. It *is*. Oh, Jason, I am so happy. I can't believe I'm this happy. Will I stay this happy?"

"Nope," he said, keeping his tone casual. "But you're there. You'll take it, good or bad. You're too adventurous a person to go back just because it might be easier."

"I know," she'd answered softly, turning to look at the gorge. Ah, the greens! soft dress, hard, cruel gorge, lucid eyes turned back on him. "I know a point of no return when I see one. I wish I knew, though, how to order my life around it. My life so already completely *is*, you see."

Now, as he sipped dusky bourbon, crazy Byronic plans formed and exploded like Mormon firecrackers in Jason's brain. Give her a new life. Sweep her away. There's that trust fund next year from your dad. You'll never find a woman like this again. *Carpe diem!* So what if she's older? So what if she's married? So what if she has this brilliant career already established? For her career was brilliant; he'd sounded Sam out about it. "Jesus, Jason, I don't understand a word she writes, mind you; but, oh, has she a manner and a tone. I'm convinced the Y chromosome is hopelessly inferior to the X; I think gamogenesis, whatever that is, is the sexiest word in the language." Fred Bunyan had volunteered that his high school used a biology textbook in which the section on genetics was "written by the Mrs. Otway we know. She talked to me about it. She's nice." High praise, from Fred.

Ah, he was desperate; he was head over heels. His body was on a rack. His body—

Two years of beautifully controlled celibacy, and what a smug exercise in pride they seemed. Now he was assailed with unexpected, ungovernable erections and wild erotic dreams the likes of which he hadn't had since he was sixteen. His body beat, it throbbed, it woke him up. He would lie there panting, thinking, The body is not important.

She was. For the first time since his own lightning stroke of belief two years before, Jason could not face the thought of being alone. His mind had touched hers; they were synesthetic—that suddenly so useful word. "I was the eyes while you were the ears," she had said so coolly. Did she have any idea how rare such a communion was, or did she take it (as she was still taking all the early glories of belief) quite for granted? Did she not know how astringent God would become?

Did she think that any person she sat down with at a miracle would automatically share her perception? The miracle. If only they could remember the details! Drawn back, Jason laughed. The details had run through their fingers like water.

In the car on the way back from Wappasenink, they'd confessed simultaneous amnesia about the miracle, and comedy overtook them; they laughed and laughed. "If anyone asks us, Jason," Chloe proposed, "we'll look very exalted and say the miracle was *extraordinary.*" The passionately vacuous word had broken them up. "And you know what Sam'll say?" she guessed. "Very ironically Sam'll say, 'Indeed.' "

Matt Bernstein had used "extraordinary" in his half-jeering, half-yearning article about "The Miracle up the Road" in the *Bugle.* Jason had read the article attentively, looking for clues to what had happened to him; he wound up thinking something might have happened to Bernstein too: "This tiny Roman Catholic church, made of clapboard and sheetrock, painted heaven-blue and gilt on the inside, selling rosaries and scapulars on a table near the holy water, has nothing to recommend it but its miracle, which is extraordinary." Hmm. Jason shook his head, remembering. Then he himself had used "extraordinary" on Esther when, suspiciously, she'd reported that Mrs. Chandler and Mrs. Thomas had seen him and Chloe *together* in Wappasenink. "Mrs. Otway was wearing a skimpy little sundress, they said." "We went to take a look at the miracle," Jason told her, as he lined up his purchases. Did Tradd really crave a lot of milk, or just think she should? Ten half-gallons a week seemed rather lavish. Sitting squatly on her stool behind the counter while Jason thought about milk and how much it cost, Esther put her hands on her hips.

"Is that damn-fool R.C. miracle worth seeing?"

"Esther, it was extraordinary."

"Indeed," said Esther, curling her short upper lip. She folded her arms across her chest and tipped her stool back against the razor blades and the cigarettes.

The miracle. It was like an Indian gift. Given, then taken back. Leaving him and Chloe with nothing but the memory of something uncannily shared. Some laughter fretting the air in a remote area of northern Pennsylvania. Why? What was it for? What do you want, God? Jason's mind called. What do you want me to do? Why give me this, why show me love when I can't have it? Indian giver!

On which bittersweet internal note, a gust of wind swept through the parlor, blowing out a screen. The screen clattered to the floor. Jason closed the window. He started to replace the screen, then put it down. He sat back in the wing chair, lit a cigarette, and closed his eyes, treating himself to another rerun of the scene at the gorge in Wappasenink.

When the knocking came at the front door, Jason at first incorporated it into his dream, a crazy dream about a hammer pounding Calvin's cherry wood statue of Queen Esther without Calvin's volition. "It's pounding without me, man!"

"All creation comes from God," the statue declared smugly. "Forbear!" The pounding continued. Thunder clapped. Jason woke up with his body perilously suspended between the wing chair and the love seat. They'd moved apart while he slept. His heels were on the love seat, his shoulders on the chair. Jason looked around rather wildly, feeling not awake, feeling late for something, feeling naked though he wasn't. He finally got up and opened the door. Both her fists still raised to knock, Elise Barnes almost fell into the manse. She was soaked to the skin, wild-eyed and frantic.

"Jason!" She threw her arms around his neck just as Tradd had the day she arrived. Ah, no belly between them, though. No sister, this. Elise was slender, small-boned, and soft as a kitten, clinging and amorous. Wait a minute, Jason's mind objected, while his body moved, couldn't help moving, pulled forward as she moved against him, so skillful, so unbelievably *experienced* he gathered that errant moment on the dance floor had been no accident. He could not remember ever so wanton a spiral of the hips.

"Honeybunch," he caught his breath to say. Lightly he kissed her forehead. "What's up?" he asked then, before he realized the absurdity of the question. Up—what a preposition! His hands went around her buttocks, he couldn't help it, couldn't bear for the exquisite pelvic contact to cease. "You certainly are wet," he inanely commented.

"Jason, I want you to make love to me," Elise returned. Her voice was light as feathers, almost singsong. Her wet clothes seemed to meld the two of them together. She moved against him in a manner almost to climb him. Her breasts softly fit wherever they touched him, like lake water.

Keep your head. What head? God, this isn't fair. "Elise," Jason said quietly, trying to sound fatherly, "I'm not sure you know what you're getting into." What a stupid thing to say, as if what she were getting into were a foregone conclusion!

"Of course I know what I'm getting into!" protested Elise. "I've done it before. In England people are much more liberated. Sex is more a part of *life* than it is here." I'll take you home, Jason planned to say, and instead he kissed her. Her tongue enticed, then searched on its own. Her body was incredibly responsive, as if to shape exactly what she wanted—long and lean and mobile—from his body. He was breathless. If she hadn't "done it" before, she sure was a natural, a part of his brain commented cynically. Ah, what else was there to do with this lovely sort of body, this soft, light, flexible body, but pick it up? Irresistible. Jason slipped an arm under her knees and held her, keeping her close to the place to which his center was ineluctably moving, blurring his eyes, pulsing in his ears, reemerging to throb against her. Ah, celibacy!

"Jason, I want you," Elise said clearly, head cradled against his shoulder. Her long hair smelled sweet and wet. He thought he might be dreaming. Holding her like a sleepy child in his arms, he turned and carried her up the stairs.

Later he would remember that, yes, he'd been gentle despite his desperate physical plight (can celibacy under any circumstances be *right?* even possible? he seriously wondered); yes, he had taken it slow, undressing her on Great-grandmother Beau's patchwork quilt that served him as bedspread; yes, he had looked at her perfect body with an appreciation that she smiled at; yes, he had touched her and gently introduced her hands to his body which she'd wonderingly explored ("Like this?"); yes, he had kissed her at the pulse points and caused her eventually to arch her back and demand him ("Now, Jason. Do it now"); yes, he'd made sure she was ready even then, and she was ready—oh, ready, oh, wet, sweet, tight—and then his mind went, his memory went. His long-denied body led him on with a vengeance; it groaned into a motion and a rhythm outside him, and then he was lost, he was gone. The pillared bandstand at Battery Park filled his eyes. The stone rolled, and the cave closed.

After, Jason kept his eyes closed against the experience, letting fragments of protest silently whirl. So unexpected. If a temptation so unfair. If a punishment for pride . . . "Jason!" said Elise. She shook his shoulder. He opened his eyes and looked at her. She had sat up, cross-legged. She was smiling. Her long auburn hair almost covered her. She looked delicious, like a dream. "It was *smashing!*" she exulted. "I knew it'd be smashing!" Her face was positively triumphant. She gracefully swung her legs to the floor and started putting on clothes. They were still wet. "I'll just tell them all I got caught in the rain," Elise told him. "I was caught in the rain, wasn't I? Jason, you'd better dress. You'll have to drive me home. You got your muffler fixed with Aunt Chloe, I know. What are these?" In her T-shirt and underpants, she leaned to look at the medals around his neck. She fingered the cross.

"Calvin made that," Jason said. He disengaged her fingers from the cross, sat up, and started pulling on his jeans. "Where do your aunt and uncle think you are?"

Elise laughed. "They think I'm at the drive-in films with Olivia and Erich and Zack. Don't worry; they won't tell. They have their own glass to guard. Especially Olivia!" She sounded like a cheeky British teenager. She pulled a torn skirt over her head and tucked the T-shirt in. She leaned to finger Jason's cross again. "May I have it?" she asked prettily.

Jason was startled. "Well, I could have Calvin make you one. All he needs is a hammer and a can." Elise looked disappointed. Did she want a talisman? A scalp?

"I'll have Calvin make you one," he repeated, buttoning up his shirt. Elise sat down on the bed to put on her shoes. So did he.

"Okay," she said, fastening the buckle on her sandal. Sidelong, Jason saw another wave of bright-eyed glee come over her face. "Jason, I feel bloody marvelous! I just knew you'd be terrific!" Elise fell back on Great-grandmother Beau's quilt and stretched voluptuously. Her laugh was exultant.

As he stood up, held out his hand to her, and said, "Come on, babe, we'd better get you home," Jason found himself wondering just who had had whom.

TEN
The Thorns of Life
Wednesday, August 21-
Saturday, August 31

Ironically it would fall upon Shelley, at his best a smart-alecky adolescent, at his worst a pretentious prig, at all times no more than a minor poet, to pen the extravagant phrase that precisely captures the spirit of the romantic.

Samuel Coleridge Barnes,
The Thorns of Life

"I fall upon the thorns of life! I bleed!"
Shelley, "Ode to the West Wind"

1 THE MANSE

Halfway up the crazy catwalk, Elise had second thoughts, felt her stomach flutter and her breath catch, completely lost her nerve, turned to flee; but coming around the turn behind her, like a roped-together team of mountain climbers, were Zack, Betsy, Kevin and Denny MacNamara, and bringing up the rear Erich, flirting outrageously with Wendy Bernstein. ("You see those tits?" Elise had heard him mutter earlier to Zack about Wendy's tight green T-shirt with the demure little lace collar, thus having caused Liz to forge proudly ahead with Selina and Fred, as if she cared as much as they did about the future of the dig.) Conversing nonstop over his shoulder with Betsy about Dungeons and Dragons and why he'd chucked it, Zack bumped into Elise. "I'm sorry, Elise. Bets, I was even playing it in my sleep. I'd lost touch with reality. Yeah, cold turkey. Elise, will you move your little ass?" Trapped. Elise turned to continue climbing. She fixed her eyes on Selina's perky bottom in bright-yellow trousers with red side pleats and tried to turn her mind off the fact that Jason would be at the top of the catwalk. Oh, God!

During the two-week-long rains that had pelted Lenni Lenape this August, tans had faded, and hair had darkened perceptibly, even Erich's. Betsy's face had broken out. Elise had read *Gone with the Wind* with an intensity designed to block out thought. Aunt Chloe's ulcer had disappeared—she'd framed her duodenal X ray and ceremoniously hung it on her bedroom window across from the Lindbergh baby. Uncle Sam had howled. "I'm going to put Blake's *Cerberus* next to our Munch. Or maybe a shot of Hiroshima!" The cottage had reeked of damp and of dill from the steeping cucumbers. The dig under the manse had virtually washed away. Hence this climb to Jason. Jason!

Elise had only seen him in church since that night. He'd treated her just as he always treated her. But he hadn't come to the cottage.

Of course, no one had come to the cottage during the rains, which were not only wet, they were cold as London. Everyone at Lake Lenni Lenape withdrew into cottages and holed up by the fire like stranded pioneers caught by snow on their way west. Proximity was everything. Selina had taken up with her near neighbors on the north shore; hence the appearance today of two of the Macs. ("Mrs. Mac said I seduced them again!" Selina had reported with glee.) Hence also the reappearance of Wendy Bernstein. Selina and the Macs had come in Wendy's big motorboat. Strange bedfellows. Oh!

The offhand phrase so alarmed Elise that she stumbled and felt Zack's hands catch her. "Easy." He smiled at her. Neither he nor Erich seemed to have the slightest recollection of the scene in the station wagon after the drive-in films. Did no one wonder what had happened to her that night? How she had got home? Olivia? In church Elise had studied Olivia's face over the harmonium and thought of what Zack said Jung called "the shadow side." All of them had shadow sides. Olivia, Jason . . . and she, Elise. Hers had just surfaced, like a common little tart! She felt her guilty secret as an actual weight on her shoulders: an imaginary scarlet backpack. All ten climbers piled up, then squeezed onto the little deck, and Fred knocked on the kitchen door of the manse. Elise suspended herself from herself; she dismissed her shadow side from the setting.

"Come on in, Fred," called Jason's voice. Elise manipulated her body so that she'd come in neither first nor last. Neither alpha nor omega. The kids filled the kitchen like pieces in the jigsaw puzzles Aunt Abbie had been fiddling with endlessly while it rained.

"Well, now," said Calvin Cunningham heartily, "this is more people than we have seen in weeks. Welcome." Aware peripherally of Jason sitting behind his typewriter at the other end of the table, Elise went straight for Calvin, who was lovingly rubbing down his sculpture of Queen Esther with fine steel wool.

"It's not a dig, it's a wallow," she heard Zack pronounce.

"A washout," said Fred grimly.

"I wept. I wept tears of rage," Selina passionately declared.

"It's beautiful, Calvin." Elise focused on Calvin's statue so as not to have to look at Jason, but, oh, the statue was wonderful. Would she ever be able to *capture* like that? The face was Olivia's, but, with the voluptuous, pregnant body, the face became altered, prouder, more aware. It had self-knowledge. Queen Esther, a work of art, knew herself, although Olivia, a real person, refused to. Calvin had captured the shadow side of Olivia, Elise slowly grasped, her sensibility groping in the dark through doubt, passion, and a touch of madness to divine the task of the artist. Calvin was an artist.

Suddenly Elise understood Olivia. Shame about her shadow side had corrupted Olivia, making her sadistic and manipulative; and, Elise thought with amazement, I am about to let the same thing happen to me! I'm on the edge of being warped. Through shame, I'm about to let myself off what happened, or to say as Liz always does that it's "no big deal," even though she's never done it. I'm about to blame the marijuana, I'm about to blame Jason for taking advantage. Oh, no, I'm not. *I don't care,* her mind shouted so loud she was surprised no one looked at her, *what Jason does!* Let him pretend nothing happened. That's his problem. I won't do that. That was me, and I did it, and it *was* a big deal, and I will not disengage myself from it. Elise reached out both hands and touched the satin-smooth contours of the cherry wood sculpture. "What kind of oil?" softly she asked Calvin, her awareness, however, ranging like feelers around the kitchen.

"Jason, we couldn't possibly start the dig over next year. With another minister? Jason, why don't you come back?"

"Jason, are you about finished with that paper? Let's see what page you're on. Thirty-two! That ain't just whistling 'Dixie,'" Liz mimicked Jason perfectly. Everyone laughed.

"Lemon oil," Calvin told Elise. "You know, Elise, the rain was just a godsend for this ruddy lady here. The wood got almost as malleable as clay. You like clay, didn't you tell me? Don't let it hook you. Just cause you're a girl doesn't mean you can't work with metal and wood. Ah, this lady's the best thing I ever done." Calvin looked at his statue, and Elise found herself smiling as proudly as he.

"So the dig failed," Zack was saying. "Things fail. Look at Mr. Otway. He worked all summer on something that might have been valuable to industry as well as science and even made him rich, and he got nowhere. But he's a good sport about it. He's not kicking his spectrometer. I think that's what growing up is about—knowing you don't get the brass ring every time."

"Bullshit, Chandler," argued Erich. "Growing up's about money, and it's about screwing—I'm sorry, Jason."

"Why be sorry?"

"I am. I just am."

"Are you going to leave the bottom rough?" Elise asked Calvin, although she could of course tell that the bottom should remain the rough wood of the log, from which Queen Esther emerged not quite as naked as Botticelli's Venus; but she wanted to blot out the other conversation.

"I'm not giving up on the brass ring," said Selina. "I'm not giving up on the dig!" Elise could see Selina's long hair toss like a shadow out of the corner of her eye.

"Selina, did you get through all the church records?" asked Jason.

"Fred and I split them up. There's nothing before 1846. Nary a word. It's as if the other years didn't happen."

"Especially 1783 when the guy was tortured and Esther was here," Fred added gruffly. "You'd think nothing happened in 1783. Selina and me were trying to find some stuff about the oppression of women and Indians, because Esther was both—"

"Jason, we owe it to Esther," interrupted Selina, while Elise, still with her back to the conversation, idly registered Fred's unprecedented concern for women. Selina must have been working on him. "We have to vindicate her memory!"

Erich hooted.

"How would you like to be a *queen*, Erich?" Raucous laughter greeted Selina's question, but she rode over it. "How would you like to be of royal blood and for people to be saying forever that you were always drunk and sleeping on porches?"

"Hell, I wouldn't mind. Just give me a bottle of whiskoo, and I'll sleep anywhere."

Elise winced at the word "whiskoo." "Calvin," she asked him again, "are you going to leave the bottom rough?"

"Yes, sugar, I am leaving the bottom as it is. You ever try doing pubic hair in wood?"

Jason's wonderful voice floated. "Tell me what everybody's been doing this rainy season. Let's see, what transpired at . . . the Barnes cottage?" Elise turned around now. Jason had his hands behind his head and was looking at Liz and Betsy, who sat on the windowsill together. Selina, Wendy, and the two MacNamara boys sat in ladder-back chairs at the table. Fred, Erich, and Zack were propped against the counter near the stove.

"Elise read *Gone with the Wind*," Liz reported. Other people looked at Elise, but Jason didn't. "I read all of Jane Austen. Aunt Chloe read the Old Testament." Jason grinned at that. "My mother did fifty thousand jigsaw puzzles and put a million cucumbers in pots to pickle."

"Hey, I thought she gave up domesticity," said Calvin. Jason laughed, then stretched and yawned.

"Ah, but then," said Liz, holding up a finger, "she wrote a poem about it. It's called 'Pickled.' " Over the laughter, Liz added, "Daddy even liked it. He wants her to send it to *The New Yorker.*"

"My brother Bill mooned around after Elise," Betsy chimed in. "I've never been so glad to see anyone go back to work." Everyone looked at Elise and grinned, Jason included. Elise felt herself color. Oh, damn! How could Jason just look smiling at her? A nagging little doubt came again. While she seemed to remember everything, even his bedspread, and she thought she had felt fine that night (if a bit wild!), what did she know about marijuana? Could she have *imagined* that night?

"Aunt Chloe talked my father into working on his Blake volume again," Liz went on. "She said, 'Why can't you just do a hatchet job like you did on poor Shelley in *The Thorns of Life?*' 'Oh, no,' Uncle Tony said, 'English literature is never going to survive Sam!' " Through Jason's laughter and the bored grumbling of the rest of the audience, Elise felt her mind cut incisively back into the weeks of rain. While Bill was "mooning after" her, she'd taken the opportunity delicately to pump him about marijuana.

"It lowers your inhibitions," he'd said.

"Could it make . . . one imagine something that didn't happen actually?"

"I don't know. Probably."

"Did you ever smoke it?"

"I don't like to mess around with my body." Suppose, Elise thought now, standing in the manse kitchen next to Calvin's statue of Queen Esther, lowering her head and through her hair looking at her feet in their ragged sneakers, suppose I came here that night and Jason just picked me up and carried me to the car and drove me home? It hadn't been too awfully late, not much after one, when she got in; Uncle Tony had still been awake, and so had Sir Isaac. "Bridge always makes me too excited to sleep," Uncle Tony told her. "Your Aunt Abbie made two grand slams." He certainly hadn't noticed anything wrong with her except the thunderstorm. "And Sir Isaac's still scared from the storm. Too bad you got caught out in it, Elise." Elise had suddenly hugged Sir Isaac, his shaggy, lightly vibrating body. "I say, Elise, let's have some hot cocoa. . . ."

Did she want it to have happened, or didn't she?

Betsy's voice impinged on Elise's memory: "Then Aunt Chloe got this letter from her lab assistant, who she says is very handsome, and her rhesus monkey is pregnant for the third time without a mate."

"Hold it," Jason said. "Run that one through again."

"This monkey keeps getting pregnant, even though she's isolated," explained Liz. "Aunt Chloe calls it the immaculate conception." Jason and Calvin laughed. The two MacNamara boys looked shocked.

"What's that?" asked Fred suspiciously.

"That's what's all over Catholic churches," said Selina, sounding indignant. "The blessed *virgin.*"

Denny MacNamara said, "Yes, that's right."

"I think it's disgusting the Catholic Church won't admit there's anything good about sex," said Selina.

"Well, is there?" Fred asked.

"Of course there is." Selina leaned forward in her chair with her hands clenched on the table. "Catholic churches are perfectly willing to show a whole lot of blood and gore. Why are they so squeamish about sex?"

"What kind of blood and gore?" asked Erich.

"Oh, all those pictures on the sides of the church, those gory things with Jesus carrying the cross and getting crucified. In some of them, Jesus's heart is even hanging out. I know; I used to go out with a Catholic boy who confessed every time he kissed me."

"The stations aren't always bloody, Selina," Kevin MacNamara told her. "It depends on what church you go to."

Jason looked at Kevin. "What's the eleventh station?" he asked him abruptly, rubbing his hand on his forehead.

"Ask Denny. He's going to be the priest."

Denny Mac frowned a little, thought, then recited, "Jesus is nailed to the cross. My Jesus, loaded with contempt, nail my heart to Thy feet, that it may ever—"

"That's gross!" cried Selina.

Elise was watching Jason. He rubbed his ear. "Jason, are you all right?" she couldn't help asking. "Jason, what's the matter?" Jason stood up. He had both hands over his ears. He looked at her.

"I reckon I could do with a little less chatter," he said. Elise drew back, stung. "Excuse me." Jason made his way past the boys, around Calvin and Elise, out of the kitchen. In the hall he bumped into Tradd, coming in with a bag of groceries.

"Jason, whatever's the matter?" They could all hear Jason's feet go up the stairs. Tradd came into the kitchen. Vaguely Elise registered her Indian-patterned jump suit, gathered at neck and ankles, enormous in the middle. The baby had grown. Elise felt numb. Tradd put her bag on the table. "What the blue blazes is wrong with my brother?" she asked, looking around. "He looks like he just saw a ghost." She started putting cartons of milk into the fridge.

"Or heard one," Calvin murmured.

"I think we ought to be going," said Liz, sliding off the windowsill. "Come on, everyone, let's go swimming from our dock. We need some sunshine. Come on, Bets, it'll be great for your skin."

"Liz, you don't have to *broadcast* it."

"We all look pale as ghosts," Liz amended. People started moving around, vague splotches of color and sound.

"Wendy, can I ride in your boat?"

"Wendy, can I try the wheel?"

"I'm staying," Fred said.

"Fred," Selina stage-whispered, "it isn't *polite*. Oh, all right, Fred, you and I can go down and look at the dig again in case Jason comes down. Then you can take me home in your kayak. It's all right, Fred; *you* didn't do anything wrong. I think it was me. I think I was disrespectful about Jesus—" Selina got Fred moving to the door. The red pleats in the side seams of her yellow trousers flashed.

Elise started to follow. "Oh, Elise," said Calvin, "I forgot. You were admiring my statue so brilliantly, it went right out of my head. I made something for you. Jason said you wanted a cross." Calvin held out his hand. In his shaded palm he held a beautiful cross of hammered tin with a small hole drilled at the top. Elise's eyes filled with tears. "I hope you got a silver chain. I haven't quite mastered the craft of making chains out of tin yet. Why, honey, what is the matter? Jason wasn't talking to *you*, babe. You don't chatter."

Calvin followed her to the catwalk door. He patted her shoulder.

Elise looked down the catwalk to where the kids were already climbing into Erich's and Wendy's boats. Greens blurred around her as she started blindly down the catwalk to the lake, her hand clenched on the tin cross.

2 THE SLEEPING PORCH

With all their rituals of getting up and dressed that so amused naturally beautiful Aunt Chloe (who'd once quoted Gloria Steinem to
them that "any woman who spends more than twenty minutes getting ready to face the world is only screwing herself," then added,
laughing, when they didn't laugh, "Why twenty minutes? Why not
five?"), with the careful shaving of legs, the plucking of eyebrows, the
painstaking removal of a mask of Clearasil (Betsy's), the slapdash curling of long hair with the curling iron (Liz's), the interminable selection of clothing supervised by Betsy ("Liz, the navy shirt with the
navy sneakers is awfully *obvious*"), it was a good half hour before Liz
and Betsy noticed, in the mirror where they existed for the moment,
that Elise had been sitting dreamily on the comfortable magenta toilet for quite a long time. Her pajama bottoms were down around her
ankles; her hands were clasped in her lap; her head was tipped
slightly to one side; her expression was one of bemused and patient
brooding. She did not look like a person sitting on a toilet, except for
the fact that she was. As Liz (curling iron still attached to a stubborn
lock of dark blond hair) and Betsy (one eye green-shadowed, the other
naked) caught eyes in the mirror and turned to look directly at Elise,
she changed position—put her elbows on her knees, cupped her chin
in her hands, and looked at the floor.

"Why are you sitting there, Elise?" asked Betsy. "Do you feel all
right?"

Elise continued to look at the floor. "I'm waiting for my period."

"Oh." Liz and Betsy turned to the mirror, saw their own identical
expressions of perplexity, and turned back to Elise.

"Are you afraid you'll get the sheets all bloody again? That's silly.
Aunt Abbie loves to clean up after us. Hey, why don't you wear a
tampon to bed, just in case?"

"I tried that."

"Are you late?" Liz asked. "Don't worry about it. I'm always late."

"I'm never late," declared Betsy.

"You have a body like a machine."

"Liz, I don't know how you manage to change all the bad things about yourself into good things!"

"I'm late," said Elise. "I'm very late." Her manner was not quite that of a girl talking to other girls. There was something dark and detached, something serious, about her tone. Liz and Betsy looked at each other, alarmed.

"How late?" Liz finally asked.

"Almost a week."

"That's not bad— Elise! Oh, my God, Elise!"

"What's the matter, Liz? Liz, you're frightening me!" cried Betsy. Elise stood up and pulled up her pajama bottoms. She and Liz headed out the door of the bathroom. Betsy followed. "What is going on?"

"Betsy, hush!" When they were all on the porch, Liz shut the door and leaned against it. She grabbed *Ulysses, Gone with the Wind*, and the Modern Library *Complete Novels of Jane Austen* to shore against the door.

"Oh!" Betsy suddenly screamed. "Elise!" She stared at her.

Elise had sat down cross-legged on her cot in the corner of the sleeping porch. Her amber eyes were wide; she looked as if she were holding her breath. "I am so scared," she said. "I am so scared, I am so scared, I am so scared, I am so scared." She clapped her hand over her mouth. Liz and Betsy both sat down very gingerly on the edge of Betsy's cot, the side nearest Elise. Liz wore a navy-blue polo shirt, red shorts, and (still) the obvious navy-blue sneakers. Betsy wore a yellow-and-green-striped polo shirt, green shorts, and was barefoot, having not yet selected sneakers. Elise wore ruffled white pajamas, patterned with little blue cupids. Her auburn hair fell forward over her shoulders like a luxurious fur vest. She looked so pretty, so like an angel, it was hard to believe what was happening. If it could happen to her, it could happen to them.

"Who?" blurted Betsy.

"Betsy!" cautioned Liz. But they both looked at Elise.

Elise took a deep breath. "I can't," she said. "I can't." Still there was something in her face that made Liz and Betsy realize that, if they pressed, Elise would tell them . . . everything. Liz alone might have resisted.

"Was it Zack?" asked Betsy matter-of-factly.

"No," said Elise. "Do you know," she asked them rhetorically, "I don't think I possess one iota of the grace-under-pressure that Zack is so keen on. I thought I would have it, if I needed it, but I haven't." She braced her head against the apple-green windowsill on the side wall of the porch. With her legs dangling from her cot, she looked like a doll someone had dropped.

"Was it Bill?" Betsy asked, then gave a scandalized gasp at her own question.

"Not Bill!" Elise covered first her eyes, then her mouth with her hand. "Don't ask, don't ask."

"Not Erich," Liz was muttering. "He wouldn't know how." Betsy and Elise watched Liz think. Liz thought almost as visibly as Uncle Sam. "Oh! I *know*." Liz looked at Betsy, and then she looked at Elise. "It was Jason."

"Liz, this isn't funny," said Betsy sidelong. "This is no time to be kidding around." But Elise had leaned forward, studying Liz's face.

"How did you know?" she asked, sounding merely interested.

"He's a *minister!*" Betsy gulped, choked, and had to be patted on the back.

"Well, that night you got in so late, you remember," Liz said to Elise. "The night you went to the drive-in, you really wouldn't talk about what happened. You pretended to—you told us all about the movies—but you didn't say much about anything else. I figured Erich had made a pass at you. Then Zack asked me the next day if you were okay, and I said, Of course, and he kind of shrugged it off, made a joke —you know Zack. I was then convinced that something had happened with Erich, two people being so evasive. But then last week, the day we went to the manse . . ."

Elise let her breath out. "What? What did you see at the manse?"

Betsy turned her head from face to face like Sir Isaac at the tennis court.

"Well," said Liz, "it was as if there were a line between you and Jason that neither of you would look at. If that makes sense." Frowning, Liz worked it out. "You both went to great pains to talk very animatedly to other people."

"Liz, I didn't notice a single thing!" cried Betsy.

Elise gave a short little laugh. "Betsy, I cannot tell you how glad I am to hear that!"

Liz reached out her hand and touched Elise's. "Elise, I don't think anyone else noticed. Even Calvin. He was diverted by you talking to him about his statue. Besides, you know I'm always noticing things; I can't seem to help it."

"You're going to be a novelist," said Elise. "You're supposed to notice things. Did you notice anything else? Tell me this," she went on, looking woebegone. "What was Jason thinking? Why hasn't he spoken to me, really spoken to me, since that night? Why did he lash out at me and then leave the room?"

"Elise, I'm guessing now—okay? I have to factor, as Uncle Tony would say, this new information into the instrument. First of all, I think that Jason must be at least as upset about this as you are—I mean, he's a minister, you're underage, and still he is not all that old. We can't expect the responsible behavior we'd expect from our parents. Jason's twenty-four. That's only five years older than Bill. I'll bet Jason doesn't know what to do any more than you know what to do."

Elise studied Liz's face. "All right," she said. "But why was he so short with me? Why be angry with me?"

"I don't think that had anything to do with you. That was something else entirely, something Denny Mac said about the eleventh Station of the Cross—"

"Probably," Betsy interrupted, looking righteous, "Jason was afraid that God would punish him, and I certainly think that God should. Jason's a *minister.*"

"Oh, Bets, ministers are men."

"I keep seeing these dreadful images," confessed Elise, "that could be from a Victorian novel. Stooping to folly. Disgrace. Going on the streets. Secret adoption."

"Abortion," added Betsy.

"Marriage," said Liz. "Do you want to marry Jason, Elise?"

"A shotgun wedding," said Betsy.

"No!" said Elise emphatically. "I do not want to ruin Jason's life. Oh, don't I sound *nice?*" She pushed back on the cot until her back was against the apple-green windowsill, her knees up in front of her. She started to cry.

"Oh, Elise, don't!" Betsy started to cry too.

"It's me!" sobbed Elise. "I'm bad. I don't. I don't want to marry Jason. I hardly know Jason."

"You wanted to do it," said Liz. "You wanted to make love with someone who knew how. It's no big deal. I can understand that."

"*I* can't!" cried Betsy, shocked.

"You haven't ever wanted to?"

"No, I think it just sounds gross!"

"Oh, it isn't," said Elise. "It's smashing."

"Smashing!" echoed Betsy. She flopped backward on her cot. "Boy, have I got a lot to learn!"

"Are you going to tell us about it?" Liz asked Elise with a little speculative glint in her eye.

Elise said, "I shouldn't. I've been wanting to. I almost must." Betsy sat up. "I shouldn't," Elise said again. "I can't."

"Elise, don't tease."

"I'm not teasing." Elise bit her lip. "I think I don't know the proper language."

"We'll ask questions," briskly said Betsy. She leaned back on her elbows on her cot and propped her feet against Elise's cot. Liz moved to sit against the sill next to Elise. Nobody said anything. "I can't think of a question," Betsy admitted.

"I can," said Liz. "Where did it happen?"

"Liz, that's not a very sexy question."

"At least it's a question."

"It happened," said Elise slowly, "in his bedroom."

"How'd you get there?"

"He carried me." Betsy and Liz squealed in unison.

"But, Elise," Liz said, "how did you get from the drive-in to the *manse?*"

"Olivia parked the station wagon near the inn, because of the thunderstorm. I got out because the boys were drunk, and please don't tell them or Olivia I told you that, and I walked to the manse in the thunderstorm, becoming drenched in the process."

"So you arrived at the manse, and Jason just carried you up to his room?"

"Not precisely." Elise had a little smile at the corner of her mouth now. She didn't look quite like the girl they had known all summer; she looked as if she had secrets, like Scarlett O'Hara in a certain scene of the movie *Gone with the Wind*. "He opened the door, and I just threw my arms around him."

"You did what? How'd you dare?"

"I was probably in a somewhat demented state of mind, because of the storm and the events in the station wagon. I threw my arms around him and wouldn't let go; and after a little, he—ah—ceased to struggle, and he kissed me. I could feel, um, well, *it* against me here." Elise put her fist against her stomach.

Both Liz and Betsy clapped their hands over their mouths to stifle screams.

"My insides went all funny, rather hot and loose," Elise continued, warming to her narrative. She shifted to the modified lotus position that Aunt Chloe had taught her and, moving her hands, looked like someone teaching yoga. "He kept kissing me, and he put his hand here"—Elise gracefully indicated her left breast—"and then he said, Honeybunch, I'm not sure you know what you're getting into, and I said, Of course I know what I'm getting into, and he picked me up and carried me up the stairs. There's a beautiful handmade patch-work quilt on his bed, which his great-grandmother made—"

"Forget the quilt!"

"Honeybunch. That's a bunch of books in my grandmother's attic."

"We sat on the bed and kissed for a bit, and then he put his hand under my T-shirt—"

"Which T-shirt?"

"The peach-colored one I wear with the challis skirt. You should know, Betsy. You coordinated it."

"Forget the T-shirt. Where had Jason's hands been before?"

"Oh, all over. You know."

"*I* don't know."

"Let her get on with it, Betsy!"

"When he did that, put his hand under my T-shirt, Jason said, all of a sudden, Elise, if you want to go, we had better go right now; other-wise I won't answer for the consequences."

"Did he really say 'consequences'?"

"Yes, but he was smiling when he said it. Then he helped me take my shirt off, and we were lying down by now, with just our feet on the floor, and then he pulled off my skirt very gently and said, Take off your pants, Elise."

"Oh, my God!"

"Did you?"

"Did I what?"

"Take off your pants?"

"Yes. He helped me, and when they were off, he looked at me for a long time. I wouldn't have believed how my body would vibrate just from someone's eyes. He lay down beside me and kissed me here"— she indicated her breasts again—"and he did something to them with his tongue and I thought that I would die right there. I could feel myself blushing all over. Then Jason reached down and unbuckled his belt and unfastened his jeans—they were blue, Betsy—and he said, Touch me, Elise."

Betsy and Liz gazed transfixed at Elise, hardly breathing. "Well? Well?"

"I was a bit afraid to. But he took my hand and guided it, and I shut my eyes"—Elise shut her eyes—"and I could feel hair, and then I felt . . . it, and he wrapped my fingers around it." She opened her eyes. "I hadn't realized they were quite so large."

"That's an erection," said Betsy wisely.

"It surely was *that*," said Elise.

"What did it feel like?" asked Liz.

"Most peculiar. Like something separate. Something alive. Like an animal, almost. It beats."

"Beats."

"And it's very soft in texture on the outside, rather like suede, but . . . hard and cruel inside. The oddest thing is the way the skin moves."

"What? What?"

"Jason moved my hand on it, and the skin, or whatever the outside is made of, slides back and forth."

"Oh, my *God*. I never heard that. That wasn't in *Ulysses*. Molly Bloom didn't mention *that*."

"After I figured out how it worked, Jason took his hand away. Slower, he said, go very slowly. So I did. Then he put his hand . . . between my legs, and I shivered and tried to get them really together —my legs—but I couldn't; and he did something with his finger. I don't know what he did." All three looked hard at Elise's pajama bottoms. The little blue cupids seemed to take on great significance. "But it was shockingly exciting, and my legs just fell apart, and he put another finger inside me and moved that too."

All three girls were breathing hard. "Oh, I can't stand it!" said Liz.

"What then, Elise? What then?" said Betsy.

Elise rubbed the back of her head on the screen. A maple branch that touched the screen moved too. "It's a proper blur in my memory," said Elise, frowning a little. "By this time I had almost forgotten him as a person; I had even let go of . . . it. Do it, I said, do it, Jason, and he said, Spread your legs."

"Ooooh. Did you?"

"I did. And he took his trousers the rest of the way off—"

Betsy interrupted, "What happened to his shirt?"

"Oh, the shirt was long gone by that time. Don't ask me what shirt, please. Where was I?"

"The trousers."

"He knelt between my legs and adjusted them. He tried with the fingers again, and then he moved on top of me, kissed me very long and deep, and then he said, Open your eyes. I opened them, and his face was very close, and he said, Elise, do you want me to go ahead? Are you sure you want me to go ahead?"

"What did you say?"

"I didn't say anything. I raised my legs up and wrapped them around him, as I read in a book once, and Jason laughed. I could see the crinkles round his eyes. All right, he said. I reckon it wouldn't be good for either of us to stop now. Then he smiled and said, Put your legs down, however, baby doll. How do you expect me to move a muscle all trapped up like this?" Elise smiled.

Betsy and Liz laughed. "That sounds like Jason."

"Hush," said Elise. "I'll forget. Then he said, Just keep your knees up and press the bed with your heels—"

"He must have done it before," said Betsy, disgusted.

"Hush," said Liz. "Go on, Elise."

Elise's voice moved light and fast. "I did what he said, and he reached down and put it inside me, and it hurt at first, but then something seemed to open up inside, and he went all the way in and just stayed still for a minute. In a bit, I wanted to move, so I just pushed up a little with my heels, and he started to move. Oh, did he move. In and out, but not all the way out, and it acquired a rhythm, almost like dancing . . ." Elise stared dreamily into space.

"Is that all?"

"Hmm? Oh, nearly. I can't quite capture how it feels. This went on for quite a time, slowly getting faster, just awfully fast, and I could feel my face get all hot and my ears pound and inside everything moved the other way from the way I was moving. It was a bit like being turned inside out. Then my bottom lifted a little by itself and inside everything began to twitch and I screamed a little; and Jason stopped moving and waited till the twitching stopped, and then he whispered in my ear, Elise, you are beautiful, and then he moved faster and faster, made a sighing noise, and moved off me very fast. I thought he was asleep, but he wasn't."

"He *came*, that's what the boys say," said Betsy. She lay back against the pillows on her cot, drained. Liz and Elise slumped their shoulders against the apple-green windowsill. "Elise, what about the 'climax'? When was that?"

"I expect I described it," said Elise. Despite the story she had just told, her British accent made her seem very prim and proper. She stretched out one slender arm and looked at it. "When Jason stopped moving—"

"You mean that twitching? That sounds icky."

Elise laughed. Her laugh had a husky undertone, rather like Aunt Chloe's. "It feels," she said, "bloody marvelous!" Then her face changed, and she looked as if she wanted to jump up and run to the ball diamond. "I can't believe I told you that. I sound just like a guttersnipe!" Elise wrapped her arms around her legs and keened. "I don't know myself anymore. I hate myself."

"What's a guttersnipe?" Betsy asked Liz, *sotto voce*.

"An urchin in Dickens," answered Liz and turned to Elise, who'd buried her head in her arms. "Elise, you didn't sound like a guttersnipe at all. You didn't use a single dirty word. I don't think there's any possible language to describe sex; I think that's what is the problem. I mean, there's this thing you called 'it.' The only other choices you had were dirty words or the proper scientific word that sounds like something you ought to pick up with tweezers."

"*Penis,*" said Betsy with great scorn.

Elise tilted her head and looked at Liz somberly. "I still sound like a common, slangy little tart. What is it your father calls Keats in *Thorns?*—'a tough little Cockney.' That's exactly me, I sound so smart-alecky!" She hit her head back against the windowsill hard.

Liz said quickly, "I think you have every right to sound any way you feel, Elise. I think it's rotten of Jason, downright crummy, in fact, not to talk to you about this. I also think you're being positively heroic. Would you like me to say something to Jason? I would dare; I really would."

"No! No! You must promise. You mustn't say a word to anyone. If you do, I won't be able to live with myself that I told you. It's bad enough to have *done* it; it's much, much worse to have told about it." Elise's amber eyes implored them. The angles of her cheekbones, elbows, and knees sharpened. She looked like she wanted to bang her head again.

"We won't tell."

"I want your hands on it." Elise held out her right hand to Liz, who shook it.

"That's a weird expression, I want your hands on it," Betsy remarked, shaking Elise's hand. "I don't think the word 'it' will ever be the same after today."

"Elise," said Liz, standing up, adjusting her shorts, "this may sound flippant under the circumstances, but I find that if I wear white pants I *always* get my period." Elise smiled.

"I do feel better, having told someone."

Putting on green sneakers with her green and yellow outfit, Betsy tipped her head back and said, as if to the heavens, "I promised, and I won't tell; but, God, I won't ever be able to look at Jason the same way *ever again!*"

3   FROM THE BARNES COTTAGE TO THE MANSE

A few days later, after a long lazy ramble with Sir Isaac through Otto's golden woods, Chloe came over the bridge in back of the Barnes cottage musing about the pipeline that cut a narrow green swath from the ball diamond possibly all the way to New York State. She walked on the pipeline, but no one else ever did. In return for the easement, the gas company had planted soft whispery grass over the buried pipes and even mountain laurel bushes at intervals to stake out its claim—a claim that made a path through the woods so soft you could walk barefoot and so eerily quiet you could be in enchanted woods, looking for trouble. . . .

Looking now for people, Chloe walked through the fragrant kitchen where basil lay freshly chopped on the cutting board (Abbie's herbed meat loaf for dinner?) and then in the living room perceived Sam Barnes wearing a tweed jacket with his bathing suit, shouting a speech from *King Lear* ("Poor naked wretches . . ."). Histrionically he waved his pipe at her, and she knew instantly what transition was upon them. When the first of September impends, a blessed rage for order descends on even the most unruly people accustomed to the skewed calendar of the academic year. No wonder there were yellow leaves in the woods. The Barnes-Otway-Wilson contingent would disband and decamp in less than a week. Minutes later, having left Sir Isaac as audience for Sam, Chloe was in her room, opening her closet and finding it full of alien clothes—bikinis, eyelet lace, red sandals—rummaging through her books and finding Bibles and Dorothy Sayers on Dante. Flustered, she sat down on the bed. It was like going through another person's things—a frivolous, religious person. She was as changed as the X ray of her alimentary canal. Ah, she'd leave that lovely photo, she decided; it belonged in the cottage with the Lindbergh baby.

Clothes—who cared? She'd traveled light. Let the girls sort out the clothes. Consider the lilies of the field . . .

Chloe concentrated her energies into clearing out her all-purpose leather shoulderbag, a not inconsiderable project, for she'd taken to picking wildflowers and stashing them in a side pocket where they dried nicely; accumulating castoffs from the ill-fated dig—four arrowheads, two canoe anchors, a most peculiar bit of bone she'd promised the kids she'd identify for them when she got back to her lab at the university (the university!)—a beautiful hunk of granite for the steel and glass coffee table at home (home!), amusing bridge scores, a golden delicious apple, a small yellow packet she didn't remember . . .

A small yellow packet pushed on her by a loudmouthed man at the little church in Wappasenink. Oh!

The wild feeling of that day in Wappasenink rushed through her, so erotic it took her breath away. Reading Dorothy Sayers had helped her to order that feeling, which resembled what Dante had felt for Beatrice. Beatrice was for Dante "the God-bearing image." Chloe's own training had come reluctantly to the fore: the body is economical, using the same materials for various organs, and also (evidently) the same physical reactions to various phenomena. The presence of God is so overwhelming it calls on all powers of the body. Look at Mary, made pregnant, transformed by the spirit—what erotic rhythms charge her Magnificat!

Chloe looked at the yellow packet again. She repaired to the fortuitously empty big bathroom and donned Elise's pretty green sundress with the drawstrings. She glanced in the mirror. Her eyes looked misty; she didn't need mascara. She sprayed some of Elise's expensive Calvin Klein perfume around her. She saw an unused tampon in the magenta toilet and flushed it away. She returned to her room and put everything but the golden delicious apple (purchased that morning at Esther's for its beauty) and the heavy chunk of granite back in her shoulder bag.

Then in her Volkswagen much too fast, Chloe, breathless, impatient, not thinking, armed with just her shoulder bag and a pertinent religious question, all good intentions thrown like seasonal milkweed to the winds, drove to the manse. The hill across the main road was beginning to burnish, punctuated with lime-green milkweed, bright goldenrod, Michaelmas daisies gaudy as lilac, and humpy maroon-colored bushes. The sun had moved so that it would set (roughly) over the Fanshawes' cottage tonight. In Chloe's shoulder bag was the unopened yellow packet handed to her in Wappasenink. Her pertinent religious question was about prayer. The good intentions she had thrown to the winds were (roughly) the following:

The thing to do about Jason Baynard: stay away. Don't be alone with him, lest you embarrass both of you. Embarrass? A shy feminine fear surfaced, humiliating as a face-lift: Jason was so much younger he could think of her as a mother figure! Maybe he just liked talking to her and wasn't attracted at all. Chloe flushed hotly and for a second felt the lines in her face as grooved into bone, then diverted herself to reservations less ignominious. Tony. Her marriage. The spiritual camaraderie she and Jason did have. Weren't physical attractions like— oh, milkweed, really—commonplace and run-of-the-mill? She was, after all, casually attracted to Sam, to her lab assistant, Mark. (And they were attracted back; they were!) Speaking of Mark, she ought to call her lab. And while her mind wildly worked out how to use Sally, the pregnant rhesus monkey, in her cytogenetics seminar—perhaps make Sally the focus, the project?—Chloe's eyes were coolly noting that Tradd's Mercedes was not in the driveway at the manse and Jason's Triumph was. Deliberately she parked her Volkswagen just around the bend near the Lenni Lenape Inn and walked back toward the manse, all thinking mercifully suspended.

Chloe ducked under the rambler rose bush. Its remaining appendant roses had dried to a ruddy tan. She plucked one and put it in the side pocket of her shoulder bag with the wildflowers. She knocked tentatively on the manse door and, waiting, began to feel awfully conspicuous and exposed. She knocked again. Tucking a white shirt into his jeans, Jason opened the door. Chloe felt as surprised as he looked, although why should she be surprised? "Chloe," Jason said. "Oh, my God, Chloe. Come in. Come on in." He put his arm around her waist and deftly drew her in. Chloe felt her shoulder bag slide down her arm to the floor. Jason kicked it out of the way, talking.

"I can't believe you're here. I'd given up hoping. Let's get out of these public rooms. That's what they call them in Charleston. People pay two dollars and come in and out. Fred and Selina are down below, playing in the mud. Come on." With gentle urgency, he steered her through the hall—cluttered with suitcases, it was—to the stairs. Laughing, Chloe let him lead her, but she protested a little, gesturing

back to where she'd dropped her shoulder bag. "Come on, Chloe."
Amused at his persistence, Chloe let Jason pull her by the hand up
the stairs through a door to the left. A bedroom. It overlooked the
lake, emerald green from up so high. She could see the Barnes boathouse. Someone was on the dock. She quickly averted her eyes so as
neither to recognize nor (absurdly) be recognized. There was an exquisite Mohawk Trail patchwork quilt on the bed.

"What a beautiful quilt!"

"Forget the quilt." Jason kicked the door shut. They stood and
looked at each other. He felt the same way. He did! They started to
laugh, doubled up laughing, holding their sides, then each other.
Chloe found her face against Jason's neck, her hands on his chest. She
could see the fine weave of the white oxford cloth; she could see the
medals that had come loose. She fingered them. An interlocked Alpha
and Omega that looked like an antique. A marvelous rough tin cross.
"Calvin made that," Jason said. His hands stroked her back, following
the ribs. Nerve endings danced where his fingers touched bare skin.

"I wanted to ask you something," Chloe said.

"I wanted to tell you something." Jason leaned his head back and
looked at her. He grinned. "I am so glad to see you. I had given up. I
reckon I already said that." He put one hand on the back of her head
and pulled it close again. Chloe felt her cheek press the cross. "What
did you want to ask me?"

"About prayer. You know, praying." Chloe's voice was muffled.

"Praying?"

"I don't know how. Could you recommend a book, or something?"
She could feel Jason laugh, then struggle to suppress it.

"Chloe, I do think a woman as articulate as you could just wing it."

"Jason, I'm afraid of—" It would sound silly.

"What?"

"I feel such a fool. I'm afraid of being *boring*." Jason broke up.
While he was still laughing, he tipped her head up and kissed her,
laughing too, both of them laughing, breath going back and forth like
honey. They came apart still laughing, both of them breathing hard.

"Try C. S. Lewis," said Jason. "He'd advise against boring God.
Catholic material is regimented and would make you mad; and I
think the, ah, well, *style* of most of the Protestant stuff might not
communicate to you."

"Style," Chloe said. "Oh, no, I love everything. The tawdrier the better. I love neon signs that say 'Jesus Saves,' I love bumper stickers—"

"I love *you*." Jason's hands moved down and pulled her close. He kissed her again, and her body turned warm, flowed to mouth, lips, tongue, and the fusion of their mouths traveled downward, the same connection replicating itself in the loins as if they were already joined. She ran her hands with wonder over the base of his spine where all the impulses gathered from the body. "Was that what you wanted to tell me?" she murmured, wanting all she could get.

She felt his breath catch. "The station," he said.

"The station?"

"The station we were at in Wappasenink."

"Dolly's?"

Jason laughed. "No, not Dolly's. The station of the *cross*. Well, never mind," he said at her quizzical look. He laughed again. "I'll get you a book." Chloe laughed too. "The place we were sitting in the church"—his hands drew her flanks toward him again—"marked the moment that Jesus was nailed to the cross. What's the matter?" Chloe had shuddered involuntarily. "You felt it too, didn't you? I can feel that you felt it. I can feel all of you. There was something about that station. It's as if we were struck by lightning together." Jason kissed her again, a spinning, wooing kiss, oh, God, and Chloe could feel his heart beat against her and then could hear a pounding sound, uneven, ultimately clattering and jarring. "What the hell?" said Jason. A loud knocking came at the door; Chloe and Jason pulled apart fast.

"Reverend Baynard!" came the voice from the hall. "We're back! Cumorah was great; we're going again next year!"

Chloe started to laugh; she couldn't help it. Jason let his breath out in a great whoosh; he ran his hand down his forehead past his eyes, over his mouth. He tucked his shirt in again. "Right back," he said. As he opened the door, Chloe heard Tradd's voice from downstairs.

"Jason, I gained eight pounds! The doctor was fit to be tied. He gave me a tongue-lashing that would have put Jessamine out to pasture!"

"Tradd, I told you you were drinking too much milk," Jason called down, shutting the door behind him.

Chloe stood alone in the middle of Jason's bedroom. No exit. The minister's bedroom in a manse suddenly full of people. God, you love farce, don't you, God? she thought, and laughed. She felt oddly wonderful, expectant and rather dreamy. The air had a golden light. The quilt on the bed was perfect even close up, the stitches that defined the rakish swirls of the Mohawk Trail as tiny as she had ever seen. The bedstead itself was iron and painted a bold blood-red. From his bed Jason would be able to see the lake (she politely resisted sitting on his bed, merely leaning to approximate such a posture) from two sets of windows. It took her a minute to chance looking at the Barnes dock again. Whew. No one there. Not that they could see her. Still—

Propped on the sill against one of the windows, Chloe found a beautiful old painted woodcarving that might have come from some dismantled European church. Shaped like a butterfly, it depicted a lissome dark-haired woman in biblical dress—faded blue-and-rose-colored mantle over a flaking white robe—against gilt wings. Whether the wings were hers or someone's behind her, they overshadowed her. Chloe turned the carving over, as if to see who was behind; the graying wood was smooth, worn fine, aged. When Jason came back into the room, she was still holding it, like a shield. She leaned back against the windows. Jason looked at her face for a long time. When her face could take it no longer, Chloe held out the carving.

"Is this seventeenth century?" she asked him softly.

"No, no. Calvin did it. It's good, isn't it? He made his own paints out of berries or vegetables or something, like da Vinci. It's Mary Magdalene, based on a girl who followed us around in Nashville. Don't tell Calvin you thought it was seventeenth century, or he'll embark on a career of forgery." Jason put his hands in the back pockets of his jeans. Chloe thought he might have the most beautiful body she had ever seen. He laughed distractedly. His body moved. "Chloe, how the devil are we going to get out of here? The Mormons are in and out of the hall, and Tradd and Calvin are in the kitchen."

I could stay, she thought. I could curl up under the quilt and live on milk and honey. "I could pretend I was in the bathroom," she said.

"The bathroom's downstairs."

"Well, how stupid."

"I didn't design the house."

"You don't think I can carry this off, Jason? Didn't anyone ever tell you how sophisticated older women are?"

"How're you going to carry it off?" he challenged.

"Just watch. Come on, we'll go down together." Still holding the woodcarving, Chloe led Jason down the stairs, chatting brightly. "I could have sworn it was seventeenth century, Jason. Why on earth is Calvin going to be a minister when he's such a talented artist?"

"I suppose you consider the ministry as disreputable as Tradd does," retorted Jason. "Or Sam Barnes." Chloe laughed. She and Jason walked into the kitchen. Tradd and Calvin looked at her.

"Aren't you all decked out?" commented Tradd. "I love that dress."

Chloe smiled. "Jason took me up to show me this woodcarving." Chloe looked hard at the carving. "It's magnificent—"

"Jason having no etchings," said Calvin. He looked pointedly at Jason.

"Tradd, when are you *due?*" Chloe almost winced at her own sprightly effusiveness. "I've been meaning to ask you—" Chloe sat down in one of the ladder-back chairs and abandoned the carving of Mary Magdalene to the center of the table. The gilt wings created an aura that was startlingly erotic. Pulling her eyes away from the carving, Chloe leaned her elbows on the table in an ingenuous manner. "What are you going to *do?* Will you go back home to your mother in Charleston?" What a dumb question! Some feminist I am, she thought.

"Perish forbid!" said Tradd. Or perhaps it was "parish forbid?" Whichever odd expression, Jason laughed. "It isn't one bit funny, Jason," Tradd chastised him. "Mother is my worst nightmare. I still keep dreaming Mother will catch me out in the bed of some young man or other." She turned back to Chloe. "I am going to Nashville, Chloe, with Jason and Calvin, who have this big old dusty apartment with a working fireplace in every room. I am going to talk Calvin into taking some art courses, as there is still hope for his future, if not for Jason's. I'll keep house for the two of them in return for room, board, and baby-sitting, which they've had considerable experience at with Fred, Selina, and company; and then maybe in the spring semester, when my baby'll be, goodness"—Tradd counted on her fingers—"three months old, and my divorce settlement should have come through if Whit DuVal doesn't drag his ass, I might just enroll at Vanderbilt and finish off my B.A."

"Or, sugar, you can sing at the Grand Ole Opry."

"She can't sing a note, Calvin."

"She'd be perfect for the Opry then."

"Or she could bartend," said Jason. "Tradd makes a mean julep."

"Just like Robert," said Chloe, remembering what Tradd had told her about the Baynard family retainers. Jason looked surprised. Tradd laughed.

"I am going to make us all some juleps right now," she declared. "We deserve them, being descended on by our resident Latter-day Saints again." Tradd took a bottle of Jack Daniels out of a cupboard. "Goodness me, someone has been at this bourbon. Get moving, Jason. Go fetch me some mint. Calvin, frost these glasses."

"I love the way you keep house for them, Tradd," said Chloe, laughing, beginning to feel at ease in this bantering company which was both like and unlike her own.

"I thought you might appreciate my definition, Chloe," said Tradd. A Mormon came clattering down the stairs.

"Reverend Baynard, did we leave any food?"

"I don't know. I'm just here to fetch the mint." Jason went down the hall to the front door. The Mormon stuck his head into the kitchen. Calvin, frosting glasses, eyed him over the refrigerator door. Tradd put her hands on her hips and turned her formidable belly on him.

"Tell you what. When you boys finish your packing you can come out here, and I'll give you something. A special treat." Tradd winked at Chloe. The Mormon clattered back up the stairs. A knock came at the back door. "Come on in, Selina and Fred," Tradd called without looking, waving her hands around wildly. "More the merrier." Selina Thomas and Fred Bunyan came in.

"I think I could get to like mud; it's very good for the psyche! Where's everybody been all afternoon? We kept knocking. Hi, Mrs. Otway! I like your sexy dress. Is it yours or Elise's?" brightly caroled Selina. She wore a black jump suit with a silver belt. She and Fred perched on the windowsill. Fred grumbled something. "Oh, Fred, you're such a pessimist!" she said sidelong to him. "Hi, Jason!"

Jason came in from the hall bearing sprigs of mint and Chloe's shoulder bag. He waved both mint and bag at the kids, handed Tradd the mint, Chloe the bag. Chloe remembered the packet. "Jason," she said, "I completely forgot what I came to show you."

As she started to unfasten her bag, she saw Calvin look from her to Jason, a look as explicit as a clothesline across the kitchen. Damn him. Chloe's hand fumbled on the clasp. She swerved her eyes to the er- ring Magdalene. The gilt wings radiated and brooded. Then she felt

Jason move behind her chair, shadowing her from the sunlight. "Show me in the car," he said. His hand caught her wrist hard. "You can drop me at the Fanshawes' on your way home. I have to pick up my pay." As Chloe got confusedly up, Jason tilted his head back and let his voice resonate through the kitchen: "Good thing somebody works around here. Tradd eats like a horse."

At Jason's outrageous (and unprecedented!) display of bad manners, a display worthy of *Sam*, Chloe saw Calvin's eyes widen. Tradd put her hands on her hips and glared. Selina grinned. Fred glowered. Still holding her wrist, Jason pulled Chloe toward the hall. "Whoops!" The Mormons clattered down the stairs into them, jumbling, then shielding their retreat; Chloe and Jason dodged suitcases and moved to the door.

"Boys," they heard Tradd declare, her exasperation diverted, "I am going to give the both of you a cool and positively *wicked* mint julep. For the road."

4 THE PIPELINE

"Hellfire, Chloe, I didn't really mean the Fanshawes'."

"Jason, where the hell *did* you mean then?" Sexual tension raddled both their voices. Just through the stone arches, Jason reached over fast and turned the steering wheel of the Volkswagen, deflecting Chloe's route from the West Shore Road. Chloe felt like a sixteen-year-old being taught to drive. Really, shouldn't the man drive in such circumstances? Assuming the "circumstances" were what she thought them to be, but of course she couldn't assume the circumstances if *he* wouldn't say. Clergymen must forget that in the real world the men seduce the women, she fumed, then mentally recanted, knowing how unfair it was that men should always be so awfully responsible for the mechanics, the logistics, the angles and rhythms of sex even when the women were on top. Well, sort of. Still, women can't rape, she thought; men *are* responsible. She looked toward Jason, quite willing to let him decide where, when, how, even if. Should we? Should we not? Maybe the Fall was sex after all, Chloe mused abruptly. Jason's profile was irritated, his voice harsh.

"This is your side of the lake. You tell me."

"How about the church?" Chloe retorted nastily. Grinding gears, she tried to turn on Otto's road, but there was Otto coming along it on his tractor. He wore a pith helmet. He waved. Panicked, Chloe swerved onto the uphill road that led to the ball diamond.

"Otto saw us," she reported, alarmed.

"Wave, just wave." Jason reached his hand over and took hold of her thigh. She could feel each separate finger of his hand balance his thumb. Desire shot through her, hard and smooth and startling as an entry.

"I know a place," she said suddenly. "I know just the place to go." She continued on the uphill road to the ball diamond.

Jason hung back unaccountably as Chloe tried to entice him through the rampant mountain laurel bushes that camouflaged the entry to the pipeline. Before them, the narrow path beckoned, the soft long grass shimmering green as a dream. "Chloe, this is the *pipeline.*"

Chloe laughed. "It is," she agreed. "So what?"

"Even the kids won't come here, Chloe. Didn't they ever tell you?" he asked, his hand on the back of his neck as if to block the ax, "how a girl was raped up here and left to die? Didn't Wendy Bernstein tell you that the publisher of the *Bugle* wouldn't let Matt write about it because the rapist was a prominent citizen with a summer cottage? Didn't Wendy ever warn you about this place?"

Laughing, Chloe flopped her hands sideways. The warm air stirred like feathers. "Wendy Bernstein is fifteen years old!"

Jason moved his hand from the back of his neck to his head. In its wake his hair fluffed up like a halo. He laughed a bit sheepishly. "I've been with the kids too much," he declared. "I'm picking up their melodrama. I'm even afraid of the human bones in their dig." He moved around her and took the lead. "Come on, Chloe," he said, turning to look at her. "I have to make love with you." She loved the "with." Jason's wide shoulders in the white shirt made a dizzy angle against the woods ahead. He slid his arm around her and pulled her forward. Her eyes hazed, and she let him guide her.

Chloe felt her hair spread out in the grass. Mountain laurel made their place a glen, a glade, a grotto. Through the silky cultivated grass over the pumping pipeline there was nonetheless a scent of the wilderness, wild and singing. Kneeling, Jason carefully untied the drawstrings on Elise's dress. He laughed softly. "They fastened underclothes like this a century ago."

"How would you know?" murmured Chloe.

"I grew up in another century," said Jason.

5 THE BARNES DOCK

Two days later, the Saturday afternoon of Labor Day weekend, Chloe and Tony lay in chaise lounges on the dock catching some of the last rays of summer. Tony had (evidently) looked in the mirror for the first time all vacation and been appalled at his pallor: "I'm the color of magnesium!" Chloe herself welcomed any respectable excuse to close her eyes and . . . dream. Near the apple-green boathouse, barefoot and in swim trunks, Sam was doing something or other annoying to the stone pilings that supported it—kicking at them, swearing at them, quoting *Oedipus* and *King Lear* to them. Chloe wasn't sure what was wrong with the stones, but she did know Sam was hot and heavy into a tragedy course he'd start teaching week after next: "Oedipus to Moby Dick." She had tried to talk him out of including Acts. "Sam, it's not a tragedy; it's a comedy like Dante." "It's a tragedy when an intelligent man like Saul of Tarsus is so misled by a fantasy he changes his name." "Sam!" "Religion attacks *identity*, Chloe. It's also a tragedy when a woman like you confuses good, old-fashioned lust with God. Never mind, I won't say another word." Sam and Calvin . . .

"As flies to wanton boys are we to the gods!" hollered Sam now. Chloe almost liked his shouting, as it broke into the nonstop apologetic monologue Tony was directing at her. Really he needn't be so abject! Oh, damn, damn . . .

"You can't know what a blow it dealt me, Chloe, to think I might have spent all summer with you instead of hovering like an anxious father over the NMR spectrometer, and have been no worse off than I am now with my damnable ligands!"

Considerable ferocity impelled the last word. Eyes evasively closed, Chloe sought rhymes for "ligand"—brigand, friggin', pig and, wig and, big hand. . . . She felt Tony's cool, limber, familiar hand touch hers. "Don't let me do it again, darling. I've taken unconscionable advantage of your good nature. Box my ears. Pluck me by the hair. Don't let me neglect you, making the bed instead of love." Eyes still closed, Chloe smiled at the clever figure of speech that touched her as familiarly as his hand, but Tony lapsed back into his biochemical lament: "Oh, God, Chloe, I wasted, do you realize, two months, not counting the initial library research that took virtually all of last semester. I also wasted all those boozy luncheon hours being obsequious to the board of directors of that lucrative company whose initials I shan't mention, and do you realize I'll have nothing to show them at the luncheon meeting next week, not so much as a hope or a prayer? Do you realize?" The question was clearly rhetorical, but Tony paused anyway.

"I realize." Her eyes still closed, Chloe managed one more languid word: "Wasted?"

"Wasted. I learned nothing. I gained nothing. I gambled on a circle of ligands and lost. Remind me never to get attached to a circle of ligands again."

"Tony!" called Sam. "I don't like the way the stones look. If I just kick at the pilings, stones fall out."

"Don't kick at them then. At least put some shoes on first."

"Tony, whatever happened to the octahedron?" Chloe asked.

"The octahedron?"

Chloe sat up in her lounge. Tony was also sitting up, she saw. His face already had some color from the sun. He looked very handsome. Chloe said, "Yes, I saw the spectrum of an octahedron, oh, about a month or so ago, in the spectrometer. I felt very stupid not to know what you were doing with it."

"An octahedron?" Tony's blue eyes caught some of the green of the water. "You thought I was using that for the central positive ion?"

"Well, yes. You were shifting them rather wildly."

"Not *that* wildly."

"Tony," called Sam again, "I'm going to have someone take a look at these stones. I don't think they'll last the winter. I'm going to call a stonemason."

"Fine!" called Tony over his shoulder. "Actually, Chloe, with the octahedron you envisaged, I was showing the Chandler boy how a spectrometer works. How you have to translate. He said it's like a word becoming a picture, or a picture a word. He's bright, a clever boy." Tony paused. "An octahedron. I say, love, you really thought I was using that octahedron?" Chloe watched what she called "the Pierre Curie gleam" come into Tony's eyes. He was onto something.

"Chloe! Tony! Aiee! It's that same spider. I'd know her anywhere! The spider just came out from the stones and bit my foot. Oh, oh! Aiee!"

Chloe and Tony both turned to see Sam, his left foot clutched in his hands, doubled up on the stone dock near the fragments he had shored against his ruins.

ELEVEN
Oedipus Sam
Sunday, September 1

1 THE LAKE

At six-thirty Sunday morning Jason cut the Evinrude and let his boat drift through the swirling thick mist that rose from the cooled lake. He reckoned he was about in the center. The drift was toward the south and the church, which he couldn't see yet. In half an hour, if he remembered correctly, the sun would clear the hill behind the manse and begin to disperse the mist. Till then, neither sight nor sound would disturb him. Jason propped his life-preserver cushions so that he could lean back against the bow, lit a cigarette not without difficulty in the moist air, and objectively contemplated his fragments. The heavy mist seemed appropriate to the void he was about to enter.

The dream from which he had just awakened in a cold sweat he had had once before, two, almost three years ago. He knew what it meant. The mist slid around his memory like cold sweat. Jason was (in the dream) a boy on his bicycle in Battery Park when the pillared bandstand unexpectedly exploded. Still on his bicycle, Jason had recognized amid the rubble bits and pieces of himself—his foot in a sneaker, an ear, his right hand, this time the tin cross he wore around his neck. Even the first time, before he was in seminary and had such words written on his brain, the dream had a spoken text: "The Son of Man comes like a thief in the night."

Suspending feeling, seeing the mist in his eyelashes like tears, Jason brought back the first occasion of the dream. He'd been in bed with a girl, an interesting, witty girl, a golden-haired psychology major from William and Mary with whom he'd been (what else to call it?) shacked up over the Thanksgiving break. He'd told his mother he was at Hilton Head with some fraternity brothers. The girl's parents were actually at Hilton Head. She'd told them she was working on her senior honors thesis. The thesis was titled, so she swore to Jason on a nearby Bible, "Freudian Phallacies." It had broken him up.

Her home, where they were, her home with the handy Bible, was in the historic district of Williamsburg, Virginia, near the Bruton Church. Ubiquitous tourists in furs prowled the brick streets and peeked in windows, even in late November. It was fun secretly to desecrate the decorous setting. The first night, after the first *time* (they had both gambled, having met at a U. Va. Beta party where she was someone else's date), she'd gone up on an elbow and told him that while making love she had visions of landscapes and buildings: "There's an apple orchard in bloom, then there's a train going through a tunnel—don't laugh, Jason! I know how obvious it is—and this big stone barn. Whenever I see the barn I know I'm almost there." She'd pulled a pillow to cover her as she sat up cross-legged. "What I wonder is *why*. Why, when I am engaged in the act on which all Freudian images depend, do I envision these polite sublimations?"

Jason didn't know. He'd been intrigued. With her help he'd begun monitoring his own visual sensations during lovemaking. "What do you see right now?" "The color red?" "You honestly just see the color red? Keep your eyes shut, Jason!" "Yes, that's it, that's architectural!" Plenty of opportunity—they didn't go out much, just once to ride a carnival replica of Captain John Smith's ship at Jamestown and once for dinner at a waterfront tavern in Yorktown. After the latter, Jason had discovered (or perhaps created, through her influence) the pillared bandstand at Battery Park centering his vision at the, ah, penultimate moment. The Freudian imagery was obvious—pillars and circles—but why, he agreed with her, see such an image when he was doing what the image symbolized? He wasn't uptight; they both agreed he wasn't uptight. Nor was she. They were wild and loose, two of a kind. They'd been fascinated, not to mention turned on by this new element. Perhaps they had stumbled on a flaw in Freud; perhaps there was something behind the behind; perhaps sex was not the center of life at all, they'd speculated, coming together again and again.

Sleeping tangled with her on Saturday night, Jason had the dream. The bandstand in the center of Battery Park exploded, leaving bloody fragments of himself mixed with the ruins. A voice said, "The Son of Man comes like a thief in the night." In the quaint Williamsburg bedroom under an organdy canopy next to a golden-haired psych major with whom he'd been (after all) playing intellectual games instead of making love, Jason had awakened in a cold sweat, a scream frozen in his throat, with a knowledge as definite and cold as stone:

my center is not holding. Packing fast, he'd left without waking the girl. She'd never tried to contact him, something he'd admired to distraction, for he was not sure he would have the same restraint in her place. He thought perhaps she knew; perhaps the same thing had happened to her. The two of them were a lot alike; her stone barn could have crumbled under psychological scrutiny. Or maybe she was using him in her thesis. Who knew? He, at any rate, had entered a void, a wilderness, a struggle to make himself whole; he'd discarded sex not just as his center, but entirely, and his life had changed.

So he'd thought. With his right hand Jason threw his cigarette in the water and, hearing its flat hiss, trailed his left hand in the cold gray water of the lake. Physically intact, he could nonetheless feel his recent breakage like crazing under the glaze on old china. He should probably talk to the rector about this; he should come clean; he should level, as he did when he was a boy. "I've done this new thing, sir. They call it adultery. Oh, and there's a little matter of statutory rape. . . ." He hadn't listened to the rector. "I'd rather be married than President." "Celibacy is a trifle drastic at your age, wouldn't you say, Jason?" Ah, he'd embraced the drastic; he'd asked for it, asked to be knocked to pieces again, just as Paul had asked for it on the Road to Damascus. Almost amused, like a person in shock, Jason contemplated the weapons that had felled him. He had fallen in love for the first time in his life, and while he was thus preoccupied, there came like a thief in the night a girl who resurrected bodily what he used to be—a lover, a seducer. Elise. What could he possibly say to Elise now? What possibly? "I'm sorry"? "Baby, you were great"? "Honeybunch, go and sin no more"? He wasn't looking forward to this week of obligatory visits and polite good-byes.

Thank God Chloe was a woman like the girl in Williamsburg, a brilliant, intuitive person, to whom he would not have to *explain.* Thank God. Jason saw Chloe's silky dark hair against the pipeline grass, saw her green eyes haze over like mist, heard her breath in his ear, and took his numbed left hand out of the water.

The mist brightened. Turning his head from the hazy silhouette of the west shore, he could see the sun fixed like a dull gold piece in the eastern sky. Sunday morning. Things to do. As superficially intact as the dreamed boy on the bicycle, Jason coolly plotted his morning. His sermon was good. Like his first sermon, it came from the intellect and not from the heart, but no one would notice. Except perhaps Fred.

Even Chloe wouldn't notice. She'd be seduced (yeah, that same old word) by the jazzy synesthetics and also delighted with the none too subtle casting of Sam Barnes as Saul of Tarsus. Jason grinned, surprised he could still feel pleasure. He rode with it. The sermon was good, it was damned good, and so was the Luke-Acts paper he'd mailed off yesterday. Okay, we start from here, thought Jason, like a pep talk. He rubbed his hands together. My intellect is unimpaired, as is my body. My soul, as has been discerned, is in shreds. Choice: either abandon the soul, or ask for it to be healed. The former would be more dignified. Jason shook his head. As he had so easily told Chloe, there was no going back. He could not unbecome himself and become Sam Barnes.

Lord, he prayed, show me what to do. I'll think later. Distantly amazed by the lack of melodrama in his plea, Jason moved to the stern and pulled sharply at the starter of the Evinrude. Godspeed. Heading toward his dock, he noticed that, on his blind side, Fred's scarlet kayak had sneaked in, like a proverbial thief in the night.

Fred lay on his stomach on the splintery dock, his right hand dangling something in the water. The biceps of his wiry arm tensed as he violently shook whatever it was in the air and then sat up like an Indian. Jason cut the motor and drifted through the lily pads toward him. Fred, motionless and glowering, held whatever he had cupped in his hands in front of him, like a live offering. Jason hoped it wasn't another bone. He especially hoped it wasn't another human vertebra. They'd found almost enough of those to make a person.

"What's up?" casually Jason asked Fred, scrambling to tie up the boat before it hit the mucky shore. On the dock he hunkered down next to Fred and tied a clove hitch. Wordlessly Fred held out one clenched hand and dropped something into Jason's hand. Jason felt before he looked; it was smooth, segmented, and moved like rosary beads. He looked. It was whitish, coiled, and dirty. The stone beads, strung on blackened metal, were woven, some broken like bad teeth, but the tarnished silver cross was still attached. Jason caught his breath.

("I can't do the lady's necklace just like I can't do her pubic hair," Calvin had explained. "Woodcarving is not that fine a craft. Wood splinters.")

"Esther's necklace," Fred said.

Enough. Get out, a voice said soundlessly in Jason's ear. Split. Live to tell the tale.

"Selina would be really upset," Fred said. "She's been telling me and telling me about how women have been oppressed. Esther is a two-hundred-year-old example, isn't she? I'm not going to tell Selina. I don't think she could handle it."

Selina could probably get a doctoral dissertation out of it, Jason was wildly about to say, but Fred went on, "The first pastor killed Esther because she was pregnant and buried her under the manse. Because who would bury a necklace? It wouldn't make sense. We've been digging up pieces of Esther's skeleton all along and we didn't know it."

"Fred, Fred," said Jason, feeling the necklace weighty in his hand, "you're drawing immense conclusions."

"They're immense because they're right."

"Maybe, Fred. Maybe not."

"I wish I had brought Selina with me this morning. Then I wouldn't have to protect her from this. I climbed up on her roof to her window, but she was asleep. I wish I woke her up." Fred pressed his lips together and shook his head. He looked as if he might cry. "I think I'll go home now," he said and, with the incredibly swift motion of an athletic adolescent boy, dove for his kayak.

"You should take this. It's yours, Fred. You can give it to that museum with the model of Queen Esther's town. They'll put your name on it. You can put Selina's name on it too." Futilely Jason held out the cold, oddly heavy necklace. "Fred, she did kill fourteen people in the Wyoming Massacre. That was one of the worst massacres of the Revolutionary War. Queen Esther wasn't exactly *good*, Fred." While Jason tried to pass the buck, Fred gracefully sliced his paddle through the lily pads and pulled away from the dock.

"She killed them to avenge her son," Fred called back. "Who was there to avenge her?" He sped away through the gray lake like an Indian.

By the time Jason climbed the catwalk and turned to look at the lake, Fred had vanished into the cove that ensconced his cottage and the Strauss fortress on the west shore. High above the powers that lived under his house, Jason leaned against the railing of his little deck and looked at Esther's necklace for a long time. If he examined it, he could control it. He strung it out, untangling the beads. The clasp was made of the same beads as the necklace proper, those beads weaving together so that, fastened, the necklace appeared seamless. Esther had worn a cross. Who gave it to her? The cross had a figure carved into, rather than embossed on, the silver. Jason had never seen such a crucifix, if crucifix it could be called; and the intimate identification of savior with cross had an effect on him he could not immediately decipher. The savior was like an embryo. Rather than saying, Take up your cross and follow me, He said, Become your cross and follow me. The cross is written on the universe, and you are written on the cross. *Tortured and lived to tell the tale.* Jason thought he might be in shock. He slipped the necklace into the pouch on his sweat shirt and went into the manse.

Less than an hour later he was wearing his tan suit with the vest and a Brooks Brothers tie given to him years before by a girl from New York. He was lugging his two duffle bags down the stairs when at her swiftly opened bedroom door he encountered Tradd. In a flowered muumuu and matching turban, she could have been selling flowers on Meeting Street. She blocked his progress. Jason dropped his duffles on the floor at the foot of the stairs.

"Tradd, what're you dressed up as?"

"Jason, whatever are you doing?"

"I'm leaving," he said, wanting to get it over with. "I'm not going to stay out the week after all. Right after church, I'm hitting the road. Please don't give me any arguments."

"Oh, good!" said Tradd. "Calvin! Calvin!"

As if he had been waiting in the wings, Calvin came out of his bedroom and down the stairs. He wore a foulard-patterned silk bathrobe and a big grin across his face as he spotted Jason's duffle bags. "Jason is leaving," Tradd told him. "I am delighted!" She clasped her hands under her chin like a pregnant ingenue. "Calvin, you look just like Sportin' Life!"

Calvin preened in his silk robe. "I was hiding it from the Mormons. You look like Aunt Jemima, sugar. What're you got up as? Jason, I'm glad you're going."

Jason looked from one to the other of them, mystified. "What is going on? Do you two want to be alone or something? I told you you could marry my sister, Calvin. High time, from the look of her," he tried to joke. "I let you use my tools and my Bibles, Calvin. What more? You really don't want me to stay out the week with you. What the hell is going on?"

"Jesus Christ," said Calvin, then, "Sorry, Lord. Listen, Jason, Tradd and I been watching you and the very beautiful Mrs. Chloe Otway looking at each other, and we have become extremely concerned, pardon our prying, to see you get out of here without playing with that particular fire, pardon us. I am, for that reason, in favor of your departure, Jason."

"I *applaud* it." Tradd visibly resisted clapping her hands. "Jason, you've always been skittish as a two-year-old colt, and there've been times I've deplored your bolting, but this time I applaud it. Do you realize what a godforsaken *mess* you could get yourself into by seducing a member of your congregation? As I have told person after person, as long as you have chosen this spurious profession, I want you to profess it right—not seducing married ladies, not breaking up homes, nor causing scandals Lake Lenni Lenape'll never forget. Didn't you tell me Chloe Otway was happily married only a little over a month ago? Well, I'll tell you something now, brother mine— the Otways might just be the only grown-up happy marriage I ever believed in, that belief coming from the way *she* talked about it, and I am not going to have you destroying my illusions and your career just because you were free as a snake all summer and poor Tony Otway was working his butt off on his ligands." Tradd paused for breath. She pulled off her turban, showing her hair in rag curlers. She looked about ten. "Oh, one more thing, Jason, if you're going to Charleston, would you please call my lawyer for me?" She smiled prettily. "I cannot get the *hang* of the phone here."

"I don't believe this," Jason said. "I don't believe it. I took you both in when you had nowhere else to go." He looked at Calvin's anxious eyes that belied his elegant robe and lounging posture; he looked at his sister's lopsided rag curlers. "Shit, I don't care that I took you in. I love you both. You know that. But talk about holier than thou, Tradd. Talk about too good for words. Hellfire, I'll see you next week in Nashville. And I'll call your lawyer for you. You want me to pay him too?"

"Don't say good-bye quite yet, Jason. We are coming to church. To see that you get off all right." Tradd went into the bathroom. Calvin went back upstairs.

Jason, somewhere in the no-man's-land between a shout of anger and a shout of laughter—between tragedy and comedy, as it were— paused in the downstairs hall at the parlor where Calvin's statue of

Queen Esther was now enshrined on the Queen Anne desk. Smooth as oiled flesh above the log from which she rose, Calvin's red lady with Olivia's face appeared to be waiting, patient as a totem and fearless. Jason made a mental note to have Olivia change the recessional hymn. Then, from his jacket pocket where he'd stashed it while dressing, he took Queen Esther's necklace and fastened it as carefully around the neck of the statue as he would have fastened Great-grandmother Beau's oriental pearls. He wondered how long it would take Calvin to find it.

2 THE CHURCH

At the beginning of the middle hymn, just before the sermon, Sam
Barnes finally stopped sneezing. Jason could feel the guarded relief of
the entire congregation. Sam himself looked surprised, stroking his
mustache as if that were where his sneezes came from and stroking
might call them forth again. Never had Jason seen a man enjoy sneezing so much. Sam had begun sneezing during the little hymn Olivia
had sung *a cappella* to open the service—a hymn she'd diffidently suggested when Jason asked her if she knew any hymns about the senses.
Singing it for him, she'd proved to have such a lovely contralto voice
that he'd persisted in seducing her into a public performance, despite
her quite honest demur: "Jason, I blush so!"

> God be in my head, And in my understanding;
> God be in mine eyes, And in my looking;
> God be in my mouth, And in my speaking;
> God be in my heart, And in my thinking;
> God be at mine end, And at my departing.

Sam's sneezes—the real thing—hearty, liquid, explosive, drawn-out
hash-hoos, so punctuated the song that Jason's mind amused itself by
composing a corny additional line:

> God be in my nose, And in my sneezing.

Since before the service started, Jason had been perilously on the
edge of the sort of uncontrollable laughter that in girls of a certain
age is called the giggles. He was getting out! Both Helen and Olivia
had been perfectly nice and accommodating about his hasty decision
to depart. Helen had gone straight to the phone to muster forces for a
farewell party on the lawn. He was getting out; the prospect made
him light-headed with relief. Then, at about quarter of ten, just as
Olivia was beginning the Prelude, Sam Barnes had lurched into the

church, managing somehow to lean on both a pair of crutches and the disparate shoulders of Bill Wilson and Chloe. Jason's initial alarm was alleviated when Liz, wearing Chloe's green sundress, detached herself from Sam's imposing entourage and came to the platform to tell him, "Jason, Daddy got bitten by a spider again." She said it in the resigned tone one might use for "Daddy got drunk again." She continued, "I suppose it was ineluctable. He's perfectly all right, except his foot's all swollen. The doctor told Mother he's a big baby."

Then, puzzling over "ineluctable," Jason had watched Sam settle importantly in the aisle seat of a pew halfway down, leaving the rest of his family to walk around the front of the rapidly filling church to the side aisle in order to get in the pew with him. He watched Abbie and Chloe politely fight not to sit next to Sam. Abbie won. Chloe reluctantly slid along the narrow pew to be awarded custody of Sam's upright crutches. Abbie, Betsy, Liz, Elise, and Bill Wilson filled the pew, Elise next to Bill. Good. Where was Tony Otway? Jason wondered. He'd been shaken by Calvin's and Tradd's perceptive reading of how he felt about Chloe. He very much hoped his feelings had not attracted similar attention on the other side of the lake. Then Jason saw Sam's left foot, swaddled in a couple of messily wrapped Ace bandages, sticking out in the center aisle, and he had to bite the insides of his cheeks to keep from laughing. Lord, he prayed, I like being euphoric, but please keep me from laughing out loud.

Sam's sneezing, which began with Olivia's plangent solo, increased in both volume and frequency during the Psalm ("Bow down your ear, O Lord, and hear me") and, despite Jason's theme of the senses, assaulted everyone's senses rather more than Jason wanted them assaulted before the prayer. He'd wanted to tell rather than show them about the senses! Recklessly he began the prayer: "Someone sneezes, O Lord, and we hear him." At that point Sam's sneezes were sabotaged by his own laughter and the delighted laughter of the rest of the crowd. Clown! Jason reproached himself, trying to remember if he had ever heard a congregation laugh during a prayer before. Comedian! "We want attention, Lord, any way we can get it. We want you to listen. We all want to be listened to—that matters, God."

When Sam finally subsided, cured by the gift of his own laughing, Jason had the blessedly long middle hymn during which to regain his composure and the shape of the whole for the sermon:

> Take thou our minds, dear Lord, we humbly pray;
> Give us the mind of Christ each passing day;

With more nonchalance than at previous services, Jason looked over the audience, pleased with its size, relieved that Fred had recovered enough from the shock of the morning to be standing between Selina and Erich, touched to see the three MacNamara boys looking like young IRA hunger strikers on the other side of Selina. Zack stood between his parents. His mother wore that big straw hat with flowers on it again. Selina's mother had somehow gotten herself next to Calvin and looked sporadically at him with mixed pity and fear. The aristocratic Laceys, who had the cottage next to the Barneses, leaned against a windowsill with other latecomers. Matt Bernstein had shown up again, this time with Wendy and that boy Joel who'd been virtually drummed out of the regiment two months ago. Now he and Wendy, shoulders touching, shared a hymnal. The lead guitarist from the Lake Lenni Lenape Inn—Denny, his name was—had brought a girl who carried a baby in a sling. Then there were the usual lake people, still quite a lot of them for this late in the season, a handful of strangers, and a couple of people he knew hadn't been before: Esther (had she closed the store?) next to a big woman with black braids around her head who looked vaguely familiar. Satisfied he was among friends and none of them were sneezing, Jason let himself enjoy the hymn, which celebrated the human flow to God:

> Take thou ourselves, O Lord, heart, mind, and will;
> Through our surrendered souls thy plans fulfill.
> We yield ourselves to thee—time, talents, all;
> We hear, and henceforth heed, thy sovereign call.

"You may be seated." Rustling noises. Coughs. Flashes of color. Mrs. Lacey's yellow shawl. Bernstein's madras jacket. Chloe's red shirt. Sam's crutches crashed to the floor. Chloe retrieved them and passed them along to Abbie. People bumped elbows, struggling to turn the page of the bulletin to the Scripture Lesson. Bill Wilson took Sam's crutches and stood them against the window on the end, making a double-cross pattern on what Jason could see of the lake. Hoping he could make the Scripture Lesson appeal to both the intellectuals (Chloe and Sam? Harold Fanshawe?) and to the kids who liked action, Jason read:

"This touched them on the raw and they ground their teeth with fury. But Stephen, filled with the Holy Spirit, and gazing intently up to heaven, saw the glory of God, and Jesus standing at God's right hand. 'Look,' he said, 'there is a rift in the sky; I can see the Son of Man standing at God's right hand.' At this, they gave a great shout and stopped their ears. Then they made one rush at him and, flinging him out of the city, set about stoning him. The witnesses laid their coats at the feet of a young man named Saul. So they stoned Stephen, and as they did so, he called out, 'Lord Jesus, receive my spirit.' Then he fell on his knees and cried aloud, 'Lord, do not hold this sin against them,' and with that he died. And Saul was among those who approved of his murder."

Jason caught flickers of interest in a spot check of eyes—Chloe's green, Fred's and Erich's blue, Sam Barnes's hazel. Enough. He began, "Nowadays when someone points out a rift in the sky to us, we don't stop our ears and stone him. No, we stop our ears and say that he is stoned." Jason waited out the laughter. Ah, he had them.

"But the assault on the senses in this passage, indeed in all of Acts, is the verbal equivalent of being stoned—either way. It hits on the nerves of sight, hearing, touch. Keeping in mind that Saul, introduced at the end, would have been present to witness the whole of this atrocity, listen to the sense words Luke manipulates so brilliantly.

"This touched them on the *raw*. The Greek word is καρδία, which means 'heart,' not in the pretty Valentine sense—rather in the sense of the naked, beating thing a real heart is." (A girlish giggle for some reason greeted this. Jason rode over it.) "They ground their teeth—an act which, like sneezing, drowns out external sound from our own ears. Stephen *gazes intently;* his is an active seeing. Stephen is *trying* to see, and the sky opens for him. He says, 'Ἰδού,' 'Look,' which in the Greek is a word that also means 'listen.' Do the witnesses use their senses to find out what Stephen sees? Hardly. Not only do they not look up, they stop their ears so they can't hear Stephen's description of his vision, and then they stone him to shut him up. The narrative of the actual stoning is muted, the action only suggested obliquely, but there's a lot between the lines. The witnesses take off their coats —why? So they can throw the stones harder. Stephen falls to his knees—why? Because he's been hit.

"What kind of man can be exposed to this and continue holding the coats? What man could watch Stephen fall to his knees and still *approve* of the murder? What kind of man could hear Stephen's last words—in emulation of Christ—and immediately go on a rampage arresting Christians?

"A blind man, you may say. A deaf man. Something of a tyrant. A man who's closed his mind because he's awfully afraid of change. Saul, who has refused to heed the evidence of his senses, a man who neither looks nor listens, 'breathing murderous threats against the Disciples of the Lord,' walks along the Road to Damascus, when 'suddenly a light flashed from the sky all around him. He fell to the ground and heard a voice saying, "Saul, Saul, why do you persecute me?"' We hear that the men traveling with Saul 'heard the voice but could see no one.' Later, when Paul tells the story and reverses this, saying the men with him saw the light but did not hear the voice, we are probably so disoriented by the sensory games Luke plays throughout Acts, so in tune with his synesthetics, that we accept the discrepancy. We're as dazzled as Luke wants us to be. Can our senses be separated?

"Saul is knocked to the ground, interrogated, and, in being forced to 'see,' blinded. A fitting punishment, one might say, for Saul of Tarsus, a man who has, like Oedipus before him, intentionally blinded himself. Do we know Saul of Tarsus? Do we know men who look neither left nor right nor up? Do we recognize him? Quick-tempered, brave to the point of being foolhardy, close-minded as a trap. A man who might say, Nothing spoils my appetite like *grace*. A man who might say, Having your soul in someone's hands is just a cut above being washed in the blood of the lamb. A man who insists that anyone who believes in God is crazy. In fact, haven't we all got Saul of Tarsus someplace inside us? the conservative, who trusts only what he cannot help seeing, who'd rather throw verbal stones than listen. *What did God want with Saul?* Why choose *him?* Why not choose Stephen, who is so full of the Holy Spirit he looks like an angel? Or why not choose Ananias, the man who baptizes Saul, who is so diplomatic even the Jewish establishment admires him? Why choose hot-headed, wrongheaded, fire-breathing Saul?

"We all have, at various levels of control, Saul's qualities, bad temper, impulsiveness, opinionatedness; but these are not qualities we are likely to admire in ourselves. Nor do we value them in others. Is it possible that God *does?* I mean, Saul must have been doing something right. He certainly attracted God's attention. Evidently God wanted Saul as He made him; God valued Saul's onliness, that which made him unique, more than we do. God used those qualities of Saul's that we tend to dismiss as unworthy.

"When the risen Jesus speaks to Saul on the Road to Damascus, he says, 'Saul, Saul, why do you persecute me?' Not why does hotheaded you persecute angelic Stephen or temperate Ananias. Why do you persecute *me?* Jesus values multiplicity. Anyone who persecutes a Christian, no matter how hot-tempered, mealymouthed, or close-minded the Christian, persecutes *me.* Jesus identifies with multiplicity; he assumes the personas of all his disciples; he is in all of them. And as Jesus does not discriminate among his disciples nor separate himself from them, neither does he discriminate among the senses or separate himself from them. He hits Saul through sight, hearing, touch, and everything blurs. The experience of God does not come neatly through one sense. We are *not* to stop our ears. Transcendence doesn't come from blocking the senses; it comes from fully *using* them. William Blake, a late-eighteenth-century mystical poet who saw heaven open again and again, said, 'You have the same faculty as I only you do not trust or cultivate it. You can see what I do, *if you choose.*' "

Jason saw Sam cover his eyes at the quotation from Blake. When he took his hand away, he was grinning sheepishly and shaking his head. Jason wound up, "I would recommend that the next time someone points out to you a rift in the sky, if you have a chance to see, hear, taste, or touch it, *do.*" Jason raised his arms. No sneeze came. "Amen."

Olivia struck the chord they'd decided on for the change of pace. "I have to be on the road by noon," Jason said, "and I want to say goodbye to everybody." There were gratifying gasps and moans. "Follow me out, please, each pew, starting at the front, as we sing the last hymn." And he led them out, Jason did, to the churchyard and the two trestle tables of coffee and cake Helen Fanshawe had set up to bid him Godspeed.

On our way rejoicing, As we homeward move,
Hearken to our praises, O thou God of love!
Is there grief or sadness? Thou our joy shalt be;
Is our sky beclouded? There is light with thee.

During the lively exodus from the church, Chloe, by dint of fancy footwork, managed to elude the clutches and crutches of lame, absurdly tyrannical Sam. Sam even called himself "Swellfoot the Tyrant," after an idiotic play of Shelley's based on Oedipus that he'd made her read last night. "Oedipus means swollen foot in Greek," he told her. "I thought you knew Greek. You didn't know what Oedipus means? You scientists have such narrow minds. Read this." She'd read it, then flung the book down, protesting the waste of her time: "Sam, the Beatles' 'Piggies' is on the same theme and much more clever." "Right!" he affirmed. "Obviously Mary Shelley published it after the poor bastard was dead just to show she was a better writer than he was, the bitch." "Oh, Sam, she sounds sincere." "Hogwash. No one who could conceive of Frankenstein's monster could possibly be *sincere.*"

At any rate, having finally shaken Sam's heavy shoulder grip, Chloe came out the door of the church and felt, heard, almost saw, the hymn rise to a rift in the sky like cigarette smoke toward a barely opened car window. Oh, the sun was hot, it was glorious, and the trestle tables under the maples, bedecked with lace tablecloths and silver coffee urns, were dappled and glinting. The vegetation, registering the slightest burn of fall, glowed as if for the first time. The ancient maples trembled on the last edge of green. There were china cups and saucers on the tables; there was silver. How extravagant to cart all that in and then have to wash it! But how lovely to have such largesse for Jason's last day; how appropriate for the bridegroom they would not have with them much longer. Was that image idolatrous, a blasphemy punishable by stoning? Clearly blasphemy had been Stephen's crime. Looking up at the sky for the contraband rift, Chloe didn't care what crime she was committing.

On our way rejoicing, As we homeward move,
Hearken to our praises, O thou God of love! AMEN

Its sound scattering on the "amen," the hymn ended. A cry came
from the steps of the church. With those around her—Selina, Liz,
Elise, and Bill within touching distance—Chloe turned to see Olivia
Fanshawe, stolid in her white blazer, navy-blue skirt, and sensible
shoes, standing on the church steps, hands out as if she were the last
just man protesting a mass theft. "The hymnals!" she hollered.

Laughter rippled through the crowd on the lawn as everyone registered an alien black object in hand. "We could throw them at her!"
Selina's light voice lilted near Chloe's ear.

"Stone her with them, you mean," said Liz. Her laugh was brittle
and cruel. Chloe turned, startled. Smart-as-a-whip Liz should keep
her whip in check. Elise's voice intervened.

"We ought to help Olivia. Bill, let's collect the hymnals. Erich,
Zack, Brian, come on! Let's help Olivia collect the hymnals." Chloe
watched Elise, wearing a blue-sprigged white lawn dress with puff
sleeves, approach Zack's burly police chief father for his hymnal. His
wary, weary face relaxed into a smile. With her long hair loose and
her pliant body poised, Elise looked like what Botticelli might have
made of "Virginity," were ever Botticelli so inclined. Liz, shamefaced
by now from Chloe's scathing glance and Elise's graceful gesture, set
about collecting hymnals with Bill and Erich and Brian. Selina, undaunted, didn't. When Erich took her hymnal, she put her hands in
the pockets of her watermelon-colored harem pants and started to
whistle. Chloe laughed and moved over to one of the trestle tables.
The maples overhead darkened the greens and shaded the contents of
the laden table. Not just German chocolate cake and brownies, lemon
pound cake and gingerbread, there were also homemade blintzes on a
silver tray with cut-glass bowls of sour cream and strawberry pre-
serves—oh, beautiful! The spread reminded Chloe of once when she'd
spoken at a Reform Temple Sisterhood on "Women and Science."
Marie Curie had dissolved into Bloody Marys by eleven o'clock in the
morning. A truly inspired speaking engagement. "Wasn't Pierre Curie smarter than Marie?" one woman kept asking. "She just helped
him, didn't she?"

Her eyes already composing a blintz, her mouth anticipating its
silken burst, Chloe heard Helen Fanshawe ask Abbie, "Dear, you'll

help me pour, won't you?" Like Olivia, Helen and Abbie both wore white blazers and navy skirts.

"Helen, I would adore to, but I really must see that Sam gets home. He's limping so, and the new semester's only a little over a week away. But, look, here's Chloe—"

Sold out, Chloe found herself sitting on a folding chair at the head of one of the tables, pouring hot coffee and watching it and random sweat stain her red shirt. The blintzes, examined with decorous wonder, were gobbled up in five minutes by the Protestant hordes. The coffee urn was on a stand, or she'd surely have dropped it. Chloe Otway doesn't bake, she doesn't sew, she certainly ought not to *pour*. Nobody looked at her, and "thank you" was all anyone said to her, although she did hear indirectly that Matt Bernstein's wife, Naomi, had made the blintzes, that Esther had closed the store for the first time since the day her father died, that Mrs. Lacey and Chief Chandler had been carrying on for *years* (Chloe found that one did startle her), that Selina's mother had made Mr. MacNamara a very high offer for his north shore cottage (and who could blame him if he took it? he had six, or was it seven, children?), and who could blame Chief Chandler for carrying on? look at his wife's *hat*. Pouring, Chloe could not look at Mrs. Chandler's hat, although she very much wanted to. Seated below the eye level of the rest of the crowd, she was as ostracized as if she'd been selected for a stoning. She refused to dwell on why she might have been selected for a stoning. This is how little children must feel, she thought instead, for the first time in her life indignant on their behalf. Then she heard Helen Fanshawe call out from the head of the other table:

"Selina, dear, would you like to pour for a while?"

"I would hate it, thank you!" came Selina's blithe reply. Chloe laughed. If a fifteen-year-old girl could get out of this, you'd think I could, she fumed. What a wonderful line: I would hate it, thank you. Useful on any number of occasions. I must—Chloe heard Jason's voice behind her, and her heart stupidly lurched.

"Oedipus Sam. Where're your crutches?"

"Probably stolen by wanton boys. Jason, was Oedipus in the sermon before you saw my swollen foot?"

"Yeah. What's it to you?" asked Jason, like a mock gangster. Mrs. Lacey's yellow shawl flicked Chloe in the eye as she bent for coffee.

Blinking, Chloe poured, passed the cup, but Mrs. Lacey stayed where she was.

"Jason, I think it's damned spooky you had it in the sermon before you knew I got bitten!" declared Sam. Mrs. Lacey laughed. Clearly, like Chloe, she was poaching on their conversation. A heavy hand landed on Chloe's shoulder. She flinched. "Excuse me. I'm a cripple. God, it's *Chloe!* Jason, look here, it's Chloe. What are you *doing?*"

"Just what any well-bred lady does of a Sunday morning," said Chloe demurely. "She pours." Sam and Jason laughed. So did Mrs. Lacey. To Jason Chloe said, "A stunning sermon," as she'd said that first morning. She looked sidelong up at him. He grinned. He took off his jacket. He loosened his tie without taking his eyes off of hers.

"It *was* a stunning sermon," echoed Mrs. Lacey with aplomb.

"Matt!" bellowed Sam. "Get a picture of this. Get a picture of Chloe pouring. I want to blackmail her." Mrs. Lacey adjusted her shawl and put one hand on her hip. Bernstein snapped the picture. Jason put his arm around Mrs. Lacey.

"Coralie, wouldn't you like to pour for a while?"

"I would just love to, Jason." Chloe stood up fast, relinquishing her chair to the adulterous Mrs. Lacey, who draped her shawl over its slat back.

"She just wanted an excuse to hang around. She's sleeping with the police chief," Sam muttered between his teeth, his left hand on Chloe's shoulder, his right hand on Jason's, as they moved away from the table.

"She's also pouring," said Chloe. "Don't knock her."

"I wasn't knocking her. I was admiring her; also her knockers. And I'm sitting down right now." Abruptly Sam let go of their shoulders, hopped five paces, and carefully collapsed on the church steps. Chloe and Jason stood looking down at him, as, groaning pathetically, he propped his swollen foot on his knee. Both Ace bandages had come undone and dangled, looking vaguely obscene, like exposed underwear. Sam took off his Harris Tweed jacket and crumpled it behind his head like a pillow. Hanging his own jacket over his arm, Jason unbuttoned his vest and rolled back his shirt sleeves. Hot, Chloe wished she had something to take off. "Jason, you're good," Sam lazily said, resting his head back on his tweed jacket. "Damned good. Boy, can you talk. My favorite word was 'synesthetics'; my favorite

line was 'hotheaded, wrongheaded, fire-breathing Saul.' Matt Bernstein just bet me fifty dollars you'll be senator from South Carolina in
ten years. Is that why you're in this preacher business, Jason?" Sam
cast a canny eye.

"I don't know why I'm in it, Sam," said Jason. "It scares the hell
out of me." Wait a minute, Chloe wanted to protest.

"You don't know how happy I am to hear you say that!" Sam
averred to Jason. "For a minute, in the church, I almost believed you
believed . . . it. I was afraid I might see that damned rift in the sky. I
didn't want to see it. You almost got to me when you said—"

"Tradd's over at Esther's having a hot-fudge sundae." Calvin, dap-
per in a white Palm Beach suit, joined their motley trio. "She was
there at the door when Esther opened up after church. I tried to stop
her. She already had three of those sour cream jobs. Here, Jason, let
me put your jacket in the car for you, so you'll be all ready to take off.
Didn't you say you wanted to be on the road by noon?" Jason laughed
shortly as Calvin took his jacket.

"Thanks. Take the tie too." Jason whipped off his tie. It stayed stiff
in the air for a second. Calvin caught the tie like a banner and went
off toward Jason's Triumph parked across the road at Esther's. Sam's
big Buick came driving right up onto the lawn. Laughing, people
scattered. Jason gave Sam a hand up. Chloe rescued the tweed jacket.
Kids and dogs gathered around the Buick as if it were important.
Brian MacNamara threw goldenrod and asters at the windshield until Selina stopped him. Bill Wilson loaded Sam's crutches in the back
seat.

" 'Bye, Jason." Sam hugged Jason suddenly, both arms tight around
his shoulders, then stepped back and leaned against the car as if he
hadn't. "Write, will you," he said, his voice gruff. "You do write, don't
you? You don't just talk?"

"Sam, Sam," said Jason, shaking his head, "you amaze me. Of
course I'll write." Sam ducked his head and got in the car.

"Good-bye, Jason." Bill Wilson grabbed Jason's hand, and then Jason went around and kissed Abbie through the car window. Abbie
flushed prettily. "You coming, Chloe?" Sam bellowed at her. Chloe
tossed his tweed jacket through the window at him. "I'll walk," she
said; and Abbie did a fast U-turn and peeled out like a teenager. Clods
of earth flew. Brian MacNamara threw more goldenrod and asters.
Then the remaining adult members of the congregation began to ap-

proach Jason to say good-bye. An amazingly deft old lady in a wheelchair told him he had taught her to dance. Huge Hans Strauss. Squat blue-eyed Otto. Cackling Mrs. Thomas. Harold Fanshawe, looking tearful. You could see their cars both ways on the road when they left.

Helen Fanshawe, Mrs. Lacey, and Chief Chandler diligently cleared the tables; Chloe, with no such admirable excuse to linger, pretended to be involved in conversation with Matt Bernstein and Elise, while actually involved in sidelong perception of Jason, talking now to Mr. Lacey, who was evidently determined to outwait his wife. They were laughing about Sam's spider bite. Chloe reacted to Jason's laugh. She was more conscious of his body than her own. This will pass, she told herself firmly.

"I'm to sit tight till he collects me," Elise was saying to Matt Bernstein. "I expect I'll be at Uncle Sam's in town the rest of the month, as my school term doesn't start till October. But, Mr. Bernstein, I promise to keep my father there long enough for you to meet him. Any fan of mine is a fan of mine, he always says." Bernstein and Elise laughed.

Damn the man, thought Chloe, meaning Mad Jack Barnes. I've a good mind to take that girl home with me and keep her. On which errant maternal note Olivia Fanshawe materialized next to her. "Fred's in the church crying," Olivia reported. "Will you tell Jason? My mother wants me to lock up."

"Does Fred want Jason to know that he's crying?" asked Chloe.

"Why else is he crying?"

"People don't cry just to manipulate," Chloe said absently. "Sometimes they cry because they're so unhappy they can't help it."

"Oh," said Olivia. "I didn't think of that." Around her, Chloe noticed that the number of adults had diminished considerably. How long could she legitimately hang around? Except for Matt and patient Mr. Lacey and those clearing the tables, she was the only person left of drinking age. Then Bernstein walked off, picking up his silver tray and cut-glass bowls and calling, "Jason, don't forget our date at the Opry in November! Chloe, say good-bye to Tony for me! See you in town, Elise! Wendy, you be home before dark, and stay away from the pipeline!" The minute his Lincoln turned onto the main road, Wendy and the hitherto despised Joel were kissing passionately. Her station wagon loaded, Helen Fanshawe drove off with the china, the silver, the lace tablecloths, the trestle tables, her daughter Viola who looked as if she were being punished, both the Laceys, *and* Chief Chandler. Hmmm. And back on the lawn, clustered about Jason like ligands in a shifting double ring (would Tony's octahedron accommodate a double ring? Chloe wondered out of the blue) were the kids. All but Elise and Olivia who (to Chloe's bafflement) stayed as close to her as two shy little girls to their mother.

"Jason, admit you'll never have a congregation like us again!" Selina was gleefully demanding. "Boys, twist his arms. Make him say it." Jason's laugh rang out as Erich got him in a gangling full nelson. Chloe grinned; she loved the way he was with the kids.

"Never again!" Jason vowed, breaking Erich's hold. Erich sprawled down Jason's back to the ground, and the three Macs swarmed all over him like puppies. "You're a congregation," said Jason, "and what I want us to do is pass the Peace now. I mean it. I mean Peace." He winked at Chloe. "Olivia, get over here." Jason put one hand on top of Liz's golden head. Olivia moved diffidently over. "I want the two of you to shake hands." Jason put his other hand on Olivia's head, as if this were a ceremony, a baptism. "I want the solidarity you all had when I first got here, no silly feuds. That's my last request, and I ain't just whistling Dixie, okay?" Looking wary, Olivia and Liz shook hands. Everyone cheered. "Now Liz and Erich." Erich, still on the ground, struggled to his knees where he was almost as tall as Liz standing. "Now," Jason went implacably on, "Selina and Olivia."

"Oh, shit. Oh, damn. I'm sorry I called you a snake in the grass, Olivia. Charlie wasn't worth it."

"That's for sure."

"Welcome back, Olivia," said Zack, kissing her. Olivia's face went a dark ruddy red as it had when she sang her solo, but she hugged Zack.

"Where's Fred?" asked Jason.

"Sulking," said Selina.

"Fred's in the church," said Olivia, still holding on to Zack. "Fred is very unhappy, Selina."

"Fred was born unhappy," declared Selina, tossing her long hair. She wore coral earrings. "Fred's my alter ego." Jason broke away and took the church steps two at a time.

"Fred, will you come out of there and say good-bye to me properly?" After a minute, Fred came hangdog out of the church and flung his arms around Jason. Jason's arms wrapped around, holding him hard as Jesus must have held his disciples at the Last Supper, Chloe's mind unexpectedly put forth; but then she felt Elise's hand seek hers and joggle her concentration. The girl's profile looked positively forlorn. Chloe squeezed her hand. Jason and Fred came down the church steps, and Jason looked toward Chloe and Elise. *We all want attention,* Chloe remembered from Jason's prayer. "Right back," she heard him say to Fred, detaching himself and coming over to them. With his open-necked shirt and loose vest, he looked like someone from Sam's Byronic era. The kids followed along behind him. "Honeybunch," said Jason, taking hold of Elise's other hand, "I want to tell you something." He bent to whisper, and then he kissed her forehead.

"Oh, ho," said the kids, except, Chloe noted peripherally, rather puzzled, Betsy and Liz, who were studying the ground. Elise's face, however, went radiant; her amber eyes gleamed as she moved away from Chloe and joined the kids. Jason took a deep breath and looked at Chloe. His smile was weary, and no wonder.

"Jason, I have something for you," Chloe said, smiling just a little. From her bag she pulled the yellow packet they'd forgotten all about the other day. "It's from Wappasenink. I haven't opened it yet."

Jason unsealed the flap and shook three small photographs into his hand. As Chloe moved closer to look, he spread them apart with a finger. For a blurred second Chloe watched Jason's hands and caught her breath as her body remembered their grace. Then she looked at the photographs. The first showed the actual tabernacle veil at Wappasenink: cheap white lace embroidered with gold thread, some white carnations in the background. The second showed the same thing slightly out of focus. The third showed it very out of focus, looking vaguely like the head of a girl with long blond hair. Chloe turned her head to look up at Jason. His eyes were cool and skeptical and in tune. "Clouds," both Chloe and Jason said in unison and started simultaneously to laugh. With abandon, Jason tore up both packet and photographs and flung them high in the air over his shoulder. They settled in the churchyard like shards of stained glass.

"What's so funny?" grimly asked Fred, coming to Jason's side. Chloe and Jason stopped laughing as all the kids circled demandingly around, drawing near with Fred. Chloe looked at Jason; he looked bedeviled. Someone had to let him off.

"Do stay in touch, Jason," she said, keeping it light. "I want to hear what happens to Luke-Acts."

He grinned. "I want to hear what happens to your pregnant rhesus monkey."

Chloe laughed. Fred eyed her jealously. "I'm planning an article," she improvised, clowning, "called 'Laboratory Management of Randy Rhesus Monkeys.' "

Jason laughed. He held her eyes. "I'm writing a sonnet. It's called" —he cocked his head—" 'Renunciation, as One of the Fine Arts.' "

"Right on." What a conversation! How mad it would look in print. Chloe held out her hand. They shook hands. "Good-bye, Jason."

"Chloe. Good-bye, Chloe." She stayed on the verge of the lawn as Fred joined the rest of the kids and followed Jason across the road to his car where Calvin and Tradd stood waiting. Tradd was eating an ice-cream cone. Esther suddenly burst out of the store and gave Jason a big hug. Another woman was with her, a tall, stately woman with black braids wound around her head. She also gave Jason a big hug. Jason got into his Triumph and, waving, took off toward the main road. When he was out of sight Chloe suddenly recognized the last person to touch him: none other than Dolly from the junkyard in Wappasenink. God, you love farce, don't you, God? she asked again upward, standing among the scattered paper fragments of "The Miracle up the Road."

4 THE GRAVEYARD

After a wild exchange of waves with Dolly, who went (thank heaven) back into the store, Chloe dawdled in the churchyard, giving the kids time to pass her, a noisy, comradely phalanx en route to Otto's for volleyball. The syllables of Jason's sonnet title ran through her mind like varicolored beads, each to be savored separately. Had he made it up on the spot?

Whimsically detouring around the church toward the graveyard, she wondered if she'd prefer the brilliance of improvisation to the loving labor of composition. Ah, who cared?

"Renunciation, as One of the Fine Arts." How she loved it that he hadn't moralized about "renunciation"; hard as religion had hit her and breathtaking as she found its breath and much as neon crosses and "Honk If You Love Jesus" bumper stickers delighted her, she'd an instinct she wouldn't be able to bear a preacher who moralized any more than she could bear a moralizing English professor like Harold Fanshawe. She had a feeling that morals were an act of man, not of God.

Chloe turned toward the church, leaning back against the wrought-iron fence that bordered the graveyard, and saw that in her dawdling she had not managed to shake Fred, who came grimly and doggedly toward her. She would have to save Jason's lovely sonnet title for later; that was all right. She would think, What is that nice thing I have to think about?

Fred also leaned against the wrought-iron fence. He had unbuttoned the shirt he'd worn to church, exposing a Vanderbilt T-shirt, a gift from Jason, no doubt. "It's awful when someone you love goes away, isn't it, Mrs. Otway? I think I might have loved him more than anyone ever." Fred's dark-blue eyes struck hers a glancing blow, then stared at the ground at their feet.

"We haven't really lost him," said Chloe, euphoric enough for the moment to mean it. "We can remember him. He can remember us." Fred's eyes darted like laser beams over her face, searching for bullshit.

"Did Jason tell you what I found at the dig this morning?" he asked, his tone darkening.

"No," she said, surprised at the change of subject. "What?"

"Esther's necklace."

Chloe thought. She remembered the lurid little parchment drawing Calvin had used to guide his sculpture of Queen Esther. The brazen lady in the drawing wore a most distinctive necklace of woven beads with a crucifix. "You're kidding!" she said to Fred.

"I wish I was. You know what it means, don't you?"

At his challenging, dark-browed scrutiny, Chloe lowered her eyes. There was rust on her white trousers from the wrought iron. "Not exactly," she admitted. Her hands closed on the fence.

"It means the first pastor, the one who lived to tell the tale, *killed* her. Killed her because she was pregnant and buried her under the manse two centuries ago. Because who would bury a necklace?"

Chloe shivered a little, not sure why. "It could be a joke," she lamely tried. "Maybe a treasure hunt or something."

"A treasure hunt? A joke?" Fred folded his arms across his Vanderbilt T-shirt and regarded her in a superior manner. His level voice had gained authority. "Mrs. Otway, who would go to the trouble to age a whole lot of stone beads and a weird crucifix, bury them under the manse, and just wait for somebody to find them? Mrs. Otway, you're just like Jason. You're not putting things together the only way they can be put together."

"Where is it? Where's the necklace? You could have it authenticated."

"I gave it to Jason. I didn't want it. I didn't want Selina to see it. She'd be upset. It means Queen Esther died unavenged, and then rumors said she was always drunk at Cayuga Lake. It means a chickenshit pastor got away with murder."

Chloe sorted through Fred's gruff tirade of chivalry and vengeance for a hook. "The first pastor was tortured, wasn't he? Why do you say, unavenged?"

"Tortured and *lived*. He should have been stoned to death like Stephen in the sermon. He should have been scalped. Fourteen people should have been tomahawked to avenge Queen Esther."

"Fourteen?" murmured Chloe, feeling stupid.

"It took fourteen commoners to avenge a person of royal blood, which Esther was on both sides. After the Wyoming Massacre, Esther herself tomahawked fourteen settlers on a bloody rock overlooking the Susquehanna to avenge her son." Fred glared at Chloe, and then his voice went singsong: "In the spring of 1833, the bones of eighty-three skeletons from the Wyoming Massacre were removed from the common grave. Almost all bore the marks of the tomahawk."

After an awed moment, Chloe asked him, "Were you quoting, Fred?"

"Yes, I was quoting. Me and Selina both quote a lot."

"Oh." Chloe nodded.

"What it means is that in Esther's day the Indians avenged their dead. Esther avenged her son. But nobody avenged her—probably because she was a woman, Selina would say."

"Fourteen," Chloe said. "Fourteen." The number nagged at her memory. The full moon in June. Oh, my God! she thought. Feeling like someone who'd wandered into the romantic and bloodthirsty world of *Tom Sawyer*, breathlessly she asked Fred, "What year? What year do you think this happened?"

"It was 1783. That's the year on the historical marker at the manse," uneasily said Fred, eying her enthusiasm with suspicion.

"Fred! She was avenged! Esther was avenged!" Chloe could not believe the youthful, excited voice was hers. "Fred, come with me. Let me show you." Like Becky Thatcher in the cave, or Selina in the woods, Chloe took hold of Fred's hand. Startled, he followed her without resisting. She led him through brambles, burdocks, and surrealistic purple bushes with white baneberries to the maverick little cemetery behind the official graveyard. The lake glinted blue at them through trees. The ground became marshy and black. "Look!" said Chloe. A shaft of sunlight illuminated the nasty little obelisk that said "1783." Out loud, Fred counted the circling sandstone gravestones.

"One two three four five six seven eight nine ten eleven twelve thirteen fourteen." A broad grin spread across his dour face. "Holy shit!" he said. "Holy shit, Mrs. Otway! They avenged her! They did. I bet you every one of those fourteen sculls bears the mark of the tomahawk!" Fred threw up his hands like Jason at the end of the sermon.

Chloe refrained from reminding him that the first pastor had nonetheless gotten off scot-free.

TWELVE
Acts
Sunday, September 1

1 OTTO'S

"Just a minute," said Elise, turning precipitously on heel and toe at the top of the cantilevered stairs, as Liz, Betsy, Selina, and Wendy, all having changed church clothes for idiosyncratic variations on shorts and polo shirts, streamed around her. "I'll be down in a flash."

"Elise, you had better be," Selina called over her beaded shoulder. "You have to seduce Bill into playing volleyball with us so we'll have an even number." Ever since Mrs. Mac had accused Selina of "seducing" her boys again, Selina used the word about as much as Liz had started using "ineluctable," thus ineluctably exposing to Uncle Sam (Elise grinned to think) the fact she had read *Ulysses*. In vain had Liz lied she'd merely started it ("ineluctable" being fairly early on), but her protesting, "Honestly, Daddy, I didn't read the end!" only made Uncle Sam all the more sure she had. "Ruined!" he'd pronounced, eyes twinkling. "A fallen woman, that's what you are!"

"Bill already left for Otto's to help the boys put up the net," Elise called to Selina over the balcony. "Consider him 'seduced.' I did it before I came up to change." Humming "On Our Way Rejoicing," she danced along the balcony to the sleeping porch. Her green sundress, which Liz had worn, and Selina's watermelon-colored trousers tangled together on Liz's bed like lovers. Caught unawares, Elise saw her own face in the wavy mirror over the communal dresser. She glowed! "You're beautiful," Jason had whispered to her. Two words that were exactly right. Not that she was actually beautiful, she hastened to think, eschewing conceit as firmly as she would have done before an audience.

From her tooled-leather jewel case, Elise extracted the cross Calvin had hammered out of a tin can for her. She'd not worn it yet. She slipped a silver unicorn Mad Jack had given her off a silver chain and ran the chain through the cross. Under the thick braid that bifurcated her back (Selina had woven the braid, fingers flying like a mother's), she fastened the clasp. She must thank Calvin for the cross! she thought, mortified, as she recollected how ungracefully she'd accepted it. It was particularly ungraceful, she divined now, because Calvin had given it to her as from one artist to another. She'd go over to the manse tomorrow (cricket, now that Jason had departed) and make up for her lapse. She would like to see Calvin's cherry wood Queen Esther once again before she returned to England, where Indians were mere myths for rock singers to pull from films. Calvin understood Esther as only a black American could, Indians now being so tamed. Would her father and Pamela really get there in time to take her on the promised tour of the American West? She doubted it.

Elise studied the effect of Calvin's cross against her burnt-sienna polo shirt. ("Exactly the color of your hair!" Betsy had exclaimed in an ecstasy of coordination.) The cross was awfully prominent. Elise thrust the cross underneath her shirt, as Jason wore his. She fiddled hopefully with her white shorts. (You're not pregnant; you can't be! Only Victorian girls get pregnant the *first time*. Like Tess of the D'Urbervilles. You are not pregnant, she thought to her image in the wavy mirror. You're beautiful!)

Elise left the sleeping porch, feeling the cross against her breastbone. Aunt Chloe was coming up the stairs. Aunt Chloe looked as dreamy-eyed as Elise felt. Spontaneously the two of them hugged each other. "Come *on*, Elise!" came Betsy's voice from downstairs.

"Have fun," said Aunt Chloe. She gave Elise's braid a tweak, then went along the balcony to her room, humming, "On Our Way Rejoicing."

" 'York-scher Marsch'!" blared Olivia to Otto over the gathering din of the loudspeaker, as she and Viola joined the girls emerging from the spruces. From atop a high stepladder, ruddy-faced, blue-eyed Otto waved. "*Ja!*" he called. Olivia could chatter away in German with Otto. Elise, who'd thought herself adroit in French and German, had discovered to her chagrin that both languages went clean out of her head in America; she admired Olivia's portable German extravagantly. As they neared the loudspeaker, the rousing, staggered brass sounds of a German marching band drove linguistic envy out of mind; Elise covered her ears till she got out of its stultifying range. Near the covered wagon, Otto had taken advantage of Erich's height and good nature to employ him (not on a ladder, but as tall as

Otto on his ladder) stringing colored lights between bamboo poles to decorate the terraces for square dancing that night. It was going to be such fun—

Elise stopped walking for a second, struck by the sudden, surpassingly odd thought what a *relief* it was that Jason had gone. His existence would no longer inhibit her. He wouldn't tug at the corners of her eyes. She could relax tonight, dance with Bill and Zack, and casually enjoy their vying for her favor. She would wear that (hideously expensive!) Ralph Lauren prairie skirt Pamela had, in an effusion of newlywed generosity, hopped out of a New York City taxi to procure for "my new daughter" (she'd squeezed Elise's knee on that one) from a window at Bergdorf's. While they waited, Elise and Mad Jack had eventually hired a horse-drawn hansom bedecked with flowers to wend them through the convoluted roads of nearby Central Park. She had seen two men come out of the bushes together and expose themselves in unison to, it appeared, the horse. Jack had covered her eyes. "America's become a zoo," he'd sighed. Later, in the actual zoo, where, transfixed, they'd read the sign about the slaughtered deer, he'd said, "Worse than a zoo. America's become a literal hell." He'd spoken not as one conversing, but as one composing.

"Liz, we gotta get them colored lights going," Zack yelled to Liz. With the unprecedentedly torpid Macs and Wendy's hairy boyfriend, Joel, he lay on the grass near the covered wagon, holding Erich's dachshund, Adolph, like a football.

"*Streetcar!*" Liz hollered back. Then, "Zack, that's dirty!" She sounded like Aunt Chloe. They all caught themselves sounding like her. How old were you, Elise fantasied asking Aunt Chloe, when you lost your virginity? Why? Aunt Chloe would counter, her eyes full of concern. "Elise, slap Zack's face," ordered Liz, pointing an imperious finger. Clutching Adolph, Zack pretended to cower. In the covered wagon, Fred was sound asleep. Selina swooped over and commenced tickling him.

"Yikes!" Fred came awake, swinging like a boxer. Elise remembered a chapter called "Violent Reveilles" in *The Best of Mad Jack Barnes* about how most Vietnam veterans awakened thus. Why should *Fred?*

"Relax, Freddy," coolly counseled Zack. He released Adolph, who ran off. As if in uniform exhaustion, the girls all collapsed amid the boys on the grass. Wendy and Joel immediately began kissing. "V,"

Zack said, tipping his head and squinting one eye at the sun as Erich always did, "haven't seen you all summer. Who held you captive?"

"My parents. I had to go to summer school." Viola tore up grass balefully. "Now we're less than a week away from school *again*."

"What'd you flunk?"

"English."

"Oh, that's hard to flunk," said Zack in a commiserating manner.

"Hey!" Bare-chested, Bill Wilson, soon to be second-string quarterback at Syracuse, jumped down from the second terrace. My, he was well made, Elise thought admiringly, her eyes running over him till she caught herself. "The net is up," said Bill ironically. "I'm glad you guys let me help. Are we going to play volleyball, or aren't we? Hi, Elise—"

"Yes!" brightly said Olivia. She stood up. She wore a gray T-shirt with a yellow happy face on it. Stretched over Olivia's jutting breasts, the happy face looked bellicose. Olivia smiled up at Bill rather flirtatiously, Elise thought, getting up immediately. Liz, Betsy, Selina, and Viola got up. The Macs got up. Zack and Fred got up. Finally Wendy and Joel got up.

"*Ja*, you may go too!" expansively Otto told Erich. "Go and play with the other boys and girls!"

Although Otto's loudspeaker was pointed toward the West Shore Road and the lake, from the dusty volleyball court on the edge of the woods, the kids could still hear faintly the lilting "Deutchmeister Regiments March" as Bill and Erich chose up teams. When just Brian Mac was left, Bill said quickly, "Brian," to give an illusion Brian had been chosen. How nice of him, thought Elise.

"Wait a minute. You call this an even number?" Erich asked Selina, who was on his team.

"I forgot Brian," Selina said, counting. Eleven-year-old Brian Mac burst into tears.

"I'm going home!" he cried and ran off in the direction of Otto's house and the West Shore Road. "I don't love you anymore, Selina!"

"Brian, it was *me* I forgot!" Selina called after him. Brian stopped running but didn't turn around. "Kevin, go get him. I don't have to play."

"Selina, we'll lose," groaned Erich.

"Erich!" said Liz.

"I'm sorry," said Erich. "I wasn't thinking."

"Ah, let the crybaby go," said Kevin and Denny together. "Don't go away mad!" they shouted at Brian's back.

Brian turned. "I hate you!" he yelled. He gave them the finger, then resumed running.

"Precocious, isn't he?" commented Zack. "You teach him that, Olivia?"

"Shut up," said Olivia amiably. She and Zack were both on Erich's team. "Let's cream these shitheads."

"You kids play the dirtiest volleyball I ever saw," Bill Wilson held back his serve to remark almost admiringly. At which pause in the action, Denny Mac, tripped under the net by Zack, who was anticipating the serve, fell to the court on one knee, then got gamely up.

"I didn't even know it was possible to play dirty volleyball," Joel, next to Denny at the net, a newcomer like Bill, concurred. Elise, also on Bill's team, looked from one to the other, surprised. As field hockey was her sport (they didn't even offer volleyball at St. Catherine's, it being an American game) and field hockey was coached by the redoubtable Sister Tekakwitha, who taught her girls how to strike devastating blows on the edges of shin guards, Elise had never thought to question the brutal infighting that went on at the net. In fact, she'd been rather impressed that a girl was as likely to be tripped up as a boy.

"Shut up and *serve!*" called Olivia from Erich's side of the net. Bill shrugged comically at his team and served.

"Side out, rotate!" called Bill's entire team as Erich's serve, twice as long as a serve should be, arced into the woods toward the ball diamond. Erich was such an uneven athlete! Elise thought. She wondered if, when he learned his own size and strength, he'd be any good. She thought not. Viola chased the ball into the woods. Elise, rotating, moved to the center of the front row between Wendy and Fred and found herself facing Olivia, who stood between Liz and Kevin Mac.

"She'll never find it," grimly declared Fred, taking off into the woods after Viola.

"Fred can't bear to hold still," Elise remarked to Wendy, who smiled. Across the net, Liz was stroking bruised shins.

"At this rate I'll be just like Daddy," she said. "Crutches anyone?"

"What happened to your father's foot?" Olivia asked.

"He was bitten by a spider," said Liz. She laughed. "Jason called him 'Oedipus Sam.'"

"Why 'Oedipus'?" Olivia wanted to know.

"I don't know," Liz returned, shrugging her hands out.

"Your mother isn't older than your father, is she?"

"No." Liz looked at Olivia, puzzled. So did Elise.

"If anyone should be called '*Oedipus*,'" asserted Olivia, her tone rather nasty, "it should be Jason himself."

"What do you *mean?*" demanded Elise, confronting Olivia's eyes through the net.

"Just that Jason had the hots for Mrs. Otway, that's all," returned Olivia without inflection. "Everyone knew that." Elise saw literal red as she'd never seen it on the playing fields of St. Catherine's. Anger rose in her like heat, so pure she welcomed it. It felt glorious!

"Why, you," she heard herself say. "You—" Her vocabulary faltered and deserted her, drawn like fire through her body. That Olivia might be called a slanderer or just a bitch became stupid, mere language. Elise ducked under the net to face Olivia directly. She pulled her elbow back as if on the archery range, clenched her fist, released, and jammed it into Olivia's stomach below the happy face. Olivia made an "oof" noise. Elise punched her again. She felt Olivia's fist hit her low. She clipped Olivia behind the knees, and soon they were rolling on the rough and stony dirt of the court. Voices were shouting. Elise could feel her braid being tugged, her arms scratched, her legs dented. Then she felt something inside her give, and grow into a cramp. Oh, thank God! Her period. What a time for it to come! Olivia kept pummeling her, although Elise herself had given up the fight, just lying there and laughing a little. Betsy's scream shrilled in the air like a slow, whistling firework, the kind that would eventually boom and fall. Abruptly released, in fetal position, Elise looked warily down at herself and saw blood—fresh, new blood flowing through her white shorts spreading around her seeping into the thirsty earth of the volleyball court. Gosh, she thought, late periods do make up for lost time.

The noise around her finally penetrated. People were shouting. People were screaming. Elise raised up on her elbow. She saw Olivia making for the path to the ball diamond, just as Liz had done on the

Fourth of July. "Liz!" called Elise. She saw Liz's worried face materialize before her spangled eyes.

"What? What should I do?" Liz asked.

"Go after her. Go after Olivia. It wasn't her fault. I started it." Elise sat up. "Liz, don't let her go away mad!"

"All right." Liz took off after Olivia. Elise saw Erich follow Liz. Betsy's face came before Elise's eyes, then Selina's next to it.

"Betsy," said Elise, almost amused that in her condition *she* was the only person present who could take charge, "you and Bill go get Aunt Chloe. Nobody else. Don't tell anyone else. Just Aunt Chloe. She'll know what to do. Have her bring me, uh"—she felt a little dizzy—"some jeans, some underpants, and a whole lot of Tampax."

"Okay, okay, Elise." Betsy's face went away.

"Don't tell *me* to do anything, Elise!" said Selina. "I am not leaving your side, no matter how authoritative your tone."

"I won't. All right." Elise felt another cramp and curled with it into the dust. She felt Selina take her head into her lap. Selina's hands were cool. Her long nails were watermelon-colored. Selina loosened Elise's braid.

"Where are you all going?" Selina shouted. "Denny, Wendy, Kevin, Zack, Joel? Where are you *going?*"

"It's the menstrual taboo," Elise woozily told Selina. "Aunt Chloe would blame it on the menstrual taboo."

"The menstrual taboo!" said Selina. "I like that. It's like Margaret Mead." Then: "You *rats!*" she hollered after those persons who were evidently departing. "You *chickenshits!*"

"She's clean. The bleeding's stopped. Her body took care of the problem very efficiently. The nurses are helping her get washed up, and you can take her home."

"But what *was* it?" Chloe could not help asking, although ticking off the dates of Elise's flamboyant periods at full moons had left her in little doubt; still, she couldn't believe it. Were all those kids . . . ?

"A spontaneous abortion. Euphemistically a miscarriage. Your daughter doesn't know; she thinks it's a late menstrual period. I leave it to you whether you want to tell her or not."

"No, she mustn't know, she mustn't! It might ruin her life," was what came out of Chloe's mouth, although various passionate alternatives were warring for expression. *She's not my daughter* would sound (and indeed feel) like a disowning. And surely it was no time to give this medical bastard a lecture on basic feminism: how *dare* you tell me and not her? *She* is the one who should decide whom to tell. The doctor mistook Chloe's angry consternation for hysteria and put his hand on her shoulder. She shrugged it off. He looked startled, and then his eyes took on a world-weary professional air, his voice a "Listen, lady" tone.

"At least give her some information about birth control. They don't stop once they've started, you know. And now that there's the pill, boys don't take the responsibility anymore."

Irrational shame washed over Chloe. She looked down, noting peripherally that she wore shorts and her favorite torn denim shirt tied at the waist. She looked like a very bad mother! I should have paid more attention to what the kids were up to, she thought, rather than drawing them out, being interested in their minds. (*Bill?* she wondered, despite herself. *Zack?*) I treated them like equals, I treated them the way I treat college students—that's why they like me. It was a cop-out. I would be a very bad mother.

Then Elise came out of the door looking like an angel who'd been in a scuffle. Tentatively, like people who've been separated for a long time, she and Chloe put their arms around each other, then held on tight. Light-boned Elise felt fragile as a bouquet of flowers, but Betsy's garbled account of her fisticuffs with Olivia told of tempered steel.

"I let them think you were my mother," Elise confessed in a whisper. "I wish you *were* my mother."

3 THE WYOMING MASSACRE MONUMENT
   NEAR FORTY FORT, PENNSYLVANIA

Jason, deviating madly from the best route south, drove north; took scenic Route 6 east (renouncing with considerable effort the western turn to Wappasenink), and late in the afternoon, nearing Scranton, saw a sign for the Battle of Wyoming monument, which marked the place where Queen Esther had tomahawked fourteen settlers to avenge her slain son. Or maybe that was where the son was slain; he couldn't remember. Still, Jason knew a gestalt when he saw one. He could not resist the perfect closure. Braking abruptly in Tunkhannock, he took Route 92 over the bridge toward Wyoming and Forty Fort. At first the blue highway wound along the Susquehanna through the "Endless Mountains" (one damned mountain after another), and historical markers laid out Sullivan's march that had decimated the Indians of the area in 1779. "Virtual genocide," the rector had called Sullivan's march up the Susquehanna. Then the road turned slow, busily commercial, and disappointing; you had to search along the side streets for a parking place near the monument. That the legendary tall bluffs along the Susquehanna were near you had to take on faith from tall green willows and picnicking families in the distance. The obelisk was ordinary gray stone: tall, squared-off-phallic at the top, and undistinguished.

   It said:

> Near This Spot Was Fought
> On the Afternoon of Friday the Third Day of
> July, 1778
> THE BATTLE OF WYOMING
> In Which a Small Band of Patriotic Americans
> Chiefly the Undisciplined, the Youthful and the Aged,
> Spared by Inefficiency from the Distant Ranks of the
> REPUBLIC . . .

Boldly Met and Bravely Fought
A Combined British, Tory and Indian Force
of Thrice Their Number.
Numerical Superiority Alone Gave Success to the Invader
And Wide Spread Havoc, Desolation and Ruin
Marked His Savage and Bloody Footsteps Through the
Valley.

Jason tried to take the Wyoming Massacre on, to bring it to life, as he'd tried with the monuments in Battery Park when he was a boy (Confederate Defense of Charleston! Explosion of the USS *Maine!* Stede Bonnet—No Gentleman Pirate!): *This really happened.*

THIS MONUMENT . . .
Has Been Erected
OVER THE BONES OF THE SLAIN

Jason remembered Fred telling him that all the eighty-three skeletons "bore the marks of the tomahawk" and shivered. The first Lenni Lenape pastor did his country a *service,* he tried to tell himself. Fourteen out of eighty-three ain't a bad night's work for an Indian lady who looks like Olivia. Queen Esther deserved to be executed. Bullshit, he thought then. Esther, the woman with child and with cross, was martyred. The stones should sing, the monument disintegrate.

Jason went back to his Triumph, parked across the busy highway in somebody's driveway. Out of cigarettes, he reached for his jacket, which Calvin had folded neatly on the passenger seat. Found in a pocket not cigarettes, but Queen Esther's necklace. Laughed a bit uneasily. Very funny, Calvin, he thought: very funny. He got into the car and slung the dirty-white necklace around the neck of the rearview mirror. The sun was setting on his right. As Jason looked in the mirror preparatory to backing out into traffic, the strange silver crucifix with its indented savior crossed his vision. Feeling the raw fragments of himself straiten into the cruciform, Jason took off southward, as if pursued by Cerberus and all the minor hounds of hell.

4 THE WEST SHORE ROAD

The sunset was smoke inlaid with gold on their left, then stippled with black-green trees, as Chloe and Elise turned through the stone arches onto the West Shore Road. The Volkswagen's muffler, unsettled by the headlong dash to the hospital earlier, clacked along the ruts. Turning to speak to Elise (what she had been about to say she would never remember), Chloe saw the girl's hand take something from the neck of her polo shirt and pull it nervously back and forth along a chain. A wayward ray of sunlight caught it, as if on purpose. Jason's cross. The hammered tin refracted the rays like a dull diamond. Elise, in profile, looking straight ahead, abstracted, ran the cross along her tongue. Jason's cross.

Random impressions clapped together like a demonic jigsaw puzzle —looks and smiles and pet names. Heat rose to Chloe's face; her scalp prickled; she nearly could not see for the atavistic emotion that attacked her like a rash. She tried to control it by naming it: jealousy! All the time— How could she? How could they? He is off, scot-free. We let him off.

Her cheekbones set like stone, her eyes still hot with primary colors, Chloe turned the Volkswagen into the lot across from the cottage that they used for parking. Sam's Buick was there. Chloe opened her window and gulped for air. Square-dance music filtered through the spruces from Otto's. He must have found a fiddler.

"Aunt Chloe?" Elise's soft voice. Chloe could not look at Elise. The images in her mind were graphic, the words vulgar. *She had him. He had her.*

"I need some air," she said, turning her head, but still not looking at Elise. Her words sounded thick. "I think I'll go for a walk."

"I'd better go in," said Elise apologetically, as if Chloe had invited her to accompany. "I don't want to miss the square dance. It's Bill's last night." Chloe looked at Elise. The girl tipped her head back against the seat. The cross was no longer visible. "D'you know what I think I'll tell him? What Aunt Abbie always says. 'Just a little girl trouble.'" Elise laughed.

Against her will, looking at the girl's lovely, animated face, admiring beyond words her *spirit*, Chloe could feel the thick knot of jealousy within her modulate to envy, refine to empathy, and finally dissolve, leaving love intact. She reached to flick a lock of Elise's long ruddy hair over her shoulder.

"Have fun, honeybunch," Chloe said. Ah, Jason's word! She hastened to erase it. "If Tony's out of the boathouse yet, do tell him I won't be long." Chloe waited till Elise had walked over the little bridge and in through the back door of the cottage; then she got out of the Volkswagen and started walking fast up the West Shore Road in the direction from which she had just come. The air had cooled rapidly in the dusk, and she could sense it around her, but it didn't quite touch her. Her bare legs, moving like pistons, were warm and strong, missionary. As she walked, she wondered, defiantly and angrily, *if God would survive this.* Will you, God? she silently shouted upward. Will you? If the God-bearing image is desecrated, what happens to God? If the church is deserted, where is God? As she passed the Fanshawes' cottage, set back on Otto's side of the road, she heard someone call her name. One of her names anyway, she thought crossly.

"Mrs. Otway. Please wait a minute, Mrs. Otway!"

Chloe couldn't believe it. Of all people. She could not believe it. God does love farce. If there *is* a God, she added, baiting God like a bad child. Temper rose in her; she welcomed it. Olivia Fanshawe caught up to her on the road, but Chloe didn't stop walking. "Mrs. Otway, is Elise all right?"

"Yes," said Chloe shortly. "No thanks to you." She knew Elise had started the fight; Elise had been most punctilious about telling her that, but Chloe could not bring herself to let Olivia off. What am I to be, she asked herself histrionically: surrogate mother to all female young? Evidently she could not bring herself to let anyone off. Damn Tony for neglecting her. Damn Jason for betraying her. Damn Sam for suspecting.

Short-legged Olivia, gamely keeping up with Chloe's stride, didn't say Elise had started the fight. Chloe was impressed, despite herself. "Sometimes I get so mad," Olivia breathed hard to explain, "that I want to destroy everyone around me. I was being destructive of two people I like, and Elise wouldn't allow it. Elise did exactly what she should have."

By the side of the road where the shortcut led to the church, Chloe stopped walking and looked at Olivia. Olivia wore a down vest; it must be cold, she registered objectively. "Have you ever considered therapy?" she bluntly asked, wondering if Olivia would hit her.

"Yes! I've asked my parents to give it to me for my birthday."

"For your birthday?" Chloe was amused. Then, seasoned adviser to students that she was, she saw a way to solve two of Olivia's problems in one fell swoop. "Olivia, do you know that if you scotched your silly fixation on much-overrated Harvard and hied yourself off to another college, there'd be psychological counseling available free?" The two of them jumped off the road as a car passed by, fleetingly lighting Olivia's face. It looked young and eager.

"I *am* going to college. I just didn't want anyone to know. There was something Liz said early in the summer about getting all A's and transferring; so I talked to Jason about it, and he said why didn't I apply for late admission someplace just in case I changed my mind. I wrote to a couple of schools in the Boston area, and one of them accepted me."

"The Boston area?"

Olivia named Chloe's university. I do not believe this. I do not believe this, Chloe thought.

"Perhaps I'll see you around," she said and started walking through the wild wheat to the church. Olivia followed.

"Where are you going?"

"I'm going to the church," said Chloe, as if it were a perfectly normal thing to do.

"But it's locked. You'll have to ask my mother for the key."

Chloe stopped walking. A kind of light seemed to emanate from the drying wild wheat that made one think words like "harvest," "gleaning," "God." "What do you mean it's locked? Churches," said Chloe haughtily, "are never locked."

Olivia laughed. Chloe thought it might be the first time she'd ever heard Olivia laugh. "Mrs. Otway, I don't think you know very much about churches. Most churches have security systems like banks."

Chloe felt like crying all of a sudden.

As if she sensed the rising tears, Olivia said quickly, "There's a window with a broken latch behind the harmonium. I'll help you get in."

"You will? Olivia, thank you." Gratefully she let Olivia walk along next to her. They emerged from the tall wild wheat on the west side of the church. Her eyes fixed on her feet as they walked, Chloe tentatively asked Olivia, "You aren't premed, are you?"

"No. Music." Chloe pictured the homely music building all the way across the crowded campus from her own ethereal science tower. Most music students were famous for their insularity.

"Tony and I'll have to have you over for dinner," said Chloe in a sudden burst of generosity.

"Thank you," said Olivia. She turned her face to Chloe's; a face cool and self-contained that bespoke equality. Chloe approved her forbearance from gush. Chloe thought that one day she might even come to like Olivia. Who knew? They went around the church to the graveyard side and moved under a sycamore tree to the back window, the one Jason had gestured from to suggest the Sea of Galilee.

Boosted up, her flanks still feeling the heels of Olivia's hands, Chloe stood on the sill to open the window, twisted through, and impatiently waved her unlikely comrade away. Then, holding her breath, she turned to confront the darkness of the church. Soft it was at first: brown and enveloping. She began hesitantly to walk and banged into the harmonium, almost swore, then used the harmonium as touchstone for what she remembered of the church. Was it an optical illusion that the darkness seemed charged, that ions of energy pierced the soft-brown like points of light on the edge of perception? When Chloe could make out the dim gleam of the bronze cross on the altar table, she was at first relieved, then unaccountably terrified. She blundered blindly to find a pew (pews being for humans!), hit her pelvic bone hard on a carved corner, tried to kneel, but there wasn't enough space (Presbyterians!), finally sat, breathing hard, on the cushion of a pew. Oh, she was thirsty; and with the thirst came a memory of how sometimes Tony, when she was thirsty, tossing and mumbling on the edge of sleep, would bring her water before she knew she was thirsty, and the water would be just right, its cool lucidity just what she wanted. Something pierced her to the heart. Not guilt, more than guilt, a pain that could be someone else's—Tony's?—if she didn't take it for him, so she took it, let the straight back of the pew inform her posture, and abandoned herself to the flow of the brown darkness that was taking on a golden hue.

"Chloe. Chloe." Her name called low like the cooing of an inventive dove gradually impinged on Chloe's wordless reverie. What time must it be? Looking hastily around her, she could discern the lattice panes of the windows and the darkness splintered into familiar shapes. "Chloe. Chloe." What kind of idiot? Chloe left her pew and went to the window she had left open. Sam Barnes stood below it, grinning up at her.

"You idiot!"

"Is that all the thanks I get? I limped all the way here." Chloe sat on the windowsill and swung her legs out, preparing to pull the window shut after her.

"Sam, catch my feet." She yanked the window, jumped before it could hit her, and felt her sneakered feet slide down the front of Sam. On the ground she looked indignantly at Sam, who was brushing off the front of him as if she'd gotten him dirty. "Thanks a lot. You didn't catch my feet."

"If I'd caught your feet, you'd have knocked your head on the church. Some scientist. Don't you know elementary physics?" Chloe made a grumbling noise. She felt like a naughty, unrepentant child being escorted home by an officious big brother. They walked in silence and slow time (Sam's stupid limp) around the church and through the wild wheat to the West Shore Road. The journey back was lighter than the journey out. There was a ragged half-moon over Otto's woods.

"You okay?" Sam asked her as they hit the West Shore Road.

"I'm okay."

"You fell for him, didn't you?" Chloe looked angrily at Sam. Sam was looking straight ahead. He was wearing a Baracuta jacket. He had his hands in the pockets. It must be cold.

"I fell for him," she admitted.

"Anything happen that night you came in all starry-eyed and disheveled?"

"I wasn't disheveled!"

"You were disheveled. What happened?"

"Nothing," she lied.

"Good." Sam's skeptical sidelong glance acknowledged the lie, and

Chloe wanted to kick him. How holier-than-thou! He was jealous, that's what he was! But then Sam went on, "I hate to see marriages better than mine break up. You and Tony. Well, I don't think I could bear that—" Sam stopped walking. *"Great thing of us forgot!"*

Chloe rolled her eyes. *Lear* again. "What's the matter?"

"Tony. I've got a message for you from Tony. He wanted to go looking for you himself, but I stopped him. Didn't know what shape you'd be in, old girl."

"What?"

"Didn't know what shape you'd be in, old girl," Sam repeated.

"What's the message, you idiot!"

Sam cleared his throat and orated, "The message was 'Tell Madame Curie she's done it again!' "

Chloe stared. All the energy in the air cohered. "The octahedron!" She flung her arms around Sam's neck, then let go and started to run down the rutted West Shore Road toward the Barnes cottage. Square-dance music came into her ears, stones flew from her heels, the cool air of the night made itself felt on her bare legs and where her shirt was torn. She saw Tony and Sir Isaac on the lighted back deck of the cottage. "Tony!" she hollered. They came together on the little bridge, Sir Isaac bumping into Tony from behind. Tony was eating an apple, a golden delicious. "The octahedron?" Chloe asked him, breathless.

"The octahedron. It was just waiting for my ligands. They settled round it like the moment of Creation. I'm putting your name on this too, Chloe."

"My part was an accident," Chloe protested. "You did all the work. Where'd you get that apple? I'm starving."

"I found it in our room." Tony held the apple so she could take a bite. "More an act of God than an accident, I'd say." Tony looked at the apple. "Some bite."

"I think it really was an act of God," said Chloe fast, bracing herself. "Tony, I've begun to believe in God," she blurted, flushing.

Tony looked at her. He took a bite of the apple.

"Tony, did you hear me?"

"I didn't know you didn't believe in God before. I expect I just always assumed you did."

Chloe stared. "Do *you?*"

"Believe in God? Of course I believe in God. I'm a scientist."

A low and mournful keen came from the shadowed darkness of the West Shore Road near the Laceys' cottage. "Chlo-ee! Chlo-ee!" Sam drew out the vowels till they winged through the air like hawks. Sir Isaac howled an answer.